Our Diligent Souls

by

Emer G. M. Lawless

Dedicated to Maura & Brendan

The right of Emer Lawless to be identified as the author of this book have been asserted by her in accordance with the Copyright, Design and Patent act of 1988 and by the Copyright & Related Rights Act 2000. All rights reserved. No part of this publication may be reproduced or transmitted by any means electronic or mechanical without prior permission from the author in writing.

www.emerlawless.com

Principal characters in Order of appearance

Mark - (The protagonist) A young Dundalk man, the logistics manager of an international shipping company who lives and works in Dublin

Ralph Mournaghan – (The anti-protagonist) Mark's nemeses and supervisor

Davin Turlock & Thomas Reeves – Executive associates to both Mark and Ralph Mournaghan.

Laura Keating – A young widow and daughter of Edward Turner- a key Management figure

Elliot – A witty pharmacist and Mark's closest friend in Dublin

Siobhan – Elliot's partner and the curator of a city centre museum

Oden – Elliot's brother; a games development student with ADHD and Asperger's syndrome

Emily – Siobhan's closest friend; an asexual singer-songwriter who captures Mark's imagination

Lucile – Oden's girlfriend and fellow student

Joyce – Mark's co-worker and right-hand man

Brian & Alfie – Mark's childhood friends who have emigrated to Australia

Jackie, Marian & Sarah – Brian's father, mother & sister

Breda, Andrew & Moira – Mark's father, mother & sister

Arthur – Mark's previous employer, friend and father figure

Michael Fitzgerald – Oden's wacky lecturer at college

This may be useful though I expect for the most part that it surplus to requirement as the characters are slowly and thoughtfully introduced.

Our Diligent Souls

Chapter 1

The long winters were shroud in darkness, a period suffocated by Christmas job hunters. The reminders of poverty were commonplace when being sent out as a boy on essential supply runs. The summer had slipped through his fingers, the five o'clock tea-time night skies of his youth found their way back every year. Mark's young bones numb and heavy from work as he lifted his attention from the fresh rain speckled pavements and walked on.

He was glad that he lived in the city; it lessened the burden of what had once been an endless journey, towards the tender light of spring. Dublin was a far cry from the open fields of his hometown where sheets of steely anger pelted from the heavens confirming widowers' belief in the wrath of God. Throughout the winter, the majestic shelter of the cities towering architecture slowed the impact of otherwise continuous rainfall. Here too, the night air reeked of dampness; the musty smell of autumn's return temporarily noted.

This particular Dublin thoroughfare paid homage to celebrity and wealth with its sparkling restaurant lights and its meandering trail of pubs. The chatter and clink of glasses, the jovial echo that oozed out from each inner sanctum conjuring images of riling, over-intoxicated troubadours. The turn in conditions had disbursed the destitute as only a few pedestrians busied themselves homewards.

Mark in truth, was not ready for what lay ahead of him that night. There was a stark contrast between the two sets of businessmen he knew, those from his past and his present. The business premise that was deeply instilled through his earlier employer had given him an unmovable sense of integrity, an acumen that seemed to amuse his new executive associates. He was not naive to the realities of global condition; they were enablers, margin expanders, corner cutters, nothing more. He made progress with his floor staff, digging deep with them to find higher levels of capability, the ceiling on which was bound by corporate inefficiency, in not meeting safety regulation, in not admitting the need for a more efficient floor plan.

He checked the time on his mobile only to discover the lateness of the hour. He had a good three hundred metre dash in front of him but that he could manage.

Our Diligent Souls

At the doorway of the restaurant, a juvenile teenager stood sniggering to himself. Mark leant over to catch his breath before moving out towards the edge of the footpath to read the signage. The air adjusted in his lungs as he allowed the boy time to take him in and make room. The sign spelt out in a golden font; La Papille Solletico.

Mark looked through the window as he tugged on his coat to distribute any lingering raindrops. The boy stubbed out his cigarette on the wet ground without, as much as a glance in Mark's direction; he turned and re-entered via the restaurant's glass door.

Stepping inside, the host was arched in welcome, his white hair and bright eyes echoing years of experience. 'Good evening, sir!'

'The Mournaghan party...' Mark muttered. He was still adjusting to the change in atmosphere, that and the gentle agility of his host, who was years his senior.

'They're straight through to the left, sir. May I take your coat?'

'Fine, yes, thank you.' Mark reciprocated, removing his coat to reveal a newly tailored suit.

The host's smile was as delicate as his placement of Mark's coat; he folded the garment over his right arm to signal with his left. He was Dublin born, an institute of identity who carried a pride of position. That much Mark had joyfully deduced.

Mark's companions were already seated, and the host to Mark's relief had enough savvy to know not to lead the way.

The restaurant was overheated. It was a dizzy contrast to the heavy undulating rain showers that Mark had left outside. Its interior had a sense of the theatrical. Comfortable booths lined the side walls, and there was a section of open tables, each table tempered by the golden shimmer of candlelight. The walls were endowed with classical artwork in whittled antique frames. He may not have noticed, but for the fact that the place was almost empty. His eyes tended to focus on high spirits rather than interiors when a restaurant was full.

Mark made his way to where his colleagues were hunched in discussion. There was an ache in his shoulders that was unshakable. He made fists of both hands to relieve the tension before sliding under the radar of the three men. At least one of them had on occasions, had relished a slice of one-upmanship at his expense.

Our Diligent Souls

He was suddenly hit by a sharp influx of hot radiated air; it was being shafted through a vent in the ceiling. 'Gentlemen...' He was attempting to control a variety of palpitations but presented with a newly sparked tremor in his top lip and a slight but unmistakable shake in his hand.

'Mark, you've arrived, we've started without you.' Ralph Mournaghan was the first to stand up; smartly fixing the cuff of his jacket sleeves before stretching out his right hand. The other two men remained seated as they intimated their welcome. The starter cutlery had been removed, and the loose cotton napkins appeared to swallow up the table top.

'I had things to see to, Ralph. I was pressed for time getting over here. You're well, Davin? Thomas?'

Mark shook their hands in turn and accepted the offer of a seat that anchored him with his back to the restaurant.

'We were talking around extending that deadline, but we won't go there tonight!' Ralph Mournaghan said snidely. Mark looked over at him with a puzzled expression. 'And that's an order,' Ralph added laughing outright. Mark knew Ralph Mournaghan was a man who loved to provoke. There was always a danger in him, divisive or otherwise.

Mark had been with the new company for six months, and Ralph Mournaghan was his superior, a key executive in T&E International Shipping. He was Mark's only access to the company directors in respect of work-related issues. They were a tight bunch, these particular executives; fluent in back watching and bundling on work. At that, he couldn't imagine anyone being able to stomach too much of Ralph Mournaghan.

'What is this extended deadline?' Mark asked politely, undoing the single button that held his jacket closed.

Thomas Reeves, who was sitting to Ralph's left, turned and shook his head. 'You're a prick, Mournaghan!'

Mournaghan laughed, Davin Turlock eying Mournaghan as he signalled to the restaurant staff. 'I'll get the waitress. What will you have to drink, Mark?'

Mark had met Davin on two prior occasions, once at work and once at a grand charity event. He had been persuaded into the executive circle three months back, but Mark's free time had since faded; his regular work was now followed by all sorts of work-related events. His primary focus was to create a better, safer work environment for himself and his team.

Our Diligent Souls

He needed to afford himself two well-cut suits to avoid some polite mouthfuls of mockery. This was a humble night out. Mark had managed higher-end experiences with these fellows; places where the entrees made him feel like an apprentice, not that anyone was given reason to pick up on it.

'I'm fine with this.' Mark insisted, directing his response to Davin Turlock. He reached over to pick up the last napkin filled wine glass. 'I'll have wine, honestly.'

From behind, Mark could sense a scurry of movement as staff approached the table. Ralph, as usual, took the reins. 'Can you serve this man his food as ours arrives, a menu might be good; he will go straight to the main course.'

The waitress had already given Mark the menu.

'Is that fair enough for you?' Davin leaned in as he spoke.

'Yes; sure!' Mark lowered his eyes as he felt the waitress move behind him.

'Your dishes are on the way out sir; I can do my best...'

Ralph Mournaghan cut her short by lifting his hand. He beckoned her with his four fingers, but the waitress stood her ground.

'How hard can it be in an empty restaurant? Yes?' Ralph sneered, reprising her with a look, Mark avoiding any eye contact with the young woman.

'Yes, sir,' she responded in a soft but sarcastic military tone.

Mark requested the first item on the menu. He spoke without pivoting his head in any direction. 'Dover sole could be good!'

'Nice choice, sir.' The waitress whispered before leaving to inform the chef of the additional main; knowing that it was likely to create stress.

'You waited tables through college, Mark?' Thomas Reeves questioned, knowing the answer.

'I did!' Mark acknowledged. 'Nice place. The menu looks good.'

'Muppet talk!' Mournaghan spouted, the man was well oiled. Mournaghan tended to get drunk, drink himself sober and then get drunk again.

Our Diligent Souls

'Is the weather still awful?' Thomas Reeves put the question to Mark. Reeves was an authority on the weather internationally as well as at home. 'We should have a window by ten.'

'You got parking then?' Mark asked; filling the gap.

'Yes, but one likes to avoid battling the elements where one can!'

'Hear! Hear!' Mournaghan voiced, raising a glass; the posture of his declaration more suited to the role of King Henry the eighth. Mark was sailing over his first wave of irritation.

The ten-minutes wait for the main course crawled by at a snail's pace. Reeves had the global time differences memorised in sync; he could list the whereabouts and schedules of company agents spanning three continents. It was a talent. The admiration of ability was one thing, his confidence to place trusts in the same man another altogether.

Mark knew that these men were meticulous in their dealings; he needed to play the long game if he was to have any chance of succeeding. He choked on the tightness of his shirt collar; avoiding the urge to tug, the sweat rolling uncomfortably along the back of his neck as Mournaghan crusaded loudly through the lower compass morality of his recent dealings.

The food was presented eloquently; laid out by both host and waitress. Mark's relief was palatable, the waft of fragrant fish reawakening his senses. The three colleagues talked their way through dinner, but Mark was not on form. His mind was still reeling from Mournaghan's snide running commentary and the effort of having to complete another impossible deadline that day.

The talk was in a grey area for Mark; much of the information consisted of the latest mergers and acquisitions of companies; none of which were in the international shipping field. More relevant to the three men were the external opportunities. This was coupled with the announcement of engagements, the measure of brides to be and the collateral worth of family alliances.

It may have been exhaustion, but Mark entertained himself with a notion of how the upper classes ate. The poised intake of wine, the delicate coordination of each mouthful. These men were generating their points, in turn, allowing for digestion. There was rarely as much as a clink of cutlery, a drop of utensils signifying disapproval; it was more like synchronised swimming. Mark felt trapped somewhere between a nauseating migraine and a royal performance.

Our Diligent Souls

'So, what have you been following in the news?' Davin investigated, as he turned his attention to Mark. Mark had picked up on Davin's traits, he found him hard to judge. Davin's questions bearing the hallmarks of condescension. It was impossible to know what side of the fence Davin Turlock sat on when it came to Ralph Mournaghan pranks. It was hard to tell if he was a party to the management dalliances that Mark had to manage daily. Mark had tried to seek support on issues from other key executives, but he was redirected back to Mournaghan with a note of disapproval in respect of his loyalties.

A young executive had gone out of his way to take Mark aside and warn him, suggesting that Ralph had his eye on Mark's position for a friend of his family. The same youthful exec could later be seen alongside Ralph, the pair entirely amused as they attempted to poke holes in Mark's naivety. The contradiction of sharing the same dinner table with the man was a hard pill to swallow. It was more than Mark could grapple with, but it was part of the course.

He took his opportunity to get a foot in on the discussion. Mark could define any economic policy that bore relevance; the political surges or risks that might affect the shipping industry. Davin Turlock tended to overuse the words 'Going forward' when analysing Mark's observations. He imitated the expression in inverted commas, exhibiting his idiosyncrasy. Mark had witnessed Davin Turlock do that to others on occasion, in a breath he decided not to take it personally and continued.

Mark's desire to explore every element of the shipping industry could further him. His groundwork and analysis aimed for the exemplary. There were new shipping systems, technological advances, port controls, petrol hikes, rising import taxes, and border controls to read up on every week. It still took guts on his part to contribute information. The executives were tight-lipped, and Mark was never sure if his research filtered through, if it was old hat, or lost on these men as they assumed incompetence.

The host and waitress were again busying themselves around the table. Mark quietly engaged himself in conversation with the host as the plates were cleared. The food was pure nectar; Mark's Dover sole melting in sweet buttery goodness. The side of vegetables was still humming in the freshly woken interior of his mouth. Thomas Reeves decided to order two cheeseboards and more wine collectively. Mark declined to join them; to wash the sensation from his taste buds could have been sacrilege. He perched his lips on the water-glass, making a direct swallow to avoid diluting the subtle residue in his mouth.

Our Diligent Souls

The talk turned to the self-build that Davin Turlock was funding; looking at the cost versus benefits of the property qualifying as a passive build. Mark had shared the same conversation with his friends Elliot and Siobhan; the couple had recently bought a two-bedroom cottage on the south side of the city. They had initially intended to pull off a self-build, so he'd been through the argument before. Mark had little to contribute to the conversation as his energy was running low.

As he watched the two men converse with Mournaghan, Mark couldn't help but wonder how much they knew about what was going on with his floor staff. To resolve the unwarranted deductions in his workers' wages; it was taking up to two or three hours of his working week. Mark, in all honesty, believed that Ralph Mournaghan was consciously managing this shortfall for two reasons; first to forge tension between him and his crew but also to impose a union-identity around his character with the executives.

There were safety concerns that the men were not shy about bringing forward. There were government standard violations that Mark had brought to Mournaghan's attention. 'Do remind me,' Mournaghan had once too often said, but months on and only a handful of these issues were resolved.

Mark combined efficiency and effectiveness in every aspect of his working life. In doing so, the output of each worker had grown by over twelve percent, no mean feat by any standards. In business, these men were competitive beyond measure; entrenched in agenda, spearing opportunity from weakness.

Mark worked an eight to ten-hour day, five to six days a week. These upstarts worked their own hours and that he envied, but enough to join their ranks as a corporate executive, that was another question altogether. It was something he had thought long and hard about; he had moved companies to advance his career, but in reality, it was a hard choice on a good day.

Chapter 2

The previous bombshell of the words 'deadline expansion' created a concern for Mark. It meant an extra workload that never balanced in his favour, but he had more pressing issues to mind. Ralph Mournaghan had taken him aside during the day and insisted that he go to the restaurant that night, he wanted him to straighten out a small issue. They would talk after dinner once the other executives had left; it was a private matter, and that was as much as Mournaghan was prepared to say. Mark had felt like he was left with no choice.

'Let's keep it quiet until then.' Ralph had reiterated.

Sitting amongst them, Mark realised that his agitation had not diminished; the assumption that he had nothing better to do was belittling to him. But for now, his concern had to rest on the fact that he had an early start in the morning, he was making no headway at this event. It was an hour later when Turlock and Reeves finally left. The conversation was that droll; he wondered if he was being broken in for what lay ahead with Mournaghan.

'I'll just get us a drink, shall I?' Ralph suggested as the two executives departed. Mark nodded, resigned to the fact that he would be there for at least another half an hour.

Mournaghan rose to meet the waitress. He waved his mobile back at Mark as he disappeared out of earshot to the other side of the restaurant.

'Was everything to your satisfaction, sir?' The waitress inquired.

Mark barely looked up from his drink. 'Perfect; thank you!' He was in need of a moment to himself. The order of business went well that day; two men had stood out and spared no effort in helping to pull up the slack on deliveries. There was still a problem in respect of the third aisle lifting machine. The long-awaited parts were inferior; they had barren threads and objectionable wiring, a fact that he had been highlighting tirelessly. Nothing had been done by Ralph Mournaghan or any other management agent to resolve the issue.

Mark knew that Mournaghan had shipped the parts in from America and the newly refitted machine was already putting his worker's safety at risk. It was Joyce who had taken the first injury; however small. He was a good man, Joyce, and besides, the problems with the poorly restored lifter were slowing down operations. It had gone on long enough, too much work was being completed manually, his men pushed beyond their limits.

'Sorry about that!' Ralph insisted as he reinstated himself at the table. 'Laura Keating will be here in ten minutes. I've ordered a taxi to pick her up.'

'I thought you wanted to talk?'

'I'll brief you before she arrives,' Ralph tried to assure him.

'Good, shall we start? I have an early morning, Ralph.' Mark turned the watch on his wrist to check the time.

'You met Laura Keating at the charity event,' Ralph continued, 'Davin Turlock was there too. It was late August fourth, what five weeks ago?'

'I remember the event, Ralph?' Mark was quietly defensive. He could feel his stomach tightening, the taste of dry acidic wine that seemed to coat his mouth now bothered him; not a trace of Dover sole remained.

'This private matter, Ralph? I have to work in the morning?'

Mournaghan pulled an idiotic expression in response. He raised both of his hands and shoulders to the ceiling in jest. Mark was losing his ability to cope. He couldn't hold back his irritation. 'For God's sake!'

Mournaghan squinted his eyes. 'She's into you, Mark.' He surrendered.

'What the hell?'

'Laura.'

'What is this? In what respect? What are you playing at?' Mark demanded as his body stiffened with annoyance. 'What has this got to do with work?'

'Everything...' Ralph announced, full of his own self-importance.

'What?' Mark was washed in aggravation.

'I said it was a private matter, you nonce.' Mournaghan snapped, losing his patience.

'I assumed that the private matter was work related, I have to go.'

'I wouldn't advise you to take that tone with me.'

Mark hesitated, desperately trying not to react.

'You do remember Laura?' Mournaghan prompted.

'You introduced me to her...from what I remember; you said you were dating the woman? What is this about?'

'One moment!' Ralph requested, cutting in.

The waitress was hovering behind Mark again. He sank back in his chair and stared at his empty wine glass as she moved a brandy in front of him. 'Thank you.' Mark mumbled realising that he hadn't looked at the girl once all night; the sum of what he had taken in was her hands.

'Can I order some champagne on ice? Would you bring it over when our female companion arrives if you wouldn't mind?' Mournaghan was uncharacteristically polite. Mark remained motionless giving the waitress time to retreat.

'Can we get down to it, Ralph?'

Mournaghan edged in closer to him.

'I can assist you with things, Mark; do you really want another deadline to add to your load this month? It's a private matter, and that's where it stays. Bring her home, show her a good time. It's not much to ask.'

'You are unreal?' Mark was no longer prepared to be reverent about the matter. 'Don't drag me out again; I have a real job to do.' He moved to get up from his chair but was sharply met by the cleaver that was Mournaghan's hand. 'You'll do it if you know what's good for you.'

Mark eased himself back into his chair slowly. He attempted to absorb the situation, feeling impatient and lost for want of some form of rebuke.

'She's bright and charming, and in truth, you're punching well above your weight but...you will do this!'

Mark was floored; he had no time to argue. Ralph Mournaghan was already getting to his feet. He could hear the host again, this time leading Mournaghan's guest to the table. He could only surmise that it was Laura Keating as his back was to the restaurant. With his stomach tightly knotted, the objection on his face would not be easy to disguise.

'This way, Laura...' Ralph brought Laura to the free seat that Mark had just moved from, she kissed Ralph on the cheek and then turned to Mark. They nodded.

'You look lovely this evening!' Ralph commented. He was right in there, and with that, the champagne arrived on cue. It was the host on delivery this time. Mark looked across the restaurant, but the waitress seemed to have gone. Ralph quickly steered Laura's attention back to him. 'How did your night go?' He enquired.

'Yes, great night, we were at Santos, not quite fine dining but it was good fun.'

She had been out on a night with some relative she explained, turning to Mark as she took off her gloves. 'We met at the Mercer Charity event, I believe?'

Mark read from her expression that she hadn't recognised his face from the event. On the night in question, she'd been drawn into another conversation moments after they were introduced. That was when Ralph had first told Mark that they were an item.

'I was looking forward to you meeting Mark again, Laura; he's a rising star in the company.'

Laura looked suspicious, and Mark's head was starting to seriously hurt.

'Can you do the honours?' Ralph requested, turning to his colleague as he stood up from the table again. 'I'll just be a moment.'

Laura's back was to the restaurant as Mark had moved over a seat. From his new position, Mark was privy to an eyeful of Mournaghan's discussions with the host. There was some dubious body language between the pair. Mark watched as Mournaghan toyed in handing over his credit card. Evidently, some agreement had been struck as Mournaghan patted the host's shoulder. Mark quickly removed his eyes from the scene and got on with pouring the champagne.

'So, you're new to the company?' Laura asked.

'I am yes, six months or thereabouts.'

'And you like it?'

'Yes! It has its moments! I'm the floor manager. Well, logistics manager.'

'You're not stuck with the boardroom contingent all the time then?' She probed.

'Not at this stage, on social occasions sometimes-deadlines permitting.'

Her smile deepened as Ralph returned to his seat. They raised their flutes and clinked glasses, Mournaghan's beady eyes checking for any development between Laura and his colleague.

'I thought we'd head over to Davin Turlock's after here, he's having a late one with some friends.'

It was news to Mark. 'I have an early start!' He said glad of the opportunity to make his excuses.

'Nonsense, all work and no play. We can't have that.' Ralph reached over to give Mark a jovial shoulder pat that left no opening for him to restate his position.

'You won't let us down, Laura?' Mournaghan added coyly.

There was something striking about the woman. Mark didn't want to see it, but she wore elegance like a child wears ankle socks. For her to be whitewashed by the likes of Ralph Mournaghan would be a regrettable shame. But maybe, just maybe she was part of the spectacle. Mournaghan was presenting like some Jekyll and Hyde; Mark reversed his thinking as he watched Ralph play charm like a second skin.

He soon concluded that the woman had no idea what was going on. She was confused if she thought that Ralph Mournaghan was a gentleman. The conversation was only getting started when they had to break, Ralph's phone was ringing. The man fumbled through his pockets, but Mark was aware that Ralph always kept his phone in his left breast pocket. Laura too appeared to pick up on the awkwardness of Ralph's behaviour. Mournaghan was a creature of habit sober or not.

'Yes, Ralph Mournaghan. Sorry, no I didn't recognise your voice...' Mark watched as the host nod to Ralph from the other side of the room. The host hung up the restaurant landline with an objectionable stare in Mournaghan's direction; he looked uncomfortable though he had been obliging none-the-less. Laura was oblivious to the interaction as she leant over to engage Mark in conversation. She was desperately trying not to overhear the discussion that Ralph was having. Her expression said it all; there was some savvy in the woman, more than she would have liked to let on.

'It's good champagne!'

'Yes,' Mark replied, 'I'm getting too used to drinking the stuff!'

It was impossible to drown out Ralph's phone conversation, but they made a fair attempt. 'No. I understand...Fifteen minutes then.' He said as he lowered his phone and placed it on the table, Ralph appeared to be convinced that his rambling sounded authentic. Laura raised an eyebrow as she glanced at Mark; she had the measure of Ralph alright.

'Laura, I can't apologise enough. I can take you home if you want but I will be straight back, and we can all go over to Davin's together. I am leaving you in the hands of someone I would trust with my life.' He turned to Mark. 'Would you mind waiting, Mark? I know you want to go over to Davin's; he hasn't seen Davin's place yet.' He said turning to Laura. 'What a situation? I'll get a waitress...'

The host again arrived, in time for Ralph to order another bottle of champagne. Laura raised her shoulders and smiled. Mark wasn't being given the opportunity to leave.

'One-hour tops, less than that possibly. Order anything you want.' Ralph kissed Laura on the cheek and made for the door. He collected his coat and shook hands with the host.

'Well, this is awkward!' Laura said smiling, her confidence untouched.

'I'm not convinced he's coming back.'

'Nor am I, but I'll enjoy his excuses. We do have something good to drink, and it's a comfortable spot.'

For the lack of something better to say, Mark thought to make a suggestion.

'It's a lovely restaurant alright, have you eaten?'

'Yes earlier. A lot earlier but I'm fine.'

He poured the champagne.

'Maybe a dessert? I had the Dover-sole earlier, I didn't want to wash away the taste in my mouth; the others had cheese to be fair.'

Laura smiled but looked unsure, the corners of her mouth shifting from left then right. Mark nodded and signalled to the host. The waitress was still nowhere to seen, but there were three other sets of customers that showed no sign of leaving.

'Can we ask for desserts, it's fine if you're...?'

'Not at all, sir, it's my pleasure.'

Within seconds they had ordered two passion fruit crème brulees.

'I do love crème brulee and if you can't be bold now and again.' Mark suggested.

'Be utterly brilliant!' Laura retorted, laughing.

Mark was surprised by her response though he had politely lined her up. It was a good idea ordering dessert, it broke up the time, and the conversation had started to flow. The warning that Ralph had made earlier, insisting that Mark better sweep her off her feet, it was ridiculous. Mark wasn't going there; the thought of Ralph Mournaghan even putting it to him made no sense.

'So where did you work before you arrived at T&E shipping?' She explored, being genuinely curious. She was an impressive looking woman. He would never have expected a woman that tender to be dating Ralph Mournaghan. She seemed authentically lovely. Mark was almost expecting her to up and leave once Ralph was gone, but he was glad now that she hadn't. She was easy to be with, and he was painfully aware that leaving her might lead to more dubious repercussions in the morning.

'Where did I work before? It was an insignificant operation in comparison. Impact on Marley Street; it was a humbler place to work but fun most days.'

'One owner?' She enquired.

'Yes.' He responded, curious as to how she knew.

'My father once owned his own shipping company. He ran it himself.'

'Go on?' Mark requested.

'My mum was ill for a while; we were in our teens. Dad sold up and bought into T&E, so he could spend more time at home.'

'Keating, you said?' Mark hadn't heard the name at work.

'I was married and widowed at twenty-six, Stephen Keating was my husband. Edward Turner is my Father.'

'Edward Turner... Sorry to hear that, widowed at twenty-six?'

'It's a long story.'

'Widowed?'

'Another time?'

Laura didn't want to get into it right then and there.

'So? Edward Turner, I've heard that name alright.'

'He's a silent partner now; he's a good man. It was a better place to work back then when he started with T&E. It was a three-man operation then outside of the floor staff. Thomas Reeves still working there?'

'Yeah, as it goes. Thomas was here for dinner tonight.'

'He's a funny egg that man; an obsessive fact finder.'

She knew a lot of the executive crowd, none of whom she seemed to have that much time for; her observations were acute, and he could verify a few home truths. Some of the characters he'd not yet gotten to know, but it was a heads up. In her Father's Day, the floor manager had a fundamental role in the management committee; there was never a meeting without a floor manager present.

As much as Mark was enjoying their exchange, he was exhausted and had to think of the morning. She didn't mind, and they left within the hour. Mark made sure that she was safely tucked inside a cab before he journeyed home himself.

It was all of twenty minutes before he fell into bed. He was thankfully not as drained as he'd anticipated, but that was down to his new lady friend. Where Mournaghan had disappeared to that night, it made no sense to him. He could only wager the man's agenda with no clue to the game Mournaghan was playing for now.

Chapter 3

'Can you get a move on, woman?' Elliot hollered from the bottom of the stairs. 'They'll be here in a minute!'

His mind was soon captivated by the radio; a snappy rift with an upbeat lyric had worked its charm. He made his way to the sink to clear any trace of laborious work first, transferring the parboiled vegetables into a roasting tray. Taking in his domain from the kitchen island, he cast an eye on the dining table with its delicate arrangement, the restored antique fireplace and the sofa at the other side of the room. 'Candles... The candles need sorting!' He reminded himself as he moved unwatched across the floor in his woollen socks.

His eyes were taken by the night sky that had crept in through the window allowing the fire to cast light on the ceiling. The ice was melting in Siobhan's drink where she'd abandoned it on the mantelpiece. The sofa's soft leather upholstery had his name written all over it. The thought of sitting back and relaxing was a real temptation, but that could wait, there were a few more finishing touches to get out-of-the-way first.

Siobhan tread the stairs as light-footed as a nun, startling him as she shifted into focus beyond the steaming hot potatoes that he was ready to tackle. He looked at her accusingly, having nearly scalded himself at the island sink. Her arms opened out as she moved in time to the tune, patiently searching his eyes for an all-encompassing response.

'How do I look?' Siobhan probed.

'You tell me, how to put it into words?'

Her dress was a new acquisition, a snip she'd found on the internet. She made it look easy, but this was seriously eloquent. The forties cut made it a vintage piece; its chiffon shoulders and neat bodes attached to a figure-hugging below the knee skirt. Siobhan's salvaged court shoes were the correct choice, her hair in pin rolls offset by a blood-red lipstick and some striking black eyeliner. The confidence in her ability to dress theatrically was undeniable as she moved with conscious agility.

'You're inspiring!'

'Stop that.' She pronounced.

'I could eat you...seriously though I'm starving!' He paused for a breath. 'It's not too ostentatious.' He was hoping to get a rise out of her.

'I'll give you ostentatious... it's very me, no?'

'Ostentatious!' With his two hands, he gently held her shoulders. His eyes were sanctioning every stitch of her new rig out. 'It's cool, the outfit, it's incredibly stylish.'

His acknowledgement was warmly recorded before she leant forward for their lips to meet.

'We'll save that for later,' he suggested, dodging a bullet as she kissed the tip of his nose.

His passion for her was never invisible though sweetly camouflaged; his flushed composure appeased only by his preoccupation with dinner. He had abandoned the dishes, to root out her hands; she had hidden them behind her back to conceal the evidence.

'Sweetheart?' He glared at her as if over the rim of his glasses.

'Yes, my love.' She spoke with a cheeky inflexion then turned out her hands to produce the gas lighter which she tapped on his dimpled chin. Half giddy, he moved in for his kiss.

'Not so quick there.'

He took her by the hips, nudged in close as he looked her into her face.

'Get a move on, love!' He whispered as he stepped back smiling.

She laughed and went to work on the table settings.

'You, and that bloody lighter?' He muttered kneeling behind the island to retrieve a serving dish from the bottom drawer; he could hear her make headway on the cutlery. He was still hunkered down when the sound of her rattling was interrupted by the doorbell.

'I've got it,' he called out. His knee cracked as he jumped up suddenly, shaking his legs to bring back some circulation. Rolling the now floury potatoes into a ceramic bowl, he wiped his hands with a tea towel and headed for the door. Siobhan glanced over as he passed, turning back to check out the playlist. There was a tangible movement in her step, that much he noticed straight off, but her figure-hugging skirt was breathtaking. It was ingrained in his genetic coding, as the festivities were due to commence, he longed to hold her, her lovely head curled up on his shoulder.

Mark was wearing jeans and a tailored rose-pink shirt. Elliot had taken that in with a quick glance through his security eye. The men embraced as Mark shut the door behind him.

'Do you both want a beer?' Siobhan called out, her voice being carried across the room. She had slipped past them and was back in the kitchen rooting in the fridge.

'Yes please!' Elliot replied. He relieved Mark of the two wine bottles, one red, and one white; both jammed between his fingers.

'I could seriously do with a drink.' Mark added.

Elliot placed the wine on the counter while Mark moved over to kiss Siobhan's cheek.

'Looking very Heath Ledger, Mark.' She suggested.

'Who's Heath Ledger?' Mark quipped.

'Go on with yah, you scallywag.' Siobhan rolled back her eyes.

'I fully intend to,' Mark replied, 'good looking this Heath Ledger then?'

Siobhan winked at Mark and turned to Elliot as she pretended to look puzzled.

'He knows who Heath Ledger is? Heath Ledger, yeah?' She asked. Elliot was the easiest of the three to wind up; it was hard to resist.

'Jesus Siobhan, he knows who Heath Ledger is.'

Mark pouted his lips in jest. 'Sure, we're best buddies, right Elliot?'

'Right, bud.'

Elliot was shaking his head at Siobhan when Mark crept in with a few choice words. 'We were great friends, Elliot,' Mark added, 'he died a few years ago, Heath Ledger.' Elliot and Siobhan stood there stumped as Mark laughed aloud.

'I can be naive.' Siobhan admitted, 'hands up!' The woman was tickled by the fact that neither of them was ready to admit that they didn't know that the actor was dead.

'The place looks great you two.'

'Glad you at least noticed...' Elliot remarked, 'it has changed in the past two weeks; it's not like you to weigh in with an opinion.' He jested. 'We've been making good ground, am I right Siobhan?' She was using her hand to cover her smile, she couldn't comment.

'It's brilliant; the place looks fantastic, guys.'

Mark had a gentle country accent. He followed Elliot who was strutting towards the brand-new sofa. 'Get over here, check this out.' Elliot was hoping for some support in his choice of suite, another new acquisition. Siobhan was busy pouring her bottle of beer into a glass. She placed two more logs on the fire and decided to let them have their time together, Emily would soon arrive. 'I'll go... we need music at this stage of the night!' She let them know as she moved away to fulfil her duties.

'Stunning!' Mark uttered tracing the line of her skirt as she swayed her glass in a humorously sultry jaunt across the room.

'Keep your eyes to yourself, mate. I'm this far away from thumping you.' Elliot stated, pinching his fingers at his eye line.

The two men watched her make her way from the iPod to the table with the gas lighter in her hand.

'Am I cruel?' Mark intimated. It had been a while.

'You know I'm no good' was the first track to kick off proceedings with Amy Winehouse on vocals, it was fun and fitting at the same time.

The room lit up in burnt orange as the fresh logs caught flame. They had lamps either side of the room and the dimmer lights on low in the kitchen. The dining table was pre-set for four with a spare chair at either end. There was a fresh bouquet of garden flowers on the table in a hand-crafted vase that acted as a centre-piece. The linen napkins wrapped, the silverware polished, Siobhan had made light work of it.

'That's a nice piece!' Mark announced, speaking with great muster. He was examining the painting that had been re-hung above the fireplace. Elliot suspected that Mark was still toying with him as he was yet to make any comment on his new choice of sofa. 'Mate, there are those of us that have it!' Elliot spouted.

'I'll give you that, smart arse!' Mark had never tried his hand at painting. A paint roller and a one and a half-inch brush he could tackle but nothing that veered away from that. Neither of his friends was into art enough to make a career of it, but Elliot's painting still took pride of place above the mantelpiece. 'He's a dab hand,' Mark thought to himself admiringly. The painting looked incandescent with the fire blazing beneath it. It was reason enough to remember that particular Autumn night.

'She's not too shabby either when it comes to painting a picture!' Elliot waffled on as he took Mark on a guided tour of the place; they had moved the entire house around. Siobhan had one of her new works hung by the dining table and another by the entrance. They went to live drawing classes together and were committed hobbyists, competitive sometimes too.

'Wait 'til I tell you...' Elliot started. He was in top form, having one of his usual pharmaceutical encounters to share. Elliot had worked for five years in the same chemist after qualifying from college. There were copious positions to be obtained in Dublin with his pharmaceutical degree, but Elliot had only ever wanted a job as a simple pharmacist. He was undeniably funny; it was his client base that gave variety to his stories. It was the truths of his punters' conditions and their frankness that brought pun to the equation.

'We'll call him Thomas Jefferson...' Elliot always starts in the same way. The pharmacy was a breeding ground for flippancy and farce; his boss was a witty eccentric. Elliot loved his job, and Mark never tired of his enthusiasm. The sciences were never Mark's thing; he didn't have the head for science, where with Elliot it was part of his natural make-up. Business hadn't always been Mark's thing either. It was a topic he took up at college because he couldn't identify any other passion. It was a good, well-rounded academic pursuit, not a dream venture; it was the same for the bulk of his classmates.

Only a small part of what Mark learned at college was of any value to him in his first job. The anarchic repetition of bullet points had left him wanting; he had felt like an anaesthetised moron in the build-up to each exam. Much of what Mark learnt proved futile in his first management role. He'd trained in accounts and web design among other things, but as time transpired, he was better able to put forward a case for new in-house strategies. Mark found it difficult to remember the systems he'd learned by the time he got around to it but once re-absorbed in the study, he regained his skill set and overtook his original college comprehension.

While Elliot regaled him with hilarious tales from the past week at the pharmacy, Mark couldn't help but let his mind wander. For a man with so many talents, Mark couldn't help but acknowledge that Elliot had settled at a young age. Mark had always been the more adventurous of the two, and now as at other times, he wondered what Elliot would have done if he had never met the lovely Siobhan.

Mark pictured Elliot on a subcontinental mission, at the far ends of the earth, sharing his antidotes with dosed up tribal members. He knew Elliot inside out, to say the man would struggle to cope with any dating scene was an understatement; he'd never even asked another woman out. There was a distinct gap in his friend's social awareness. It was not that Elliot was naïve, but he knew nothing when it came to courtship rituals. Mark had this picture of Elliot, wondering where to put his hands, a skinny bloke in a white coat surrounded by natives with sticks in their noses. He could see him gulp at the sight of bare-breasted women bejewelled in ancient turquoise with face-painted children on their hips.

From Elliot's perspective, there were concerns about Mark's well-being. Elliot was aware that Mark had jumped into this new job. His earlier employer had practically been a father to him. To one extent or another, he knew that Mark felt that he'd betrayed the man. The new job had started off rough, but Mark had a natural flair for business. He was a prompt delegator; seriously organised and ultimately keen to learn.

The floor staff at T&E International Shipping had taken it in the neck from the other floor managers; so, they were at odds with Mark from the start. It didn't sit comfortably with him. He was spoilt by the four years of camaraderie he had experienced in his first job, and by the mutual respect there that had been so unshakable. Not knowing the details of what his new team had been through made it harder to fix. Mark soon grasped that much of the upheaval was being created by upper management.

'How are things, work wise?' Elliot made his enquiries. Having finished up his drink, he had just returned with two fresh beer bottles.

'Everything's shipshape.' Mark responded. Elliot had such a trustworthy face.

'And the office goons?'

'Still goons, but hey thanks for reminding me.' Mark didn't want to talk about work. He would have needed to turn them away in the first place, refusing to venture out on a night with the executive circle was near on impossible now.

'You're still eating out then?'

'Choking on my suppers, but yeah! Point that out!'

'Tonight, you will eat in the company of good friends.'

'Well, thank you for that, Elliot. I'm bloody famished.'

'I have some warm bread.' Elliot informed him, but Mark just smiled and shook his head.

'Leave it, no. I want to wait.'

'It's not a bother.' Elliot pointed out as he went to the kitchen and returned to show Mark the bread. 'It's a new recipe. I have a second batch in the oven.'

'I'll wait but thanks, yeah, it smells divine.'

Elliot was famously biased when it came to restaurants. He could decipher the frugal mastery of one kitchen, from the pretentious twee of another, be they low-budget or high-end. Few restaurant owners were driven by a passion for serving excellent food. It didn't have to be Michelin star to be inspiring. Few chefs, Elliot had decided, were offered the opportunity to cultivate a talent outside their own homes, forced to focus on repetitive production line agility.

'You can handle these guys, Mark', Elliot reassured him, noticing that his friend had gone quiet.

'I'm a man of many talents, Elliot.'

'That I know, mate, you will find a way to conquer it and handle these guys! You've always got there in the past.'

Elliot sensed uneasiness in Mark since he'd started this new job, growing insecurity. He had been forced to bring Mark back to his old self more than once, but tonight he was fine. He was neither distracted nor cagey. Elliot had been concerned.

It was up to Mark to control the expectations of his floor staff, he had pushed his crew to their limits and wanted to follow that up with incentives and further raise the bar. But, Mournaghan had dismissed his suggestion without looking at the advantages. He was amused by Mark's naivety, quickly sounding out the prevalent attitude of upper management; the more you gave the workforce; the more entitled these people felt.

Mark had watched executives run up elaborate expense accounts as if they were buying groceries. They were players in suits with highbrow attitudes and expensive tastes. He knew the form. These same executives acknowledged their equals while strutting from office to the carport, otherwise wearing a distant glare that the men on the ground had grown accustomed to seeing.

Chapter 4

'I'm going to give Siobhan a hand, are you okay there for a drink?' Elliot asked, not wanting to abandon his mate.

'I'm fine for now!'

'Can I help?' Mark called over.

'No please, stay where you are. I'll be back in a minute.' Elliot hollered, as he checked on Siobhan's progress. She was busy basting the fondants in butter and putting the finishing touches to the deserts. She could take a selection of sweet morsels to work on Monday; it was amazing how well a slice of desert went down at lunchtime, arriving with her dedicated tin put a smile on everybody's face.

'Hey, I forgot to ask, have any voluptuous babes cropped up on the scene?'

'Nothing exceptional happening here, mate... You'd be the first to know.'

Mark met Elliot once a week and sometimes twice with Siobhan in tow, they usually went for an inexpensive bite to eat and hit the local for a few drinks. Mark had been fighting off office colleagues who expected him to attend all form of evening events. The executives that were married with kids could bail out easier, needing to get home to their families.

These executives could be underhanded, arranging future dalliances with women who were already out on dates with their other work associates. If a woman was not yet married, there was no line to cross; that was the unspoken policy as far as Mark could see. Merely a handful of women were deemed eligible in their circles; mutual attraction was affiliated with status and the necessity of an extensive third level education. Ralph Mournaghan's "stand-in" business that night with Laura Keating was another matter altogether. Mark saw fit to share the situation with Elliot though neither could fathom what Mournaghan's agenda was just yet.

Elliot was quick to announce. 'The guy is a leech, definitely one to watch your back with.' Mark had already told Elliot stories about Mournaghan and the menagerie of cluck heads that hung on his every word. Mark knew that his friend's eyes had been opened. Elliot's world was much simpler than Mark's; his life revolved around the punters at the pharmacy, Siobhan's family, his own and their wide array of colourful friends. 'Have you heard from the lads?' Elliot asked.

Mark's two other best friends, Brian and Alfie, had emigrated to Australia in the downturn. Except for the occasional Skype, his school buddies were virtual strangers now. Elliot had hung out with them when they lived in Dublin, and the four lads were inseparable for a good two years before the guys left. Alfie had settled in straight away to the Australian life. He'd obtained a job as a bartender in a joint on Bondi beach, but Brian was finding it trickier. Brian was an electrician by trade, but that stood for very little in Australia without the right paperwork. He worked for six months as an apprentice before his full licence came through. It meant working on a basic salary for a while, but he loved being a sparkie.

'Brian's got a job with a new construction company. He's finally on a full licence. He's bought a greyhound to train with his new girlfriend too. Can't remember her name?'

'Melisa.' Elliot replied.

'That's it. Brian's working the stadiums with her at night. Alfie's still in that beach bar.'

The two lads had split up with their respective partners in Ireland before they moved abroad, so they were free as birds, at least until Brian met this Sheila.

'Bondi beach, ah!' Elliot shook his head.

'Bondi beach!' Mark reiterated smiling as both men clinked their glasses.

Elliot had no idea how out on his own his friend was feeling. The apartment that once filled Mark with optimism had become a restless place. There was no one to come home to; he rarely had the time or energy to invite anyone around. Elliot and Siobhan's friendship had become a constant lifeline, a reminder of his humanity while the pressure and game-play of the office execs grew more intense.

Elliot knew that Mark loved the practical side of his work; he had a recognisable talent at last and ran a tight ship for the company. But little did Elliot know that it didn't count for much, there was always another experienced floor manager waiting on the sidelines, a colleague from the boy's club who happened to be between appointments. There were no funny antidotes and no human stories in meeting impossible deadlines. Even his sister had enjoyable tales about the kids when she called on the phone.

'How are the folks?' Elliot prompted.

'Yeah, good... I haven't been home in ages.'

'Mate, it's been two months.' Elliot was quick to point it out. He knew how important it was for Mark to stay in touch, his family would be concerned otherwise.

Mark's sister had married a man that had a habit of berating her; they had two girls now. It hurt Mark to see her losing her backbone; there had been a time when they were close, but she was blindly in love now. His parents were preoccupied with their grandchildren and who could blame them, his nieces were incredible.

'Remember that guy with the varicose vein thing?' Mark voiced, attempting to distract himself.

Elliot was soon in full swing with another hilarious story from the pharmacy. It was just what Mark needed.

'Will I top you up there?' Elliot suggested.

'Yes, that will do nicely.'

Siobhan was suddenly in front of them. What a picture, he hadn't adequately taken her outfit into account. She was generally in the thick of it with them, but she was busy sprinkling her metaphorical glitter on the dishes tonight. She had made the potato fondants from scratch. Elliot had given the lamb an extra hour to allow for the probability of Emily's lateness. The starters only needed ten minutes; the lamb shanks were tenderising slowly in the oven; all the other preparation for dinner had been done.

'She's always late Emily, these music things can run over time,' Siobhan stated, both men nodded. 'Will I turn down the stove?' She asked.

Mark knew Emily as Siobhan's closest friend; he knew that they related in ways Siobhan and Elliot could not. Elliot had forgotten the conversations he had shared with Mark about her, and the stories of Siobhan's adventures that had brought Emily to life, Mark had long since been intrigued, he felt suddenly flushed by the thought of meeting her.

Looking at Siobhan's new fashion statement, Mark agreed with Elliot that not everyone could carry that look off. 'No, you look good, Siobhan.' Mark commented. Siobhan scrunched her forehead, she rarely trusted compliments.

'Enough said.' She blurted out.

'I think I'll shut up so.' Mark retorted.

'She's a lover, not a fighter, mate' Elliot shot back in laughter.

'Emily won't be long,' she promised as she smiled and stuck out her tongue to retreat.

Elliot had invited Mark over at Siobhan's request and let him know that Emily was planning to attend. Strangely, Elliot had talked Emily down; apparently, she was not the sophisticated kind of woman that Mark was used to, describing her as deep but impersonal, politically sharp and in no way romantically inclined. He reiterated the fact that she worked for a couple of hours a week with a local lawyer as a part-time legal secretary, she waitressed and wrote the odd song, not a big achiever he had said.

Mark frequently enjoyed Elliot's summations but not that night; he already had a clear understanding of Emily in his mind. Mark had gone to dinner parties in Elliot and Siobhan's before, and for one reason or another, Emily had never been able to make it. She had also been over for dinner when Mark had to cancel due to work.

There was no tackling Elliot on the night of the invite; he was prohibitive and jumpy, not wanting to give away anything about Emily's history. All three of them Elliot, Siobhan and Emily, they were great friends, and he was protective when it came to her. Elliot wasn't attracted to the woman, that much Mark knew, but there was something that didn't gel with him around the invite. There was no issue; it was just unlike Elliot to knock someone or talk them down.

'Oden's on his way over.' Elliot whispered with his back to the kitchen, 'I organised it during the week but say nothing.'

'Okay?' Mark replied.

Oden was Elliot's younger brother. Though Mark and Oden had met several times and knew each other's lives inside out, they had never sat through dinner together or hung out in Elliot and Siobhan's place before. Oden wasn't one to stay long anywhere where there wasn't an Xbox, and in Elliot and Siobhan's, the Xbox was banned.

Mark's first thought was of the table setting, preened for an intimate occasion.

Elliot had taken away the beer bottles and transferred a glass into his hand as Siobhan crossed the room with an open bottle of wine. She wasted no time in pouring before returning to the kitchen to turn up the stove. Mark sat back in the chair and began to realise how hungry he was. The smells from the kitchen were intense. The juice of the meats merged with the herbs and spices, the waft of warm bread offset by the fragrant wine now in his hand. He was a happy man if a hungry one.

'Emily's on her way,' Siobhan called out.

Elliot had mentioned that Emily had this enormous maternal love for Oden; she had a knack for getting him to slow down and relax apparently. She listened to the scientific depth of his understanding and even quizzed him on it. He was enormously insightful. Mark was pleased that Oden was joining them but was curiously struck by the idea that the boy may have been a decoy. Siobhan had planned a romantic couple's night, and she had no idea that Oden was coming. The doorbell rang. Elliot was up, and on his feet but he wasn't quick enough to catch Siobhan who was already at the door.

'Oden!' Siobhan's voice was strained. She was finding it difficult to disguise the surprise in her voice.

'Yoh, bro!' Elliot had made it to the door. 'Come in, me auld compadre!'

Siobhan was astonished as Oden approached and gave her a swift kiss on the cheek before he proceeded to wrap himself around his brother, the lad was oblivious to the scene.

'I thought I said Thursday; you're a muttonhead.' The tension was palatable as Elliot brought Oden over to Mark. 'I cook, and this guy turns up without fail,' Elliot explained, 'there's nothing wrong with his sense of smell.' 'Or timing?' Mark added. Elliot glanced apologetically at Siobhan over his brother's shoulder as she attempted to close the door, still stunned. Her night wasn't going to plan.

Mark jumped from his seat to greet the lad.

'What's the craic with you, Oden?'

'White and hairy!' Oden responded with a smile.

The lad had an under-chin beard. He had a crazy stretcher earring embedded in his right lobe, the kind that would leave him with a gaping hole in his ear if it was worn too long. Mark struggled to listen when the lad set out on a verbal rampage. He was careful to conceal that fact as Elliot would forever rise to his brother's defence. Oden had been diagnosed with mild Asperger's Syndrome as a kid. He was relatively sound now, everyone agreed.

As a young lad, no one could touch or hold him, but adolescence had put an end to that; for the most part, he was an affectionate sort of lad now.

Mark was pretending to listen to Elliot as he ranted on about the wonder that was his brother. The atmosphere was still intense, and Siobhan still visibly flustered; Oden was relaying new technology reports at top speed, news had arrived in through social media; an entirely new arena for artificial intelligence. To Oden, it was a matter of life or death getting the information across before he forgot it. They had little interest in the topic but that never registered with Oden.

Elliot glanced back to discover Siobhan mouthing the words 'Holy shit' in his direction. This turn of events had shattered entirely, her hopes for the night.

'A drink, brother?'

'Beer would be incredible.' Oden proclaimed.

Oden wanted to get a photograph, the photos Elliot had of his brother were dated, and he had none with Mark in the frame. He had promised not to leave the stretcher earring in too long, so a quick snap was vital; he was building on a collection of stretch earring photographs involving all his friends.

'It will only take a minute, shush, come on.' Oden shimmied in as the three lads linked shoulders together, laughing as Oden took a photo with his phone.

The doorbell rang again, but this time it was Emily's turn to step into the mix. As she entered, the tension abated, the frantic atmosphere melting to a mellow lull. Mark was startled somewhat, too embarrassed to look her straight in the eye. The edge of his vision transfixed on the softness of her jumper as she brought a new disposition to the event. There was a natural courtesy that he recognised in her. The presence of her unusually animated soul was what lead him to believe that he had met her somewhere, he reckoned.

'I'm so sorry everyone, it ran late as per, I'm a nuisance.'

The two women embraced. Emily pulled away at once to check out Siobhan's attire. She raised an eyebrow and smiled affectionately. 'You look perfect, girl.'

Elliot spoke out. 'You look like you need to get close to the fire!' He took the coat from Emily's hand, allowing her to produce a brown paper bag filled with chutney and jams.

There was a shy veiled recognition in the way she acknowledged Mark. She turned to him again and nodded, her warmth then given in equal measure to that of her friends.

'It's something and nothing Siobhan, I picked them up at the Saturday market in Clontarf; sweet pepper chutney, lime curd and rhubarb and apple jam.'

Mark watched as everyone gravitated towards the dining table. Emily possessed a rare but natural nonchalance. Her soft cream mohair jumper and tight straight jeans were cosy and casual. Her eyes were decidedly blue, cerulean blue. Mark felt somewhat awestruck as she approached, his stomach growled loudly to his amusement as he thrust forward to stretch out his hand.

'A pleasure to meet you,' he acknowledged.

'And you, we've managed to miss each other on a couple of occasions.'

'I hope we've seen the last of that,' he said.

'To great friendships!' Elliot announced as he raised a glass.

'To tonight!' Emily expressed openly, with resounding approval.

Siobhan and Elliot got to work on the dinner. In unison, they moved in a light-footed fashion from the kitchen to the table with every form of delight. Oden and Emily had a good thing going on; it was witty and tender. Oden was asked to leave his shoes by the entrance; he would be free then to make contortionist shapes in his chair. They had lots of news for one another. Oden erased in Emily's presence any notion of sarcasm; she had a mellowing effect on his mood from the moment she entered the room. Mark watched on as Emily connected with Oden like a great aunt, and the lad was evidently at home with that. A wry look silenced his need to impart endless realms of information, allowing him to join in rather than be central to the conversation.

Mark was mesmerised and fully aware of Emily's every motion. He didn't want to be predatory though he was unravelling in the allure of her complexion, body shape and consciousness. Little did he know that her detachment was ingrained, she took his occasional flirtations as nothing more than friendly gestures.

Emily was apt at egotistical disengagement, reshaping romantic overtures while putting everyone at their ease. Her voice was earthy, and her words punctuated with sharp humour. Elements that naturally melted into a sophisticated form of benevolence, a benevolence that he could not pinpoint. Mark was a more sceptical person than she was, he realised. He would soon see that her understanding of the world was filtered with empathy.

Politically, she was well-informed. There was talent in the way she could pinpoint the prevalent outlook of a nation, defining their belief system in historical development, exposing the lack of cultural insight of one country in respect of another. People were under-concerned or preoccupied with their betterment, he knew that much. To Emily's thinking, everyone needed to know themselves better, including herself. People would be well advised to dig deep and question their behaviours in a world so filled with chaos and numbed generic responses. Siobhan couldn't wait to talk about the recent breakthroughs that were achieved in primary schools, where children were practising mindfulness.

Siobhan and Emily were enjoying the food, but beyond that they shared some snappy banter, pulling witty character descriptions out of the bag. They could unearth the funnier side of people and stay relevant which wasn't easy; the warm-hearted mannerisms they detailed, their animated thought processes, they were hilarious. Their humour fitted well with Elliot's pharmaceutical tales, they were different, but one seemed to compliment the other. Emily was comfortable in their company, and Mark between laughs was searching for a place where they might have met. He suspected that he knew her from somewhere or maybe it was the stories that Mark had heard, regardless he was enjoying himself.

The food was beyond fabulous; the greens were unlike any vegetables he had ever tasted, sweet and savoury mouthfuls of deliciousness served with the lamb falling off the bone. The butteriness of the perfectly tanned potato fondants genuinely joyful. The accompanying jus was made to dance on the taste buds. A hum of good humour galloped across the table as they freely shared wit without any trace of self-consciousness.

Emily had caught Mark's effervescent curiosity at different stages; she wasn't shy but took no notice. Both Emily and Siobhan had acute emotional intelligence, Siobhan taking great pleasure from the naive way that Elliot sometimes acted. Mark was glad to be able to back what they were saying with his observations as an array of desserts flooded the table. Oden was sliding off his chair laughing. The guests were asked to try everything. There was a baked blueberry cheesecake, white chocolate and almond tart, and a plate of tiny, crispy cream profiteroles with a salted caramel sauce.

They had enjoyed a goat's cheese starter on home-made sour-dough bread with a balsamic and onion reduction, so it was a good half hour before they got around to tasting each luxurious surprise. The coffees were up, and the wine momentarily slowed, their sighs of delight and laughter memorable and rewarding.

Chapter 5

The night air was dizzying, at first, its crisp immediacy kissing their cheeks with a blushing smack. As they closed the door, they were alerted to the potential free-fall of those undulating steps. The alcohol was taking new effect as they steadied themselves on the railings. Mark buttoned up the heavy grey duffel coat he had borrowed from Elliot. It was an ugly mismatch with his rose-pink shirt, but his vanity had no defence against an evening that had turned so bitterly cold.

He watched as Emily pulled down on her scruffy woollen hat, she hadn't expected the chill in the air. She stood exposed, wavering as she acclimatised to the atmosphere, slipping a pair of gloves from her pocket, she used them to indicate a way forward. The idea that she was now alone with Mark was momentarily daunting. He was a great friend to Elliot and Siobhan, but he was still a virtual stranger to her.

'I'm getting over a head cold this week. Thus, the crazy hat!' Emily announced awkwardly. She explained that she was canvassing for support as her workmates had already knocked her choice of headgear.

'I didn't notice. Your head cold that is, not your headwear.'

It was the ugliest hat he'd ever seen, and yet her face was even brighter in it, her eyes softer still. He wasn't easily enamoured, but his attention at different stages of the night had been fixed on her, he could admit that much to himself. He hoped he'd been discreet, having more than once employed an expression of cynicism to shield his fascination.

She was astonishing to watch. She had an air of innocence yet there was depth, a sharpness that was brutally profound.

'I hope you don't mind me walking you home. Elliot is protective but has good intentions. I can get you a cab?'

'No, Mark. It's fine; I enjoy a walk. Besides, I need to work that meal off before I sleep.'

He couldn't have agreed more; it was a gift to be able to share her company for a while.

'Their cooking would put you in a blissful coma.'

'That's for sure.' He entirely agreed.

'They're great, aren't they? Good friends are a deep blessing.' She said. It was for both a means of fulfilment that existed nowhere else outside those four walls. Siobhan and Elliot were always insightful; they celebrated life, even with Oden riding gunshot beside them. Limits and boundaries were off the table for the night as they dodged bullets to avoid the mundane. Neither tragedy nor oppression could suppress their need for joy; Elliot and Siobhan were untouchable on such nights.

The two walked on, spellbound by the closeness of the night sky, quietly cherishing the finale of a great event. Both of their lives revolved around the inner city with its monumental buildings and tower blocks. These few rows of tenement house were authentic Dublin. It fitted that Siobhan and Elliot should set up home there. These were the streets where ballads were conceived, born in the minds of its long passed local legends.

'You warm enough?' Mark inquired.

'Thank you, yes, I'm fine. Siobhan and Elliot give a great party! I can't begin to tell you how much they mean to me. It's such a wonderful place to set up home, yeah?' He turned and smiled. As Emily talked, he captured the gist of what she was saying, though to him her voice was more like a gentle melody on the radio.

'Oden too,' she continued... 'I often sense that I'm in a new place when I leave their company. I know that sounds hipped out.'

'Even after coffee?' He asked.

She nodded, surprised by the truth. 'Even after coffee...they do, they inspire me.'

The two of them walked on and conversed without trepidation, but it was simpler to talk trivia.

'So, are you from Dublin?' He questioned her. 'I do know you were at boarding school with Siobhan.'

Mark's words were met with a quick despondent glance. What odds did it make if she came from Dublin or not?' She wondered what else Siobhan or Elliot might have told him? She was conscious that she looked like her knickers' drawer had just been rifled, her private life she cherished above everything else. Siobhan was discreet though she shared most of her thoughts with Elliot as couples often do, and Mark was Elliot's key confidante beyond Siobhan.

'No! I'm not from Dublin.' Her tone was sour; her behaviour out of sync with how he had seen her that night. Her tone no longer gentle or elegant, but stern.

'I was curious, sorry.' He was surrendering his desire to know more. 'You don't have an accent; it's the only reason that I asked.'

Mark waited, but Emily made no further comment. He knew when to quit. They walked on in silence, avoiding the more populated route. They stuck to the residential areas, made up of cobbled streets and row upon row of red-bricked cottages. They passed an old grey stone building, a factory that still had its old livery stable doors and a matching wrought iron sign that hung over this arched relic of a gateway. It reminded her of a painting by Bill Ennis, an artist she admired from Stoneybatter.

There was the occasional rustle of leaves, the wind blowing in a light south-easterly direction. The occasional house light was left on as the street outside whistled faintly; there was little or no sign of life. It was way past the hour. Narrow footpaths ran along rows of front doors with curtained windows; there was the occasional ornament that suggested the orientation of its occupier. A hippie relic in one window, a plastic sacred heart figurine in the next, more than one cottage with a faceless clay model wearing wire wings.

Mark's attention was captivated by a bunch of sweetpeas that tumbled from a hanging wicker basket. It was very late in the season for a thriving sweetpea. It was rare enough to happen upon sweetpea even in the late summer months. He'd identified with the flower long since; it symbolised for him where he wanted to get to in life, having dreamt up the garden in his ideal of home.

Emily's mind was elsewhere; her eyes were tracing the overhead power lines on the other side of the street. The birds were silently observing them from their private perch, pecking at each other's feathers between glances. It was pleasant walking without having to talk. Mark had a Chet Baker song in his head, 'My sweet Valentine'. He chuckled to himself at that moment; life was playfully promising just then.

Startled suddenly, they both looked up at each other. The insidious rustle of a plastic bag had grabbed the pair's attention. Emily instinctively touched Mark's arm. She was caught off balance for an instant. They listened intently, both puzzled. There was something eerie afoot, something out of kilter that provoked an unexpected curiosity in both.

Mark edged forward, and she followed, both shuffling towards the strange noise as they pinpointed the crackling sound three cars ahead of them. They made their way through litter and leaf, stopping cautiously to confirm the sustained presence of this peculiar reverberation that had captured their minds. Nervously, they moved in on the car. The wind whistled softly down the street as the moonlight cast shadows on the front of the car bonnet. Emily stepped back in quick motion, her chest leaping with fright. 'Mother of God!' She whispered as he followed her gaze.

There in front of them, majestic and wild-eyed; stood a fox, frozen to the spot, just as blindsided as they were. A city fox that had been rummaging through the litter, his eye line fixed as he took them in, in full measure. He appeared to be evaluating the danger. The three stood there, frozen in time until, with a swift turn to the left, the tangerine coat disappeared between two parked cars. 'Holy crap!' Mark muttered. He could just about speak.

'Too right!' Emily belted out in a whisper. 'That was something. I've never seen a fox close up.' She shared.

'Me neither,' Mark mumbled in response. 'We don't get them in the town that I come from, none that I know of at least.'

'Uhm...' She gasped for breath, raised an eyebrow then touched his arm again before they made their way further along the road. They had a shared experience now, an unexpected happening to relay to Elliot and Siobhan. They were vigilant as they turned the next corner, scanning a hundred yards ahead to either side of the road. It took two blocks for their excitement to subside. By then, they both conceded that a second viewing was unlikely. As they walked a further block, conversation again began to open up between them.

Mark did most of the talking as they discovered that they both shared a love of Wicklow with its exceptional scenery. Strawberry Beds was another favourite location and a place they both cycled to on a warm summer's day. They had more in common than Emily wanted to admit. They both loved 'The Piano' and 'Betty Blue', they were great movies. Talk again faded, but Mark still wanted to know more, he thought to ease her in on a more practical topic.

'You work as a legal secretary, from what I can remember Siobhan telling me.'

'I temp, part-time.' She paused and looked puzzled before saying another word. 'I've been getting work to take home lately; it suits me though I get distracted and end up staying up to write tunes. But yeah, it's good. You work for a big shipping company, right?'

Mark was relieved that the conversation was flowing.

'The job has its ups and downs.' He shared. 'I was happier where I worked before, but there were fewer prospects there. I don't know. I expected more of myself, I guess.'

Emily chuckled before lowering her face. They continued to walk and talk, remembering concerts they'd both been to, books they'd read: Paulo Coelho was an author they both liked and then fell out with for no good reason. They loved Steinbeck's book, 'The Pearl' which was by Emily's standards one of the great tragic novels of their time.

She was passionate when it came to 'Love in A Time of Cholera' by Gabriel Garcia Marquez, but that was mostly for its prose. He thought Florentino was too seedy a character for his liking. She strongly made the point that this was because Florentino had lost hope of a relationship, a relationship of any depth having lost his Fermina. With the possibility of Fermina's love returning, he abandoned his way of life on the outside chance that he might get to care for Fermina again. When her situation changed, he was right back to where he'd been as a young man, on a quest for their happiness. Mark laughed. 'Jesus, but that was one impassioned argument.'

Her eyes near popped out of their sockets. 'See you!' She shot out at him; Mark laughed again.

She was starting to get the intimate form of provocation he seemed to naturally exude. They talked of the great poets, writers and musicians that had been and gone. Mark knew that Emily had lost both her parents, how that came to be, he had no idea. He remembered that Siobhan had said they were involved in the arts.

Emily had some insight as to why these masters of the arts were only granted short stays, having read studies on the matter.

'Your folks were artists or musicians?' He asked curiously. Emily was appalled. He hadn't thought the comment through and genuinely had not set out to upset her.

'I didn't tell you that, I didn't mention them.'

'Siobhan and Elliot were at their anniversary a couple of months back? I just remembered. I'm sorry; they said they were involved in the arts.'

'They did, did they?'

'I didn't mean to offend you.'

She quickly realised that she had overstepped the bounds in attacking him when he was just acting out of concern. They walked on in silence, and once he let go of the questions, she relaxed again. She relayed a few lines of a song that had been preoccupying her mind, wanting to break the tension.

'There is nothing more powerful than a song entering your mind out of nowhere.' She had a sense of composure even when riled and was with every curve a woman. Her skin mocked the aesthetic of porcelain, still young, untouched by pollutants or time.

The women that Mark was accustomed to were easier to read. They gave him signals to let him know if they were interested in him or not. Emily's view of him was unreadable. He thought of kissing her every time she looked his way. There was no way of telling; innuendo would sail past her; he knew that without trying. He thought to ask her to dinner, but she spoke before he had the chance.

'I'm going to cut off here, thank you so much, sincerely!'

'This is you then?' Mark did not expect the ending to arrive so abruptly.

'It's been a nice experience!'

'I'm with you on that one.' Mark stated unapologetically.

She moved closer. 'Thanks for walking me home!' Leaning forward, she kissed him on the cheek as she took his hand to shake it. For the first time that night her perfume reached him, it suited her with its citrus note and sweet, subtle tone. She drew back and nodded a goodbye without saying another word. He thought to linger and watch her as she walked away, but that was not the thing to do.

It took him another twenty-five minutes to make his way home. Mark walked back the way he came, ordinarily he'd have waved a cab, but he wasn't ready for his place yet. His apartment wasn't a place he'd have wanted her to visit; it lacked charm, it was sparse and uninteresting, bland, soulless and easy to clean.

His books were still packed in a box at the bottom of his wardrobe. He had a painting that Elliot made for him; it was not yet framed but abandoned in a paper portfolio case under his bed. There were other paintings boxed away that he'd collected. The linen curtains and duvet were neutral. Neutral was a way to describe how his life had been. It was time now for some form of colour, some vibrancy. Emily. Sweet Emily.

Chapter 6

'Boss, there's a problem. You need to get over here quick.' The new trainee accompanied Mark across the main loading dock and further on as they made their way past aisle two.

'It's the parts,' Joyce informed Mark, joining them as they approached the vehicle.

Four workers stood stanchly, arms folded as the smoke billowed from the back of the lifting machine. One man had a fire extinguisher resting against his foot. Mark's eyes focused on the man's vein protruding hands, the extinguisher hose and nozzle, tight in his grip.

'You didn't get to use the extinguisher?' Mark put the question to him.

'Not yet. These things are unpredictable.' Spraying down the lifter meant putting the machine permanently out of action. Mark could only do that if his staff or the building were in jeopardy. In retrospect he thought, it may not have been the worst idea to finish off the damn contraption, but the opportunity for doing damage had passed, valuable piece of kit or not.

'One of you, please. Get the coolant and a wire brush.' Mark insisted. The new apprentice scuttled off; eager to please. Mark's frustration was apparent. 'Joyce, can you head over to aisle one? Take two men with you. If you can get the top shelf items cleared?'

'Not a problem, boss.'

'You can move the aisle one lifter over here when you're done.' Mark added.

'You'll be okay here, boss?'

'Yeah! I'll work on the lifter. We can ship out this section together when you get back.'

With his instructions in hand, Joyce left.

One of the men had received a blister burn to his wrist, and Mark insisted on having a look.

The worker was feeling awkward. 'It's fine, not worth the worry but it was luck that prevailed here. It seriously kicked off, Mark. We got off lightly.'

Our Diligent Souls

Mark was adamant that this team player needed to report his injury to Imelda at the reception.

'Get her to write it in the incident book. Make sure it's recorded, have her spray the burn.' As the guy walked away, Mark called after him. 'Take ten or as much time as you need. Have a cigarette and some sweet tea. Just make sure you're alright when you get back to work!'

The new trainee arrived with the coolant. The machine's engine had cut out a full ten minutes at that stage. Though the smoke had vaporised, its pungent smell still filtered the airwaves. The engine was roasting; it took an hour to refill her with coolant and scrub away the sticky sinew that had been created.

Joyce was quick to arrive back with an extra man in tow.

'Aisle one is looking good. The men reckon they can take it from there, Mark. You go on ahead. You haven't stopped!' Joyce suggested. 'We had lunch earlier.'

Joyce was the one team member that cared about Mark; he recognised that Mark respected his work ethic. Mark was never critical of those who worked at a slower pace; he just encouraged them; it was all but miraculous the way they had grown in confidence. Mark was in no form to head off; he needed to push on regardless.

'Thanks, Joyce, but if we get this out of-the-way, we might just make it out on time today.'

Mark understood that his standard of work had to match that of his best team member and more where he could show it. You lead by example, his father always said. With their instructions in hand, the afternoon flew by, and they were looking at the last hour or so. Mark was an animal for work, the sheer enthusiasm he used to complete a task was heroic. He dug in with a zealous pride though he was never harsh on the men that surrounded him. He helped where others fell short in comparison. This simple action had bonded his men. The more capable lent a hand to their less industrious workmates to fall in line with his work ethic.

'Come on, guys. We need to push this. Aisle five boxes 27543-29543.'

He checked his clipboard briefly while Joyce wrote the numbers on a pad and tore out the piece of paper.

'Right, we've got forty minutes.'

Our Diligent Souls

The workers disappeared, duty bound. Mark was left standing with one foot on a pallet, the other secure on the poured cement floor. He had a further set of instructions to give to the others through his blue tooth; he clicked the side receiver.

'Yeah! Aisle eight?' He said as he checked the list. '83216-93216 has to be clear; we have sixty minutes. The sooner you're done, the sooner you're out of here and home. Keep me posted!'

Mark turned to make his way over to join the lads when he came face to face with Ralph Mournaghan. Ralph just laughed.

'Something funny?' Mark quipped attempting to get back to his work. Ralph had a habit of creeping up behind him, but he was in no mood to pretend that it was okay with him, not today. His hatred for the man squeezed at his throat; the liable lifting machine was for large part Ralph's doing.

'Here!' Mournaghan stated, handing over two envelopes. 'I resolved those salary payments for your men.'

'Good!' Mark responded, as he stopped in his tracks and took the envelopes from Mournaghan's hand. He was half expecting an absurd grip game, but the cheques were freely passed.

He tapped the envelopes in his hand. 'We still have issues that need addressing. The parts for that lifter, I've said it before, the lifter's not doing the job we need it to do. One of my workers nearly lost his foot to that machine last week. It was smoking today, and we had to bring a lifter over from aisle one. It's hampering operations, and I have a man with a burn on his hand.'

Mournaghan sneered while nodding his head. Though Mark was disturbed by the man's twisted expression, he continued.

'We've had to make up two hours today, moving a lifter from one aisle to another with men doing the bulk of the work manually. You'll have a walk out on your hands.'

Mark was making sure he got the point across but so was Ralph Mournaghan.

'No, Mark, you will have a walk out on your hands.' Mournaghan moved away before turning on his heels. 'I'll do what I can when I can, Mark, that's as much as I can promise.'

'It's a serious safety risk to my men. Do you understand that?'

Mark lowered his head as Mournaghan re-joined him.

'Are you attempting to make light of my authority?'

'Do we want a lawsuit, Ralph? None of these men can afford to be out of work with an injury.'

'And that's why we have insurance. You're quick off the mark, Mark.' The sarcasm was dripping from Mournaghan's ill-shaped mouth.

'None of my men want to lose a body part. Trust me on that.'

'I'm not here to make people happy, mate; I'm here to make money.'

Mark realised that arguing with him was pointless. He pulled a folded sheet of paper from his back pocket.

'Here. I've researched the parts that are needed. There's a reputable dealer on the south side of the city, with proper trading papers. I talked to him on the phone. He could deliver the parts tomorrow.'

Mournaghan removed the paper from his hand. 'I'll have a look when I next get a chance.'

Mark filled his nostrils and turned, walking off in the direction of aisle one. He'd wasted enough time.

'So!' Mournaghan called after him. 'You had your slice of fun with Laura? You enjoyed her?'

Mark could not believe his ears; he stopped in his tracks and turned ready to answer Mournaghan.

'I'm terrible,' Ralph said sarcastically, 'I feel bad that I didn't get the chance to call and say I couldn't make it back. But, I'm sure you convinced her that something must have come up, being the amenable fella that you are!'

'I'm guessing there was no after party in Davin Turlock's place then?'

Mournaghan smiled and looked at him with a shifty expression. 'Why, were you hoping to fall in love with a lovely lady?'

Mark's thoughts were at once of Emily. He removed her image from his mind with as much grace as possible before he stood glaring at the buffoon. His picture image of her was too precious; he couldn't think of her in the same room as Mournaghan. Right there, he understood how distorted Mournaghan's idea of beauty was.

'I thought things might happen for you and Laura.' Ralph commented, smiling as he stood back, smug and yet full of cowardice.

'She was pleasant company, Ralph. I made sure she got home safely.'

Ralph sized Mark up. 'Safely out of your league, my friend.'

'Then why push me into that? What was that about?'

'Just testing the water, Mark.'

Few of Mournaghan's actions ever made sense. Mark chose not to retort. As Mournaghan started to walk away, he naturally turned to throw in one last comment amending his stride. 'There may be a bit of a whore in there?'

'Fix the part!' Mark stated plainly not able to stomach another word.

Mournaghan grinned. 'In my own good time, Mark. In my own good time!'

Chapter 7

It was the first of the poor weather, heavy showers with intervals; you'd expected Dublin bus would have given this bus stop a shelter. If the planning office had applied some common sense who knows, Oden reckoned. The bus stop was fifteen minutes from the closest college exit. The added frustration of no rain cover when you arrived, was just too much for him to grapple with, in his opinion. The buses were scheduled twenty minutes apart, but they appeared two at a time, every half hour or so. Oden didn't care for random, haphazard services; he needed a bus that was scheduled for two twenty, to arrive at two twenty. That way all was right with the world.

He thought through his schedule for the rest of the afternoon. He had an assignment to be handed in soon and had written the due dates in his journal. The last place he used the notebook was in his bedroom, finding it was a priority. He could pull an all-nighter where necessary. He just needed to remember to check in his journal.

'It's a pain in the ass, right?' A muffled voice was in his ear. The lashing rain wasn't helping the girl he thought as he turned to face her; her mascara rolling down her cheeks. Oden was unaware of Lucile up until that point though she shared a classroom with him for one of his modules.

'Bloody snakes, they could have at least put up a shelter, right? City planners, they don't care for students; we're a threat for sure. Someday we'll steal their jobs; that's the issue here. That is the issue.'

She was wearing a heavy anorak, her wet curls peeping out from under the hood. Oden instantly felt uncomfortable, as was often the case with the opposite sex. He was trying to figure out why on earth she was talking to him?

'Do you have an opinion?' She quizzed.

He was doing everything in his power to conceal his embarrassment; the whole deal left him utterly confused. How to respond, thought Oden. She had it lighter than him because she was articulate. This experience measured seven out of ten on Oden's Richter scale of awkwardness. He had a knack for offending people as he understood a limited number of social cues, this he openly acknowledged. It was only ever around established friends and family that he could be himself. Otherwise, it was a case of trial and error.

'Awful weather,' he remarked.

She lifted her face up and smiled.

'I haven't seen you in the college bar,' she pointed out, 'they're doing a two for one on Wednesday.'

'Two for one?' The words came out of his mouth though he hadn't planned to speak.

'Two cocktails for the price of one! Not that I drink much!' She asserted. 'I enjoy cocktails because they don't taste of alcohol. It's good to be social, keep your hand in, what do you think?'

Oden shrugged his shoulders at her then, immediately regretted the weakness of his gesture. 'Social is good,' he said when he spoke again. It was his second regrettable remark.

Oden hadn't taken in the four or five others that had gathered to get the bus. The schedule that had been essential minutes ago was forgotten, and he was only now aware of the crowd that had built up behind him. He hadn't seen the bus arrive but suddenly everyone bunched forward. This part of the bus journey was usually the hardest; it always made him jumpy. The same irrational fear made a return; that he might get crushed in the stampede.

'Can we call it a date? Cocktails, on Wednesday? I'll come find you!' Her voice echoed from behind as he stepped up onto the bus.

He was dumbstruck, and while he wanted to turn and say something composed and original, girls were not his forte. He didn't look back. His hand was trembling as he made his way to the card scanner and then proceeded to the nearest available empty seat, just where he liked it, at the back of the bus. He was grateful that there were no further comments.

An old woman with a plastic see-through rain scarf slowly placed her bag on the seat in front of him. He watched as she squeezed past her belongings to take the window seat before raising the parcel to put it on her knee, freeing up space for another passenger. The raindrops were still fresh on her plastic scarf. As she took the damn thing off, it splashed back at him and got him right in the eye.

The girl from the bus stop again came into focus. She had paid her fare and was struggling to balance, the bus already in full motion. He saw her gain ground, not knowing where to fix his eyes. The next thing he knew she was beside him, but not before he rubbed away a layer of skin from his sweaty hands.

'Shuffle up, shuffle over!' She insisted.

His face was glowing as he made room for this odd girl, a cookie chick, he thought. Elliot had warned him to steer clear of cookie chicks.

'Ah now!' She sounded out in relief as she lowered herself into the seat.

Oden needed to hold onto his bearings; he had that notebook to find so he could check out those due dates. His professor had refused to put the exam details online as class attendance was low. His mind was racing, and he was beginning to question where he had last seen the notebook, he wasn't sure that it was in his bedroom at all.

'I guess you must think I'm a stalker, right? I'm Lucile, L.U.C.I.L.E!' Oden's newest acquaintance stretched out her hand to greet him. 'I'm in the same room as you for computer architecture on a Monday and a Thursday. I've seen you there. I don't understand why I took up basic computing; I should have done coding, got into the gaming end of things. Just impulsive, that's me. I might transfer over, but it means losing my grant for a year. I want to do what I love.' Oden gripped his shoulder bag for dear life. He sat in silence before he finally got up the nerve to ask. 'You like games then, league of legends?'

'A lot,' she replied.

A Romanian couple started arguing in what sounded like double Dutch to them. It was far from playful. The Romanian girl was refusing to hand over a bag that she'd been holding behind her back. The guy that was with her was beyond vexed, he was trying desperately to get his point across. The entire bus was registering a blank expression, pretending not to notice. Oden and Lucile smiled at each other. They lowered their heads, instantly owning a sacred space together. The rain was pelting against the windows as the bus driver steered along the avenue. He took the corner with near wheelie effect, and Lucile and Oden were jammed against each other in the gravitational pull.

'Too much!' Oden grunted. He was angry with the driver. The spell they were under was broken as Lucile jumped up.

'I'd better go!'

Oden looked surprised; they hadn't even reached the next stop.

'Is this your stop?'

'No,' she acknowledged, 'I have to go.' The girl was struggling to get her footing. She gripped the top rail of the bus; it was still in transit towards the next bus stop.

'Wednesday then?' Oden called out after her, braver now.

She heard him alright; her face lit up in agreement. 'I'll come and find you,' she shouted back.

Her voice lingered as he examined his hands; he had a way to go before his stop. He caught her face one more time as she smiled back and pressed the yellow button to get out. He hadn't asked if she played League of Legends or if he had he couldn't remember. Oden again tried to think back to his schedule. The rocking of the bus and the pelting rain had left him distracted. It was lashing out there. She'd be soaked.

He was another fifteen minutes on-route before the bus finally got to his stop. It was a five-minute walk to his house from there, but he was ready for the chaos. The gang cooked dinner at seven and the latest episode of Game of Thrones was on the box tonight at the same time. He managed to make it to his bedroom without getting distracted. He found the notebook and the due date for the assignment; mission accomplished, Oden thought, falling on his bed in relief. But his mind soon shifted back to the girl with the runny mascara, who might be into League of Legends games.

Chapter 8

The five band members had been plugging away at the same song for under an hour. There were fifteen minutes left of studio time, and the vocalist was very nearly there. It was just one note in the bar of the chorus that kept running amuck. Emily was zoned in on what she expected to hear through the microphone, her frustration visible. The sound engineer knew precisely how to soften the blow, congratulating the musicians at every given opportunity. It was always different working alongside songwriters, it wasn't him at the helm, and they liked to take over his microphone.

'And echoes from a place... Lift it,' she instructed, 'and lower for the word, where. Are we on board with that, guys?'

The vocalist nodded at Emily in agreement.

'You're doing great, lads,' the engineer stated once she had moved back out of his way. 'From the top then...' They counted in the song.

Emily stood up in the glass booth with her arms folded, watching the engineer's fingers dance on the sound levels through the corner of her eye. The vocals were crisp and heaved with emotion. The golden hue of the sound booth with its heady blend of leather guitar cases, mixed with patchouli oil and tobacco, it was utterly intoxicating to Emily. With the right mindset, fifteen minutes and they could resolve this 'one off note'. There was just that last bar to get right. She held her breath as the singer moved in on the chorus.

'And echoes from a place... where.' There it was again; it was throwing the effect. What they had was good, but they had time for one last shot, studio time wasn't cheap.

'Enough! I'm going in there.' Emily stated. Before the engineer had time to respond, she was already the other side of the sound booth running through a fresh approach. He checked his watch; the man was now looking forward to his lunch break. Emily's friend Siobhan popped her head around the door; he'd met her a few times.

'Is she here?'

'Come in... faster,' he whispered, 'keep your head down, please, and shut that door tight.'

He looked straight ahead and leant into the microphone. 'Can you stay in there, Emily?' His voice was commanding enough to grab Emily's attention. 'We have time to run this through again. Sing the full chorus yourself. Take the microphone, Emily.' The engineer evidently knew his stuff. 'It's the only way we're going to get this done, trust me. He's a better chance of getting it if you sing it through first.'

He held the booth microphone to one side and leant over to where Siobhan was crouched unseen.

'This, you have got to hear,' he whispered. 'Shush now!' He raised a finger to his lips before he sat back up in his seat.

'We ready?' He counted in a verse of instrumental before Emily's voice filled the booth.

Siobhan's knees weakened as she listened. It was her bloody Emily. It had the same sweet sound, the rich soulfulness that was there when they laughed together. It was Emily at her most vibrant. In the chorus of a song, Siobhan discovered a whole other side to her friend; the woman had an incredible voice but the fact that she had kept her talent a secret, it was hurtful to Siobhan; she felt like she'd just had her face slapped.

'Quick, go!' The engineer demanded, still smiling. 'Emily will not be impressed if she finds you here. Quick...' Siobhan was ushered from the booth.

As she got up on the other side of the door, she wasn't sure if she was hugging or gripping herself. Emily had something rare in the sound of her voice though she had only ever denied that she could sing, she had stood in front of Elliot too and flat-out rejected the idea. Siobhan knew that bringing up the issue would make Emily defensive. Her friend would be in a far better position if she were to use her God-given talent and talent it was, Siobhan was now in no doubt.

Waving her hands in front of her eyes, Siobhan blew upwards to stop herself from crying. The band had one more shot at the song, and that was it. The guys were ordinarily sprawled across the sofa, she made her way over and slowly took a seat. She was left alone for a minute or two when the drummer fell through the door.

'Sorry, love!' He smiled with his eyes. He looked a real rock and roller, a cocky sort, winking at her as he made his way to the exit. The others weren't long behind him. They had finally got the track to where Emily wanted it; they had a perfect recording in the end. Even Emily agreed it was a good session.

'Will we go?' Emily suggested, appearing suddenly at her side. Siobhan stood there, half-heartedly wanting to hang out, but Emily moved her forward, manoeuvring her friend to the door.

'Thanks, guys!' She linked Siobhan's arm as she curled in and whispered, 'I want some normality at this point of the day!'

'Normal? Shucks thanks!' Siobhan shot back in response.

'Grown-up conversations then, come on you.' She was brimming with anticipation and relief.

It was a ten-minute walk to the bistro where the girls regularly did lunch. The place had taken off lately, and they realised on arrival that they had no hope of getting a table. They stood at the window glaring in for longer than they should have, appearing dejected and abandoned. No one came to rescue them, unfortunately, so they decided to leave. With the autumn rain still holding off, they ventured further than usual.

They soon came across a new deli, with bar stools in the window. It looked just the ticket. They spied flapjacks and a decent coffee machine behind the counter. The girls always opted for independent traders; the whole corporate coffee chain thing didn't gel with them. Besides, their custom was better valued in less incriminating spots. They were famished.

The lentil soup was a pure feast with some warm pumpkin seed bread. The veggie burgers and miso soup were just as tasty. Everything was wholesome, wholegrain or organic, with decent fair-trade coffee and juices, as well as herbal teas of every description. They were too hungry to talk much, at least until they had ordered second coffees and pastries, rounding off what had been a fabulous lunch.

'So, what did you make of Mark?' Siobhan queried.

Emily had anticipated the question. 'Fun, curious!"

'In what way?' Siobhan probed. She was intrigued.

'He asked plenty of questions!'

Siobhan laughed, amused by her friend, she was an odd girl sometimes.

Emily was independent, but girls that had been to boarding school ordinarily were that way inclined. She never did boy talk, not ever. Her friend was a real entity in that way; it was unusual for a woman of her age to still show no interest in the opposite sex. She wasn't silly about it or anything; it was a private part of her, she had no fears in that respect and never came across as inhibited.

Our Diligent Souls

Siobhan had only met Emily's parents once; she visited the year before they died. Unlike Siobhan's parents, Emily's travelled internationally with their separate jobs, and they would formally entertain when Emily was home on visits. Siobhan had spent two days in their company and was witness to a strange, almost unnatural distance that existed between the couple.

Emily's mother and father were unusually independent of each other, and Emily loved that about them, she seemed to admire the fact that they both led separate lives. It was a different set up in comparison to Siobhan's family, her mum and dad habitually finishing each other's sentences.

Emily talked to a bereavement counsellor at boarding school after they died, and Siobhan was the one person that she could count on not to bring it up, not ever. The car crash was a tragedy that was felt by everyone at school on Emily's behalf. To lose both parents in the one fowl swoop was unusual, but even Siobhan felt her classmates' empathy a touch overwhelming at times. They were competitive when it came to who should be there for Emily, measuring their degrees of compassion in corridor arguments, it was too awful.

Emily's grandmother was all that remained then, a warm, tender woman who loved Emily dearly. The grandmother was widowed early in life, and Emily's mother had grown up the only child of a single parent. Her father was an only child as well but his mother, her other granny died before Siobhan even knew Emily. She had talked once about her granny's wake to Siobhan though she would now remember her parents' funeral more vividly; the passing of her father's mother had been quite the event too.

When her parents died, Emily and her remaining grandmother became inseparable; they never lived together, but Emily visited every second day. They regularly cooked lunch together, her grandmother passing on recipes while sharing stories of Emily's mother from when she was growing up. Her grandmother was there to answer a plethora of questions while Emily pulling together the missing pieces of her parent's life. When her second grandmother died, Emily was truly alone with no living relatives to speak of in this world.

Siobhan and Elliot attended the funeral as they had been a couple for a few months by then. Emily didn't allow anyone but Siobhan to see her sorrow. Siobhan was there when she picked herself up and dusted herself off. Emily had been flat on her face with grief for a couple of weeks, but the girl just kept running to the light, what choice did she have? In Siobhan's eyes, Emily could climb any mountain, and she was behind her every step of the way.

They'd been friends all this time, and yet Siobhan had no idea that she had this superb singing voice. Emily had gone to great lengths to disguise her talent, and Siobhan needed to speak out, to tell her what she felt and heard in that one chorus. Every ounce of her wanted to encourage and congratulate Emily, but Siobhan knew that it was essential to hold back for now. Emily was stronger than any woman she'd ever known but fragile when it came to people knowing what she deemed as private. No one had the right to mess with that, though Siobhan's heart was breaking. She reached over the table and took hold of her friend's hand.

'What's up with you?' Emily was intensely concerned.

'I'm barmy, don't mind me.'

'You have your period again? You do get it rough.'

Emily had no clue, Siobhan realised. The two girls were always of great comfort to each other. The world and its mother could look on, but they didn't care one iota.

'So, tell us what happened at the recording session?' Siobhan asked, attempting to pull herself together as she sat up properly in her chair.

'Yeah, it went well. You okay?'

'I'm fine don't fuss.'

Emily got back to business with one eye on her friend's emotions. 'He's got a strong voice.' She'd mentioned that before. 'He can carry the tune, but it was written for that other girl and since she dropped out?'

Siobhan wondered if the last female vocalist had heard Emily's voice. She might have decided that the song was something Emily should do herself. 'Do you know why she took off?' She asked bashfully.

'Heaven knows, I'm beyond asking, but what the song loses in vocals it gains in translation. It's so good to hear the lyrics from a male perspective, brings a whole different lilt to the story.'

'Are you working tonight?' Siobhan pretended to be interested. She was hoping to change the direction of the conversation. She was wound up tightly, still wondering how her friend could keep back so much of herself, especially something that significant.

'Seven o'clock I'm in at the restaurant. I've to drop in and pick up paperwork at the law practice; I've loads to get on with before then, but we've time yet. The food was something else the other night, Siobhan; I had the best night.'

'Mark was cool when he walked you home then?'

'He was kosher, but before you ask, I'm not interested.'

'You're never interested.'

Mark was all of fifteen minutes away from the cafe where they now sat. He had taken time off work to gather a few things together for his flat. It had taken him forty minutes to decide on a feature wallpaper, and he was now stretched time-wise. From there he went straight to the art supply shop that specialised in picture framing.

The shop was busy when he arrived. It was all that he needed as he was already on edge. He scanned the choice of frames while he stood there, his eyes drawn to one particular frame but the picture had to be mounted beyond that. The other frame shoppers battled back and forward on prices with the owner while he thought it through.

Mark waited his turn, agitated he checked his watch several times within clear view. The more small talk these customers made, the harder he had to work on controlling his temper, it was torturous. Mark hated shopping. He had lots to do beyond the wallpaper and picture frame; there were cushions, a quilt cover and curtains, and fixings for the shelves to gather. But wait he would, he needed the shopkeeper's full attention.

The picture that Elliot had made for him needed thoughtful consideration when it came to its framing, getting it right was vital. Elliot had worked hard on the piece, and it would need to meet with his approval at a later stage. Mark was utterly confused; the mounting boards came in all sorts of colours, complicating the decision. His head space was so wholly in the wrong place as he tried to match the shade of the feature wallpaper and frame.

When he finally got the shopkeeper on his own, he took out the painting and placed it on the man's workbench before he pulled the wallpaper roll from his bag. 'It's got to work with this too.' He announced sweating as he struggled to strip away the plastic wrap to reveal a meter of its design. With his free hand, he tapped his finger on the frame he'd chosen.

'You have an eye for texture.' The shopkeeper remarked.

'I didn't paint it.' Mark muttered defensively. He wanted to be in and out of there as quick as possible. 'It was a gift, from a talented friend.'

'I confer...this painting is right up my street, but it's as much about the setting as it is about the picture itself.'

Mark nodded though his head was pounding.

'You have an eye,' the shopkeeper said, 'we'll tune into the matching mount that will do them justice. It's got to work with the wallpaper too I'm guessing. The paper and frame are for the same room, right?'

'My head is genuinely melting.' Mark shared in a matter of fact fashion, realising that his mouth was dry. He focused. 'I'm conscious of what the piece originally said to me, the wrong colour combination and the emphasis could completely change.'

'The colour of the mounting board can change the mood alright.' The shopkeeper agreed. Mark tightened his lips knowingly.

'Take your time there,' the shopkeeper whispered as he handed Mark a set of colour cards, 'that's not a cheap frame.'

'That's not an issue...' Mark replied.

The shopkeeper nodded. 'I've enough to contend with,' thought Mark.

'You want to get it right.' The shopkeeper reiterated.

'No pressure then.' Mark watched as the shopkeeper tipped him on the shoulder and smiled before he placed a shimmering burgundy mount and a soft green one beside the arrangement. Mark scrambled his way through the colour cards before latching onto a golden turquoise. The shopkeeper disappeared for a few moments to give him time to decide, but in the end, it was the soft green mount that won the day.

'You can't beat a bit of expertise.' Mark said, lowering his head apologetically while proceeding to take out his credit card. The framing would take three days and could be delivered, an option that Mark was only too glad of, he'd enough to do without having to waste another lunchtime on the project, and they delivered after six, so he'd be home in time.

'Thank you.' Mark mumbled as he headed for the door.

Back in the cafe, the two women sat back and took in their surroundings; they'd enjoyed every mouthful. It was a real discovery; the café, with Richard Thompson playing in the background on the stereo. The staff were folksy, a sesame seed crowd, Siobhan surmised. These were folk that had humble ambitions. They had plenty of workers and images of happy faces in timeless photos on their walls. The photos spoke of musical capers, full of life and camaraderie.

The bakery end was small but had a good variety of bread and pastries. No two chairs or tables were the same. No two tablecloths for that matter. But it was a painting in itself where the characters appeared to be living the dream.

A picture of Shiva - the revered Hindu deity of destruction and change, it was blue tacked to the back of an antique cash register. On the bookshelf sat an assortment of classic reads. Emily spotted 'The Shack' by William P Young, a novel that she knew Siobhan had recently finished and enjoyed. They both looked at each other in approval.

A girl called Annie floated around with new product offerings on a plate. 'Simply-wonderfuls,' she called them. They were powdery white balls of icing sugar and clarified butter that had been rolled with angelic tenderness; they were lightness exemplified.

According to Annie the opening week had been chaotic as was expected, but they were starting to find their feet and create a sense of connection in the local community. It was a south side cottage cafe on an ancient cobbled street only fifteen minutes' walk from the city centre. For Siobhan paying up felt awkward as everything sounded so under-priced. She put an extra three quid in the tip jar for the aesthetics alone.

The girls were the other side of the street when the owner chased after them with an umbrella. They just then felt the first touches of rain.

'No worries, it's the remnants of an American tour bus that visited on our first week. There's no chance they'll be back now. Please put it to good use.' The owner darted back to the cafe and took cover as the two women looked up at the sky. It was still early in the afternoon.

'See you both again I hope!'

Emily and Siobhan waved back as they took off, both gripping the same handle at first. They made their way through a shower that had risen out of nowhere, to become hard and relentless. They lowered their cover at the gates of Trinity College as the passing shower filtered to a stop.

It was only then that they had the chance to appreciate the humour of the situation. They were baffled by the cafe owner who had spotted the rain from inside the coffee shop before they had. Siobhan's feet were squelching in her slip-on shoes, and the wetness had risen to knee height on Emily's jeans. They were bent over laughing when they saw Mark. He was stunned to find the two women in front of him. The poor chap was laden with bags and dripping wet.

'Ladies?'

The women were trying not to laugh, but he was soaked to the skin. There were beads of rain on the tips of his dark hair.

'Look at the state of you, Mark!' Siobhan hollered, busting her sides.

'What can I say? My arms were full.' He was put out by her remark.

The brown paper bags in his hands were beginning to disintegrate. Siobhan pulled out two scrunched up plastic bags from her jacket pocket and handed them over, much to his relief.

'You're a saviour. Where did you two come out of?' He looked back over his shoulder. He had rounded the right side of Trinity's surrounding wall, as had they.

'It was lashing before I realised it, there was no cover.' Mark was babbling now.

Siobhan's curiosity spiked. Mark was not a shopper by any stretch of the imagination though he looked as if he'd just done his Christmas shop.

'What's going on here?' She quizzed, raising her eyebrows at the contents of his bags. 'Are you decorating?'

'Have you caught your breath?' Emily explored.

'I'm fine. It's nothing, just a few pieces for the flat. I was thinking of having everyone over for a bite to eat. It doesn't see enough action my place.'

Siobhan nearly lost her footing; this will be news to Elliot, she thought; home improvements, shopping, and guests? She found herself checking for any chemistry between her two friends. He is such a lovely guy, she thought. If anyone had a chance with Emily; maybe it was him. She sighed with anticipation before she spoke again. 'That might happen?' Siobhan whispered, barely believing the words that came out of her mouth, blushing, she rushed in to cover her tracks. 'Just let us know in time, yeah?'

'Sounds good,' Emily declared, 'I'll do my best to be there!' Her words left both Siobhan and Mark momentarily stupefied, neither of them had expected his invite to be accepted so freely. Siobhan decided then and there to go on ahead; she knew she couldn't contain what was plain over-excitement. She feared she might say something off-putting if left with either one of them especially after her visit to the studio.

'I have to go, guys, I'm late!' She surprised Emily with a kiss on the cheek and asked, 'Are you getting the bus?' Folding her friend's hair in behind her ears, she needed to check with her before she left.

'Yes, of course, I'm getting the bus.' Emily responded, flushed in the face thanks to Siobhan's unusual behaviour.

'Great, take care then!' Siobhan mumbled, rolling on her heels in amusement before she spread into the distance. Emily and Mark watched on in confusion until she vanished into the crowd.

'Coffee?' Mark asked without any hesitation. Emily told herself she had little choice; he was in no state to be abandoned.

'I don't have long but yeah, why not; we'd better get you dried off, my friend.'

'Magic!' Mark replied, as he pointed in the Dame Street direction. He had a favourite café on Georges Street, about ten minutes from there; they made a great carrot cake, and it gave them a few extra minutes to walk and talk.

Emily started in on her story about the cottage café and the owner appearing with the umbrella. Just then the sun crept back out of its hiding place, stopping them dead in their tracks to gaze up at the sky. They were glad of each other's company; both were smiling as they made their way down the road.

Chapter 9

The stretch of thin corridor that lay ahead was always fascinating. It had four large windows to the right and four or five office doors to the left; each office shared by more than one residential lecturer. It was the quietest part of the college; a place where the extension of deadlines was begged for on occasion.

The Venetian blinds were probably cleaned twice a week, but it made little odds. The dust particles danced in the sunshine, the light reaching through to hit the far wall. These multicoloured speckles all but disappeared as the clouds slipped by momentarily shading the sun. It was a day's let up in autumn's advance, and the sun was pledging its attention.

Ireland invited all four seasons in the one day on occasion, but it had a mysticism of its own that corridor; fairies could easily commander it in the summer months, Oden thought, amused by his imagination. These ghoulish shadows climbed above the lecturer's door frames and onto the ceiling; students making unintentional shapes with their rucksacks as they scurried past him.

Oden's books were heavy, his back arched forward with the weight in his arms. He'd intended to make his way to the library where he could off-load three of the more substantial manuals. He wasn't sure how much further he could manage when he crash-collided into his favourite, though strangely eccentric, lecturer. Oden's books went tumbling to the floor, his eyes still fixed on the lecturer as he attempted to pick them up.

This physics lecturer, Gerry Fitzpatrick, was as always frantic to communicate his love for the place. The bounty of talent that had made its way through the college gates had never failed to impress him. He was engineering the idea that Oden might have grasped his latest lecture straight off the bat.

'Ah, but did you appreciate it, Oden. Did you assimilate the magnitude of what that says?'

Oden was still trying to find his feet and re-balance his books. 'Do you mean the friction and gravity formulas on a slope or plane?' He piped up and spoke thinking back.

Our Diligent Souls

The lecturer's expression contorted; you would swear by his face he was struggling to pull a string of bile from Oden's throat. 'And what does that say, Oden? In no uncertain terms?'

The pace of the lecturer's articulation was often slow and surreal. Oden visualised the guy shaping every phonic word by candlelight. His lectures resonated; most of the students had formed that opinion.

'You appeared to absorb it on the first lecture, Oden; it's hard to tell from my standpoint until it gets to the exams. Students while they know their stuff, they can have difficulty getting it across on paper. It's fundamental that you can translate these things into your own verse.'

There it was the fundamental verse thing again as if any student could translate something that specific, into their own words.

'Define the theory, right here, right now, while it's still fresh in your mind, Oden.'

Oden gave him an unmerciful glint, took a deep breath and began. 'The friction and Gravity formulas.' His start was impressive though his exhausted expression was evident. He stopped to exaggerate the weight of his books but was sadly ignored.

'You start with three variables and assume gravity.' Oden began again. 'The normal is the direction that the plane is facing, and gravity is 9.81. What you need to find is the force of the objects into the plane. Then check using the 'givings' to see if it's static or kinetic.'

'Not bad.' The lecturer muttered to himself; his eyes bright and alert as he held the boy in his gaze. To his right, Oden felt a familiar shadow pass him by, watching with intent.

'Go on, talk!' The lecturer prompted.

Oden focused himself, determined to complete the definition.

'Using the formulas, you then find out the amount of force you lose by friction. You add these forces together to get the net force. Then divide the net force by the mass of the object in motion to get your acceleration?'

The lecturer looked pleased.

'How's the physics engine coming along?'

'Good. Yes!' Oden responded.

'You now have an initial acceleration,' continued the lecturer. 'You know from your last step where the position and velocity of the object is?'

Oden's heart pounded as Lucile briefly popped her face up from behind the lecturer's shoulder. She appeared to be amused.

'I do.' Oden responded.

'And your gaming idea?'

'It's a car that moves from land to water.' He announced.

'What you need to make sure of...' The lecturer was cut short as Oden jumped in to explain. He was attempting to rush ahead, eager to get to the end of what felt like torture.

'That the acceleration is recalculated when the car enters the water.'

He watched Lucile step back from behind the lecturer. He could see she was doubled over, covering her mouth to silence the laughter. He must have looked a state; he knew at this stage that his face had turned a beetroot colour from the weight of his books.

'Yes, you're making progress.' The lecturer stood there tapping a pencil on his hand. 'You're starting to get a handle on it, good for you. I'm very impressed.'

'Do you mind, sir? I have to go?'

'No, that's fine.' Gerry Fitzpatrick looked flustered; he'd clean forgot where he was going. 'I'd better be off, gone.' He laughed. 'I have to go.'

Oden felt sure that his hands were developing welts in his effort to stay standing. The strain was affecting his knees as he approached Lucile in a lopsided fashion. His whole body was about to give way, and he didn't fancy picking up the books a second time.

'I'm going to the library,' he declared in a gruff voice.

'I'll help.' She insisted.

He thought he should refuse, but he didn't. Without a second thought, Lucile removed the weight from his arms. The stress lifted from Oden's face with a light blush as he blew the hair from his forehead. He followed as they made their way past the canteen.

'I'll buy you a coffee when we're done. You look as though you might need it?' She suggested.

'That won't be necessary.'

'Fair enough!' She answered, standing cold face and thoroughly offended.

'We can go for coffee together. What I mean to say is that...'

Lucile butted in. 'The less you say, the better, agreed?' He could have been upset by her response, she wasn't sure, but as they walked on, she decided to keep quiet. Instead, she studied the three books in her hands; they were well-thumbed as were all the essential manuals from the library.

'That stuff with the lecturer sounded tough.'

'You still want to do games development?' Oden enquired.

'I think so, maybe.'

'You'll pick it up, Lucile.'

He was daunted by much of the games development lingo himself when he started out; he thought it best to inform her.

The librarian knew Oden well. Two books had arrived that he had ordered; science books for his own reference though she wondered where he had the time in third year. Lucile suggested coming back for them when he had less to carry. Even with the three books that he had left back, he still had his arm's full which was odd for a gaming student, as overall; they had fewer books to carry than most students, with most of their study being transferred online. He was in no mood to be questioned; she knew that much.

'Is tomorrow alright to collect them?' He asked.

'If you can collect them by two o'clock, Oden? I can't hold them any longer?'

'To the canteen so...' Lucile exclaimed, expressing a note of impatience as she moved towards the exit.

'Hold on! What time is it first?' Oden demanded to know as he followed behind her.

'Ten past two, why?'

'I don't want to go around there when there are big crowds; I just don't.'

'Fair enough, but lunch hour is over by now.'

'Right, to the canteen then...' He decided.

When they arrived, there was no queue at the hot food cabinets, but the earlier offers of interest had been claimed. They had dried up chicken goujons or spaghetti Bolognese that was it. Oden went to the cold counter and got a Caesar salad while Lucile opted for a coffee. She followed as he made his way to the far corner of the hall, avoiding a bunch of party revellers who were messing around in onesies.

Once he knew he was a safe distance from any other life form, he got into a groove. He talked and talked, and for now, Lucile was the one listening. He made little to no connection between topics that she could figure. It was mostly factual-information; she adapted as best she could. She was intrigued by what he was saying though she did find it hard to keep up with him. There were technical terms that she still hadn't grasped.

When Oden had information, imparting it was a matter of urgency before he lost track of what he was thinking. It could be something he'd discovered on reddit.com or darker less factual accounts of the League of Legends match he'd been playing. He could talk forever about the character's abilities and the dimensions of the game, strategies too, he'd been surprised by manoeuvres.

He could always see where something could be bettered. It was a trait that Lucile recognised in herself. Oden was rooted in theory, but he was still the most light-hearted individual she had ever met. The guy was awkwardly inappropriate sometimes, but none of that registered with him, she had gathered that from afar. People just loved or hated him, hated was too harsh a word, he did tire the odd person with his information overloads. Those who liked him loved him because there wasn't a cynical bone in his body. He could be endlessly entertaining in his own right.

'So, do you want to go to this cocktail hour in the student bar?' Oden asked her.

'Yeah, that sounds good.'

She couldn't keep her eyes off his marvellous face. He had a quirky fashion sense with his funky gamer look; the boy had swag by Lucile's reckoning. He was stocky and handsome and was bold enough to wear a stretcher ear piercing. He showed her the retro '*game over*' sign tattooed on his heart. She had visions of him being wheeled in on a hospital trolley with nurses opening his shirt for the big reveal. Game over like.

He'd done well in his art classes at secondary school. He learnt from the techniques he was given where most of the students believed that art was a gift that you were born with, a belief that left them unreceptive. His art teacher had given him a greater understanding of colour and balance; he knew how important the use of white was, all of it contributed to freeing his artistic abilities, it taught him how to be expressive in the way he dressed.

Lucile loved to talk through her emotions and Oden admired that. He wasn't good at reading signals, and the ins and outs of her personal dilemmas were insightful to him. She was cute too and outright with her feelings. After two meetings she told him that she thought he was suitable boyfriend material. He agreed with her, but they hadn't got around to getting it together yet. There was no hurry; the moment had not yet arrived.

Lucile lived in a house not far from his that she shared with three other girls. They were more conservative than she was, so the prospect of linking in with his gaming pals appealed to her. She was out on her own in the fact that she was hooked on games; girls who loved gaming were regularly thin on the ground.

The Caesar salad was excellent as was the coffee and it wasn't long before they were heading for the door.

'We have a few hours to kill before happy hour, and I'm done for the day lecture wise, you?' Oden asked.

Lucile smiled sincerely, excited by what Oden might suggest. 'Yeah, I'm done here.'

'Do you want to meet my housemates?'

'Sure do. I'd love that.'

He led the way to the bus stop, giving her a blow by blow account of the lads, primarily covering what score average they were at in their gaming. He listed them in order, starting with who was the laziest when it came to them cleaning the house.

Chapter 10

'That was a great day's work, gentlemen! Thank you.' Mark was glad to see the back of what had been, a troublesome day. They were right on the bell, five o'clock which suited him. It wasn't bright creating the habit of letting everyone go twenty minutes early, but the men understood that where there was work that needed doing, they had to be there to see out the day and that was the end of it. Mark made sure they never ran over, where they did it was he alone that stayed on.

'Have a good one!' Joyce called back exiting through the main door.

Mark had arranged to meet up with Elliot at eight o'clock in the local pub. He had enough time to go home and put a few finishing touches on the sitting room walls. He could grab a shower and still be there on time. It wasn't every day that Mark had no paperwork to complete. The thought of a night off filled him with an equal measure of promise and relief.

The warehouse felt cavernous, the crackle of electric pulses sounding out above his head. The royal blue night sky streamed through the large holding door where the delivery van came and went throughout the day. There was nothing, but a warbling bird left to penetrate the relative silence.

Mark sat motionless, taking it all in before moving off on his rounds. The power points had to be checked, the lights and switches turned off for the night. He had just finished up when he noticed the receptionist making her way over to him. Reluctantly, he forced a smile.

'You're still here, Imelda. I thought you'd be long gone. You're lucky I didn't lock you in here.' He was joking, but Imelda looked as though her face might implode.

'I was finishing up when the call came through,' she commented.

'What is it?' Mark asked. 'You okay?'

Mark hadn't been within earshot of the downstairs phone extension, so she was forced to come and look for him. She had berated herself for not having his mobile phone number for such emergencies. A member of Mark's team would usually pick up the receiver on their end when Imelda dialled down to talk to him at ground floor level. She had enough to do without the hassle of having to chase after Mark.

'Laura Keating is on hold upstairs. She needs to speak to you.'

Mark was curious but nodded Imelda on as they turned their attention to the task.

'Not a problem! Let's get a move on then.'

As Imelda reached the stairs, she turned around to him. 'Will I let you go first?'

'No. I'm fine, Imelda, lead the way there.' She was uncomfortable with that.

Imelda was the receptionist come superwoman that glued the strands of activity together for the company. She was a hearty family woman with grown-up kids. She had a vibrant country glow and curly brown hair.

'I'll follow you up, lead the way.'

Mark was curious as to why Laura might be calling him? He guessed it had something to do with Ralph Mournaghan. He had a good conversation with Laura that evening in the restaurant. If Ralph hadn't called to apologise for his disappearing act, she might have been offended. The last thing Mark needed was to be drawn into any crossfire between the pair of them.

There was still the possibility that she was dating Ralph. On the night, Laura had laughed off Mournaghan's disappearing act, she was eloquent and witty, and so that couldn't have been it. Mark had found her easy to be around, and if he could help in any way, he'd try. He did hope she wasn't in any difficulty.

Imelda flicked the downward switch. The receiver was positioned at her ear as they stood behind the reception desk. 'I'm transferring you over, Mrs Keating, please forgive the delay.'

Mark was reminded that Laura was a widow. He took the receiver from Imelda's hand and waited for her to leave the reception with her cup of tea.

'Laura, how are you?'

'It's good to hear your voice, Mark.'

'Is something wrong, Laura?'

'No!' She insisted. 'I wondered if we could meet for a coffee. I'm at a loose end, and I was looking for advice. Imelda happened to say that you were finishing up there.'

Mark processed the idea in double-quick time; this whole meeting up concept was not a good idea. She might want to seek advice on Ralph Mournaghan, and a character assassination was as much as he could offer. The last few comments that Mournaghan had made about her were offensive, a warning enough for Mark to stay away.

'I have a friend to meet, Laura; it's not something I can cancel. But you're okay, are you?'

'I don't know, Mark. I don't know. But that's not a problem; you have arrangements made. I enjoyed our conversation. I'm surprised I felt the need to talk to you myself.'

Mark was taken back. 'Oh, okay?'

'No, please don't get the wrong idea! I have a series of decisions to make in the next few days; I'm overwhelmed by the whole thing. Please don't get the wrong idea.'

'My mind is completely blank at the minute,' Mark assured her, 'it's been non-stop here since seven this morning.'

'It's fine,' she told him again. 'Another time, I do apologise.' She was trying to get off the phone as soon as possible. 'I must go.'

Mark didn't want to come across as cruel. They had connected on work topics that night in the restaurant, and she could prove to be a good contact in a selfish respect.

'No, look!' Mark responded, acting with haste. 'I'm not meeting my friend Elliot until eight. I had intended to go home after this and finish painting my walls before I head out, but it can wait. Where will I meet you?'

'Are you sure, now? I can't think of anywhere?' Laura was busy trying to keep up with the sudden flip in resolve.

He blurted out the first place that came to mind. 'Bewley's? On Grafton Street. Half an hour okay?'

Now, it was Mark's turn to get into a tizzy. To be there in a half hour meant he would have to shut up shop in the next ten minutes. Imelda was still floating around somewhere with a cup of tea in her hand.

'That should work out fine,' Laura commented. 'I'll see you then.'

He had to think sharp, checking on the time. 'Give me ten minutes leeway just in case, yeah?'

Our Diligent Souls

Mark scanned the reception for any sign of Imelda while Laura chuckled the other end of the phone. 'That's not a problem.' She replied, amused by his panic.

Mark was left trying to disconnect the line; he had never worked a switchboard. Whatever it was that he'd touched, it didn't do the job. The line was still live though Laura had gone.

'Imelda!' He called out, 'Help!' There was no response.

He found Imelda in the toilets but not before scaring the life out of her with an almighty holler through the door. The locking up took seven minutes. He checked and re-checked everything before setting the alarm.

Poor Imelda didn't know what had hit her. She was bundled out of the place in double time, muttering to herself as she legged it through the holding door. She threw a dirty look back at Mark before disappearing beyond the gateway. You didn't dare discommode Imelda. Mark stopped to think for a second; the woman was Mournaghan's eyes and ears. He had neither the time nor inclination to worry just then. He said goodnight to security guy as he reached the gates of the unit and hailed a cab.

Mark's thoughts drifted back to the night before; he was being bounced around in a bruising ride of an old taxi by then. He had worked hard to transform the flat. The statement wall was the unexpected surprise; he had learned to wallpaper when he was in his teens, but wallpaper had seriously come on in the past ten years.

The further on he got in his renovations, the more likely the possibility of a relationship with Emily seemed. He was already heavily invested in the idea of Emily. The fact that he had only met her twice, it was difficult to equate, he had heard so much about her over the years. Looking back, he'd been intrigued by Emily from the outset, his notion of her deepening with every story that Siobhan and Elliot relayed.

The taxi driver pulled in but had to repeat himself twice before he got a response. 'Seven-euro, mate.'

Mark scrambled through his belongs reaching a full sweat before finally touching the leather of his wallet.

'No problem.' He muttered.

'It must be love.' The taxi driver commented, looking to the road ahead.

Our Diligent Souls

'Keep the change,' Mark requested, as he handed over a tenner. Disgruntled by the driver's perceptive observation, he hoisted himself from the back seat and closed the door without another word being said.

Gathering his thoughts, he made his way through Grafton Street. The weather was holding. This place had held a special magic for him. He had often taken the train down on a Saturday with one of his mates from home to play the guitar on this street. He wasn't great on guitar and had long since given up but thinking back, the day's takings only ever covered the cost of the adventure if they were in luck. Although, it had always been worth it.

Grafton Street was a place that was full of possibilities, a place where you never had to account for your next step in life. He recognised a few old faces, the fortune tellers at the Molly Malone. The Quaker, Mick, he was no longer on the jewellery stalls with his fingerless mitts. The poet busker nodded.

Mark was now a shadow in a tiny chapter of an epic read. There was a time when he was recognised there, but not any longer. He had heard the songs of one or two of the other buskers who had made a career for themselves in music; their songs bringing him back when he'd been walking through a shopping centre or sitting at the kitchen table with the radio on.

Laura was waiting by the door of Bewley's bathing in the lamplight, a brilliant blue-sky cascading overhead. She was temporarily transfixed by a colourful array of life that was positively new to her, going by her expression. She was standing to the right of the entrance with a multitude of foreign-students packed in behind her. To her left were some world travellers, adorned with piercings, Indian neck scarves and bright alpaca jumpers.

Laura was wearing something elegant and understated. When she caught sight of Mark the relief on her face was visible; she was starting to wonder if she might have got the address confused, there was a second Bewley's on West Mooreland Street just down the road.

'You made it!' She called over, rising-up onto the front of her heels. Mark laughed as he knitted his way through the crowd to get to her. 'Will we go inside?' He asked still smiling, having passed by her to open the door.

The two were only inside when they were transported then to a world within a world, Bewley's on Grafton Street. The shiny gold display cabinets were framed in mahogany, a heady blend of coffee and chocolate wafting through the ventilators. At a glance, the glass display units which were flawlessly assembled and fully stocked seemed to whisper seductively, promising all forms of dark chocolate delights.

Mark led the way across the mosaic floor through to the dark interior of the back room, its massive expanse and high ceilings epic in proportion, resembling an antiquated college food hall with its panelling and hard wooden mahogany cubicles. The likelihood of thoughtful debate having transpired there was significant, discussion on the politics of Sigmund Freud even more likely.

Laura wasn't that keen on Bewley's coffee; she was a Costa girl herself. Mark wasn't that concerned either way; he was still focused on sharing a few pints of the black stuff with Elliot later in the night.

'So, how have you been?' He asked.

'I'm not sure that I want to tell you in this place. I'll have to whisper; they might decide to take me out in a straitjacket after the week I've had.'

Mark took another look around the room. It was full of stiffs alright, Guardian and Times readers. People were seated alone pondering deep thoughts and taking notes in hardback copies. Mark had been to Bewley's on many an occasion. It was a royal monument to the city; a place that spoke to the literary mind. It had undoubtedly seen through many changes in its decades of time there; having co-existed with Grafton Street and the cascading ramble downstream towards Trinity.

'So where is this head of yours, Laura Keating?'

Mark was concerned about the time he had to give her; he initially thought he had no more than an hour to spare. Elliot was never late and wasn't one for sitting around in a pub on his own. Mark attempted to calm himself as he caught sight of a clock; it was just gone a quarter after six; they had loads of time yet.

Laura leaned in to gain Mark's attention. 'I'm selling up a small company that I started. I'm buying into a new venture. It's all happening in the next few weeks.'

'That is news,' Mark openly decided.

'It's Stephen's anniversary today, the anniversary of my husband's death. I was halfway through the day without realising it. I don't know why it should leave me feeling at odds; it's just another day without him, but a lot is going on in fairness.'

'Oh, okay!' Mark wasn't sure how to respond.

'Is it an expectation that we buy into, does an anniversary have to be that hard like?'

'Are you alright?'

'Yeah... I've been wondering if I can ask you a question; it's theological?' She added. 'It's just today of all days, these recent notions I've been having are getting in the way of my regular thought processes.'

Mark chuckled. 'Go on then, spit it out.'

Laura paused. 'Do you believe in heaven, hell? The stuff you're not supposed to bring up?'

'That's a loaded question for a Friday afternoon, Laura.'

His humour was ill-judged as she looked at him, startled. There was a brief flash of desperation in her eyes. Maybe this anniversary was affecting her, he thought, and she just wasn't aware of it yet. It was an odd line of questioning.

'You know what I believe?' Laura couldn't hold back; she needed to air her current views.

'I'm not sure, Laura. That guy over there looks like Freud.'

'You don't even know what Freud looks like; I'm betting?'

'Caught rapid!' Mark joyfully admitted.

She shook her head in disapproval before taking another sip of her coffee.

'Go on then, I'll hold it together, Laura, come on spit it out.'

She lowered her cup. 'Okay, well. I believe in community, be it at work, with friends, family. As deep as that goes, that is where goodness needs to reside, right?'

'Okay!' Mark replied, pulling back in his chair. He wasn't sure there was a point to this.

'I haven't always believed in god. There were times when I felt I deserved so little that I formed empty bonds. I wanted a loving relationship with everyone, to live in that abstract world of coincidence. We reach for the same thing at one stage or another, don't we? We get despondent with the world?'

Mark was reviewing her statement carefully. He wasn't sure if he was just intoxicated by this revisit to his youth, but her talk was impassioned.

Grafton Street held the romantic mysticism of coincidence, of the great novel, the notion of peace. Laura was foreign to such madness, surely? She had gone straight to college, was married and had a mortgage at twenty-six, with a career and prospects of children.

'My relationship was everything, Mark. But then the only place I saw God was in ceremony and duty. It was the same for Stephen.'

'Is this a covert mission you're on?' Mark inquired, with a wry smile.

'I was doing my bachelor's in business when I met Stephen. Right to the end, we were completely infatuated. It was just us and our duties to each other, our duties to our immediate families. That and what the world threw at us.'

Mark was now listening attentively. He could barely grasp what it meant for love to be reciprocal, let alone to love and lose in that way, it was a stressful day for her. Mark was a long way from being with Emily, assuming that something would even happen. He was also curious as to why Laura had gotten married so young but not enough to ask how that came to be.

Laura was adorable and savvy, but she came from a wealthy family that could offer any range of opportunities. For her to marry so young, it just didn't fit with his preconceptions. As if she had read his mind, she lowered her voice.

'We didn't give our families a choice. We married two years after we graduated. We wanted married life then and there when I think back, it's as if we knew?'

'That his life would be short lived?' Mark asked tenderly and with great concern.

'We were three years together as a couple and living apart; there was always this urgency that we shared. It was full on sometimes with one or other of us up to our eyes in commitments, but it worked beautifully for the entire nine months that we were together in our new home, and the wedding was great.'

'How lucky were you?'

'I was, and then everything was wiped away. All our plans, they were completely shipwrecked! I won't lie, it's been intense... I did more than teeter on the edge. My doctor had the best advice. He said, look forward more than you look back, as a practice. He talked about negatives and positives, and it's curious. Positive is positive, right? But what is negative, that's what the doctor asked me. To my thinking, you examine the negative and weigh it up before you throw any of it out?'

'Okay. 'Mark was stumped.

'The doctor defined it for me; he said to keep well I needed to change my thinking. Negative he said, is where you metaphorically put your hand out and say. "Halt"!'

'I could be doing that right now, in my mind's eye, Laura.'

'Why, am I annoying you?'

He smiled, and they started to laugh.

'I still love and miss Stephen, Mark, regret, remorse, it gets you nowhere.'

'I can only imagine how tough it's been, Laura.' Mark felt humbled by her openness and transparency. They were strangers to each other, but there was a genuine connection between them right there. She was out there a little, in so far as she was open, not your regular business associate.

'I should get to the point.' She remarked. 'After he died, I got through the first few months. The two sets of parents,' she explained as she shook her head, 'his and mine, they'd enough of me trying to go to hell.'

'Had you a reason to feel guilty?'

'No not really, but grief is hell enough to convince you of anything.'

Mark's face fell silent.

'They loaded on the pressure; I had given up the idea of going back to work. The mortgage on our home had been cleared, thanks to the insurance, and I didn't want to deal with the outside world. A few months in and I had doctors, and the pending threat of hospitalisation to contend with alone. I needed to prove something to my family, to myself, so when I got home; I started a small card business. It was just to keep my head right at first, but it went wild. By the end-of-year one, I was busy, and it was clearing a substantial profit; it took on a life of its own. I was fully occupied.'

'You were through the mill?'

'It's the past.'

'So, you were saying? That's unusual for a business in its infancy. Go on, tell me more.'

'The card company was born out of what Stephen and I shared, I was attracted to the quotes that reflected us, and I sent out those affirmations in card form. I thought that meant something, it did to me at first, especially when it was going so well.'

'Fantastic, that's amazing.' Mark was impressed.

'It was deeply spiritual at first like maybe he was still there; it was like we were still together in a kind of abstract sense.'

'Right.' Mark was baffled.

'It's all commercial bullshit now; I hate the cards that I produce. It's as if I'm betraying Stephen's memory no matter what way I look at it.'

'Your business runs on demand, Laura. So, what if the card production is nothing to do with Stephen anymore? It doesn't take away from what you shared with him, does it?'

'You don't get it, the cards I'm producing; they're diminishing my faith in the world. I tell people I'm in stationery, just stationary, not because I necessarily care what people think. I just have no interest or enthusiasm for what I do. We need a reason to get out of bed in the morning, right?'

'I can relate to your frustration, Laura, but it all too often comes down to the dollar when you're in business.'

'I've been lucky.'

'That you have.'

'Well no, but yes and no, I've been lucky with the card business in the past few weeks.'

'In what way?

'I got an offer out of nowhere, more than I ever expected. I didn't have it on the market which stood to my advantage. Thankfully, the buyer had no idea that I felt lumbered. I want to manage something more robust again, with a serious crew maybe?'

The coffee was by then, cold enough to taste. Mark and Laura talked and drank while shifting their attention from one incoming individual to the next. They chatted about her card business and the feeling of exhilaration she had felt with its initial success. Laura had believed in her product, as did others, it appeared. She had a few bad ideas, but they were selling, quicker than her more enlightened best sellers. It became clear that there was a market out there for offensive, mindless dribble, literally the lower you go, the higher the demand. 'It was sacrilege for the mind.'

She was now looking at several established firms and planned to investigate them properly before taking anything onboard. She wanted then and there to lay out a skeleton of options, but for now, there wasn't the time.

'Shall we head out and get a taxi?' She suggested once they'd guzzled the remains of their coffee. 'Are you okay if I pick up a few things at the counter before we leave, Mark?'

An hour and twenty minutes had passed, and he was starting to go off the idea of a pint. He checked the time as the server carefully wrapped up Laura's selection of sweets to take home. The early evening light was peeping through the ancient doorways as the sounds of a tin whistle from the street slipped in and out of earshot. He was spellbound by the well-polished gold of the railings, by the floor tiles, by the sheer sense of time past. The coffee beans and chocolate, yet again, proving a heady mix.

'We should head toward Stephen's Green,' he said, as they stepped out into the fresh air, 'there's a taxi rank up this way.'

'I wish we'd more time.'

'Me too,' Mark admitted. 'I can take some time out later in the week to go through these options of yours. Don't worry.'

The street was alive with activity, buskers lining the doorways at intervals, with jugglers and hair wrappers scattered in between them. A flower seller with rare and delicate blooms sat on the first side street. There were two real funky middle age punks selling prints from the doorway of a derelict building. A young girl was playing the fiddle with her mum looking on from behind her. They barely shared a word on the way there, enough was going on to keep them entertained. The simple interaction in body language said everything they needed to say.

Mark gave the taxi man a blow-by-blow set of instructions as to where he needed to go before turning to Laura for her address. She was heading in the same direction at least; he'd only thought of it then and was reminded of the night outside the restaurant when he'd put her in a taxi to go home. It all came flooding back, the fact that Laura could be dating Ralph Mournaghan. He suddenly found it difficult to see her as the same woman that he had just shared coffee with moments before.

He was within minutes, over-rout by a notion; the idea that Ralph Mournaghan could have a hand in any deal she might strike was frightening. She was capable but vulnerable too, and Mournaghan was such a crook. He had a game plan in respect of Laura on the night they met; Mark was sure of that.

The pair of them were safely tucked into the back seat of the taxi when he turned to her pointedly. 'Promise me something?' Mark pleaded. Laura childishly agreed in one defining nod. 'Laura, you have to keep your head and double check the books. You'll need to do homework, practice checks. anyone can be whitewashed in business.'

'Do you think honestly now, that I'm naive or vulnerable, Mark?' It was a genuine question.

'No, but people are fickle, Laura. Keep your eyes open. Please do that for me. When you zone in on a business, just...'

'How have you been getting on with Ralph?'

Mark was instantly flooded with aggravation. He threw her the sharpest of glances. 'You'll only touch a nerve, Laura. I'm off on a night out with my best friend.'

Laura had questions that she was not going to let go of just yet. 'Workwise. I know his figures stack up. He's making headway on the floor at T&E from what I heard.'

Mark couldn't figure at that moment, where she had gotten her information from or for whom the enquiry was being made. Now, he was worried. He could feel the blood rush to his head. 'He hinders every process on that work floor, radically, Laura.'

'Ralph Mournaghan?' She retaliated.

'Yes, Ralph Mournaghan.'

'And Davin Turlock?' She quizzed.

'He has very little to do with it. I make the floor work, Laura. I'm not saying this to be at any vantage point; it is what it is. Davin's alright, but at that, I don't know him well enough to vouch for him.'

The sky opened, and the rain began to beat heavily against the roof and front screen of the taxi. The wipers were switched on, reminding them that they had company.

'Bloody Irish weather!' The driver stated, having overheard their conversation, sarcastically airing his views as he pulled into the kerb. 'Mother of the holy sweet Joseph, sure you can count on nothing. Am I right, son? Six euro twenty, young man.'

'Where did you get that accent from, the tourist board?' Mark looked demented as if he might strangle the driver. 'I want to pay for the full journey for both of us.'

Laura lodged herself in the gap between the two front seats. 'Give me peace and let me pay. Go, please. You got the coffee. I needed to get that nonsense out of my head, and you didn't patronise me, that's what I'd have got had I have gone to my usual sources. Go, enjoy your night. You're late.'

Mark reluctantly nodded and checked his belongings.

'It was lovely seeing you again,' she reassured him. 'I hope I didn't offend you with the questions?'

'Please Laura, don't trust Ralph. He's not a good guy, no matter what you've been told.' She took him at his word. She had needed more time to relay the plans she'd been looking at, and Mark reminded her that he'd offered to meet her later in the week. 'Call me if you need me, yeah?'

She nodded before he closed the door. Lifting his jacket up to cover his head, he waved goodbye and darted to the door of his local. Elliot was waiting inside, and his thirst for a pint had returned without question.

Chapter 11

Elliot was standing at the bar waiting for his drink; he turned instinctively as Mark came through the door, catching his attention. There was a tired, confused expression on Mark's face so by Elliot's reading, the man could do with a nice cold pint.

'Guinness?' Elliot called out. Mark nodded in agreement as he lifted a smile and tilted his head to the far end of the lounge.

Mark took his place behind a small circular table while Elliot made light talk with the bartender who they both knew well. Elliot didn't have long to wait. As he stepped away, he watched the bartender throw a curious glance in Mark's direction; it was unlike Mark to arrive and not say hello. Elliot held the two pint glasses by their wide necks, he was attempting to preserve the liquor on the glass. It was traditional to run a finger along the icy cold circumference while they waited for the head to settle. Trade was brisk, and the bartender was already busy with a gang of students who were lowering shots at the bar.

Three decades had passed, and they still hadn't renovated the place, but that was part of its charm, too many pubs were over-designed. The skinny rustic toilet cubicles were intense, the broken vintage tiles and high Armitage Shank cisterns were something to negotiate when you were a few sheets to the wind. The sweaty odour of a bygone era still assaulting the corpuscles of your nose. It kept the tourists to a minimum, in this pub that they had sponsored for so many years.

'What's up, dude?' Elliot enquired as he circled behind Mark to find his stool. 'You look done in, mate.'

'I'm fine,' Mark replied. 'Cheers!'

Elliot had placed a pint in front of him. Mark's finger caught the overspill of its creamy top before he stroked the chilled ice liquor from his pint glass. He wasn't ready to converse, nor was Elliot. It had been hectic in the pharmacy.

The entire pub felt dishwater dreary, and he hoped his friend was in better tune. Mark had seen out a hard day though everything had gone smoothly. Although he hadn't made it home to finish the task of painting, he'd enjoyed his trip down Grafton Street and most of his chat with Laura. Elliot looked well; he'd just got a new haircut.

'Nice trim, mate,' Mark prodded, as he boyishly ruffled Elliot's hair.

'Go easy.'

'You got the hot towel treatment, huh?'

'I did, and very nice it was too.' Elliot confirmed.

The two pints were ready to roll. They lifted them in unison, congratulating each other on a drink well-earned.

'I do look forward to a Friday,' Mark said proudly. He was full of bravado, but it was good to be at the end of a hard week's work. 'Any plans then?' He asked.

Elliot looked at him with a vacant expression.

'For the weekend?' Mark continued. 'I have jobs to finish in my apartment. Will Emily be round at yours?'

'Emily?' Elliot's eyes lit up with intrigue. He chuckled without sound, half choking on his pint. It took seconds to recover.

'Siobhan said they met you out doing some shopping, when did all this happen?'

'Nothing's happened, not yet anyhow.' Mark confessed.

'It's not likely to, mate. Emily's her own woman.'

'And what's wrong with that?'

'She's not into relationships, mate. At least not physical ones. In fact, I was sure she was more of a woman's woman until we all went to a pride night with another of Siobhan's friends. She's not a lesbian.'

'Well then.' Mark was on the stir for information, sitting pensively on his seat. He could wait. Elliot shook his head and gave himself time to think. He stroked his chin in jest. Elliot loved Mark, so there was no issue, but he needed to be careful. Emily was a very private person. 'I don't know, Mark, it's just that she doesn't date.'

'What do you mean she doesn't date?'

'Simple as - she doesn't date, she's oblivious to men in that sense. It's hard to get your head around when you don't know her. She's not frigid, more preoccupied. But, if she still hasn't gone there at the age of twenty-seven. I think you can safely say that she's asexual, mate.'

Mark sat motionless; he was intent on taking in every word, ready to scrutinise any small detail that could prove vital in winning round Emily.

'Look, mate. Emily's social, approachable you've seen that. Maybe, it's just that she keeps her relationships completely private. Siobhan says no, she insists that Emily has never been with a man. Look, from what I can make out Emily's an enigma that way. She is secretive.'

Elliot had a gut feeling that his friend was going to fall hard for Emily long before he'd introduced them. Mark's relationships were transient at best. He would struggle in convincing Emily to get involved with him that, could turn into a headache. It also had the potential to affect the dynamic that Elliot and Siobhan had long since built with both friends. Now he was trying to remember why he had ignored his gut feeling in the first place.

'I can't get my head around her, Elliot.'

'I get that Emily can have that effect on men initially.'

'I can't get her out of my mind.'

Elliot was taken aback, and yet there it was. Mark was a guy that women quietly pursued, he'd gone along with a few of them, but none had ever made an impact.

'I'm a wreck around her. I'm in trouble, Elliot.'

'Winning her over won't be easy.'

Elliot was still trying to take in what he'd just heard. Mark was a solitary creature. The dinner party, the shopping, doing up the flat, it wasn't like Mark. He enjoyed a few pints and the odd football match. He attended the occasional dinner party, workwise or with friends; it was his management post that was his primary focus, his orientation. Settling for family life or even finding a partner was a distant prospect for Mark and the same could be said of Emily if she ever thought that way.

'She's an incredible woman.' Mark wasn't letting go. He was never a guy that expressed feelings, observations alright, focusing on friends and colleagues but this was different, these emotional outbursts had never been part of who he was. Mark chuckled.

'What are you like?' Elliot demanded though he couldn't help but wonder. It wasn't Mark, though it was slightly amusing to hear him talk that way.

They were heading towards the end of their first pint when Mark caught the barman's attention. He ordered the same again; standing up out of the seat; he circled the two pint glasses with his finger.

'What's the story with the apartment?' Elliot asked as Mark sat back down.

'I couldn't bring Emily back to the flat as it was. I had it in my head after walking her home from your place that night. It feels good to have made changes though.'

'Nesting, it's primitive that. Did you put my painting up finally?'

'I even got it framed.'

The shock struck Elliot's face; Mark chuckled as Elliot strained to look at him.

'I was thinking of putting a meal together, an evening for you and Siobhan, Oden too if it gets Emily around. What do you think?'

Elliot couldn't find the words.

'Here. I forgot to mention I seen your fella the other day up Rathmines way.'

'Who?' Elliot asked. 'My brother you mean, Oden?' Elliot was still trying to grapple with the dinner idea.

'He was with a funky looking chick?'

'Not Oden, trust me.'

'It was Oden.'

'She will have been a friend then.'

'Fair enough, but they looked pretty cosy.'

Elliot groaned. 'What is with you tonight? He's too odd for that yet, in case you hadn't noticed, Mark.'

Mark lowered the last of his pint with pleasure. Elliot was still trying to pull himself together. 'You want me to invite Emily to yours?'

'That's right, for dinner.'

'You can't cook?'

'I can cook, Elliot. I do cook.'

'No, you don't?'

'From a jar, I do... you can show me.' Mark retorted, as he stood up and got the okay from the barman to go and collect their pints. 'You want peanuts?'

'Bacon fries.' Elliot replied. He was left sitting alone long enough to absorb the information. If he could help his friend in any way that was fine, getting with Emily was going to be a challenge, without a glimmer of doubt. Siobhan had filled him in on Emily's history, but that was not his to divulge. Defining the woman's background could lead to a potentially explosive situation. Mark was taking his time with the drinks.

'So, are you up to much the weekend?' Mark quizzed him again as he returned with the two pints in hand, the munchables in his trouser pockets.

'We're full on the entire weekend, mate.'

Elliot had a list of events that he was in no form to attend; he just wanted a lazy few days with Siobhan. There was a garden fete in Wicklow, and a country market planned for Saturday morning. Then they had a visit to Bray. They were going to see an amateur dramatics thing. A 'Woman of No Importance' by Oscar Wilde. He'd seen it last year and was being dragged there for the second time. Then it was Siobhan's turn to have her family over on Sunday. All that considered, complaining to Mark wasn't going to help matters, so he continued with his pint.

'I have an idea?' Elliot whispered. 'Why don't you swing by the restaurant tonight, where she works? I know she finishes up at eleven.'

'Tonight?' Mark nearly came out of his skin. 'That's coming on a bit strong?'

'You can ask her to join you for a quiet drink. It's Siobhan's birthday in three weeks. Tell her that you're organising a party and you could do with her help? Women love that stuff.'

'That's so underhanded, but they do, don't they? I'm not sure that's a great idea?'

'If you do get a chance to chill out with her, just don't make any sudden moves, maybe take it slowly, yeah?'

'I don't make moves?'

'That's right... Hey, I don't think she does either.'

Elliot hoped to leave it at that, as it was all a bit too much to take in at that point.

'I have seriously felt the urge to kiss her.'

'Okay.'

'On the walk back from your house that night, I couldn't hear what she was saying; the thought of kissing her was that strong. That's not me, right?

'Right!'

'She's intoxicating. What is that?''

'Leave it out, Mark; I'm starting to worry about you.' Elliot was serious.

'She's just there, on my mind!'

'Enough, yeah?'

The two men dug into their pints and bacon fries and again became aware of their surroundings. The early afternoon drinkers were now thin on the ground. Punters that were dressed up for a night out were starting to arrive. A few boisterous yobs were being put to rights as they entered. The rain had stopped they realised; the young women were no longer attempting to shelter their hair as they came through the door. Girls in scant dresses made their way to the bar, the lads trailing behind them wearing freshly ironed shirts and hipster jackets.

It wasn't Elliot or Mark's scene tonight, but the Guinness was not just average, it was the babe's breath. Their pub was as good as any, how many times had they come to that conclusion? They laughed.

'How was work?' Mark looked as if he could do with a funny anecdote, but Elliot didn't have his heart in it.

'Everything's good there; it was just a slow week.' That was not the case, it was nonstop, and he'd filled more flu and cold prescriptions than he cared to think of with the change in the weather. He'd been filling the same antibiotic scripts from morning until closing time. He'd been thinking about Brian and Alfie, the two boys in Australia, his mind locked on the notion of moving to the other side of the world. He'd no idea if Siobhan had ever entertained the idea. He never mentioned it for fear that three months later he'd find himself on a plane.

'How was it over at the shipping company?'

'It was an easy week as it goes. I had Ralph Mournaghan in my ear at the start of the week, but he was good enough to stay away beyond that.' Mark stopped himself there. 'Laura called today, oddly enough.'

'The widow woman?' Elliot was surprised.

'Jesus man, don't think she'd fancy being called 'the widow woman'!'

'Laura then, that's her name, right?' Elliot made up for the comment by offering up his full concentration.

'I met her for coffee after work.' Mark eventually admitted.

'So, what's behind that?'

'You're seriously cynical sometimes. When the woman rang, I assumed it was something to do with Ralph. I was about to turned her away, but she needed advice.'

'Sounds ominous?'

'She started up a greeting card company shortly after her husband died. As it goes, it took off in a big way.'

'Good on her.'

'She's selling the business up this week, she's trading it in to start a new project. She got a good offer; it's been making a tidy profit the card business.'

Elliot looked confused. 'With the Irish economy as is, where are these pastures new?'

'We didn't have the time to get into that. It's her husband's anniversary today. How does a person cope? A widow after less than a year of marriage? They were three years together before they got hitched.'

'Doesn't bear thinking about, Mark.'

Mark had never covered that ground with Elliot. It wasn't his place. Elliot and Siobhan had to have talked about marriage and children. But how do you sit and try to converse with your partner about the possibility of their demise, especially when you're in love? That was way out there for Mark, a million miles from where he was in his life.

'I got a phone call from the lads in Australia.' He announced, remembering the event. Elliot was a friend of the two men, but it was Mark they usually called. He had grown up with the lads, he knew their families, and so he had more to exchange on the home front.

'Brian's father is not well, though he's being told it's nothing major. I promised I'd take a jaunt home on Sunday and check in with them.'

'Nice one.'

'I know I haven't seen the family in a while. It's just a flying visit. I must ring my mum so she can organise dinner. I'll drop by Brian's on the way back to the train.'

'Siobhan's folks will be gone by eight on Sunday so I can pick you up at the station, just ring me when you're set to come back.'

'I might do that. Here, before I forget, what's the name of that restaurant where Emily works? I'll have to find my way there later.'

'La Papille Solletico. I think. It's...'

'On Parnell Street?'

'Yeah, you know the place?'

'The Papille Solletic, you're sure? And she works two nights a week?'

'Yeah, Wednesday and Fridays, it's always the same. It's a decent restaurant, pricey for what it is, but yeah, she's been there every Wednesday and Friday since she started.'

Mark looked lost for a moment as the blood appeared to drain from his face.

'Are you okay, mate?' Elliot was concerned.

The waitress's hands were all he could remember. He hadn't even looked at her face with all the bullshit that was going on that night. It dawned on him on several levels at once.

'Hold on,' Mark asked, 'the night before the party in yours, the week before, was there any talk of Emily being unwell?' He solicited.

'That girl never gets sick, mate. Let me think. She was in ours that Wednesday before she went to work. She had to drop back books. She called on Friday too.'

'Was she sick that week, a head cold even?' Mark was beside himself.

'No, she's healthy.'

'She had no flu, no cold?' As Elliot shook his head, Mark dropped his chest onto his lap. After a negotiated silence he pulled himself together and sat up again flushed. 'I have to get out of here.' He whispered shaking his head.

'What is it?' Elliot asked, wanting information.

'I was at the restaurant, with Mournaghan and his cronies, that Wednesday night I told you about it. The Wednesday before the party of yours. I knew I recognised her, it was vague, but I felt it. No, she recognised me. Hell no...'

'So, where's the problem?'

'I recognise her voice now. I don't know what she overheard. Ralph Mournaghan was full on rude to her.'

'Were you?'

'No!'

'What was going on?' Elliot enquired.

'The whole set up thing with Laura and Ralph Mournaghan. '

'The widow woman?'

'Will you stop saying that?' They briefly looked at each other and looked away.

'When Emily stepped outside your place that night. When I left to walk her home, she said she'd had a head cold that week. I'm confused.'

'I don't get you?' Elliot was concerned.

'She had this woollen hat on her. I knew when she said it there was no sign of flu on her, or it was the way she said it. I knew she was lying; I just didn't know why.'

'Man, you're going way deeper than you need to go with this.'

'You think?'

'I know! We have three hours before she finishes work.'

'I'd have to go home and get changed; I don't know.'

'You can grab a shower at mine, Siobhan's out. There's no big deal here, chill.'

Mark half-heartedly agreed and lowered the end of his pint. They said goodnight to the barman once they reached the door, but he was too busy to notice.

'Hungry?' Elliot asked.

'Yeah, I should eat.'

'I'll put something together when we get back to the house.'

After a long chat, it looked straightforward enough, and that was assuming Emily recognised him, he could clear that up with the truth. Finishing her shift, she might be too tired to join him for a drink. If she wasn't interested in going out, at least he could manage to get her to help with the party, he'd have the chance to get to know her better then.

Our Diligent Souls

   By the time they got back to Elliot's place, they were both in better form. Mark was handed a pair of jeans and a shirt before he hit the shower, they were both about the same size. Elliot made supper and they talked through any eventualities before he left, or so they thought.

Mark made it over to the restaurant by a quarter to eleven. Through the window he could see Emily gather her things, she was busy saying goodnight to her workmates. He was nervous, but that was partly because he was minutes away from seeing her again. A few days had passed since they met up outside Trinity. It was pouring rain, and he hadn't thought to take a brolly with him. He stood at the window waiting for her to finish up.

   'Later!' She called back before the door closed gently behind her.

   'Emily!' He called out through the rain, and then again, 'Emily!'

   She turned around, frightened. 'Mark! What are you doing here?' She was startled and upset; her posture braced in defensiveness. 'What is this?' She asked.

   'I wanted to...'

   'You wanted to what, Mark? You knew that I worked here?'

   He was struggling to find the words. 'I need to talk to you... I'm having a party...'

   'Why show up here?' She questioned.

   'I thought I should talk to you in person.'

   'What?' She demanded, 'what's going on? I'm out of here.' She spat the words out at him. Emily was fit to kill as she side-stepped him and moved to the edge of the road to grab a taxi.

   'Why are you so upset?' Mark asked, following behind her with his hand out. He was utterly confused.

   'I have to go.'

   He was stifled, his urge was to grab hold of her and try to calm her hysterics, but he knew better than to do that.

   'I don't want to talk to you. I don't know why you're showing up here?'

   He began to panic when he spotted a taxi heading in their direction. 'You're getting this wrong; I just need help with Siobhan's birthday.'

She didn't take in what he said; she was focused on getting the taxi drivers attention, she wanted out of there.

'What gives you the right? How did you know I was working tonight? How?' She was livid, shouting at him through the rain. Mark stepped back afraid to bring Elliot into the equation as the taxi drew in beside her. She opened the door to the front seat and put one foot inside her ride.

'You knew it was me who served you that night. It's not just weird; it's bloody creepy. What were you expecting showing up here?'

'No.' He pleaded.

'What do you mean, no?' Emily then turned her back to him and climbed into the taxi.

'What I meant to say is...'

'I have to go!' She repeated before she shut the door. She turned to catch his eye-line while he was bent over, his face peering in at her through the window. His hands were jammed in his pockets as he withstood the rain. She hit the electric window button in a temper as he waited for the glass to roll down. 'Stay away from me, you hear me, Mark?'

The taxi driver leant forward and took a good look at him from the driving seat as he checked her safety belt.

'I can explain. You have me all wrong.' Mark called out as the window rolled back up again. Frustrated, he kicked a puddle of rainwater and soaked himself as she was driven off into the night.

Chapter 12

As Elliot reached the top of the stairs, he met Siobhan on the landing in her robe. What was the attraction with women and scalding hot baths? It was unfathomable. The steam was rising off her red raw skin, a potent blast of aromatherapy oils wafting from her dressing gown. When passing the bathroom earlier, he had heard her shriek as she attempted to brace the hot water. Stepping into that tub was ridiculous. Women!

'What, are you doing to yourself, love?' Elliot started out of concern. 'Having the water that hot is not healthy.'

'I haven't an ache in my body, babe.'

'What, had you pain before you climbed in?'

'Don't knock it until you've tried it...eh Elliot!' Her book, her glass of wine and the fresh linen on their bed, were all that she wanted for now. 'I'll sleep like a baby and be ready for the week ahead.' It was their usual sleepy Sunday evening, her parents not long gone. She kissed Elliot on the cheek and made her way to their bedroom.

Oden was finishing his energy drink when Elliot returned to the sitting room, the lad's cyber connection being intravenously fed through the laptop. Elliot lifted his coffee off the kitchen island and guzzled down the remains. His coffee plunger had seen better days, he had to avoid the sediment that had settled at the end of his cup.

He had another ten minutes before they had to leave, enough time to finish up the few dishes that needed drying. It didn't take much effort. A single lamp would provide sufficient light for Siobhan. She might decide to come down and make a brew or refill her wine glass. He tackled the other switches one by one, collecting his keys and their coats at the door.

'Will I shut it down?' Oden asked, without turning from the screen. 'I could run that new windows programme? It'll be installed by the time you get back.'

'Not tonight, mate! Just shut it down, yeah?'

Elliot had put in a long day; he just didn't need the hassle tonight. He had spent the entire afternoon with Siobhan's parents. They were always pleasant if somewhat dull. The constant acknowledgement of each other's characteristics had been mildly irritating. Elliot feared that he and Siobhan might end up that way. It was reason enough to hold tight to as diverse a bunch of friends as possible.

Oden was as always dilly-dallying. Elliot stood waiting with his brother's jacket in hand; history had taught him that patience would serve him best in this case; any banter and Oden would get distracted. He was going to bring up that funky chick that Mark had mentioned but thought better of it. He loved the boy, and he would know if Oden was romantically involved with someone. Oden was too preoccupied to recognise the opposite sex unless they were opponents in a League of Legends match.

Elliot securely locked the front door and made his way to the car with his brother. 'Can you drop me off after you pick up Mark?' Oden requested as he climbed down the steps, he had plans, but not being one to share too much of his private life, he left it at that.

'Suits me, mate! We're going to have to figure out a plan to help Brian in Australia; his dad's not feeling the best.'

'He has Skype, yeah?'

'That reminds me, bro,' Elliot sparked, 'I'm having difficulty with mine...next time will you remind me to let you have a look at it.' The words were no sooner out of his mouth when Elliot realised how bad Oden was at reminding him of anything. He found it impossible to retain information, let alone focus on something that did not entirely hold his interest.

Elliot needed to get out of his parking squeeze. He was being well and truly challenged tonight. It was not every day the man got to park outside his front door. When he did the next-door neighbour came right up his tail end. Elliot meticulously etched his way backwards and forward before finally pulling out.

'Neighbours, huh?' Oden sniggered. Elliot had told him about the car situation on a previous occasion.

Oden as per usual timed the journey. It was seven minutes from door to station. The lad jumped out once Elliot had grabbed a space that was close to the main entrance. Elliot couldn't help but acknowledge the nature of his brother, endearing as it was. Oden's naively adventurous expression was that of a man on a mission. It was simple, find Mark and bring him back to the car. He would be swift in the way he completed the task. Elliot didn't even have to ask.

Our Diligent Souls

It took all of three minutes before Oden and Mark were in full view. Mark trailed behind Oden, carrying a stuffed plastic bag in his arms. The visuals were comic. His brother was making strides towards the finish line with the mindset of a young boy that had smelt a medal.

There was no immediate rush, no one barking up Elliot's backside for a parking space. In a bid to be helpful, Oden jumped into the back seat. Mark rounded the car and checked the road traffic before he slipped into the front passenger side. There wasn't room for his plastic bag on the floor, rhubarb and celery sticking out either side.

'My dad sent this lot over from the allotment for you and Siobhan. Guessing he wants you to make him another Bakewell tart the next time I'm heading in his direction.'

Elliot indicated and drove out, his eyes on the traffic. 'I should have thought before you left!'

In truth, Elliot had had a busy weekend ahead of him the last time they'd met in the pub. It wasn't unusual for him to send Mark's old man any number of homemade treats, but this was the first time Elliot was given produce from the allotment.

'You do a thing twice for anyone over a certain age, and they expect it as routine.' Mark laughed. Elliot was too chuffed with his allotment pickings to care.

'I had to hide the allotment bag around the side of Brian's house. I didn't have the time to visit and go back to collect this.'

The two men smiled at each other.

'You okay, mate?' Elliot asked.

Mark nodded and turned around to look over the headrest; he was hoping to bring Oden into the conversation.

'So, how's Oden?'

'I'm fine? College is good.'

'What's the craic otherwise?'

'White and hairy.'

Mark waved his finger. 'No women on the scene then?' He asked being coy.

'You two would be the last to know about it.' Oden replied.

Mark laughed as Elliot checked his brother's face through the rear-view mirror.

'Defensive wee bugger, isn't he?'

'He has other fish to fry.' Elliot stated. 'He'll find himself a nice girl at some stage. Am I right, Oden?' Elliot asked, his eyes shifting to Oden's expression and back to the road.

Oden's attention was fixed on his iPhone as he spouted bits of trivia for the full journey. The lad completely monopolised the conversation, again timing the trip, from the station to his house this time around. It came in at fifteen minutes. Oden sat in the car until he had arrived at a figure for their journey to follow. With the lightness of traffic and distance, he estimated that they would make it to Mark's in no less than twelve minutes. That would give them an arrival time of two minutes past ten.

'You're an incredible source of information, Oden.' Mark commented, marvelling at his friend's younger brother.

'A walking encyclopaedia, am I right, mate? You name it, he knows it, this brother of mine.'

Elliot had always been protective of Oden; he instinctively defended him against anyone who found him a handful. It wasn't long before Oden was safely inside his front door, knowing his brother had set off for Mark's flat. The two friends would save their serious discussion, for now, it was better to wait until they were both in front of a cold beer. Elliot instead filled Mark in on Oden's living arrangements.

Mark was happy to listen to Elliot talk about his brother; the man's love for the young lad was enormous. The boy had moved out of their folks' place about a year ago and moved in with a bunch of gamers, all computer geeks. They all had consoles and computers in their rooms and a wide-screen in the sitting room.

Oden was easily distracted and struggled to keep his stuff in order. His mother had long since given up on him but having to live with a bunch of scruffy pre-pubescent students suited him fine. He found it easier to assimilate himself there to a degree and learned how to do the dishes. They had lots of rotas in the house and all night online gaming tournaments to turn their hands to as well.

Study wise; he did everything at the last minute. He was as sharp as a razor blade, Oden, but it had to hold his attention. He had unbounded faith in his ability to a point where he thought he didn't have to hand up assignments. That was where his mother drew the line; she was safer avoided for the entire month of May when Oden lived at home. His approach to study slowly drove her to the edge when it came to the end of every semester.

Mark's family were doing fine. His sister had joined them for dinner with his two nieces. They had perfect roast potatoes, and the kids were very well-behaved. The sister's husband had gone to the pub to meet some friends. That had given Mark's dad the opportunity to have a word with him, in respect of tensions between him and the father of his grandchildren. Mark had convinced his dad that there was no argument between them. His sister never burdened her folks with the antics of her partner. It wasn't for Mark to highlight his failings to them.

'I didn't know she had trouble there?' Elliot quizzed him.

'You don't know the half of it, mate.'

The dinner was delicious. There was always a distinctive taste of Mark's mother's cooking; in fact, it all had the same distinct flavour. That was part of its charm. If you were letting her down in some way, her agitation would be echoed in her cooking standards, with a Sunday roast that was tough as old boots.

Elliot was as always glad to see his friend. That said, he knew by Mark's humour that there was something troubling him. It was exactly two minutes past ten when they arrived at Mark's place. He had a bunch of twenty keys, so it took some searching before he finally found the right one. Mark was entirely organised when it came to his job, but in respect of his home life, he had a more relaxed approach.

Elliot had wholly forgotten the decorating buzz that Mark had been on, so he was more than surprised when he walked through the door. It was very Mark. The cream canvas sofa had been brought to life by some well-chosen cushions. It was way more masculine than Elliot's place, but there were feminine touches that he didn't expect. There was an ornate picture frame that his mother had sent him, a herb box by the window and a vibrant chilli plant. Elliot loved the box shelves that displayed the old vinyl records, and Mark had created a statement wall with some art deco wallpaper that impressed.

There was a story behind almost everything in the place. Mark had put effort into Elliot's painting, using a green frame with a tarnished effect that picked up on the mood of the piece amicably. Some sincere congratulations were given, and it wasn't long before they were facing each other, beers in hand.

'So! Brian's dad, Jackie, he's not so good then?'

Mark had phoned Elliot on his way to the train station with a brief snapshot of the situation. It was a head-scratcher when it came to what to do next. Brian's father was much sicker than he was letting on. He was far sicker than his family were ready to admit. Nothing that had happened during the visit sat comfortably with Mark.

'Jackie's not well, Brian's mother too, her nerves were frazzled. She sent me upstairs.' Mark began. 'Jackie was in bed, propped up by pillows either side of him. He looked a good ten years older, mate. The weight has just fallen off him.'

'Was there a prognosis?' Elliot's enquiry should have been anticipated; being a pharmacist, he had more insight into these matters than most.

'According to Marian, they found a tiny spot of cancer but nothing that would account for him coughing up blood.'

'Does Brian know this?'

'Not that I know of...' Mark wasn't sure. 'Jackie did six weeks of chemotherapy and testing before they let him go home from the hospital. He was still coughing up blood. In saying that, the doctors expected that to pass in a week to a fortnight with the medication they'd given him to take home.'

'Christ!'

'Three weeks on and nothing had changed. So, the doctors brought him in for another few rounds of chemo but still no proper diagnosis.'

'Can you remember the name of the medication?' Elliot enquired.

'Sorry mate, I wasn't thinking. He's lost thirty odd lbs and most of his hair, but the doctors are still not calling it cancer. The tumour was shrunk to almost nothing.'

'And Brian knows none of this?'

'His father doesn't want a fuss. Jackie is convinced that Brian doesn't need to know. I didn't like the way he was talking. He was rambling, going on about how proud he was of Brian. I couldn't believe my ears. Brian was out seeing the world, doing what Jackie himself never had the guts to do. You know how he was about Brian leaving a decent job?'

Elliot was feeling as concerned as Mark at this stage.

'How did the rest of the family seem?'

'They were avoiding my eyes, fussing around like butterflies over making a cup of tea for me. It was like watching something in slow motion. Brian's just has the one sister, Sarah, you did meet her, she's a decent sort. Jackie and Marian were always rock solid.'

'Go on.' Elliot urged him.

'Marian repeated the news carefully with Sarah looking on nervously. The doctors didn't expect any complications. They said there was no reason for him, not, to make a full recovery.'

'That could be the case.'

'I asked if they were comfortable with the prognosis. Marian didn't like the question, and Sarah didn't know where to look. What choice do they have? They're living in the hope of Jackie getting better, and Marian was adamant that Brian should not be told, that's what his father wants.'

'So, what to do?'

'I am going to tell Brian, they're not stupid, they know Brian sent me to check on his father. They know that I'm going to relay the truth. Sarah was relieved that I called in that respect.'

'There's no panic though, is there?'

'You didn't see him, Elliot. He's in bad shape, and the way he spoke. He was reminding me of stories from our youth. And then the way he left things. I filled up like I'd never see him again and he acted as if he knew it. I was trying to convince myself that it was in my head, but I genuinely don't know.'

'People talk like that sometimes when they're frightened, Mark.'

The two friends sat in silence. Mark swiftly killed the beer and went to the fridge to get two more.

'How much does Brian need to know?' Elliot enquired. 'He's only getting settled now, and if he's dragged home, he may not have the funds to start over.'

Mark just tucked into his beer. He was already carving out the words in his head. It felt like his task. There was no running away from it, and on top of that, he couldn't take the risk of waiting. Brian would ring anyway, and he knew in his gut that if it were him, he would want to know. The fact that Brian left for Australia on bad terms with his old man didn't help.

'The facts are all you need, everything that's happened over the past ten weeks. Just stick to what the doctors said, the good humour, and the expected recovery. Don't mention the hair and weight loss.' Elliot felt he needed to intervene.

'And if he asks?' Mark quizzed. 'He will ask.'

Elliot needed to pull his friend back for the minute. 'He'll end up coming home, when he may not need to.'

'And he has commitments over there.' Mark reinforced, knowing the issues.

'Has he even got the airfare? We could offer to help,' Elliot suggested. 'That's not a problem, but you need to think before you get on that phone, Mark.'

'I don't want to do this. Are you going to hang around or what?' Mark was agitated as the urgency of the task was real. 'It has to be done.'

Elliot nodded before Mark turned around to look for his laptop.

'Maybe we can catch him on Skype? What time is it there?' Mark reiterated, 'What's the time?' The pair stood up as Mark's phone began to ring. His coat was in the far corner of the room he realised as he tried to follow the sound. 'It's Emily.' He relayed lifting the phone. Elliot had given him her number before he left for the restaurant that night. Desperately hoping for some solution, Mark answered the phone. On hearing her voice, he realised how off his thinking was, he was in no fit state to talk to Emily.

'Mark?'

'Emily.'

He wished he hadn't pressed the receiver. Elliot's face lit up with enthusiasm, but Mark turned his back on him, attempting to maintain some composure.

'How are you, Emily?'

'I got your number from Siobhan, she admitted it straight off, I've been thinking, Mark. I should have said it myself when I met you in their place; I should have said it was me that served you in the restaurant that night.'

'Emily!'

'I was shocked when you turned up; genuinely, I've been stalked in the past.'

'It's a bad time right now, Emily!'

'What do you mean?'

'Look, I wanted to put a party on for Siobhan's birthday, and Elliot suggested that I ask you for help. He told me what restaurant you worked in so that I could get things moving. When he told me where you worked, it was then that I realised who you were. I thought I'd get the chance to explain when I turned up.'

'Okay!' Emily was trying to take it in. Even Siobhan hadn't been able to explain why he'd shown up at the restaurant.

'It was crossed wires.' Mark stated coldly.

'Look, I shouldn't have lost the head,' she asserted. 'I should have given you the opportunity to explain yourself. It's just that table; it wasn't the easiest table to work and...'

'Emily, you don't have to explain. I know what it looked like, they're a bunch of office goons, and I've had to play along with that sometimes.'

'I'm sorry that I judged you so harshly, that much is visible I know, it was more about the company you keep. I knew it was a business meal and I didn't want to make you feel uncomfortable at Elliot and Siobhan's, that's why I kept it to myself. I was just blown out when you showed up at work like that; it completely spooked me.'

'It's fine.' Mark insisted, but Emily needed to continue.

'I didn't think you recognised me at Siobhan and Elliot's place.'

'I didn't know that night, Emily.' Mark promised her. 'I swear to you; it was when Elliot told me the name of the restaurant where you work that I realised who you were. I was so embarrassed that night when Mournaghan berated you; I didn't want to look up. I didn't properly take you in.'

'Okay.' She whimpered.

Mark was afraid of digging himself into an even greater hole, he needed to walk her through the situation with his work colleagues, and it was not a good time. Elliot was hovering inches away from him.

'I have a situation here, Emily. I'm sorry...'

'Mark, look you're a great friend of Elliot's and Siobhan's and...'

He stopped her there.

'Can we meet and talk this over properly, Emily? I want to be able to give you my full attention.'

There was a deafening silence both ends of the phone.

'I hope you'll allow me to help with this party. I'd do anything for Siobhan.'

'Can I ring you tomorrow, Emily? We can meet up for a coffee and if you'll allow me to explain.'

'There's nothing to explain, Mark, its fine.' Emily stated plainly.

'There is,' Mark replied. 'But, thank you... Talk soon, yeah? You're not upset or anything?'

'No, I'm fine.' Emily confirmed.

'I'll talk to you soon.' He insisted.

'Okay then, okay.' She hung up the phone.

Elliot was beside his friend again, he put his hand on Mark's shoulder and spoke. 'It's all fixable, mate?' Elliot had picked up on some of the discussion; he was already uncomfortable knowing what he knew. 'Things didn't go so well with Emily then?'

'We didn't go for the drink, put it that way.'

Elliot hesitated before opening his second can of beer.

'I feel utterly sick here, Elliot.'

'I can see that but calm down, mate. What time is it now, eleven? We need to look at the time difference?'

'Ten hours... It's nine in the morning there. He'll be an hour into work.' Mark informed him.

'It's better if you hold off telling him until the evening when he has time to absorb it. He can go and be with friends. You're in at eight, yeah? What time is Brian in from work?'

'Seven normally, but he heads to the beach or the dog track after that. He usually leaves the house again by around eight o'clock.'

'Mark, call him on the phone from work, your best bet is to ring between nine and ten, you'll catch him then. Just call him, forget Skype yeah, it's too much juggling.'

Mark had a task on his hands, and Elliot was developing a migraine. It was time for Mark to go to bed and Elliot to make his way home, they both had early starts. Abandoning his three-quarters full can, Elliot stood up. 'You need some sleep. I'm going to go.'

Mark followed him to the door where Elliot wrapped his arm around his shoulder. 'It'll be alright, bud, and we'll sort out the Emily stuff another time, yeah? Just try to get some sleep.'

Mark locked the door and turned to face the room that he had created for Emily. He couldn't think properly, his head was in a muddle, with Brian, with all of it. It had to wait until tomorrow, and that was if Mark was able to sleep. He had no overalls organised for the morning, but then again, he could always wear a suit. That much was ready; it was unlikely that anyone would pass any remarks, he decided.

Tomorrow can wait he thought as he stripped down and fell into bed. He was too exhausted to dwell on what he was facing, but the issues stayed with him as he tossed and turned for a further hour, making little headway with sleep. When he woke the following morning he still had part of his dream intact, his sister Moira arriving at his door with her bags and two children in tow.

Chapter 13

Mark arrived at the warehouse ahead of time, his head heavy. He had managed to put together a tight morning schedule for the crew. He would need to abandon his post by nine to phone Brian. Ralph Mournaghan walked through the holding door where the delivery vans were waiting to be filled with cargo. He ignored the greetings of two passing execs and made his way up to the offices without a word, which was suspicious Mark thought.

The new trainee was the first to arrive at Mark's side, the other workers assembling behind him. Two of the team were finishing the remains of their early morning smoke, as it was they still had a few minutes left on the clock. No one mentioned Mark's suit though their eyes were on him. The team had only ever seen him in his overalls and were reminded of the fact that he was a businessman, a man above their station in his well-tailored suit.

Mark congratulated the young trainee on coming to grips with his duties and went on to give concise instruction on how the morning was to run. There were a few quips from the crews, not their regular early morning banter as he officiously got straight to it. Mark's new modus apparatus was being met by waves of dubious curiosity; the men appeared unfocused and mildly suspicious. But, Mark wasn't buying into any of it. He had a significant task to get to right then and wasn't sure that he'd be able to face a full day's work after his phone call to Australia. His shoulders were stiff with tension.

Unimpressed by his worker's attitudes, Mark decided to skip out on a pretence. It wasn't like him, but he wasn't on form. He'd heard there was an urgent boardroom meeting later that morning which might have explained Ralph Mournaghan gruffness. Making his way up to the office, he cleared his departure with Imelda. The plan was to get home, call Brian, reorganise his work clothes and get back to work after lunchtime. He ran into Davin Turlock at the bottom of the stairs.

'Wow!' Davin cried, as he stepped out of the man's way to take in his suit. 'Where are you off to?'

'It's not any of your concern.' Mark responded, though he immediately recognised that his tone was unjustifiable. 'You'll have to excuse me, Davin. Sorry, it's just I have a funeral to attend.' He was ruffled, embarrassed by his deceit, he had never felt the need to lie to anyone in as many years and his cheeks were flushed.

'I'm sorry to hear that, Mark. No one too close I hope?'

'No, sorry, I'm sorry.'

'I wanted to run through a few things with you regarding general operations.'

'My heads not on right. What do you need to know, Davin?'

'What would you change if you were given a choice?'

Mark was surprised by what he was saying, on today of all days. 'What's going on, Davin... Please?'

'Are there problems on the floor that we're unaware of at present? There's a board meeting this morning. What can I do to help? Have you any ideas that might make room for further efficiency?'

Mark shook off his sense of despair and leapt on the opportunity.

'We have a critical lifter that needs proper parts and professional servicing. The other lifting machines require servicing too if we're to work to full effect. They need to be maintained on a weekly basis. We could bring the team in some Sunday to re-organise the aisles, but the floor staff need time and a half for that. I've been analysing the general layout here, and I've plans drawn up that should create more fluidity. It would leave us better able to cope with the nuisance of broken lifters or any delays we might encounter. It would streamline the activity on the floor.'

'That sounds achievable.'

'I have to go,' Mark interjected. He turned on his heels. 'I need the men to be paid their full wages without miscalculation. I hand up perfect time sheets and keep copies.'

'That's Mournaghan's remit?'

'You'd think.' Mark retorted. He had given Davin enough of his time; he had noticed that two of his workers were standing idle.

'Are you in need of something to do, lads?' Mark spouted.

Mournaghan stepped passed Davin as Joyce approached Mark from a separate aisle. 'Is everything alright, boss?'

'Can you take charge until after lunchtime?'

'Not a problem, Mark.' Joyce nodded.

Davin Turlock was already on his way back up the stair when Mark looked back. He handed over the clipboard to Joyce and ran through his proposed agenda one more time. Mournaghan had slowly been approaching them from behind.

'Can I have a word?' He enquired as Joyce stepped aside.

'Yes, Ralph.'

'You're away again? That won't sit well with the board of management. Do you have an aversion to this place, Mark? A straight answer would be good.'

'I'm going to a funeral, Ralph.'

'Who's funeral?'

'That's my concern, now if you'll excuse me, Ralph. I'm running late.' He attempted to leave.

'Hold on there, just hold on a minute. Who do you think it is you're talking to, Mark? Who have you left in charge?'

'Joyce. Why?'

'It's me that you turn to for approval on that. I am your supervisor, or has that escaped your attention?'

'Not for one minute, Ralph.'

'You're aware of that?'

'I am fully aware of your position.'

'You don't go anywhere without getting my approval first. I want to talk to this Joyce fella; get him here until I have a word.'

Mark hesitantly called Joyce over to join them.

'Yes, boss?'

Ralph weighed in. 'He's not your boss, I am, and I'm here to warn you that if you fall short of your workload today... I'll see you gone out of here before you know what's hit you, we're up to scratch on that now?'

Mark stepped in between Joyce and Mournaghan. 'I'm not allowing you to speak to my staff in that manner, Ralph.'

'And you're the captain of this ship?' Ralph was pleased with himself.

'Joyce, go back to your work.' Mark insisted, but his authority was short-lived.

Mournaghan growled. 'Do not move.' He snapped at Joyce before turning his attention to Mark. 'If you think you're telling me what I can and cannot do around here, you're very much mistaken. Let's be crystal clear about that, Mark.'

'Are you finished, Ralph?'

Mournaghan turned to Joyce with a filthy look before he left. The two men watched Ralph's movements in silence as he headed towards the stairs.

'Do not fall behind!' Mark whispered before they got back to the work schedule.

It was ten to nine when Mark jumped into a taxi at the gate. He found and readied his key before opening the door to his flat. The stale smell of the two empty beer cans, it needed to be tackled. He emptied the cans then flung his overalls and a few loose sweaters into a quick wash before throwing his jacket over the chair. Undoing his tie, he sat at the laptop to open his Skype.

Brian's face animated the screen for a few minutes before decent sound was established. He was just in from work. Mark was relieved to see that his girlfriend Melisa was floating around in the background. They covered the opening pleasantries.

'So, how was he?'

'Not great Brian, in good form, but they haven't given you much of a picture.'

'I know he was coughing up blood, but that's resolved itself, yeah?'

'He still has that going on, mate, but it's not as severe as it was.'

'Don't spare the details, Mark. I need the full picture.'

'I don't want you to be alarmed, Brian.'

Brian sat patiently at the other end of the screen. 'Go on.' He eventually said.

'They found a spot of cancer, but it was too small to be the reason Jackie was coughing up blood. To be on the safe side, they treated him with chemotherapy and radium; it's practically gone, the treatment has shrunk the tumour to nothing.'

'A tumour? When did this happen?'

'They kept him there to run tests, so he was in the hospital for a good six weeks. The doctors were sure that the coughing up blood would stop, given two weeks at home on the medication they gave him.'

'But it didn't work?' Brian enquired. He was ready to hear the worst.

Mark hesitated. 'He was home for three weeks and no change, so they brought him back in for another few rounds of chemo.'

'So, the coughing up blood, that's still happening?'

'The doctors said that there's no reason for him not to make a full recovery. He was in good spirits, weak, but in good spirits.'

'I've just landed this job. The timing couldn't be worse.'

'I didn't want to give you this news, Brian, but if I were in your position, I'd want to know the truth.'

Brian wasn't stupid. 'He's lost weight? His hair too I'm guessing?'

'They don't want you to worry, Brian. He doesn't want you to find out. You'll need to talk to the family.'

'When they've been putting off telling me it doesn't sound good.'

'They know you struggled to find your feet without the permit, Brian, and Jackie could make a full recovery. The doctors said to expect as much.'

'Doctors differ in opinion, and as a result, patients bloody well die, our fella?'

Brian was right. The two friends sat in silence.

'I thought something was off when he was never on Skype. He was too upbeat when he was on the phone.'

'You have to think this through; there's only scrap work here in the building trade. This new company might not hold onto the job for you in Australia. I can help with your airfare if you decide it must be done. Elliot wants to help too if that is what you decide.'

'You're a good mate. I might have to consider that.'

'Is there any chance that they'd give you a hall pass and take you back? That's the question. It wasn't easy for you the past few months there, and your dad could have another thirty years, Brian.'

'And mum, and my sister?'

'Yeah, Marian and Sarah they're both doing fine, no worry there.' Mark finally had something good to relay. Having given it some thought; Marian's wobbler was a gut reaction, she knew he was going to spill the beans to Brian.

'Look, Mark, I appreciate you going over there. I need time to absorb this. I'll talk to my manager in the morning and call you in the next twenty-four hours once I know where I'm at over here. I've got to talk to Melisa too. I'll work out the time variations. No worries, yeah?'

Mark could tell that his friend was straining under the news, but that was to be expected. He said his goodbyes and disconnected.

Elliot was at work but was glad to take Mark's call. 'You've done the right thing, Mark. Just give him time to digest this. You okay?'

'I'm grand. I've clothes to dry, and I need to get back to work.' He heard his spinner stop. The flat was chilly, so he threw the overalls on one of the radiators, set the thermostat to full whack and put the kettle on the boil. With a strong cup of coffee in hand, Mark lifted the phone one more time to call Emily. He was planning to apologise and fill her in on what had been going on, but his call went straight to messenger.

'Emily, it's Mark, I've called to apologise. I was hoping we could meet for a coffee. There are circumstances I need to explain. I'll try you again later... I'm not sure of your work hours; I'm hoping after six will suit. Take care.'

With an hour or so to kill Mark decided to finish that second coat of paint while his clothes dried. Before long he was rearranging pieces of furniture. His work overalls were ready, and he still had time to go into town for lunch. The phone rang. It was Emily returning his call.

'I'm glad you called, Emily.'

'I don't understand where the problem is, Mark. I thought I'd put you straight on everything last night.'

'Put me straight?'

'Sorry. That sounds judgemental. I was shocked when you called to the restaurant, and I've no problem helping with Siobhan's birthday.'

'That's great, but I want to explain in person. Will you meet me for coffee or even a drink? At least give me the opportunity to redeem myself. Can we do that?'

'I feel as though I'm being railroaded here, but I guess that's okay, fair enough. I'll meet you in the next day or two.'

'Great!' Mark finished up once he'd made the arrangements. 'Tomorrow, at six, is that okay then?'

'I guess.'

'Outside the solicitors?' He asked.

'Yes, sure. It's on Upper Abbey Street; McGill & Associates.'

'I'll find it, no worries. Talk to you then, Emily.'

'Such bother, and for no good reason but fine, I'll see you then.'

She was disgruntled, but Mark was sure he could win her round. Hopefully, he'd get to buy her dinner.

Mark had barely got through the door at work when Mournaghan barged his way past him. Davin Turlock was close behind and making a bee-line towards Mark.

'How did the board meeting go?' Mark enquired, remembering their earlier conversation.

'Good. Mournaghan found a reputable dealer on the other side of the city for those parts, so it's been approved. The faulty lifter that you mentioned that'll be repaired, that's due to take place sometime next week.'

Mark had of course been the one to locate the supplier, but he had no interest in drawing attention to that. The problem was finally solved. 'That's great news!'

'The lifters are serviced regularly, Mark.'

'No, they're not.'

'Are you sure of that?'

'A hundred percent!'

'It wasn't my place to bring up the wages issue; you need to tackle Ralph Mournaghan on that count. But you've got time and a half for your men on Sunday if you're still interested in bringing the team in to reorganise the floor.'

'That's great. Well done.'

Mark was elated; it was good news. A morning off and more had been accomplished than if he'd worked his socks off. The men were interested in the Sunday overtime the following week. Joyce had a wedding to attend, but Mark figured he could write Joyce in and say something to him on the quiet once the event had passed off smoothly. He was feeling less apprehensive in respect of his position.

Mark decided that once they'd finished for the day, he would go and visit his old boss Arthur. It was a good idea seizing the opportunity while he felt he had a handle on things. It had been six months, he had missed Arthur and his nettle like observations.

Chapter 14

A cuckoo made its call, scattering seagulls off to distant boundaries. Mark approached the towering green gates, beyond which lay the haven where he had once worked, the old industrial shed where Arthur had set up his shipping company decades ago. He was a proud man Arthur; his routine had not changed in all the years that Mark had known him.

Arthur arrived every morning an hour ahead of everyone else and left an hour after the last clocking card had been stamped. What he did with those hours of grey space was for him alone to know. Mark had missed the place. When working there, he would never have thought to break the inner sanctum of what was Arthur's private time. But times had changed.

Arthur had gone from a lightly silvered mop of hair to a creamy white mop and beard. Nothing else had changed in the four and a half years that Mark had known him. His eyes ever wistful, his skin deeply lined with irreverent good humour. He always wore the same soft lamb's wool jumpers. They were light blue or green, sometimes beige but never did he veer from that, or the light cotton shirt he wore beneath it.

His slacks were not negotiable, even when playing badminton, those slacks, they never came off him. He wore Clarke's leather shoes, loafers, and the obligatory wind-shield jacket on a rainy day. That was it for Arthur, a man of simple pleasures. Every day he carried in his lunch box with ham, cheese or tomato sandwiches with a slice of Madeira cake or a cherry tea cake, it was always the same.

Mark loved the nostalgia of it. The building hadn't changed since he had worked under Arthur's proprietorship. Mark's attention was promptly drawn to the still standing safety precaution signs that permeated the building. Fire resistant devices and exit points were posted in excess, way beyond government regulations. The men's safety was always paramount to Arthur.

The radio was playing as Mark approached; it was as always neatly positioned on Arthur's desk. He was partial to the green scene, a radio slot of traditional homespun merit. Arthur was sitting in his armchair inspecting a parcel with an ancient magnifying glass. His jotter and pencil on his desk poised to receive any information.

Our Diligent Souls

Occasionally a package arrived with an element of mystery, a parcel without fitting receiver or return address. These warm bundles of curiosity were put aside for late claim, only to be examined after the extended duration of two months. The noble task of investigation fell on Arthur's shoulders. Never were his finds shared though the occasional parcel was redelivered where details were enclosed. Otherwise, their secrets remained safe with Arthur.

'Did I miss you, Arthur?' Mark called out as he approached the desk.

Arthur did not move an inch but spoke as if he were expecting him. 'You knew you would miss us, Mark. The question is, was it a wise decision?'

'Today it was, Arthur. For the first time since I left, today it felt right.'

'Sharks, Mark, they never swim in low margins. It was never my place to stand in your way.'

Mark moved closer as Arthur lifted himself from his seat. He waited for Mark to come to his side of the table so as he could stretch out his arm and touch his shoulder. Mark wrapped his arm around the man; he held on tight to the auld fella that he had loved and missed so dearly. Arthur stood back and took him in before passing comment. 'Climbing a tall tree, you've got to understand the risk of falling, my friend. You sometimes have to spread your wings to reach the highest fruit.'

Mark nodded understanding all too well what Arthur meant.

'How have you managed, Arthur?'

'Well enough as it happens, but I'm getting old, and my grandchildren like my children are growing up without me around to play lip service. You wonder what it's for sometimes, my friend.'

'Your son never stepped up then, Arthur?'

'He did for a while to help, but business was never his passion, Mark, you know that. I couldn't hold him here. Your services are still of use; you might bring the place alive again, I reckon. I fear for the men's jobs now; we could do with a return of my prodigal muse.'

'So, what am I now, a prodigal muse? You haven't eased up on the shit talk, I see.' Mark was enjoying the banter.

'You have a cool-head, Mark.'

'You were the one that trained me for something bigger, Arthur.'

'I did, and it was a privilege, but you're missed.'

'I am?'

'Without a doubt you are. So how are the family?'

'Well, my father's allotment is bursting at the max, leeks and gooseberries, spuds. Mum's busy with my sister's kids, the two girls. They're great. You still visit the dog track on a night?'

'I do... myself and the rest of the old cronies.' Mark's smile went straight to his eyes.

'Brian found himself a girlfriend in Australia who trains dogs!'

'For the track? In Australia?' Arthur asked. 'They finally got settled in then?'

'Alfie's still bartending on Bondi beach; it's a great spot they say. Brian, you knew it would take a while for him to get accredited as a sparkie, and now that he's finally got a decent job, his father's been taken ill. Seriously ill! That's all in the pipeline at the minute.'

'Is your sister still with that sad case?'

'She is.'

'It's funny the cards that life throws at you, Mark. You've to make the most of things sometimes, like it or lump it. I've missed you here. You always brought debate, and that you can't give away. Walk with me a while?'

As Mark walked past the old workstation, he noticed that standards had not been maintained. He lowered his eyes to the floor, broadly realising as if for the first time, that Arthur was ageing. Life was full of choices and leaving Arthur had been harder than Mark anticipated.

His present job was sometimes without spirit, without bonds, but it was elevating him into a position where he might soon afford to buy his own apartment. Arthur wasn't tight. There just wasn't big money in the way he did business, not enough to squeeze single mortgage wages from the pot. A lot of the floor staff had partners that they could afford homes with, others were renting, but Mark had always wanted to buy a property. There was the opportunity to advance at the new firm.

'So, any lady friends as of late?'

'I did meet someone.'

'Good, she's a nice girl then?'

'It's hard to tell. I barely know Emily yet but yeah, she's something else is Emily.'

'So, you're smitten.'

'I guess so.'

'Good for you, Mark, it is a long time coming. How is Elliot?'

'He's good; himself and Siobhan just did a heap load of renovations to the house they bought. Evidently, it upped the value; they did most of the work themselves.'

Arthur smiled, he was glad to hear that they were making progress. He was stiffer in himself, slower in the way he moved. He was still as sharp, his memory fully intact but slower, physically slower. Perhaps, it was just their time apart; Mark wasn't sure.

'So, you might come back to us?'

'I have a decent position, Arthur. I miss the place, but I have to try to move forward with my life, selfish as it sounds. I owe you everything.'

'You owe me nothing, Mark. You're a talent, don't you ever forget that we're evens!'

'There's a fella called Joyce that I'm working with; he has great potential. A post here would be a step up for him. You need a good floor manager to help you.'

'I need to retire, Mark.'

'You don't mean that.'

'I might do. You having walked through that door again, has given me a reason to consider.'

'Nonsense!'

'I'm tired, Mark. It's not the same when I don't have an annoying little bugger on my back.'

'You'd be bored senseless in a week.'

'I could slip in and out, just to keep my eye on you.'

'You say that now, Arthur, but you need this place. Joyce could be a fresh set of eyes for you. He's not as good looking as me, but you can put up with that.'

'We've seen some ugly faces here in our time.'

The two men smiled.

'I think we should leave this conversation where it's at for another couple of weeks? Go on now. I've things to do before I get home. There's a charity night at the track in three weeks, let me think over an offer for you, and I'll see you there. Will you do that much for me?'

'I will. I'm not sure I'll be able to come back but...'

'Enough. I'll talk to you then.'

'No problem, Arthur.'

'My respects to Brian and his father, yeah... You stay well.'

Mark could only think through Arthur's proposal. There were occasions when he wished he could turn the clock back. A month ago, he'd have jumped at the suggestion of a return to the old firm, but he'd stayed away for six months with good reason. The principal thing to do was not to return for Arthur's sake. Nor should he abandon his new position for fear of becoming an office goon. He had a chance to resolve the standing issues at T&E in the coming three weeks and see from there. He might stick his nose out this time; now there was the choice to return from where he came.

He left Arthur in better humour. It had been a while since Mark felt secure in himself. There was more to life than working for capital gains. As he reached the bus stop, his phone rang. It was Mournaghan, and he was drunk.

'You need to get over here. We're in that Papille Solletico again. Davin's on his way over, big meeting! We need you here in ten minutes. If you jump in a taxi, it won't take you long. I'm laying the law down here now, you'd...'

Mark hung up the phone and knocked it off while he was at it. He wasn't going to the restaurant. Mark would call into Elliot's for a warm cup of coffee and fill him in properly on Brian's reaction on Skype. He would then go home to his newly decorated apartment and his freshly made bed. He'd had enough of work for one day.

Mark felt carefree on the journey to Elliot's. For once his mind was blank. He watched people clamber on and off the bus in quick fashion. He cherished the anonymity of the city; it suited him. The capital was more colourful than his hometown. People in Dublin were always going places, not just heading to the chipper or the pub. He could slip in and out of places in the city without being questioned. It had a completely different air, not that he didn't enjoy going home. His sense of pride would always rest there, in his hometown.

Our Diligent Souls

Elliot and Siobhan's house was only two streets away from the bus stop. As he approached their door, Emily stepped into view from the other end of the road.

'Great minds, eh?' Mark voiced, delighted to see her. Emily picked up on his valid good humour.

'You're looking lovely.' Mark remarked, moving past the comment with a nod and a smile.

'Thank you, I guess. I was calling for a quick coffee before work.'

'And I was calling with news of a mate.' Mark filled her in on that much.

Emily had already been brought up to speed. 'Brian, he's in Australia, and his father's been taken ill, yeah? Hence the drama?' She was in good form herself.

Mark stood quietly before her; he was pondering something.

'What's up?' She was curious.

'I don't think I'm up for going in here tonight now that I've arrived.'

Mark wanted to saturate himself in her company, never to move from her side truth be told, but his gut instinct advised him to step back for now. He suspected that Emily might cancel their meeting for the following day if they talked to any extent that night, she had resisted, in agreeing to join him in the first place. He was happy and alive with anticipation around her. Elliot would be all over him for an update on the Brian scenario. His desire to be with her was profound, but he was looking forward to a more open, undisturbed exchange on a one to one. He juggled the conundrum in his head.

'Could you do me a favour and not let on you've seen me?' He asked before he lost his resolve. 'I'm going to go home and figure a few things out if that makes any sense?' The idea of leaving her was abhorrent but wise under the circumstances. It wasn't long before she'd have to be at work anyway. He had planned to take her to dinner after picking her up from the solicitor's office.

'Are you okay?' She whispered.

'Yeah... I need to sit back and take in the details of what has been an interesting day. Are we still on for tomorrow? We'll need to put our brains in gear. We've got to figure out what we're going to do for Siobhan's party.'

'Sure. I was going to have a cigarette on the steps here. Do you want to join me?'

Our Diligent Souls

Mark had the occasional cigarette when he had a drink. Emily herself wasn't much of a smoker, but the urge was on her today. 'I even got strong mints and hand cream, so I don't get a telling off from Elliot.'

Her smile brightened her face.

'Go on then.' He whispered, sitting on the step as she lit up in front of him.

'I enjoy a smoke after work.' Emily revealed.

'How was your day?' He enquired.

'Thankless to be honest, Mark, and I have to waitress for a load of bloody tables tonight.'

'My work crowd are there now.' He admitted. He could feel himself sink into her eyes but managed to pull back and keep on talking. 'I was invited over there,' he said, 'I hung up the phone on my boss and turned the damn thing off. I'm sorry that crap happened the other night. I don't enjoy any of them.'

'I've had to deal with worse.'

'It's something I need to get out of right now. I've had enough of corporate execs. It was a mistake getting involved with them in the first place.'

Emily tipped her cigarette ash and watched the tiny parcel of dust roll away on the step. 'I've another hour before I start. Your executive crowd will be getting the early bird. I'm on late tonight, thank goodness.'

Having taken the first few drags of the cigarette, she passed it to Mark. 'You upset over Brian then?' She sounded like she already knew his friend.

'You know Brian then?' Mark inquired.

'Yeah... Siobhan and Elliot introduced me to Alfie and him before they left. I was on the phone with Siobhan today, she filled me in. It might be good to see Brian again if he comes back, yeah?' She suggested.

'Maybe so?' He agreed. 'Don't tell them I've been here. Brian will ring tonight, and I should wait until I get a better picture before I talk to Elliot. I don't know why I drifted over this way. It was one of those days.'

'You sure?' She asked.

'Yeah.'

'No worries then, Mark! I have your back.'

Our Diligent Souls

He passed back the tail end of the cigarette, but she refused as she was already applying the hand cream and had taken out her mints. They both looked up as a taxi rolled into view. Mark jumped to his feet and to his delight the driver stopped. She stood up too.

'Thank you!' He said as she fed a mint into his hand. He held her eyes and leaned in to kiss her lips just barely. There was no struggle, no glimmer of surprise as he bent towards her. It was a gesture that appeared to barely register though his heart was pounding, as he peeled himself back he could feel the moisture of her rose scented lip balm on the edges of his mouth. The idea of them as a couple felt so right to him that the flippant move of a farewell kiss seemed appropriate.

'Thanks again.' He stated as he said goodbye. 'You didn't see me, don't forget.' He called back as he reached the cab.

Within minutes, he was gone. Emily watched him leave as she rested her bag on the step to sort through her belongings. She shook her head as she lifted her bag again, taking a last look across the street to watch the taxi turn off at the first corner.

Emily couldn't remember the last time a man had kissed her on the mouth, but that was as much thought as she was prepared to give it. He was handsome and kind and where that came from she had no idea. It was just a peculiar twist in a day that had already been as odd as they come. She climbed the steps and knocked the door to her friend's house. The weather was perfect, just perfect.

Chapter 15

Emily left the office for the nearest deli to grab two takeaway coffees. The solicitor's doors were shut when she arrived back, scalding beverages in hand. She was amused to see Mark standing outside, he was smiling and flushed as Emily approached.

She wasn't ready to say goodbye to the summer light or the habit of taking a coffee with her to the park after work. The rain hadn't shown its face all day, so she had no intention of letting a decent evening slip through her fingers, not while it was still bright.

'Thought we'd go to the park, it's not far.' She said as she stood in front of him.

'I thought I'd take you for something to eat,' Mark relayed, a little too quickly. His plans to take her to dinner were being dashed.

Emily shook her head.

'You're not hungry?' He asked.

'No, it's early for me, I had lunch. Shall we head on so?'

'Okay, will I take one of those coffees? Let me carry your bag.'

Her bag looked heavy and cumbersome. She had a tonne of paperwork inside its folds. There were a million bits and bobs that she didn't necessarily need to carry around with her. She passed him his coffee and loaded the heavy bag onto to his shoulder with gratitude.

'Cheers you, I'd normally manage myself, but I'm shattered today. So, is there any word on your friend Brian?'

She was curious to know how the situation was evolving with his friend, having talked through the issues with Siobhan and Elliot at length. She had discovered that Brian and Mark went back as far as primary school and was made aware that Mark had a close relationship with Brian's father as well.

'Yeah, as it goes, he's working off a week's notice before coming home on compassionate leave. He has three weeks to get back to Australia if he's to keep his job. I'm looking forward to him arriving home.'

'Any word on his dad?' Emily asked.

'Brian's been in contact with his family, and they're well enough under the circumstances. He hasn't told them he's coming home yet, but he plans to tackle that during the week. He's pretending that his workplace is closing for three weeks and that he's jumping on the chance to visit home.'

'That's good.'

'It could destroy his family if his father's condition worsened. He's a great guy Jackie, still young in his early sixties.' Emily smiled as not every thirty-year-old thought that sixty was a young age.

Mark had given more than enough thought to his friend's predicament. He needed to avoid the issue as it already weighed far too heavy on his mind. He was glad to be with Emily, though the dinner suggestion hadn't gone to plan.

'I hope it turns out okay! He's a nice guy Brian.' Emily voiced sincerely.

'He helps keep me grounded, or he did until he decided to wander off to the other side of the world. I miss him sometimes, Alfie too.'

Mark still felt the loss of what was once a male orientated scene.

'Alfie kind of fancies himself from what I remember,' She laughed, covering her mouth. 'He's a sweet guy, though.' That was Emily's experience.

'He's a sound head, Alfie. Brian and I linked up with him at secondary; the three of us have been friends since.'

'You're a tight-knit bunch then?' Emily investigated.

Mark raised an eyebrow being playful, and that got a smile. They had already made their way down the side street and through the park gate. As they walked on, they approached what looked to be a comfortable bench, and so he offered her the seat.

'How long have you known Elliot and Siobhan?' She enquired.

'Four or five years now, since I moved to Dublin. I met Elliot through other friends that I know here, and by coincidence, he happened to be my pharmacist. He's comical, Elliot, animated when he tells the stories from the chemist. Siobhan's great too, they suit each other.' Mark was convinced of that.

'Oh! I don't know?' Emily prodded, attempting to be funny.

'Have you something to say, you don't think they're compatible?'

'You don't get out enough, Mark. Is it me or is this bench sticky?'

Emily was looking displeased, pretending to be upset at where he'd landed her. Mark frantically checked, but the bench was spotless his end. Emily rolled over laughing covering her mouth again to muffle the sound. Mark was royally confused.

'I was joking.'

'It's not sticky?' He asked.

'I know, and they're a great couple.' She answered still amused.

'Are you prodding holes in me?'

Emily couldn't contain herself. 'I was joking.'

'Jesus Emily, I'm starting to wonder if this was a good idea.'

'We should put some thought into this party?' She suggested 'Brian will be home around then I'm guessing?'

'Most likely.' He thought as much.

'So, numbers?' She took a sip of her coffee and glanced sideways at him.

'Are you okay with this?' He asked sarcastically.

'I'm alright as it goes.' She smiled again.

Poor Mark didn't know how to conduct himself. 'We're talking between ten, twenty people. Twenty tops.' He insisted.

'You have a big enough flat to fit that many?'

Mark was feeling more confident of the flat since he'd made the few changes. 'It's cleverly arranged, so yeah. There's room for a good few.'

'Fair enough.' She said.

'If it were left to me, I'd do snack food, but seen as its Siobhan's birthday; the event needs some pizzazz.'

'I'm with you on that one.' Emily knew her friend well.

They talked long and hard recalling what dishes Siobhan particularly liked. They both agreed that the buffet should be hot though that could prove to be a hassle on the night. Spicy salads were Emily's forte. She suggested that they do cold salads as well; to lessen the burden. The air was as refreshing as the company, and it wasn't long before they strayed off topic.

'I listened to one of your recordings. I didn't expect the vocalist to be a male, that was surprising, but I enjoyed the tracks. I might have got to know you a little better.' Mark was entering uncharted waters, and he knew it.

'Jesus, don't say that to me, I spend my life trying to disguise who I am.'

'Why?'

'Musically it's different. I think I try to get across stuff that is relevant to everybody. I'm not sure that I show that much of myself. I do have a fear of being misunderstood. People can misinterpret what you say. So, I keep what's deeply personal to me under wraps, maybe that's betraying my craft. I'm not sure though, there's plenty of other stuff to write about.'

'Do you mind me asking, I know this sounds odd… but do you ever cry?' Mark wasn't sure why the question had risen in him.

'What? Where did that come from?'

'I've been thinking about Brian and his dad a lot.,' he was piecing it together, 'and just the way people react to things. Just humour me?'

Emily sat back for a moment. He was playing devil's advocate by putting her on the spot, she reckoned. 'I very rarely cry, not while I have one solid friend in the world.'

'Just, one friend?'

'Mark to my way of thinking, too many people are chasing their tails trying to expand their circles. I've seen people on a rescue mission, dragging themselves down into the bargain. It's very Irish, and it's not me. I have cried, of course, I've had reason to, but I keep busy.'

The pair lowered their heads before looking up at each other again.

'How do you fair out?' She asked.

'I get pressure at work.' He went quiet. 'Jackie, Brian's dad, I like the man, maybe even love him in a way, we go back.'

'So, the work is stressful?' Emily brushed past it. 'I can barely manage myself. It's enough.'

'I am good at my job.' He admitted.

'I wish I could say that of myself.'

'I'm sure you can.'

'Not really, Mark. I write a song and put everything into it, and it's still not where I need it to be sometimes. And yet…' She shrugged her shoulders.

Our Diligent Souls

'Go on...'

'I have this need to keep scribbling. I've been writing songs for a long time, six, seven years now. When you put that much into an enterprise, it's hard to give up on it. You look back at a song, and it's grown into something else, it's soul-crushing sometimes, but it's interestingly curious too.' She stated. 'The regular work gets me out of the house; it eliminates the isolation. It focuses my mind on other things. Waiting tables is fun, but it's like a begging bowl tips wise after a while. Maybe I'm too proud, but that's why I only do the two nights and play the legal secretary otherwise. There's nothing to law, its common sense at my level. I'm typing and copy editing most of the time.'

'So, the song-writing is a side-line?'

'No, I have real ambition there, but I still have to balance my life.'

The night was creeping in around them, even though the clocks hadn't yet gone back an hour. It wasn't long before they had both finished their coffees.

It was Emily who decided it was time for them to get a move on and call it a night. Mark was not impressed by the fact that she was heading home so soon; he'd had bigger plans for the night. In any case, Emily didn't give him any time to wallow.

'I've enjoyed this mini excursion, Mark, but it's bloody cold.'

'We could go for a drink somewhere?'

'Not tonight, Josephine.'

'You're kidding me; it's still early?'

She wrapped her coat in tight and stood up.

'Come on.' She whispered as she began to walk. Their pace was slow, but they were enjoying themselves, it took twenty minutes to walk all of three hundred meters to the park gate.

'How about a joke?' He asked. 'I heard a good one today.' Mark was hoping to finish on a high note; he needed to know if she took herself too seriously and knew it could go either way.

'Go on then.'

'Okay. Michael's distracted, noticing this; his teacher posed a question to him in class. 'You have three doves on a fence, you shoot one, how many have you left?' She asks him. 'None,' says Michael. 'No.' The teacher quizzed him. 'How did you get to that answer?' 'You shoot at one,' he suggested, 'and they all fly off.' 'Very insightful,' the teacher said. 'Lateral thinking, Michael, I like it.' So, Michael wondered if he could ask her a question. 'Work away,' she said. So, Michael starts. 'You have three women in an ice cream parlour, one sucks the ice cream, one licks the ice cream, and one bites the ice cream. Which one is married?'

Emily looked to be enjoying Mark's efforts. 'Go on then?' He was tickled by her enthusiasm.

'The teacher scratches her head not sufficiently convinced that this joke is appropriate, but she went ahead after a little coaxing and having no real clue she opted for the woman who sucks the ice cream. 'No,' says Michael, 'it's the one with the ring on her finger, but I like the way you're thinking.'

'Very good,' Emily applauded him, 'very good.'

Mark was thrilled. 'Yes,' He said out loud, 'the woman has a sense of humour!' Mark was delighted.

'I've been known to tell a few jokes in my time.' She admitted with a coy twinkle in the corner of her eye. They laughed hard.

By the time they made their way toward the gated exit, the park was empty. In the space of twenty minutes, the light had gone, and it had gotten undeniably chilly. Emily felted uplifted somehow and was in better form than she had been in earlier.

'Let me buy you dinner?' Mark pleaded.

'I have mountains of work to do when I get home, and honestly, I'm not hungry.'

'What are you like? Would you give a man a break?'

'I'm wiped, Mark. I'm enjoying the craic, but I'm done in, and again I'll repeat myself, I still have work to do when I get home.'

'You're not refusing me for the sake of it?'

'Ah now. Some people, really?' She shook her head.

'You're sure you won't eat?'

'We could go for a drink another night. I'll write a shopping list for the party, not tonight though. I'm exhausted here.'

'Alright, then I can take a hint.'

'I thought time in the park might perk me up, but it's wiped me out in truth. I'm in good spirits now, but I know myself, Mark, given an hour I would be sour company.'

There was no mention of the kiss from the night before, but Mark was okay with that. They were building a relationship and having secured the promise of another date for drinks; he thought it safer not to bring it up just then. It might have felt forced to try to kiss her again.

They walked along the path, both dithering, not wanting to go their separate ways. It had been nice. They watched a group of children being called into their respective homes for the night.

She directed him to her bus stop as he was still carrying her bag. They talked about Christmas and how it was fast approaching. She liked to get away on holidays, to save herself from unfavourable concern and avoid the unwelcome invites over the season. It was the whole build up to Christmas, it dragged on forever, that's what Emily couldn't face.

She was planning on taking a trip to Morocco this year. He'd never been away for the Christmas season. The idea delighted him. To be a million miles away from the hassle of work and family was just what he needed. The bonus of Emily being there, the whole idea was delightfully promising, or it would be if he could wrangle his way into joining her.

He let his mind wander; the shipping industry worked right up until Christmas Eve and into the New Year, he'd have to put in for holiday leave soon. From Emily's point of view, her mention of Morocco was nothing more than small talk. It would never have dawned on her that he'd be cheeky enough to invite himself along.

She liked travelling alone, being somewhere new and yet undiscovered, somewhere she could catch the cultural details and become ensconced in another way of life, it was utterly inviting. She loved sourcing and bartering for traditional pieces that were otherwise overpriced in Ireland.

She liked the quieter, scenic restaurants, where she could eat and take in the surroundings at her ease. The bustle of foreign markets was always exhilarating; she could ramble by day through the streets that were typically eastern.

She had regularly met fellow travellers on a break who were forced to share a table with her in a cafe. As it happened, these fellow travellers usually filled her in on their experiences, where they had gone, who they had met, what they had encountered. Bumping into characters was something that she could almost guarantee would happen.

Our Diligent Souls

She always looked forward to that book that she'd been saving, usually a book that one or more of her musician friends had recommended. The headspace to read a book in one sitting was not something she ordinarily had.

The bus wasn't long coming, so they said their goodbyes with a detached handshake, leaving Mark forlorn at the edge of the pavement. The afternoon had not gone as planned, and nothing was going to happen quickly between them although for him a tender urgency remained. She hadn't allowed him to feel too at home with her; the conversation was witty but somehow distant. Boy, was she beautiful?

He walked away and deliberately turned his thoughts to Elliot, he needed to let him know that Brian was on his way home in the next few days. It would be news to Elliot that he had met the ever-elusive Emily, but it was news he would keep to himself for now.

Chapter 16

When the flight left Australia, Brian's father was still alive. Making it through passport controls at Dublin airport, he had a sick sense of what was awaiting him. As he searched along the stretch of faces beyond the bollards at arrivals, his eyes were drawn to his sister's face. That first glimpse of her was enough; her expression conveying the sad truth, a truth he didn't want to acknowledge.

The sudden thought of his mother alone with neither son nor daughter at her side, it appalled him. His father Jackie was gone, there was no denying it. His feet kept moving in a forward direction, but it felt as though he'd left his heart a hundred yards behind. It was then that he registered Mark. His friend's empathic eyes greeting him from a distance, Mark was standing uncomfortably, allowing Sarah to partly shield herself behind his arm.

The entire journey to their hometown was erased from mind though it had taken the full hour. Neither Brian nor his sister had any recollection of the stretch of road from Dublin airport as they pulled up at the gate; they were sure not a word had been spoken. Mark parked up alongside their family home, feeling daunted as he glanced back through the rear-view mirror.

Brian and his sister Sarah had been immersed in their own separate worlds; they were positively startled by the fact that the car had stopped at their front gate. Their grief or maybe the shock; it had snatched the journey from them, though that experience was not for him to acknowledge or admit. Mark jumped out of the driver's seat and went to the back passenger door, from where he gently ushered both brother and sister along the garden path to their front door.

Silent as the sky, he couldn't hear a single breath on either of them as they looked at each other in bewilderment. Going through that door felt like the hardest things that Brian might ever have to do. That was the house that he'd grown up in, a place full of precious memories, a place that now stifled him with dread. An unavoidable delay at Sydney airport had robbed him of the opportunity to share a final few words with his father. It was inconceivable.

A congregation of people blocked the hallway. There were others in the front room; they were relatives primarily. Relatives he still recognised though it had been years since he had seen any of them. Sarah was quickly engaged in conversation, but Brian was not ready to talk. His instinct leading him through to the kitchen in search of his mother; it was her outline that he caught first. Her face appeared to shift beneath her skin as she moved closer to acknowledged him in a clutched vacant manner, her arms stretched out as he made his way to her.

'Mammy...'

She laid her head on his chest without a word but instead held him then in a gripping intensity. He needed to know if she forgave him for not being there on time.

'He tried to wait,' she whispered. 'I should have let you know earlier.'

'No mum, please, I was delayed at Sydney. I was at the airport, remember. There were security issues; my flight was delayed.'

'Mark's a good friend; he's a good friend. I can't believe you're here.'

She loosened her hold and looked up at him, her eyes filled with grief and disbelief. She pulled away and moved toward the kettle, steadying herself as her fingers wrapped around the edge of the countertop. Brian's sister stepped in to help, touching his shoulder. 'I'll see to her love, please. She's taking it badly. He's upstairs.'

Brian had felt his sister pass him; her movement like a flutter of wings; his feet rivet to the floor.

'He's upstairs.' She was referring to his dad Jackie as if he was up there reading a paper. He was gone. Whatever was left was upstairs, he wasn't ready for that.

Mark stepped in to assist. 'You okay, mate! Do you want me to go with you?'

Brian was scrambling to gather his thoughts. 'Go with me; I just walked in the door, Mark.'

He watched his mother move like a ghost, being bundled from one condolence to the next. She looked lost in herself. Where was she, why was she not holding onto him, why was his father upstairs? It was too much to question. A coffin was ordinarily placed in the front room; Brian wondered if he was laid out in bed. His compulsion to check became all-consuming.

Mark followed quietly behind his friend as they re-entered the hallway. As they reached the stairs, the front door opened. It was Elliot, followed by Siobhan.

Our Diligent Souls

'I'm so sorry, mate!' Elliot said as he touched Brian's upper arm.

'Thank you,' Brian's reply to him was dazed.

Siobhan leant in to kiss his cheek. The couple nodded as they acknowledged Mark who was still at his friend's back. The two men climbed the stairs, arriving on the landing to stand in relative silence at the door to his parents' room.

'Siobhan and Elliot, how did they get here so quick?' Brian enquired.

'I rang them from the airport earlier.' Mark whispered.

A rumbling sound was echoing from his parent's bedroom. It took moments to make sense of the noise. A rosary was being offered up for the deceased. Brian's first thought was to knock as was the tradition in his house. It was still his parents' room. He checked with Mark before he walked in. 'It's okay, mate.' Mark needed to comfort him.

The room looked different; they had redecorated since he'd left. The bed too was gone, and in its place stood a new oak coffin on a silver fold up stand. Brian's eyes inspected everything but the coffin. There were three seats against the wall, the curtains were drawn to block out the natural light, and there were candles, candles and a wreath.

At a glance, it didn't look like his father. Brian shifted his eyes to the floor. His aunt was sitting alongside the coffin finishing up a last decade of the rosary. Her hands and eyes locked on her prayer beads; as soon as she was finished, she turned to attend to Brian.

'You're here, Brian, I'm so glad. Marian hadn't left his side for two days, your poor mother. He left peacefully at the end, thanks be to God. We managed to get her to go downstairs to eat something. You must be exhausted.'

'Hi!' Mark whispered an introduction. 'I'm Mark, Brian's friend and a friend of the family.'

They shook hands as Brian stepped closer to the coffin. Jackie's hair was the first thing that caught his eye, the grey quiff worn in the same way it had always been presented, though his hair was thinner, much thinner. Brian checked his face for markers; he recognised the small indent on his left eyebrow and the freckle on his upper lip, a freckle that was usually disguised by stubble. Brian's aunt leant over and touched his arm.

'He didn't want to leave without saying goodbye, Brian.' With that she stood up touched his shoulder and left the room, nodding at Mark as she exited.

The two friends clumsily stood together taking in the remains. Mark was conscious of the fact that someone could arrive in at any minute; his friend needed time to adjust. Brian was shaking with annoyance, Jackie was really gone. Mark watched as Brian reached into the coffin to touch his father's face.

Brian's tears came fast, and when they did, they fell without any whaling. His father was half the man in stature due to the weight loss. He was laid out in front of them, his face dark and drawn. The degree of his suffering was wildly apparent, his father having lost the deadliest battle of them all. Brian was chocked up with tears, trying desperately to hold down the emotion.

'Can you hear me?' He lent in and whispered. Mark clenched to hold back the tears. 'Daddy?' Brian hadn't used the word daddy since he had needed him as a child. In his mind, it was his last chance to catch what photos missed; the little indentations where Jackie regularly cut himself shaving. He was taking in the size of his father's hand and the shape and texture of his nails.

Mark watched as his friend's body bolted upright to stop his chest from heaving, breaking through the grief to calmly stroke his father's hands, Jackie's fingers and thumbs intertwined and resting on his chest. The disbelief at what had happened rising like vomit in his throat. Mark let his arms fall limp, the tremors in his hands fighting to take visible hold. The door opened but thankfully it was Brian's mum.

Mark acknowledged her as his eyes welled up, he gently passed her, leaving Brian transfixed by his father side. As he shut the door behind him, Mark tried to quell his own tears, gripping the bannister to silence the roar that wanted to escape from his chest. He was overwhelmed by all that had already happened in those first few hours. He loved Jackie and felt heavily involved in his passing.

Mother and son were in there a good half hour before leaving to join everyone downstairs. Mark had stood on the landing patiently waiting. He had wanted to avoid any small talk with the posse downstairs. He knew that Elliot and Siobhan were down there among strangers, he just couldn't find the strength to leave Brian and his mother alone.

Our Diligent Souls

Sandwiches were being passed around the kitchen. Elliot and Siobhan had brought homemade tarts. The Dublin couple were properly taken back by the country wake. There were at least thirty people in the house paying their respects at any given time, and the faces kept changing, people endlessly introducing themselves. It was a different set up in Dublin at funerals they had attended, where the remains went from the morgue to the church and then straight to the cemetery. It was a different ball game here, at least for them.

Everyone had a way of defining Jackie's character; he had a great belief in family, and his love of traditional sports was always evident, even as a young man he never missed a match. He favoured home-made food, and his wife's baking as he had a very sweet tooth. The fact that he could never arrive anywhere empty handed was repeated through the crowd. He had a hatred of things that were showy. The Ford car, Clarke's shoes and cottage loaf bread, they were his favourites. He loved his cottage loaf.

Everyone was sharing a different scenario of the first and last time they met, the speech Jackie had made at someone's wedding. A neighbour had bumped into him the week before he got sick and Jackie, it struck him, had acted out of character, he'd gone and had a drink with them to salute old times. It was the very odd occasion that Jackie had alcohol at all.

Brian and Marian were feeling better after being upstairs for a while, and Brian was soon bombarded with questions about Australia. Elliot and Siobhan explained that they would be back and forward over the next few days before they left. Siobhan had won that battle with Elliot, though wanting to be there for their friend on all three days was completely unnecessary. They hoped that once the funeral was over, he might visit with them in Dublin and stay for dinner, it was great to have Brian home. They left him with Mark who was hanging in for the duration.

The funeral directors were weaving their way past visitors. They were waiting on the schedule of proceedings; the time of the mass and burial was yet to be confirmed by the priest. The immediate family were asked to consider the running order of the ceremony, the prayers of the faithful and the readings. There were decisions to be reached. It was one o'clock when Brian arrived home to be at his family's side. Six hours had passed, six hours of endless callers and trays of sandwiches. The fact that what remained of their beloved would soon be gone was starting to weigh heavy.

Mark knew that he needed to be at Brian's side throughout the entire wake. Brian's sister Sarah was at her strongest comforting the crowd. She disappeared off to weep privately at Jackie's coffin and returned to hand out tea and coffee. There was no alcohol served until evening when Brian retrieved a few bottles of stout from the fridge. There were only one or two takers as Sarah's seven-year-old son had arrived. Sarah's boy was not permitted to go upstairs to see his grandpa, upstairs was out of bounds. But as with everyone else, the boy needed time to process the fact that his grandpa was gone.

The boy's father had partaken of one too many drinks earlier in the day. It wasn't his style as he wasn't into the bottle, but it was his way of coping with the circumstances, or so they discovered. He was capable of minding the boy, and no one was going to dispute him taking his son home. He was made to eat a curry that a neighbour had prepared; it was being warmed in the kitchen. The food brought him back down to earth, and he was soon sent off with the boy in their great aunt's car. She would make sure that they were settled before she left.

In the garden, before he was taken away, the seven-year-old lifted a tin whistle. He played the lonesome boatmen, a tune that was recognised and appreciated by everyone. He had learnt the melody in high infants, and nothing could have felt more fitting. Jackie had listened to him play it a hundred times.

Brian went up to see his father, again and again, that evening. There was a melancholy love in the air thanks to the intimacy of good neighbours. Marian was despondent, barely lucid as she wandered up and down the stairs. In saying that, by late evening Brian's exhaustion and grief took hold of him too.

'Thanks for hanging in, Mark. It means so much that you're here.'

Mark had called in a family death at work on Friday postponing the Sunday overtime event for now. He was grateful that the wake took place on the weekend and was not a midweek affair as it gave him more scope to be there.

'I should have moved quicker, Mark. If I'd responded at once to the first call that you made?'

Mark intervened. 'If you hadn't responded when you did, Brian, you'd not have been here for any of this. It is sad that he went before you got back, but you're here when your family needs you, and he knew that you were on your way. He knew that you were on that plane, he knew that for a fact.'

Old Paudie from up the road sang a favourite tune, 'Fisherman's Green'. The expression 'his worries are over', rang out above all other expressions.

Our Diligent Souls

The comment was irritating Brian's sister as her father had no worries in the first place or none that he minded having. He loved life she explained.

The talk softened, and the family finally got around to making the crucial decisions about the funeral mass. The hymns, the eulogy and the prayers of the faithful that needed to be read by immediate family, they got through it all. The offerings were to be brought by the younger members of the clan. The priest had gathered enough information. He could now portray an honest and well-rounded assimilation of Jackie's character at mass. The funeral director organised the flowers and transport to the church. Getting involved in the arrangements appeared to help Brian cope as he chatted with his cousin to arrange something special for the burial itself.

Marian made toast and tea and gazed out the kitchen window into the night. She was joined on either side by her son and daughter. They didn't say a word. Mark phoned his mum and dad's and booked the spare room for Brian just in case. They both needed to sleep at some point, especially Brian who was now slurring his speech; the passing had taken its toll on him.

It was ten o'clock at night when Brian's mum and sister agreed to get some shut-eye. Brian decided to stay up, jet-lagged or not until they woke. It was customary for one member of the family to be at his father's side through the night; they wouldn't have it any other way.

The visitors kept arriving, and every condolence seems to wound Brian even more profoundly, his heart lost in the tenderness of people. By twelve o'clock, there were two cousins on patrol, and Brian caught a nap on the sofa. Mark covered his friend with a blanket. He advised the two cousins of his departure before getting ready to cut across home for a few hours rest. It had been a tragic day, and he too was making no coherent sense.

He hoped that Brian could manage to sleep and promised to return early in the morning. He had tried to persuade him to come back to his parent's house, but Brian was having none of it. Marian was back on her feet and had returned to her husband's side. There was no convincing her to stay in bed; she couldn't sleep and leave the man alone in his final hours. Her son needed the rest after his flight.

The relatives hoped she would tire and let them take over, but for Mark, there was no part to play in that. He looked in on Brian before he left saddened to his very depths by everything that had gone on that day. He needed the arms of his own mum and dad, though as a grown man he'd never dare to ask.

Chapter 17

After a quick chat with his parents, Mark returned to the wake the following morning. He was relieved to hear that Brian was still asleep. His friend had been up twice in the night to take over from his mum, and she had slept if only for a short time.

Marian and Sarah were back in the kitchen with extended relatives. Time was getting on and sooner or later they needed Brian awake to free up the front room. Jackie's remains were to be removed that evening for six o'clock mass. Then from the church to the graveyard the following morning.

Mark brought a breakfast tray into the front room. He placed it on a side table before attempting to rouse his mate. Brian's eyes were encrusted with sleep. Saturated with sweat, he tried to adjust again to familiar surroundings. He sat up, trying to hold onto the tail end of his dream; where Jackie had peered over the front gate attempting to give him advice. Brian was standing on his tipped toes shading his eyes from the sunlight, he was trying to capture every sonic word. He was a boy in the dream, but the message was unclear.

'Is it me, Mark... Is this surreal to you as well?'

'It's a huge amount to adjust to in the space of a short time, mate. Have you a suit with you?' Mark asked.

'It's in my luggage; I had been in two minds whether to bring it or not. It seemed neurotic then to think that I might need it for my father's funeral.'

'I brought your suitcase over to mine last night. I'll give my mum a ring and get her to pull out the suit and give it an iron if that's okay with you?'

Brian attempted to straighten himself up. 'That's a good idea!'

'The mass is at six. The removal will start at half past five, the family reckon.'

'Is mum still asleep?'

'No. Your ma's in the kitchen.'

'They got the doctor for her last night after you left, and she agreed to take two sleeping tablets.' Brian explained.

Our Diligent Souls

Mark filled Brian in on what had since happened. 'Sarah slept straight through and was up at seven. They're both fine.'

Brian hoisted himself out of the sofa and rose to his feet; he needed the bathroom but returned minutes later. He ignored his coffee and toast. The chatter from the kitchen was growing louder. They knew that they only had a short time before they'd have to join the gathering.

'Do you want to head over to my parents' place, grab a shower and get changed there? It might be a better idea.'

Brian took a moment to consider.

'I think that's wise; I'll just let the family know.'

Mark removed the tray of coffee and toast and went to the kitchen. He needed to give his friend a few minutes to gather himself. Brian had slept in his clothes, a grapple of his chin and he understood that he was rough with stubble.

He went upstairs to pass a few minutes with his dad. He wanted to confirm more than anything else that his sanity was still intact. He somehow needed to be sure that this was still happening. Jackie looked peaceful. Again, he studied him laid out in his best suit with his white shirt and his pastel tie. Brian knew that he was gone, but still, he spoke to him.

'I'm sorry I left, dad. I'm sorry I left when I did... I'm sorry,' he repeated.

He reached out to touch his father's hands again to compare them in shape and character to his own. He would have cast them in bronze if he had known that they were to disappear so soon into a hole in the ground. A man's hands say everything about him.

Brian wondered how deeply haunted he might feel in the coming months. Questions about an afterlife were again playing havoc with his senses. He had spent the past few days on two sides of the continent; the details were still confused. The question of his family and the domino of these recent alterations, they still hung in the balance.

He touched his father's lips, moving his thumb from one corner of Jackie's mouth to the next; it was a sign of affection, a tenderness that was so hard to display in front of his father when the man was alive. He needed to be with him alone this one last time.

Mark had walked over to Brian's house that morning. With car parking at a premium, he had thought it wise. Besides, Mark's father was never comfortable when it came to handing over his car keys. It was sharp outside and a brisk ten-minute walk back to Mark's family home, with both men glad of the air.

The house where Brian had been reared felt dank; the air stifled as if the walls were closing in on them. They met no recognisable neighbours on the way to Mark's, but a few people were going out for their Saturday shop, whole families piling into cars. A gardener was attempting to get the end of his summer plants under control.

Mark's mum was at the door filled with empathy and ready to meet Brian with open arms, they could see her as they approached.

'Welcome home, Brian. We were sorry to hear the sad news, love. Come in please, come inside, love.'

'How are you Breda, it's great to see you again.' Brian had known both of Mark's parents for the more significant part of his life.

'Mum, if I get you Brian's suit from his case here, will you give it a press? Mine's in the wardrobe. He needs a shower too; mum, if that's okay?'

'Andrew's wash stuff is on the table as you go in, Brian.' Andrew was Mark's father and a loving husband to Breda. 'I insist you eat a proper breakfast when you get out though, and while you're at that, I can press that suit. You can slip into my husband's robe; it's hanging up in the bathroom. It's was just washed so you'll be nice and fresh.'

'Thank you.' Brian was grateful for her maternal kindness.

'Get me your suit, Mark, I'll run an iron over the lot. While you're at it get your dad's black tie out, it's in with the socks in his drawer somewhere. Let me look…' Mark's mum disappeared but not for long. She was back with a warm bath towel, a clean razor, and a toothbrush that was still in its plastic wrapper.

'Thanks, Breda.' Brian mumbled before he went on up to the bathroom. Safely out of earshot Mark's mum was free to express her concerns.

'How is he coping?'

'I don't know. Okay, I guess.'

'And Marian and Sarah?'

'They're shattered, mum.'

Mark got a full embrace. 'How would I cope if I was to lose you, son, or your sister, or your dad for that matter?'

'Do you think I'd cope so well with losing you?' It was not like the thought hadn't crossed his minute under the circumstance. Mark wrapped his arms around her and stood back. 'The doctor called late last night and gave his mum something to help her sleep; she got a few hours. The removal's leaving at half five to St. Joseph's for six o'clock mass.'

'They'll get peace tonight.'

'I wouldn't bet on it. The removal from the church to the graveyard is tomorrow morning.'

'I didn't realise they were very religious.'

'I don't know. I don't see Brian staying here tonight. He'll want to stay with his family. The funeral people will be putting his parent's bedroom back once the coffin has left I'd imagine.'

'God help us, are you okay, son?'

'I'm fine.'

'And work?'

'Yeah, it's good.'

Mark helped while Breda cooked. He pulled out the ironing board and gathered together the suits. He filled a bucket of coal to save Andrew his father from having to do the job later. A full Irish was placed on the table as Brian descended the stairs.

'There you go, Brian. Tea or coffee, love?'

'Coffee, please.'

'I'll have tea, Ma', Mark announced, as he took his place.

'It's busy over there I take it?' She asked.

Mark was not impressed by his mother's questioning though Brian took no offence.

'It'll still be quiet for a while yet.' Brian stated as he looked at his watch.

Breda meant no harm; she blushed and lowered her face. The ironing board that was now up in the kitchen dwarfed her as she reached over it to iron the shirts first. She was a short, stout woman and the ironing board was enormous. The iron itself, Mark had tried to replace on many an occasion, but he was never allowed. She loved the old one though it had only one setting.

Our Diligent Souls

'We should get back there by ten. What do you think, Brian?' Mark questioned his friend, anxious for his mother to get a move on with things.

'Sure,' Brian responded, though he barely looked up from his plate. He ate very little but did his best to hide the fact. Breda made little of it where she'd usually give you a talking to over wasted food. The boys slipped on their suits in the front room and reappeared again in the kitchen moments later.

'We'll see you at the church, love,' she addressed Mark first, 'and Brian if at any point in the day you find you want to rest, Mark's room is made up and ready. Day or night you hear me, don't be afraid to knock the door.'

It was time to head back.

The house was full, everyone was busy organising, teas, coffees and food. Flowers were arriving and were laid out primarily against the wall in the front room. A couple of family friends had made their way upstairs to where the reposed was still resting. Brian's mother was at peace by his father's side, engaged in silent prayer to avoid any conversation.

His sister was busy locking horns with someone in the kitchen. She was attempting to comprehend their idea of a day's grace. According to Marian's friend, the dying always knew instinctively or otherwise, that they were nearing the end.

'They often get the chance to say their last goodbyes.' The woman insisted.

Jackie had been up and in town doing messages after the first rounds of chemo. He'd bumped into a few people. Apparently, the things he said indicated that he knew he wasn't long for this world, Sarah had missed the signs. The woman was rubbing her up the wrong way, which was what made no sense to her, the woman wasn't blind to the fact that her father had just passed.

Time was moving fast; the impending five-thirty deadline was drawing closer. The trays of sandwiches and cakes were still arriving. There was mention of a meal on the way back from the graveyard. It was a new tradition that was brought in during Ireland's Celtic Tiger years, but Marian was having none of it. They would come straight back after the cemetery, and she could rest then.

The funeral directors were much more to the fore than the day before, their visible presence reminding everybody that the church service would soon be underway. The priest was still collecting testimony on Jackie's way of life, hoping to perfect his speech. The suits were out, everyone looking their best.

The last hour crawled at a snail's pace with the kettle beside the cooker continually on the boil. The descriptions of Jackie's condition were compiled and repeated tirelessly; the reasoning of the doctors, the coughing up of blood and the tumour that had all but disappeared. He was taken to the mortuary to establish the cause of death, but that was old socks to Brian and his mum as they moved through the crowds without a word.

'He's at peace now!'

'At least it wasn't a drawn-out thing; he went relatively easy.'

'He was holding on; he knew you were on your way back.'

'He had his views, but he loved you dearly.'

Everyone had something to say, and Brian was taking it all in his stride. Mark was struggling with the fact that he couldn't quite remember the event that Jackie had mentioned to him, on the night he'd called over to check on him. This whole thing had started just over a week ago for Mark and Brian, and yet Mark couldn't remember the stories that Brian's father had shared, Jackie had reminded him of an event from when they were boys, but it was gone.

Mark took himself out to the garden and looked over the fields. The intimate part of their last conversation had vanished, he'd been surprised by Jackie's memory, it was something he hadn't thought of in a while. Baffled by the short circuit in his brain he lent over the fence.

Before they knew it, it was time to close the open casket. Brian, his mother Marian and sister Sarah were left alone for what seemed like the hardest part of the process. It was their final opportunity to say a last goodbye. The five-thirty deadline felt to them as if it had come out of nowhere.

An uncle after a few minutes popped his head in to see if they were ready. Marian politely told him to fuck off and mind his own business. It brought a smile to her children's faces as it was totally out of form. They hunched up together and held each other tight.

'That's our Jackie.' Marian whispered, 'We'll never forget him, but this is something we have to do, agreed?' The three of them welled up, each dropping a tear on Jackie as they leant over to say goodbye. The funeral directors were ushered in as they left the room, and the coffin was closed.

Our Diligent Souls

The men in the family carried the coffin on lowered shoulder down the stairs, Brian to the front of them. They moved through the front door to the back of the hearse where a large crowd gathered waiting on the green and nearby footpaths. The church was only two estates away and a short walk from the house, so most decided to follow on foot. Marian, Jackie's two sisters and Sarah travelled in the car while the immediate families walked directly behind the hearse. Brian wanted to walk. His young nephew moved in solemnly beside him to take hold of his hand.

The flower displays in an array of colours covered the hearse roof and coffin inside of it. There was little talk. Cars stopped as the procession passed, strangers blessing themselves in the driver's seats. The steps of the coffin followers were echoing from the back of the hearse.

On arrival at the church, the coffin was slowly hoisted onto the shoulders of the six closest to the family. Mark was one of the men called in to help; he was brought over to link arms with Brian at the front of the casket. He could see his father in the distance, hold up his mother who was in tears at the sight of her son. The other parishioners formed a steady queue as they made their way inside. First names and nods were shared by everyone but the immediate family as they carried their grief to the altar.

Once the coffin was in place at the top of the church, the mass began. The family had taken up their positions in the front two rows. To the depth of their souls, the family felt the cool stainless sword of reality as they faced the event that their hearts and minds had battled to avoid.

The sermon was a humble one; the prayers of the faithful were emotionally recited to spare no one, there was not a dry eye in the house. The priest summarised Jackie's personality with acuteness and humour. The choir passionately sang one of Jackie's favourite tunes. Sarah was heavy with emotion, Marian distantly watching on; unable to shield her daughter from the pain.

People acknowledged each other warmly as they rose from their seats for communion. Otherwise, it was the same rhetoric, standing up, sitting and kneeling. Brian was numb, but it was how his father would have wanted it, a dignified last stance.

At the end of the funeral mass, the congregation formed a procession to the top of the church. They gave their condolences one by one to the family with handshakes and solemn words.

Outside on the church steps, everyone congregated under umbrellas in the rain. Old friends were catching up, friends that rarely met up otherwise, everyone had busy lives and too much to contend with on a typical day. The family returned to the house, drained but willing to converse after the proceedings, with a handful of close relatives to keep them company until they were settled. Mark handed Brian a spare set of keys to his parents' house and told him that he was going home.

'Just let yourself in, mate, or whatever suits... you need time with your ma' now.'

Siobhan and Elliot had attended the mass but once acknowledged they had left to make their way back to Dublin. It was a real show of friendship to appear on both days, above and beyond the call of duty. Mark needed space on his own now, as did Brian. It had been a trying two days.

Brian talked to his mum for a while and was relieved to see that she was more herself. Keeping his eyes focused and his head from nodding off, took everything he had in the church. He could no longer defeat the exhaustion. Upstairs, the beds were being organised back into their places, and Brian took over the sofa for a quick nap this time. The distant sound of chatter in the kitchen was soon drowned out, and Brian was deep in slumber.

Chapter 18

'Get up son; you have guests.' Mark's mother was leaning over him at the side of his bed tapping on his shoulder. He took a moment to absorb the fact that today was the burial.

'It's Elliot and Siobhan... I'm making them a cuppa.'

His mum left a hot coffee beside his bed. Cupping it in his hands, he took a long gulp before he wandered down the stairs in his pyjamas.

'Morning guys,' he mumbled, rubbing his eyes with splayed fingers.

Siobhan and Elliot were amused by his appearance; he had the balance of a boy who had just crawled through a hedge.

'I won't be a minute,' he announced, as he finished his coffee, banged it on the table and reached for a piece of toast. He grinned as he headed for the stairs again to go and get dressed. 'Three minutes.' He said as he ruffled Elliot's hair in passing, Siobhan tried to contain her laughter; his mother was standing with her hand on her hip.

The morning was crisp as the three friends set off, and though the early frost had vanished, their breath was still billowing fog.

Brian was seated with his family in the first pew when they arrived. Mark made sure to catch his eye and let him know that he was there. The turnout was enormous. Brian's father was well known; having worked at the post office and in charitable practices for a considerable part of his life.

The post office was a job that he loved but having watched so many disenchanted, walk through its doors; he'd trained in his spare time to become a councillor with the Samaritans. He had for twenty-two years offered up his Friday night to man one of the helplines for the organisation. He was a stranger to the people that he helped, but a close comrade to the ones who worked alongside him. They were there to say their last goodbyes and honour a man who had given back so much to the community.

The mass was short and impersonal in comparison to the six o'clock ceremony at the church the day before. A friend of Brian's sister with a powerful tenor voice was employed to sing 'Ave Maria' as the proceedings came to a close. The priest swayed his golden incense canteen as he followed the coffin along the central aisle.

Everyone was gathered on the steps of the church as the coffin came out, people were either watching on or engaged in shaking hands in condolence with the family. Elliot and Siobhan climbed into their Volvo to follow the trail of cars to the graveyard.

The hit of frankincense had overwhelmed Siobhan in the church; she wasn't feeling well. They had been on the road since early morning. The journey to the graveyard was less than a mile, but it took twenty-five minutes for the cars to trickle through the graveyard gates.

The priest was in a white gown with a sacrament scarf draped over his shoulder. As they reached the freshly dug gravesite, the two young altar boys stood to attention, one wielding more frankincense. In Latin, the priest rattled off a ceremonial blurb. He swung the frankincense vessel over the open ground once the coffin was being lowered. A brief prayer was shared, and a decade of the rosary began.

Siobhan at this point had turned a lighter shade of pale. The heavily perfumed air was more than she could take. The pair had overdone it having attended three days in a row. It was Siobhan who had insisted that they do so, so she couldn't complain.

Mark was finding it difficult to bear witness to the family's pain. He admired his friend who was playing a blinder, supporting his mother and sister, physically as well as emotionally. The two women were finding it hard to keep hold of their emotions. Mark could see his friend's mindset.

As the soil was lifted and thrown on top of the coffin, the final goodbyes were shared, Brian stood firm taking in every word. His sisters seven-year-old was ushered on to say a parting prayer. The boy wiped his eyes on his sleeve, choking on the second line of his verse. He had to stop to gather himself but finished strong. His words were met with tears, and as the lad finished up, he was proudly acknowledging.

A large wicker bird carrier was moved into position, it was opened and with that several doves were released. Silence fell as these symbols of new life spread their wings, the crowd following their flight as they soared upward, circled the party and spread out past the boundaries of any visible sight. The doves in truth had deserved some round of applause, but relatives un-phased by the poetry of their flight moved swiftly in a cluster to surround the family.

'Oh my God, this is awful, how they must feel, 'Siobhan said softly.

'Different strokes for different folks,' Elliot whispered in retort.

Mark looked up from his refrain agitated by the pair of them, lost as to what might have amused Elliot. It wasn't long before Brian made his way over to the three who were standing back a little from the crowd. 'If you want to come to the house, there's curry ready and more sandwiches. I guess it won't go on that long.' Elliot and Siobhan gracefully bowed out though they were more than grateful for the offer.

'We have to get back, we have people calling later and work in the morning, but we're looking forward to seeing you. We're hoping you might arrive at Siobhan's birthday gathering at Mark's next week?'

'Thank you for coming. It means a lot to me, thank you.'

Elliot took his top arm. 'Not a problem, Brian, it's good to see you home. I'm sure you'll give us a bell and fill us in on your plans for next week or Mark will. We'll get together at the weekend hopefully.'

'It's just four or five of us for dinner in Mark's place, but it might help lift your spirits.' Siobhan added.

'It means the world; you guys made an enormous effort driving here three days in a row, it is very much appreciated.'

Brian and Mark were left to their own devices; they had a lift back to the house, courtesy of Brian's uncle.

Brian turned to Mark. 'Can we have a few beers in the pub tonight? I need to come back down to ground level after the past few days.' He suggested it, knowing that the night he was facing could be a restless one at home.

Mark was doing his best. 'I need to see how things come together at my folk's house but that sounds good.' Mark thought it best to leave and go back home for a few hours if that were okay with his friend. 'Just ring me twenty minutes before you're ready to leave the house, give me time to throw on some fresh clothes. I want to spend time with the folks when I'm here, and it'll give you a chance to talk to your mum.'

Mark got out at Brian's house, and after thanking his uncle for the lift, he headed straight home.

The four walls of their family's refuge felt familiar but empty when they got back from the graveyard. The relatives were gone within the hour, and

Sarah took off once their mother saw fit to go to bed. Left alone in the kitchen, Brian hugged a cup of coffee, taking in his surroundings. He felt like the caretaker of a venue. The punters were gone, and he was left on security watch with the keys to a vacant lot. Beyond that moment he had no idea as he sat in the ghostly stillness of the sitting room, the spirit of his father again a question.

He thought back to the story of a local character that he knew, Charlie, he was a well-known greyhound trainer in town. After Charlie's funeral, his friends went to the track. Coincidentally, a dog was running called Charlie's dilemma, a long shot at fifty to one. They lobbed every penny they had on the dog with the bookies, half wanting to get home with exhaustion and grief, but the same brindle bitch galloped home. It was a parting gift as they seen it, confirmation in a sense that Charlie was still with them in spirit.

Thinking back brought tears to Brian's cheeks as the words; 'Jackie's dilemma' fell from his mouth. A message from his father was what he needed, what he'd been waiting for throughout the weekend. Ever since the dream that he had on the couch where his father was gazing down at him over the garden gate, he'd been searching for any indication that he was forgiven for running off to Australia, for abandoning the family to chase hopes and ambitions that may have never come to fruition.

He never needed his old man's say so until now. The idea that his father wasn't there anymore, it was hardly right. Brian felt the anger swell in his chest. He knew his father would still speak to him in a sense though he could never pre-empt his father's response to things. That in effect was the crux as to why they were so often at odds with each other.

The house was quieter without his dad. His mum was still young, but that would fade before she'd ever recover he thought. Jackie was the noisy presence, and she was the whispering by his side. She loved the man thoroughly, never disagreeing, always comprehending his workings and arguments.

Brian began to sob uncontrollably, attempting to keep it to a whimper, not wanting to disturb his mum. She was brave beyond what he expected, but she had folded in disbelief at moments. He was overwhelmed when he saw her display glimpses of dementia. He could not go back to Australia and leave her on her own, how cruel would that be.

Gathering himself together, he went to the cupboard. He started to make soup from the ingredients he found there. His father liked his soup old style with chunks of carrot and even lentils or barley with it. Marian often fed him his and then used the blender on what was left for the rest of them.

Our Diligent Souls

Brian thought to taste the chunky version before he blended the rest for his mother. At first, Brian thought the idea was thoughtful but then unthinkingly cruel. He almost flushed it down the sink when out of nowhere Marian came to his side.

'Don't throw it away and don't blend it, not tonight, son.' She whispered in a croaked voice as she took the bowl from his hand. 'Sit with me a while, love... It's been so long. I've missed your beautiful face.'

The pair ate the soup in silence before she took his hand.

'I always thought he'd do me the kindness of letting me go first. I've been so angry at him. It comes in waves.' She pulled a tissue out from where she'd placed it under the cuff of her sleeve, she wiped her nose. 'Am I a hypocrite? I could see he was going, but I couldn't accept it.'

'Don't talk like that mum; it's not the truth.'

'It's funny. The past few weeks, they're like a block of time lost somewhere. I should have called you earlier. It was all the plans we made. Sixty-three years of age may appear old to you, but we thought we'd at least another twenty years in us yet. Your grandfather was eighty-seven when he died. He smoked sixty woodbines every day since he was eleven.'

'You're a bit better in yourself, ma'. It was a nice ceremony, yeah?'

'Your father swore that there were two things essential to a happy life. One, believe in yourself. Two, never forget to celebrate life. In saying that, he was so easily drawn to tears. You never got to see the full extent of how much your father loved you but, you will in the coming days. We will sit and talk, properly talk. You and your sister can share what went on over the years. I know you both have your secrets. He had his ways, but only because he acted with the three of us in mind.'

'We should watch an old movie tonight, mum. You need to relax.'

'This place is full of his voice tonight, son. I want to rest; he's still with me when I close my eyes. I need that right now to get through the next few days. If that makes any sense to you?'

'It does ma' if it makes sense to you.'

'We'll talk again in the morning. Stay at Mark's if you want, son. I know I'll sleep through the way I'm feeling. I can be left alone.'

'I want to be here in the morning. I'll sleep in my old room, but I might go with Mark to the pub once I know you have your head on that pillow.'

'Whatever you think is best, son, I'm going back upstairs.' She took his head and kissed him on the forehead.

'You're a good lad.'

'I love you, mum.'

'I'd better sleep, son.'

Brian was frightened by her parting comment somehow. Nothing seemed to make sense. His mind was playing tricks. He drifted around the house for the following hour, trying to find something to tidy away. Everything was as it always had been, in its place. He went upstairs to check what had once been his bedroom, but it was now laid out in more neutral tones as a guest room. It lessened his guilt for some reason.

He was listening at the door of his parents' room when a rush of sheer adrenalin hit him. She was sleeping in the room where his coffin had been. The same room where she'd nursed him in his death-bed. It hadn't dawned on Brian that it had been their private chamber for over thirty years. It was time to call Mark and hit the pub. There was no other option if he was to get through the night.

An hour later and they were at the pub. A handful came up and gave their condolences, but the two men were left to their own devices after that, apart from a few drinks that were sent over.

'I needed out of that house. I feel like a tractor just ran over me.'

'A few days, Brian. Give it a chance to settle. I have work next week but I can commute and get back here, or you can stay in Dublin with me the odd night.'

'What am I going to do, Mark? My head's all over the shop. I can't remember where I was before this kicked off.'

'Don't worry, Brian. It's all natural, man. Tell me everything about Australia.' Mark was trying to take his friend's mind to a place beyond the wake.

'It's hard to explain; it's another world away. What's happening with you though, how's the job, is it okay now?' Brian enquired.

'Work's okay; I might go back to work with Arthur. I'm waiting to see what offer he puts on the table.'

'That's news?'

'There's a charity night at the dog track on the twenty-third. I said I'd be there to hear Arthur out on a proposal.'

'That could be a good night. How is Arthur?'

'He looked tired... He's slowed down, the reason for the proposal I'm guessing. I think he wants me to run the place for him.'

'I want to be there for that. I'd enjoy a night at the dogs. I think of Shelbourne now and again when I'm in Australia.'

'It's Siobhan's birthday coming up too. I'm having a party for her. It's a quiet event as far as she's concerned, just a small dinner gathering. That's not the case so, definitely a few old faces, yeah? Tell me what this Sheila's like, Melisa right?' He hadn't given Melisa that much though in the past few days.

'She's sound. I've never been as happy, but since this...'

'Have you rung her yet?'

'Yeah, I called her before I came out tonight! She's a great attitude, Mark. Australian women don't need to be in charge all the time.'

'Nor do Irish women, Brian.'

'It's different there. Melisa gets me. I don't know when I've met anyone as straightforward, but I'm not sure I'm going back, mate.'

'You don't have to think about that right now.'

'Settling with an Aussie girl means settling there for life, for me anyhow. It could be because it's Melisa, she's like me in that she's family orientated. I don't see her ever leaving Australia, not long term anyway. I'm not a hundred percent sold on Australia, not yet, but she knows that. You're right though; I don't have to think of that for now.'

'So, tell me then, what's work like?'

'Yeah, it's good. You go in, no bullshit, everything's very laid back. Aussies work hard, but it's straightforward. The wages are good but the price of living, it's not cheap, you knew that. If you're not a big spender, you can tuck a few quid away. There's no pressure, you finish up early with the sun still shining, the surf is free. She has lots of friends Melisa, and everyone in Australia can cook without exception. I've come on in that department, believe it or not.'

'Now that's a laugh.' Mark had reason to find that funny; he'd shared a flat with the guy once upon a time.

'I lived on beans for the first five months with Alfie in that bedsit. The qualification was a long time coming.'

'You got there.'

'It wasn't that tough. I have a nice place of my own now so, yeah!'

'Good.'

'How... do I leave my mother again though?' He mumbled shaking his head.

'Let's take it one step at a time. We should get through planning next week first.'

The two men talked over two pints before exhaustion kicked in. Brian's eyes gave the game away. Mark wanted to tell him about Emily, but he had made little ground with her and besides Brian had bigger things to think about right then. Mark insisted that Brian come home with him. He offered to wake him at seven so he could get back in time to make his mother breakfast.

They both needed a good night's rest. There was little doubt; Brian was spooked. He agreed in the end. Mark still had the old bunk bed in his room, so they stayed up to sneak in a few cans. The nostalgia wore thin very quickly and they slept, they both had been through the mill.

Chapter 19

Mark had taken time out; time owed in fact, the weekend of the wake he'd needed, he'd left Joyce in charge while he went to the airport. The pre-scheduled Sunday overtime had been postponed on Friday, and he was back in action by the Monday.

He arrived in this lunchtime, having met Brian off the train. He'd safely settled him into the flat. It was by then the Wednesday after the funeral.

The floor staff stood their ground as he walked through the holding door, he was met by a wall of blank expressions, one malice filled worker to the front. Joyce was nowhere to be seen.

'What's going on here? Where's Joyce?'

'The hospital would be our best guess at this stage, with or without his right hand,' a worker replied having come from the back of the crowd to stand face to face with Mark. 'How many times have we said that the hydraulic cylinder is faulty, the hose is shot, and the thread joints are worn to nothing?'

A second worker intervened. 'He got us to work on and tried to fix the bloody thing himself, it was that or have us spend the remainder of the day lifting manually, we didn't have the manpower for that.'

'Christ!' Mark muttered as he slumped his head in disbelief.

'He was stuck in trying to get the hydraulics back in action, it near on took his arm off, Turlock left an hour ago to take him to the hospital,' the man continued.

Mark was still putting it together, but there was sharpness in his eyes.

'No one touches the lifters, you just stay as you are until I see about this. Christ!' Mark spoke again heading towards the stairs. "Just have a smoke...go!' He called back.

Mark rocketed up the stairs before making strides towards the reception desk. He was not yet aware that Ralph had skipped out of the building when the accident took place. Ralph had made a quick exit, making sure to bypass the drama on the floor where the men were gathered around their injured co-worker.

Ralph had quickly questioned Imelda before he left; he needed to know when Mark was due back, and why he had taken leave of absence. Ralph knew that Mark took hours off on a regular basis without his consent, that was the ace up his sleeve. In truth, Mark was not expected to be there twenty-four seven and rarely left for more than a few hours at a time, even Joyce would have struggled to manage the team beyond a couple of hours.

'Where is that Ralph Mournaghan fella? Now! I want him now!'

Imelda lowered her head. 'I can put you through to his mobile; he's not in his office.'

'Does he know?'

Imelda nodded her head. She dialled and put the receiver to her ear. 'I have an urgent call for you here Mr Mournaghan, hold the line please.'

She handed the phone to Mark. 'Mournaghan?"

"Speaking."

"I will have you for this; there is no stone under which you can hide. Are we clear on that count? He is a good man with a decent family and if your antics have cost him his hand.'

There was silence the other end. Mark handed over the phone. He waited a moment until the switch was flicked.

'Thank you,' Mark whispered before going back downstairs to gather the troops.

'We're going to have to do this manually. That is the last thing I wanted. My hands were tied but not for very much longer. Let's be clear here; it should have been me who sustained that injury. We need this done today and done right, Murtagh you're in charge. You know how to read this schedule, right?'

'I do.'

'We'll just get on with it. That machine will be fixed before the end of the week and never again will this happen on my watch, never. I know exactly who will pay for this, and by Christ, he will pay.'

'But boss?'

'I'm calling in some extra hands; I'm damned if you're carrying the load off their back. Go!'

Mark made a handful of phone calls; no one dared to go near him. Within ten minutes he had three extra workers on their way.

'Murtagh, you have three men arriving in the next hour. I'll be back as soon as I talk to Joyce.'

'No bother!' Murtagh returned.

'I'll let you know how he's doing when I get back.'

Again, Mark headed up the stairs, this time to let Imelda know that he'd be out, he took the steps two at a time and was met at the top by Thomas Reeves.

'Why didn't you let us know there were difficulties with the parts on that lifter, have you any idea of the damages this might set us back. Where were you?'

'This is down to Mournaghan, and I will quote him in front of the heads of management until they know the filthy liability that he is, do you get me?'

'But...' Reeves appeared flustered.

'It's none of your concern, Thomas. The machines have long since needed servicing, and you're backing him up like he's somebody; that lifter needed a new cylinder, hose and thread joints all of which were brought in on the cheap by Mournaghan. I did everything but knock that indignant shit out of his standing to get the point across. I knew that this would happen; eventually, I warned him.'

Thomas Reeves was by no means satisfied. 'The new parts were just approved but not in time. You should have spoken up sooner, Mark.'

'A big mistake, I should have gone straight to the top and to hell with the chain of command. I've been too bloody patient, the cost of which has fallen on Joyce, my best man when it should have been me. If there is permanent damage heaven help him. Get out of my way, Thomas, I mean you no harm.'

Thomas had a different standpoint. 'But you left Joyce in charge?'

'I'm not even dealing with you, Thomas. I wasn't contracted to do an eighty- hour week. This is Mournaghan's doing, and I hope the wrath of God comes down on him or better still, that he loses his job.'

'He has shares, Mark, he is a partner in this firm, and right now, he's not here. It's you that's on the firing line.'

'Would you ever get away from around me and cop yourself on! Seriously! I warned Mournaghan time and time again, the parts he brought in were inferior and deadly dangerous, they needed replacing. I sourced a supplier of legitimate parts; they said they could deliver the next day. It was two

Our Diligent Souls

weeks back when I gave him that information but what; another week on before he presents the research to the board as his own.'

'You be careful where you cast your accusations, Mark, Ralph Mournaghan has a lot of clout around here.'

'I have workers to organise and a man to visit in the hospital; I haven't time for this codswallop, can you move?'

Mark made his way back to Imelda's desk and found her steady as a rock. 'Oh, Mark... Would you have any suggestions for the Christmas party? They want to have it early this year, any ideas?'

'The dog track,' Mark threw it out there, not giving a toss if she was listening or not.

'Oh okay, they do meals there, right?'

'Shelbourne does, there's a big charity night there in the next two weeks.'

'That could be good.'

After a brief exchange concerning his departure, he headed back downstairs to call Joyce on his mobile; there was no signal. Directions were being handed out by Murtagh as Mark made his way onto the floor. Mark sorted out the protective headgear and gloves for the staff that were due to arrive and highlighted the aisles they were to cover with Murtagh.

'Send them straight to it.'

As Mark was getting ready to leave, Davin Turlock arrives in through the side door.

'How is he?' Mark asked.

'He'll live, but you're down your favourite stand-in.'

'I wouldn't start on me if I were you; we're up to our tonsils here. What did the doctors have to say?'

'They had to pick scraps of metal from his hand. It's bad, they might have to keep him in overnight, possibly even for a few days. Do you need help here?'

'Murtagh has it all in hand but ask him the same question. I'm going there now.'

'To the hospital?'

'Yes!'

Our Diligent Souls

Joyce will recover, Mark. It will work itself out. It's Mournaghan you got to look out for now, he won't take responsibility for this, and he's a blaggard.'

'Don't I know it?'

Davin shook his head, took off his suit jacket, left it on a bench and set to work.

Mark tried Joyce's number one more time on the way out the door. 'Hello.'

'Joyce, It's Mark here. How are you feeling now?'

'It's not good Mark, the cylinder snapped and near took my hand clean off. My right hand too, so I'm going to be out of action for a while. I should have just let it be and got the men to work on manually, but we would have come in well behind, I can only imagine how late you're running now.'

'You don't need to concern yourself with that, it was the faulty parts in the first place that created this. Did they give you something for the pain?'

'Don't worry about that; I'm not feeling very much at the minute.'

'Can I call someone for you? I'm on my way over now myself.'

'My wife is already here, Davin Turlock rang her for me earlier. She's more than a little upset.'

'Have either of you eaten, I'll pick up something on the way.'

'We haven't actually. I'm trying to get the Mrs to go and get a cup of tea, but she won't leave my side with all the fussing.' Mark could hear her in the background telling Joyce off.

As Davin Turlock joined the team to stand alongside Murtagh, there were a few comments thrown into the mix. 'He's a bloody good floor manager.' 'A tenacious dog that fella when they're messing us around.' There was a definite change in their attitudes.

Mark left and walked towards the gates; he felt instantly drained when he saw Mournaghan turn the corner and waver slightly in his tracks.

Mournaghan knew to tackle the situation in a dignified manner, any one of the executives could have been watching on, it was no time to play dastardly. Mournaghan put his hands out, shaking his head as Mark approached. 'It's unfortunate but these things happen, Mark, these things happen.'

Our Diligent Souls

    Mark refused his handshake and met him face to face before opening his mouth, even then he spoke calmly. 'I'd love to break every bone in your body, but you're not going to bring me to that. You just continue to stand there without one shred of remorse. If I'm to stay with this company, you will be made accountable for this, simple as now move out of my way.' Mark had come right up in his face. 'Now!' He shouted.

    Mournaghan jumped back, his cowardice on full display.

    Mark marched on fearlessly, disconcerted, though relieved that he had managed to keep control of his anger.

Chapter 20

Mark called into Joyce's place on the way home from work and was relieved to discover that he was on the mend. The arm might be stiff for a while, and he was looking at a three-month sabbatical, the scars given time could fade. The company had proposed to cover three months paid leave, resting on the advice of the medical professionals. They also offered to cover his medical bills.

Mark advised him to get a solicitor to find out what he was entitled to before agreeing to sign any papers. The company should have replaced those faulty parts. They should have taken measures straight away. It was a deplorable act not to have secured the health and safety of their staff.

There would be no fees for Joyce's solicitor at this early stage, they would take a cut of the settlement, and if he had any issue in finding a solicitor to take it on, on that basis, then Mark would cover the cost, no argument.

Mark knew it wasn't a straightforward work accident claim. They were slippery when it came to Joyce's compensation, and Mark couldn't stomach the way they had handled things. Offering Joyce, the bare minimum to stop him from processing a claim, was nasty. If the company wasn't covered by insurance, that was their fault. Management had not served his workers well. He was relieved when Joyce finally decided to seek legal advice.

As Mark walked through his front door, he was convinced he could smell Emily's perfume. With the Joyce situation under control, he was free now to carry on with his notion of her. The flat had never looked so immaculate, neat to the point where Mark wondered if he needed to rough the place up a little. He had long since anticipated this evening's event. It was the night of Siobhan's party, and Emily would soon be on her way.

She regularly wore a delicate gold link bracelet, a plain simple chain. Mark sat to recall the playful turn of her wrist. The way she placed the clasp on her pulses, satisfied only in the interim until it had shifted again. He remembered the conversations they had covered, the way she looked at him when they spoke, the expressions she wore and the movement of her hair. Her long delicate fingers that wrapped themselves around her coffee mug.

Our Diligent Souls

She was to arrive at six. That would leave them with plenty of time to prepare the food before the gang landed at eight. Mark had washed and prepped most of the ingredients just in case. She had given him a list earlier in the week on their fourth coffee date. It was beginning to feel like the start of something. Mark wasn't sure what, but it was something.

With his glass in hand, Mark listened to the last of the album he'd been playing. John Martyn was his favourite musician from as far back as he could remember. In a world that never had enough romance, it was his indulgence. The album took him to places he had no idea existed as a boy, the same way books did, the music painted images. The longing that John Martyn created in every strum of his guitar; it put Mark in the epicentre of an atmosphere that carried him away in his mind, just as Emily did.

He could replay this album until she arrived and spotted something in his collection that she might like. The rain stopped thrashing against the windows. It was twenty to six. She was frequently late; he expected that. The cake was in the fridge. There was a stack of party bites in the freezer, and the falafel mix was an easy one to pull together himself if she didn't show up on time. He had basic salads prepared, and he knew how to make a mean hummus. His readiness brought him no cheer; he just wanted to find her in front of him.

Brian was to work with Elliot to keep the event a surprise. He was due to meet up with Elliot and Siobhan at seven for drinks in their local. The plan was to head over to Mark's place at eight for what Siobhan thought was going to be a small cosy dinner. Emily arranged to meet them at Mark's apartment, it was more convenient for her coming from the studio, or so she'd said.

Mark threw on a coat and took an umbrella as he flicked the door snip to grab a quick smoke at the front door before Emily arrived. He was ready to spark up when she met him on the steps. It was an awkward moment as he was fully aware of how foolish he looked, juggling cigarette, matches and umbrella, all at the same time.

'Emily!'

'Nice night for it?' She announced.

'Well, that's thinking subversively. Get in there out of the rain.'

'Yes, dear,' she responded neatly, as she slipped under his arm and inside, into the bright, warm interior.

He stood for a second to let the night air cool his blush. He made an effort to put the cigarette back; it was half soaked and refusing to go into the box. He followed her inside.

'Let me take your jacket.'

'I got it.' She insisted. 'Your flat is very homely. I didn't take you for someone who spent much time at home. It's lovely.' She stated, removing her soaked cover as she looked for a place to hang it. He took the jacket, hat and scarf from her hands.

'I need to be able to relax here sometimes!' Mark acknowledged. She handed over a bottle of wine and her pre-wrapped present for Siobhan.

'Can you put that somewhere?'

'Sure... no problem.' Mark disappeared into his bedroom, putting the present on top of the locker, he hung her things on the back of the door.

'A glass of wine?' He asked as he returned.

'I'll have a quick glass. I haven't heard John Martyn in years. I think he might have been responsible for putting me on the songwriter's trail.'

'He inspired you then? Great stuff. I have the prep done; we have time yet.'

'It was a battle getting over here; the traffic was crazy.'

'You're right though it's not a great night for it, weather-wise. Make yourself at home, please.' Mark was tried to dispel visions he'd had of her draped over the couch. He quietly observed her as she wandered out to the kitchen. His heart was pounding; he hadn't noticed how loudly until she was out of his gaze.

'You've been busy.' She called out.

'I'm at home since three with the groceries. I wasn't sure you would show at all, so I thought it best to be prepared.'

'You're a regular boy scout you.' Emily laughed.

There was an awkward pause.

'I'm glad you have... arrived that is. I think I got everything we need.'

It had now been several weeks since they had first met. Mark's mind was focused on her steps as she confidently moved around his home, so much so that he forgot her wine.

'Guess I can do without that glass then?'

Our Diligent Souls

'Sorry, what was I thinking? I'm not accustomed to having guests.'

He lifted the wine bottle, got her a glass and poured slowly before handing it to her.

'Have you a playlist organised?'

'Better! I've old vinyl, there are playlists too on the iPod, and you name it radio-wise. You can change the frequency buttons as it suits, folk, jazz, funk, I'm an old hand. Pick out what you want, and we'll get going on this food whenever it suits you.'

'I'm happy with John Martyn for now. I do love John Martyn.'

They sipped at the wine, making small talk until they lost interest in sitting. Both Emily and Mark turned their hands to the task ahead of them. Emily was at home in the kitchen, a waitress's trait. She knew her fennel from her fenugreeks seeds and encouraged him to inhale. Mark hadn't heard of half the spices on her list.

Their laughter was active, the ingredients tasted, with a touch of double dipping involved. They were very much at home with each other. It was pure alchemy as the fusion of spices came together; the heat and aromatics in the kitchen filled their senses. It was a dance of dishes as they weaved their way from pot to bowl, from cooker to table. Time was of no relevance; he could have worked through the night with her in that same fashion, he thought.

They were left with twenty minutes before the first guests were due to arrive; everything was ready. It will be a quiet reunion to start, they thought, introductions and so on. At least until Siobhan, Elliot and Brian walked through the door.

Emily had invited three couples that both Elliot and Siobhan knew well. Three other friends of Siobhan's were coming too; one girl from Siobhan's workplace, the two others women Siobhan went for drinks with occasionally. Oden was invited to bring a guest, and Mark had asked along two lads from his hometown to support Brian. The driver was a teetotaller, and the other lad was Brian's cousin. Two electricians that worked with Brian might arrive. Siobhan and Elliot knew them as well. There was enough food to go around as many as twenty guests.

'Maybe you could put some other music on now. It's not my place and forgive me, but John Martyn back to back might not be everyone's cup of tea.'

Our Diligent Souls

She was disarming; the energy between them electric. Mark's humour was remotely childish at one point, she gave him a glance that left him flushed with embarrassment. She smiled as she attempted to lift the atmosphere, moving in the direction of the radio, reminding him that they would soon have company.

'Can I get you another?'

'Yes please,' she responded.

He had imagined her sitting in that chair more than once, but the reality was much more animated. Contrary to what Elliot believed, she was beautiful beyond measure. She was stunning, and she knew it too, but not in a cocky, arrogant way; she made him feel utterly relevant.

It wasn't long before the bell was hopping off the front wall; they were piling in, seizing that first drink while waiting for Siobhan and the crew to arrive. Oden was the first one through the door, introducing Lucile. Brian's cousin was next to call with his pal. The other three couples appeared together having hired a minibus. The girl from Siobhan's work trailing in behind them. Ten, fifteen minutes later Siobhan's two other friends arrived.

On the other side of the city, Brian oversaw the text alert. He was soon informed that the party was in full swing. He was to message Mark when they were getting into the taxi. A good half hour had passed, and Emily was beginning to wonder if she could even calm the crowd for the surprise entrance.

She let everyone know that they were making their way in the taxi. The cake was taken out of the fridge, and just before Siobhan arrived, the thirty candles were lit. Fifteen people had turned up, and there were a few that had called ahead to say that they were running late. It was a bigger turnout than they had expected.

A hush sailed across the room again as the doorbell rang. When Siobhan walked through the door the entire room burst into a roar, 'Happy Birthday.' Streamers, bells and whistles were released, filling the space.

'What in God's name!' Siobhan exclaimed. She was blushing, though delighted in the same hand. Elliot was there at her side.

The air was full of chatter, beer cans and wine bottles flowing; people were digging into the finger food, the odd person sitting with a plate on their laps taking full advantage of the offerings. The food was exceptional; Emily and Mark had surpassed themselves. There was a stack of presents on the coffee table for Siobhan and another few in his bedroom.

Brian was relieved, at least tonight; there were people here who knew nothing of his circumstances. Oden was drilling the head of one of the country boys; talking about a perfect cube that was two metres long and two metres high, 'it contains eight meters of cubic air,' he went on to explain. That was Oden's idea of small talk, but Lucile was lovingly eating up his every word. She was a social butterfly as was he in his own way. In unison, they were creating humorous connections that were hard to fathom.

Brian's cousin made a move on one of the single girls, and as anticipated he fell at the first hurdle. The room was full of good humour. Siobhan was the centre of attention with Brian following a close second. The couples were mingling and having the craic.

Mark's eyes were never far from Emily. He could sense her movements and hear her voice over the rest. Brian couldn't have been happier to see everyone enjoy themselves. He thanked Mark for inviting him more than once, several times in fact, to a point where it was becoming a concern. Brian was usually very laid back, practically horizontal most of the time; the kind of guy who was invited everywhere.

The girl that arrived from Siobhan's workplace was bubbly and full of wise craic. She started flicking through Mark's record collection and was no doubt taken by Mark and his home as she kept him locked in conversation for a good fifteen minutes. She was what Mark ordinarily went for, a girl who cornered him in a sense, a girl that he had no reason to turn away. But this time he had cause to steer clear, he couldn't ever have imagined feeling grateful for that.

He watched as Brian and Emily struck up a connection that quickly looked intimate, they were engrossed in conversation. He found it hard to watch and made himself useful in the kitchen. The idea struck him that if Brian and Emily were to fall for each other, there was no way he could contest that. He hoped that when he went back into the room, they'd have moved on to chat with someone else, but no such luck, they were now close to intertwined. Mark had not yet mentioned his feelings for Emily, not to Brian. As a last resort, he made his way over to join in on the story.

'You okay here, anyone for a drink?'

'We're fine, Mark,' Brian replied.

Elliot had caught what was going on from a distance.

'I'm fine, thank you!' Emily stated, somewhat concerned about the idea that Brian had spoken for both of them.

Our Diligent Souls

Mark was delighted. 'What's this, tales of the outback?'

'Some.' Emily stated.

'I was quizzing her on her songwriting skills; we have a serious talent here, my man.'

'Don't mind him; he has strange taste in music.'

'He has, has he?' Emily was smiling as she sneaked in a look across the room. Elliot and Siobhan were making their way over to them.

'Having a good night?' Mark asked Elliot as he joined them. Siobhan called out over his shoulder. 'Yeah! It's great!' She was swerving and dancing, splashing some of her drink onto the floor.

Oden joined them.

'Who's the girl?' Elliot asked his brother.

'Lucile.'

'Just Lucile,' Elliot tried again.

'I wanted to explain this new site; you have a zombie game; the difference being that they aren't ravenous, human flesh eaters okay, but...'

'Oden?' Elliot interrupted.

'What? It's a game.'

'Enough, Oden. Are you having fun?'

'Yeah, it's not bad.' Oden admitted.

'You're having a good night, Oden?' Siobhan asked, releasing a faint burp before covering her mouth.

'Yeah, why not, it's crowded for me?'

'Did you bring Siobhan a present?' Elliot had lent in and whispered.

'Yeah. It's on the table.' Oden whispered back, disappointed by his brother's question.

'I'm not driving tonight!' He advised his younger brother. 'Who is the girl?'

'I know you're drinking. I can make my way home.'

'So, Lucile; is she at college?'

'This zombie game is gravitational, just a tweak to the overplayed concept and boom! It's a curious thing.'

Our Diligent Souls

Elliot withdrew from the conversation, nodding his head as he stepped backwards, he was getting nowhere fast.

They moved back the chairs once the food was demolished; the room pulsating to the sound of Cuban music.

Mark turned to Elliot. 'You two better show them how it's done.'

Siobhan and Elliot knew the moves where the rest of them just gave it a whirl alongside them. Mark retreated from the crowd to watch Emily dance; she was a natural in the way she picked up the moves and was utterly unaware of the effect she had on people as she swapped one partner for the next.

The music had gone from folk to salsa to samba, from funk to frenzied and back to folk music to taper in the night. Mark finally moved Emily back to the makeshift dance floor for two last songs. It was a given, and the arena was theirs as he held her lower back. He was energised by the warm sensation of her body as they moved humorously with dramatic poise. They were elegant and well timed, and after a moment of undeniable affection, she politely disengaged.

Brian was convinced that the party could continue for hours, but no matter what party they were at he always thought the same. The last of the cake was wrapped in tinfoil; Oden lent a hand so that everyone could take home a slice, it was his idea.

Brian's cousin and neighbourhood friend were the first to go; numbers were exchanged with a real sense that they would stay in touch. Brian hung in, though he was supposed to travel home with his cousin, he turned down the lift in the end. He was delusional, refusing to believe that there was no more to be squeezed out of the night.

It wasn't long before Elliot and Siobhan took a taxi back to their place. Emily joined the couple, quietly saying good night as she attempted to slip away. Brian did his utmost, pleading with everyone to stay for one more drink.

Mark tried to get to Emily's coat before she reached the door. 'Thanks for your help. I can't begin to thank you; you'll let me take you to dinner and return the favour I hope?'

'We'll see, Mark. We'll see.'

'Why wouldn't you?' He asked as they were disconnected, the others piling up at the exit.

Our Diligent Souls

'Night, folks. And thank you.' Elliot patted Brian on the back and hugged him before moving on to Mark. 'Thank you, my friend. Seriously, she was genuinely surprised.'

'Love you, people,' Siobhan added, half cut, drenched in sweat and enthusiasm after her dance showdown.

'Better get her home,' Elliot stated, still smiling.

The music was ringing in their ears when the room finally emptied. There was plenty of cleaning left to do.

Brian announced that he reckoned Emily liked him.

Mark felt his heart sink but did not have the energy to debate. 'Have you spoken to Melisa?'

'This morning, she's fine. Mum wants to get us together for a big discussion, so I need to get back home early morning. I'll call Melisa again tomorrow night when I've more news. I still don't know where I am with things.'

Mark was cleaning as he went. 'What's the discussion about?'

'No idea, but mum's making a large fuss over it. Everything's still tense at home, raw even, so it was a serious blessing to have had the party, mate. Thanks for having me and on Wednesday as well.'

'What's with the thanks for having me bit?' Mark asked.

'I'm coming to terms with the fact that my father is dead and I'm adjusting to being at home. I don't know if having fun is even appropriate. I feel like my confusion has a ten-mile radius. I'm saying the wrong things to everyone I meet. My heads here and in Australia at the same time...'

Mark felt foolish. 'Forgive me. That was bloody thoughtless of me.' He admitted, ashamed of his questioning. 'It's early days... Will you manage to get to sleep on the sofa?'

Brian took the quilt and pillow from Mark's arms.

'I'm sorry. I'm zapped.' Mark whispered, finishing up the cleaning before he made it to bed.

'I'll be fine.' Brian replied as he tapped his friend lightly on the back.

Mark lay there still picturing Emily. He weighed up the time they had shared before and during the party. Joyce was in his thoughts again as was the work agenda. He needed his sleep; he'd get five hours, tops. Brian was in the other room listening to his friend's favourite records on the stereo.

Mark had the re-organising of the warehouse in the morning. The floor staff would be on time and a half for being dragged out on a Sunday. It wasn't long before he was asleep.

Chapter 21

Brian arrived home minutes before his sister. The train had been manic on the way there, with every seat taken. Once through the door, Brian flopped straight into his favourite chair. His mother was not willing to be drawn into a conversation until his sister Sarah arrived. When she did speak she was agitated, but that could be expected, these were unordinary circumstances.

In Australia, Brian pictured his family home in vibrant colours but now in the cold light of day, it was the complete reverse. It was brown and blue that predominated as he glanced around the room. Everything that belonged to his father stood out, from Jackie's high back chair to his reading glasses, taunting reminders everywhere that Brian wanted to banish. Jackie was sixty-three years of age, and yet everything that was Jackie's seemed to tell the story of a much older man.

It was when both brother and sister sat at the kitchen table that Marian joined them. She moved uneasy, her unwashed hair and timid frame reminding them of what had just passed. Marian had always dressed smartly, but today her clothes hung on her, her face drawn, her posture still slumped in disbelief. She had long since worked as a care assistant; she had left the nursing home to look after their father and had missed her colleague's interaction and companionship.

It was time to pull things back to some resonance of reality. Three months ago, the man she loved was in perfect health. He had enjoyed his job at the post office and was, by all accounts as fit as a fiddle.

Before Jackie falling ill, Brian's parents had decided to use the house as security for a loan, Marian went on to tell them. 'It was a loan we got on the back of our mortgage being paid for outright. With our life insurance in place, the loan repayments are now cleared. Brian and Sarah sat in silence. Now was the time to listen; the strategic plans their parents had made were being put into action. Sarah was saving up to get married having secured a home with her partner; they were struggling and had been since they bought the house.

Marian and Jackie had been planning a surprise trip to Australia. They were planning to cover Brian's health insurance over there. One of Jackie's colleagues had a son in Australia, and their family had been financially devastated when he was injured in an accident; diving into the shallow end

Our Diligent Souls

of swimming pool. 'You've always had a fearless nature, Brian. You're prone to taking risks. Your father thought that you living over there was a ticking time bomb.'

She talked through their thinking and the fact that they had hoped to help fund Sarah's wedding. They'd planned to keep money aside to do renovations on the house. As the conversation progressed, Marian let her son know in no uncertain terms that it was up to him if he wanted to go back to Australia or not. She would not hold him back. Marian intended to get on with her life; she was happy to travel to Australia for a visit but either way she expected to go somewhere warm to recuperate, at some stage.

'There is twenty-five thousand euro in the kitty for each of you, and you can do with it as you see fit. I won't interfere with your choices. If you do return to Australia, Brian, you damn well better get good health insurance. You'll have to stop and think before you act, you're a responsible adult now.' Marian looked relieved to be getting these issues off her chest. 'That's it; the money is in the bank, you can have it whenever you want it.'

'What do you plan to do, mum?'

'I want to get back to work. I miss the girls. With or without you, I'll be missing your dad. Someone told me about a bereavement group; I might join that. The house will be empty without him; look, I'm making no big decisions for now.'

She had held the news in for over a week until she talked to the insurance company. It wasn't something she'd been especially looking forward to telling her children. The whole idea of doling out money to them when her husband had just died felt a tad morose.

She had been given strength throughout the week from the stories her children had shared. Their father had quietly resolved difficulties for both, and she could see him in a whole new light, even now. Jackie had come to their rescue on more than one occasion; she understood that.

He had hidden much of their youthful follies from his wife, making sure to keep their secrets to his dying day. She was finding even deeper levels to the man, standards that she had never known existed; she was only now learning how much worry and anguish he had spared her.

'Dad won't be at the wedding.' Sarah realised.

'I can come back, our lass. I'll be there to give you away whether I move back to Australia or not.' Brian's response was swift and was enough for his sister at that moment.

Our Diligent Souls

They both knew that Marian's grief was very close to the surface. She was going to miss her husband in a way they couldn't understand. Nobody said another word on the matter. It was not something that either sibling had expected, but it had the power to change much of their plans. Twenty-five thousand Euros was a sobering amount of money.

Marian was a very independent woman, she had good friends and was in a number of societies. She had plenty to keep her busy outside of work, from book clubs to badminton tournaments. She might see Brian as a burden if he was to move back into the family home, he was aware of that. Mark might be willing to share his flat in the city Brian thought; he could always get himself a place later. That way at least he could be near enough to call on his mum and return some support.

If he were to stay in Ireland, it would almost certainly mean the end of his relationship with Melisa; it was unlikely that she would move over herself as she was very closely tied to her family. There was much to question. Twenty-five thousand euro could go some way to set up a business here with Mark. Alternatively, it could be a comfortable safety net in Australia.

Sarah left soon after hearing the news. Probably, Brian surmised, to share the details with her other half. Marian and her son had dinner together, and afterwards, he gave her a hand with the dishes. It was nice to have time alone with her; mundane tasks were welcome after the frenzy of the past week. There were other issues too, their father's things needed to be cleared away. That wasn't going to be easy. A touch of redecorating could help, Brian thought. If he decided on Australia, he'd only have a small window of opportunity if he was going to assist.

'So, what had you planned renovation wise?'

'I don't know, son, a lick of paint, new wallpaper. We need a new kitchen counter, and the shower, the shower needs to be fixed.'

'You could let me do it later in the week; we can look at wallpaper and whatever else we need.'

'I've decided to go back to work on Monday, and your dad's things need sorting.'

'No one will expect you back so soon.' Marian fell silent. 'We could tackle dad's stuff tomorrow. You always enjoyed projects; it would be good to decorate. You said it yourself; the sooner things get back to normal.'

'That's not normal, Brian, that's moving on. I'm not sure that's appropriate. I'm not interested in having the place turned inside out... I'll give it thought.

Marian was ordinarily enthusiastic about getting stuck into things. This time though, she knew that it was unlikely to take her mind off this incredible loss and besides she was far too drained.

'Think about it tonight, mum, and we'll see where we are tomorrow. It's better than letting a stranger into the house in a few weeks.'

'I said I'd think it through.' She was exhausted by him through his intentions were good. They were both wiped out.

Later that evening, Brian brought a mug of hot chocolate and the paper to his mum in bed; it was far too early for him to sleep. He headed into the spare room and climbed into bed with his mobile.

He was glad to hear Melisa's voice. They had everything in common in Australia; both were sparkies, they drank the same beers, had the same love for greyhounds, it was uncanny. They were very similar in their idea of family. In a few short words, she got what he was going through in a way no one else had. He missed her intensely just then.

They talked for twenty minutes; he didn't mention the money or the party, but they spoke plainly without drama. He enjoyed her company even if it was short lived. Brian knew once he hung up the phone he would sleep; she'd allowed him to rest his mind. When he did, he lay there and felt as if he had betrayed her by even contemplating the idea of Emily. His head had been all over the place since his father died and besides, nothing had happened.

He needed sleep, and possibly tonight he could dream of his father in a way that was useful. It was hard to credit that Jackie was gone. He wasn't sure if any of it had hit home yet.

Chapter 22

Mark had twice sat before the board of management, the first time for his interview, the second when he was given the job. Being called in front of the management committee for no apparent reason was unnerving. He had pushed Joyce into getting a solicitor to make a proper claim for his injuries, but he'd acted as his conscience seen fit and he knew that Joyce would not betray that.

It was speculative to think that the meeting was arranged because Joyce had decided to retain a solicitor. Mark was more determined than ever to prove his worth. He needed to make his case with Mournaghan plain. That was what he needed to concentrate on with management. Thank god, he wasn't kept waiting long.

'Mark, can you take a seat?'

Present were three of the company key pins. Ralph Mournaghan was thankfully nowhere to be seen. Mark waited for questions from the other side of the table.

'Do you know why we have called you here, Mark?'

'Not specifically, gentlemen, no.'

It was Mr Turner himself that spoke first. He was Laura's father and usually a silent partner in the company.

'We need to discuss the incident with Mr Robin Joyce and the lifting machine. We believe he sustained an injury that will keep him off work for three months?'

Mark needed to take care when speaking his mind.

'I have seen Joyce, and I believe his injuries are substantial. It was an injury that could have been avoided. He is an honourable man, and I know that he wants to get back to work as soon as possible. He has been my key worker and has on occasion stepped up to take charge when I was called away.'

'Have you ever asked Ralph Mournaghan to stand in on such occasions?'

'No, I'm afraid not, I wasn't given the impression that it was within his remit as my supervisor.'

'And why not?'

'I don't know how to answer that question, I never asked.'

'I see. Mark, we believe that Ralph Mournaghan put his faith into an overseas company; importing parts that were sub-standard.'

'That is correct. There were issues with the parts.'

'And you were aware of this fact when precisely, Mark?'

'I was aware of the fact straight away, as were the workers on the floor.'

'And did you bring this issue to Ralph Mournaghan?'

'I did promptly, with immediate effect, alongside other issues that I had.'

'Can we stay with the problem of the parts for now if that's okay with you?'

Mark was beginning to sweat; he had the urge to take hold of his throat but held back. 'Yes, that's fine.' He replied in a croaked voice.

'So, the parts arrived on the eighth of May, and you believed that they were faulty at that point?'

'I did, the treads were worn, and the cylinders warped. They didn't match up with other lifters; the machine kept snagging. The mechanic stated the same; he wasn't comfortable fixing the lifter in the first place. His objections were versed in front of Mournaghan. I was aware that there was a danger of someone getting injured by the machine at that early stage. The mechanic also made it clear.'

'And you voiced your concerns with Ralph Mournaghan?'

'I did and again on other occasions when the machine presented us with difficulties.'

'There was more than one occasion?'

'I warned Ralph Mournaghan several times, regardless of the grade of the injury sustained. I made sure the men logged each event in the incident book at reception.'

'There's a separate incident book for the floor staff?'

'I asked Imelda to write up a book for me. Ralph Mournaghan informed me that no such book existed. I needed to make sure that records were being taken. I felt I needed to do that.'

'So, this can be verified, Mark? And there were other injuries?' Turner appeared dismayed.

Our Diligent Souls

'They were something and nothing, claim wise you don't have to worry. The men report their injuries to Imelda; she writes in the details and I sign it later. The first aid box is kept at reception and Imelda tends to the injuries. I know that the new parts were approved. I had given Mournaghan the name and contact information of a reputable company, eleven days before Joyce's incident,' Mark attempted to lay out the facts. 'They had offered us next day delivery.'

'And who told you that the new parts were approved?'

'Davin Turlock?' Mark replied.

Turner tapped his pen on the desk.

'Is Davin Turlock your overseer?'

'No, Ralph Mournaghan is. Look, every time I tried to convey the urgency of the repair to Ralph, it was dismissed.'

'Did you seek permission to set up an incident book?'

'No, but where would I be if I'd not established one. I couldn't give you the accurate dates or the extent of the injuries if they were needed. It is in my remit to protect the floor staff under my command and if the company has fallen foul on its insurance policy; I'm not to blame for that.'

'Do you have issues with Ralph Mournaghan, Mark?'

'On a professional level, I do, yes. Ralph's actions or the lack of them have put my men at risk.'

'Have you personal issues with Ralph Mournaghan?'

'In what respect?'

'Do you go out on nights with any of the management?'

'I have done in the hope of resolving these issues for my men, but it has never proved helpful.'

'Mark, you mentioned other difficulties?'

'Yes, Sir. We need a mechanic to do a weekly maintenance check on all the lifters. We need to keep the hydraulic lifters fully operational. There's the shortfall in wages that my men still experience as well. A shortfall in wages doesn't inspire drive when you're trying to build confidence in a team. It takes up too much of my week chasing monies owed to my men. There were other issues too.'

'Mark, Ralph Mournaghan has made several statements. He claims that you had never highlighted the need for new parts. He assured us that maintenance had been carried out on the machines on a weekly basis.'

'This is frankly not true and not difficult to verify.'

'The first we heard of the sub-standard parts was early last week. It was put to us that you had not brought this issue to Mr Mournaghan attention, he was backed up in this regard.'

'That is plainly not the case. Weekly maintenance of the lifters does not exist. In respect of unwarranted deductions in wages, I kept a record with double entry time sheets. I started to record these after twice being accused by Mr Mournaghan of incompetency.'

'It's obvious that something is amiss, Mark. Ralph Mournaghan has payments receipts for the weekly maintenance of the lifters.'

'It has never happened.'

'The company is required to service our lifters on a weekly basis. It is a necessity for insurance cover. If the substandard parts were the cause of Mr Joyce's injury, then our insurance cover is in jeopardy. Ralph Mournaghan has stated that he asked you not to use the lifter with the inferior parts. According to him, he gave you that instruction directly after being made aware of the issue. We may need to settle outside of insurance if it can be determined that this particular machine was being used.'

Mark could barely believe his ears. 'Ralph Mournaghan did not ask me to stop using the lifter; he knew our regular workload could not be complete without the partial support of the aisle one lifter. We have been forced to use the lifter as, without it, my men cannot manually complete the work within the necessary time frame.'

'You are saying that there was no weekly maintenance of the lifters, Mark?'

'Gentlemen...There have been no maintenance checks on the lifters. You can verify that by consulting with any of the floor team. I use the machines every day as do the floor staff. I open the place in the morning and lock up here every evening. I have not seen any maintenance in respect of the lifters, not at any point. The lifters have kinks that have worsened over time; any mechanic can verify that. It comes to this, gentleman. If I can't resolve these work conditions for my team, then I will gladly give you my one month's notice from today.'

Our Diligent Souls

Mr Turner swung round to his left and briefly reviewed the notes his colleague had been assigned to take. He scolded the company representative as a note had not been taken on two separate points.

Mark could not hold back trying to impart every detail. 'The sub-standard parts, I reported straight away. I have been in a constant battle over new parts. Again, I'm sure you'll find any number of witnesses among the floor staff. The men can relay open debate that took place between Ralph Mournaghan and me on this issue, as can Imelda at the reception.'

'We will promptly investigate the case, Mark.'

'My worker's experience miscalculations in their wages, shortfalls, that diminishes morale. I'm fighting a losing battle to make headway. To re-work an out-of-date loading process we needed one day of extra overtime. That was approved, and we now have a better functioning layout downstairs. I have brought in new clients and brought up our efficiency by twelve percent. Much of this work, we completed manually while using tired under-serviced lifters. You need to figure out who is telling the truth here?'

Mr Turner placed his pen on the counter and intertwined his fingers.

'It is evident, Mark, that you are passionate in respect of your work and your collective team. You have made advances with the floor staff, and I will finish by saying that we do not wish to see you leave.'

Mark could not contain himself, as there were still points to drive home.

'It is obvious to me, gentlemen; the floor manager needs to be part of the management meetings. This stands regardless of whether it applies to the next man in line or me. Management will then be fully aware of what is happening at ground level. We want this company to succeed, but without the right strength in communication we are spinning on a wheel.'

Turner looked at the men either side of him as he moved to his feet and stretched out a hand. 'We will talk again in the coming weeks.' Turner stated as he nodded his head. The businessmen offered the same congratulatory handshake. Mark confidently retreated from the room having thanked them.

Our Diligent Souls

Chapter 23

Mark gently placed his paperwork and phone next to the computer. He pulled out a chair; the office surroundings frequently helped him to work with a clear objective. His eyes scanned the room, taking in the rows of desktops, the junction boxes and unsightly computer cables. Every desk was covered in paper files; the aftermath of a hectic day in the sales room. The cleaners had been in with the polishing machine; they had left behind a hum of French lavender wax.

He mentally walked himself through the lockup jobs that he had completed downstairs. Most of the tasks were done and dusted; everything except the last few light switches. He had work yet ahead of him, the bookkeeping end of things that he refused to bring home, for one. He was wading through the ledger, ensconced in his findings when his phone rang. He answered the call without removing his focus from the page.

'Hello.'

'Mark, I have a plan.'

'Brian, is that you?' Mark was struggling to hold the phone between his ear and shoulder. He was trying to keep an eye on the transcripts, not wanting to lose track of where he was.

'Can you meet me in the pub? I've news, Mark.'

'I can be in Brannagan's at eight,' Mark replied, giving himself time.

'Are you alright there?' Brian had picked up on Mark's drill sergeant response.

Mark had seen Ralph Mournaghan strut by with his executive crew three or four times that day. They hadn't uttered a word to each other. Mark was nervous after the meeting. He'd been busy reprimanding himself for pushing Joyce into seeking separate counsel. He knew it was the right thing to do, but he was nervous.

'I hope its good news, Brian?'

'It is good news alright.'

'I might need a job soon; I'm not sure where I stand with this crowd here after today.'

'That might be for the better.'

'How are Marian and Sarah, Brian?'

'It's a one day at a time thing, but in the middle of it there's news, substantial news.'

'Fair enough. I'll see you at eight so.'

Mark had work to get through. It wasn't long before comments from the meeting were playing havoc with his head. Turner was an impressive man, diplomatic, Mark thought. He was not unlike Laura in his facial features either. She hadn't crossed his mind since that day in Bewley's.

Laura hadn't sought his support in the end, but she was an insightful woman, so hopefully, the apple didn't fall too far from the tree. He smiled to himself recalling his staff at home time, they'd made their way out the door like speeding bullets. Mark was in no mood for staying at work. Again, he was on the defensive wondering if Mournaghan might appear. It wasn't as if he hadn't dropped him in it, he had.

He went to the canteen to grab a mug of coffee; to perk himself up and continued with his work. He had two hours left before meeting Brian in the pub, but it was hard to concentrate. Mark's hatred for Ralph sat squarely. He even pitied the man to some degree. He was a low life, and that hadn't risen out of anything that was decent; he had no idea what had inspired Ralph to become such a vile individual in the first place. The dilemma still stood; it was Ralph's word against his, and he knew just how quick Ralph was to turn on the charm.

Imelda appeared out of nowhere and made her way over to say good night. Mark almost fell off his chair; she'd been doing overtime unbeknownst to him. Imelda reminded him that the booking at Shelbourne Park had been made thanks to his suggestion. She couldn't go herself, she told him. Mark suspected that a bunch of thirsty work hounds was not her style, not that Imelda would have said as much. She had confirmed the event with both management and floor staff. Mark checked the date with her and realised that it was on the same night that he was due to meet Arthur.

Imelda was gone when he hit the last light switch. Mark was not usually granted the time to enjoy a leisurely walk, he always had somewhere to be and was customarily in a hurry. The city was at a sleepier pace now that the six o'clock rush had passed. He wasn't up for a massive drinking spree, but he doubted his friend was either.

Brian had stayed in Dublin the night before with friends he hadn't seen in a while. Mark genuinely hoped that he had decided to return to Australia. Staying at home with his mother could be a difficult choice. Being greeted by condolences for the next six months might drive him mad. He could avoid that in Dublin, but there was no work in the city, not as an electrician, not with the new tax embargo on the building trade.

'Brian, mate!' Mark touched his friend's shoulder momentarily; Brian was busy digging into a second pint.

'Mark, my man!' Brian was lit up to see him, the barman was stretched forward waiting to take Mark's order.

'Pint of Guinness when you get a chance, mate. You have a fun night last night?' Mark asked Brian.

'Quiet one but, yeah.' The lads were both in top form. It was nice to catch up with each other.'

For Brian, the word great had been watered down; good was acceptable, great was a word that people used when they hadn't recently been bereaved of a loved one.

'So where are you, Brian, you said you had news?'

Brian's tired face lit up, 'Did we have a dream to open up our own shipping company one day?'

'Back when we dreamt aloud I guess we did,' Mark suggested. The bartender swooped in with his pint. He swiftly slid a beer mat underneath the glass.

'Thank you.' Mark said, handing over a crisp ten Euro note.

'Dad left us money,' he lent in and whispered. 'He left us twenty-five thousand each. It's more complicated than that; it's from both, both parents.'

'That will help, Brian. I know it doesn't replace your dad, but it will give you something new to focus on.'

'A shipping company, I've been looking at the figures, and we could rent a place to start.'

'Brian, when I was working with Arthur that was the dream. But if I knew then, what I know now, I'd have felt a right fool. It takes hundreds of thousands to come up against the likes of T&E shipping. With the small market share that Arthur owns, we'd have to knock him out of the picture before getting a wage for ourselves, and again you're talking more than the hundred grand to get started.'

The joy in Brian's face began to melt away. He needed the engagement that came with a potential new project, but Mark couldn't feed him one word of a lie.

'Besides that, it's something I just couldn't do. There are so many other dreams, Brian. Twenty-five thousand doesn't go far in setting up any new business.' He said. 'You need a ground floor insight, experience to drive a new venture forward.'

'We could do that together, Mark.' Brian stated without giving much thought to what he was saying.

'I thought you loved being a sparkie?'

'I do, but we could thrive in business together? You're a full-on businessman now. Think about it.'

'Don't be daft. We're not kids anymore, Brian. You'll always be my best buddy, but you have to put your dreams to bed as have I, what does Melisa think?'

'She could get some work on the black in the greyhound industry.'

'She has family commitments, Brian? There's no work here, there are fewer people training dogs, the whole country is desperately trying to hold on to their jobs. People are working for nothing just to get out of the house. It's impossible here, that's why your dad didn't want you to leave your job, we're in the thick of it now, and he could see it coming. It has worked out for you in Australia, but if it hadn't, you were coming back to nothing. You knew that in the first place.'

'Hear me out at least, Mark. I have a couple of ideas I jotted down for you.'

'Twenty-five thousand is an easy thing to dwindle away over here, Brian. Australia gives you a decent wage and a good future. It's not that I don't care, I'd love you to stay, but you have to look after yourself.'

'I have eight days left here if I'm to go back, Mark. I have one day to let them know.'

'Talk to Elliot too, Brian, maybe he'll have a better perspective. As much as I'd miss you, it will be tough on you if you stay.'

Brian looked drained of life. He knew as well as Mark did, the inevitable conclusion. There was nothing for him in Ireland; he was clutching at straws.

'Do you think I'm foolhardy?'

'You enjoy life, Brian. You take these enormous leaps of faith and then struggle to find your feet. Then you take another leap of faith in a totally different direction. It's hard to find the energy to keep up with you sometimes.'

'If I go back, mum wants me to get good life insurance.'

'Wise woman Marian! No telling which end of the pool you'll dive into head first.'

'That's what my dad thought!'

'So, are we making the night at the dogs you're going away party or are you going to stay at home?'

'It's a baptism of fire no matter where I look, pal.'

'Drink up then, man.'

The two sat in contemplation. Mark gathered up his change before moving from the bar. He sat at a round table with two small stools and a comfortable corner seat. Brian hadn't thought to ask Mark about what he'd said earlier on the phone.

'Was there trouble at work?'

'I was brought in front of the management committee. It was a full-on inquisition.'

'Go on?' Brian nudged the news forward.

'It's that Ralph Mournaghan eejit again. He's skimming extra cream off the top; at least it looks that way; non-existent maintenance for the lifting machines, and he has receipts. I might have dropped him right in it. I offered my four week's notice.'

'You did what?'

'I know.'

'What did they say?'

'Not much. It's a case of my word against Mournaghan's. If they investigate properly, the twat should be caught red-handed but where that leaves me is anybody's guess. Mournaghan has shares and receipts from a mechanic that never did a day's work. The lifters are still only half operational; I told you what happened to Joyce.'

'The arm thing?'

'Let it blow up in their faces, I no longer care. Arthur has offered me my old job back, and I'll find out at the dog track how much he can afford to pay me. I've long since been wondering if I'd be better off back there.'

'He's still training a few greyhounds for the track?'

'Yeah, one or two I'd imagine. Is it much different over there in Australia then, the greyhound track?'

'A lot more Sheilas there on a nightly basis.'

'Shielas, at the track, do they wear anoraks?'

'Um, don't be biased, they have eight dog races, different lingo too. It took a night or two to pick up the changes, but their concern is keeping the tradition, the same buzz.'

'Sounds cool. Listen, I have something to tell you, Brian; it's between you and me, yeah?'

'What?'

'I've had a crush on Emily for a while now.'

'You what?'

'More than a crush, I'm seriously into her. We've been out for coffee a few times. I didn't get a chance to tell you.'

'You let me make a twit of myself, you should have said.'

'Just do me a favour, yeah, and don't be acting out. I'm not saying don't talk to Emily, but you know what I'm saying. I want this to happen with her.'

'It's not you to be taken by a woman, but she is an interesting creature, I can see the attraction.'

'Cheers, mate.'

'So, what do you reckon, is it going anywhere?'

'I hope so, but she's not easy to read. I'm going to take her out one evening, let her know where I'm at with her.'

'I'm glad you told me. I'm glad for you, mate.'

Brian was a decent sort and knew too well that Mark wasn't easily set alight. He listened as his friend talked about her. The walk in the park, the

Our Diligent Souls

night they cooked together in the kitchen, the coffee shop met ups. It didn't just end there, the trouble outside the restaurant, the fox on the way home from the dinner party at Siobhan and Elliot's.

Brian talked about Melisa too; how they had met, how grounded she was. She also was a very earthy, natural sort, nothing too crazy or shallow. Maybe, Brian suggested, they were growing up at last.

'So, I was talking to Elliot on the phone,' Brian let him know. 'Both, Siobhan and Elliot, they're up for a night at the track. They're bringing Oden and Lucile too. Lucile's Oden's girlfriend now?' Brian asked. 'I assumed from the party in yours, but I wasn't sure... Elliot was odd with me when I brought it up; he has some oppressive ideas about Oden.'

Mark didn't care too much to get into that, what went between Oden and Elliot wasn't their concern today.

'What about Emily? Will she come as well?' Brian was curious.

'I guess so. I must invite Joyce too, although he might not want to be seen; he is still on sick leave. It could be a big night if Arthur's proposal is put on the table.'

'It might be a big night for me if I decide to up and abandon you for the sunny coastlands of Australia.'

'It might at that, Brian, see as you go.'

They managed four more pints of Guinness each before heading home. They had a hot and spicy kebab from the chipper on the corner. Mark had backed out of his free dinners with the executive crowd a while now. He was revelling in his takeaway treat. It had been a while since he had felt so at home in himself. Brian had rectified that for him, or at least the event of his father dying had. He was starting to remember the old Mark though now he felt ready to tackle something more meaningful in his life.

Maybe he was wrong, and maybe Emily wasn't all that interested, but one thing was sure; he wasn't just setting up camp where the opportunity arose, not anymore. Emily had a rare substance. There was something about her that brought the notion of serious longevity into play.

Chapter 24

This night had the makings of something special, and to add the boot, it was Brian's last night on the cobbles. The decision had been reached; he was heading back to Australia. Mark's floor staff had been transported to Shelbourne from a pickup spot in the city. They were met at the track turnstile by the executive chef. The men were having dinner and drinks on the company with a few betting tokens thrown in for good measure. Mark was collecting Joyce before meeting up with Elliot and the rest of his crew on the stands.

The upstairs restaurant with its glass enclosure gave quality views of the track. The tote betting clerks were weaving their way around the tables with ticket machines in hand. The executives took up one large table and Mark's floor staff another. It was a brightly lit restaurant, everyone in their favourite clothes. The entire party were seated a good twenty-five minutes before the first race, giving them plenty of time to get stuck in an early round or two of drinks.

When Mark arrived, he brought Joyce straight through to meet Elliot and the gang. They were waiting in a huddle outside on the stands just in front of the bookies. Both bookies and clerks weighed up the news with the regulars while standing beside their pitches, all of them, fully rigged out and ready to brace the cold night air. Frank Finnegan was the most decent soul among them, laying bets for 'winner come second' not far from Bernard Barry another Dundalk bookmaking legend that Mark instantly recognised.

Elliot and the crew were up for a stupendous night out with the whole gang in attendance, Emily included. There was a decent chipper with seating on the ground floor, a tea and coffee stand and the bar. Mark knew he had to head upstairs for dinner once Joyce got a feeling for the front of house. It wasn't Joyce's first time at the track, but he kept that to himself.

The grey cement stands were atmospheric and the only place to set up camp. Emily blushed as she caught sight of Mark.

'Mate!' Elliot called out.

'Elliot, Siobhan, Emily, guys!' Mark did the rounds as he moved in beside them. 'Oden, what's the craic?'

'White and hairy!' Oden responded; the pair of them laughing hard.

'Is Brian here yet?' Elliot inquired.

'I haven't spotted him.' Mark returned, 'No worries though, he'll be here soon enough.'

'When is he flying out?' Siobhan asked before cocooning her gloved hands against her mouth to blow warm breath on them.

'Tomorrow. Marian and Sarah are taking him to the airport. Elliot, let me introduce you to Joyce.' The gang gathered together and shuffled in close. 'This is Siobhan, Elliot's partner, Oden, Lucile and the lovely Emily.'

'Pleased to meet you,' Elliot said, stepping in to grip the man's shoulder, a handshake was way too complicated with his injury, but the situation left Joyce with a smile. 'Can I call you Joyce? That Mark fella forgets his manners sometimes.'

'Joyce is fine. My first name is Robin, but everyone calls me Joyce. It's a good night for it, I'm glad I came.'

Mark started to explain to Joyce how the regulars could get good odds; the tote pot was for some part made up of first-timers; betting on whatever dog names tickled their fancy. The dividends were often higher on the tote than with the bookies if you were betting in small money.

It wasn't easy to make money, even for those who were there without fail and they knew the dogs better than most. Moreover, to regulars this was a lifestyle; they had the dog form well studied before they got to the track. Joyce didn't mention that he was familiar with the industry; it was his first time at Shelbourne though he'd grown up practically next door to Harold's cross and had regularly attended meetings there. He was entertained by Mark's assumption and did nothing to dispel the notion that he was a novice.

'We heard you injured your arm. You okay now?' Siobhan quizzed him, seeing that his hand and arm was still bound up in bandages. 'You don't want to have them bumping into that arm upstairs. It's a tight squeeze up there sometimes, especially when people have one too many jars.'

'I'll manage but thank you; it will give me an excuse to get back down here later. It's been years since I've gone to the dogs.' Joyce pouted his lips and Siobhan lit up with happiness as they laughed pressing shoulder to shoulder and lowering their heads before turning to greet the others. Elliot pointed them in the direction of the trainers and their dogs that were by then being paraded. Mark was preoccupied; going out of his way to attract Emily's attention.

'You are doing okay?' He asked.

'I will be if I win a few quid.' Emily quipped.

'I'll be upstairs and back down to you lot throughout the night, I'll get to scan Arthur's card for a few possibilities. He's my old employer; he knows his stuff.'

'Sounds good to me,' Emily whispered. 'I'm pissing against the wind here otherwise.'

Mark nodded at her as he moved off with Joyce to join the crew upstairs, holding her eyes as he retreated. Elliot saw the exchange and disapproved. By his standards, Mark was way too obvious, but it hadn't taken a flicker out of Emily, he then observed.

Joyce arrived to a fanfare as they reached his workmate's table. There were two places kept aside for them both and a single chair waiting at the executives' table. Mark suspected that the executive chair was saved for Mournaghan who was yet to show his face. He was still wary of the executives, and as of yet had no idea what way his appraisal had gone since the big management meeting. Mark was fighting a growing concern. Arthur could just as quickly have decided not to take him back. The likelihood that he could be blown out from every angle was real. He had no choice but to wait it out.

The waitress took the orders in quick time, trying to get a move on before the next race started. The bartender was serving them their third round and already finding the lads a challenge. Mark let the waitress know that he'd be eating with his crew, before heading over to square it with the executives.

'How are you, Mark? Good of you to bring Joyce. We have a seat here for you.'

'It's not for Ralph Mournaghan then?'

'No, Ralph Mournaghan won't be joining us tonight.'

'I'll eat with the crew if you don't mind. It's more fitting. I've ordered from there. I'll join you later if that's alright?'

Turner winked at him and sat up. 'We can talk later. We didn't expect the noise or the bright lights for that matter.'

'I'll go downstairs shortly to get my card marked if you're interested.'

'You have friends here?' Turner shouted, trying to be heard above the tandem.

'I do, yeah.' Mark called back as he glanced over at his table. He made his excuses and returned to his team.

The men were in top form, unconcerned by the management's tired expressions. They were engaged in their usual style of devilment as the drink flowed and bets were placed. It wasn't long before the first course started to come out.

'So, the lifting machines have been fixed.' One of the men couldn't wait to tell Joyce. He was championing him as the instigator of that provision. 'It's a much safer place to work. That's down to you, my friend.' Joyce lowered his head and tucked into his deep-fried brie; he'd always been a man of few words. Once the food was eaten and a quick shot of Jägermeister was lowered, Mark headed off downstairs.

Arthur was talking to a trainer when Mark approached; he passed Mark his calculations and watched him retreated to score the projected outcomes on his card. Mark knew it was too early in the night to inquire about his decision work wise. Arthur had a dog running in the fifth race which he predicted to have a good chance of winning. Mark explained that he was upstairs for dinner, but he could talk to him later in the night.

'Go ahead; enjoy your night, Mark, we'll get a chance to talk later.'

The bookies were out in full force, 'Four to five the field, three to one the top dog.'

The lingo of these legendary bookmakers jolted the punters into action, big spenders or otherwise, it was time to start plying for trade. The tote tandem called out. 'Three minutes to bet.' The shrewder clientele was holding steady, pensively waited to pounce on the shifting odds. The track tandem compounding the urgency. 'They're going behind the boxes.'

A few rustled their way in between the hungrier punters, making sure that they weren't blocked at any stage. The opportunity to bet was easily missed by amateurs, but in the foray, the regulars moved slickly. The newcomers to the track tended to get their bets on early; they didn't hold back to see what way the stakes were going. There was a last-minute flutter as the bookies upping the odds; the dogs being bundled into the traps.

'We're talking evens now, evens the two dog! Three the one bar! Last chance to bet, folks.'

There was a better view from the stands. Mark stepped up behind Emily and held her shoulders; she didn't flinch. She was on the top dog which was coming in at four to one on the tote. 'Go on, yah beauty!' Mark hollered. 'Come on you good thing!' The dog, in the end, made good time to come in second to a long shot, with the favourite following in third.

'So is the nature of the game, Emily, you can't win every race.' Mark was attempting to comfort her.

'I'm not keen on losing.' Emily replied, with a touch of bitter desperation.

'But that's the magic of it... Look, you can make your money back in a single race especially if you're doing cross bets, forecasts and the likes.'

He had just started to explain when Brian's face rounded the corner.

'Brian!' Siobhan yelled out, waved joyfully.

His arrival was celebrated with plenty of back-slapping. It pained Mark to have to leave them again; the humour amongst his group of friends was infectious.

'Brian. I have to go, catch you later. My dinner will be coming out upstairs; I must go. I can leave you with this bunch of yahoos, yeah?'

'You can do that, Mark.'

Dinner was served when Mark reached the table upstairs. The lads were too distracted to notice what had happened to his food, but the waitress wasn't long in retrieving his plate from the kitchen where it was being kept warm. Everyone was on steaks with a few at the executive table having duck; it was the sirloin steak that had caught the men's fancy, no expense being spared.

Joyce was in the best of form; you could see that he'd missed his mates, he was yearning to be back working. They were doing their utmost to ring up as big a bill as possible on the company, and the drink was flowing.

After dinner when the dust settled, and the dessert orders were placed, Mark made his way over to the executive table with his card, but the management showed little interest. Turner was doing the talking.

'Mark, we have given what you said serious thought. We have investigated the claims that you made about the lifting machines and their maintenance. There will be a new maintenance team starting next week. We have a proposal for you.'

Our Diligent Souls

Mark fell silent.

'When you started this job, we informed you that there was room for you to advance with the company.'

Mark straightened up, holding his breath.

'We can see that you have done justice to your appointment as logistics manager. We're now proposing that you become more connected to the board of management.'

Mark stood his ground, staying silent.

'What I mean to say is that we need more correlation between floor and management, Mark.' Turner had to talk louder than he'd have liked too.

'Please, go on,' Mark responded, encouraged by what he was hearing.

'We are suggesting that when Joyce comes back to work, he might take up the role as supporting floor manager. The job will give him a six percent pay rise and will allow you to take time out of your week to work with us on operational improvements. It should free up your time to gather new clients; your financial position will improve with an additional percentage of our end-of-year profit. That will include this year ending.'

'Right... Can you give me any idea of how much that might be?' Turner nodded. He took out his pen and wrote a figure on an envelope before sliding it across the table. 'That is what you might have received with your share of last year's profits. But the first three-quarters with you on board, we are up twelve percent this year which has yet to be added to the figure.'

'Right, that's excellent... that would certainly make it worthwhile. And Joyce will have a new position?'

'We are planning to offer him a small lump sum on top of his sick leave and medical expenses. He is free to come back earlier to manage logistically without the use of his arm if he so wishes. We thought you might want to give him the news yourself.'

'I will do, thank you.'

'We can take it then that you accept the offer?'

'It may be hard to refuse; can I ask where Ralph Mournaghan stands with this?'

'Ralph is leaving the company for pastures new. He will be retaining his shares in the company, but otherwise, he will be taking a step back.'

'Okay.'

'So, you accept the offer then?'

'I'd be very honoured to...' The words weren't out of his mouth when he thought of Arthur downstairs waiting to speak to him. 'There's someone I need to consult with first if that's alright?'

The gang downstairs were heading back later to Elliot and Siobhan's. They were having farewell drinks with Brian, and he could bring them up to speed then. The staff table was getting louder and louder. The winning ticket holders had lost all inhibitions. At this rate, Mark thought that Joyce might be in danger of receiving a blow to the arm.

He hesitated before leaving the management table, Mark had one last enquiry to make. He asked if they might be prepared to pass on to Joyce the figures regarding his lump sum as he was planning to escort him downstairs out of harm's way. They agreed, and Mark managed to bundle Joyce over to the executive table without too much ado.

The offer was written on the other side of the same envelope. Joyce weighed it up for a moment and agreed. The executives got up and stretched out their hands to congratulate him, he pulled his bandaged hand back and smiled, they genuinely did not know where to look.

Mark and Joyce made it downstairs having battled through the crowded ground floor to make it to the stands. Mark stood tall against the night sky at the stadium; it was breath-taking. To the right of the concrete stands was an apartment block overlooking the grounds, in the distance the Aviva stadium was just visible.

Arthur was ready to talk by the time Mark caught up with him again. The fifth race was over, and his dog had put up a mammoth effort and sprinted home first by three-quarters of a length. There had been a steward's inquiry into the second and third places, but that didn't concern Arthur.

He was playing it down as if it was an everyday occurrence, but Mark could tell he was delighted. Apart from the prize money, he had a sizeable sum on her to win with one of the bookies. It paid a handsome dividend which put him back in front for the month.

'Congratulations!'

'I'm thinking of taking it up full-time, kiddo.'

Mark was dismayed and lowered his head. 'I take it you've made up your mind then?' Arthur asked while Mark looked warmly into his old friend's face. 'You're staying with the other company before I even get a chance to lay out my offer, young man.'

Our Diligent Souls

'I couldn't take the money they're offering from you, even if you could afford it, Arthur.'

'No worries. I've offers of my own on the table.'

'What, you're selling up?' Mark quizzed him.

'Am I a quitter?'

'Never!'

'Well, there you have it.'

The tandem rang out, 'three minutes to bet.' The bookies called from their stands, 'six to four the field.'

'We'll talk again, Mark.'

'No hard feelings, Arthur?' Arthur put out his hand, but when Mark took hold of it, he pulled him close. 'I'm proud of you, lad. Never doubt that.' Arthur whispered.

Mark and Joyce re-joined his friends to share the rest of the night with Brian. Joyce was happy to receive an invitation to go to Elliot and Siobhan's, but he knew better than to accept. Joyce felt at home with the lads, they were a decent bunch of young ones, and without any question, they were there for Mark, they were firm friends. He finally made his way back upstairs with Mark to say goodnight to his work pals and make a quick exit.

Before they reached the taxi rank, Mark filled Joyce in on the news. He let him know of the offer of a position as supporting logistic manager with a six percent pay rise. Mark explained his new agreement with the board of management as well. Joyce could take the rest or come in and work on logistics without using his arms if he pleased.

'It will mean getting paid on top of the three months leave, that's how these things worked.' Mark advised him. 'But, you're better advised to start with logistics a week or two before you're due back. It will give the hand time to heal. You should enjoy the time off.'

'Time off!' Joyce pulled back. 'You're kidding me; you have met the wife?'

Mark chuckled happily.

Joyce thanked him if it weren't for Mark's efforts none of this would have happened. He was more than happy with the lump sum.

As they made their way to the front door for a taxi, Mark spotted Laura Keating in the distance. He was sure it was her, but double checked what he was seeing. He hadn't laid eyes on her all night, and now here she was, talking intimately with Arthur, but Arthur knew everyone. They might have even been related. The timing was strange, but he had enough on his mind.

    He delivered Joyce back safely to share the news with his family, following on to Elliot and Siobhan's. Emily was going to be there, and at last, he could celebrate. He couldn't make too much of his promotion though; this was Brian's big night as well.

Chapter 25

The rest of the gang were only kicking off their shoes and coats when Mark arrived. He was glad he hadn't missed much. Siobhan was busy tackling the music while Elliot was getting the fire up and running. The heat was welcomed and as they gathered around, the flames casting dynamic shadows across the ceiling.

They'd had a great night having thrown back a few pints at the stadium, these guys were thinking 'bananas after party'. The sound was whacked up to high volume, and the beers passed around, their chat animated as they huddled in subgroups, everything being discussed except Brian's imminent departure. Mark chose not to tell his friends the good news just yet; it was neither the time nor the place.

Emily joined Siobhan in the kitchen as they warmed up the seafood chowder, Brian's favourite.

'Mark's keen on you, you know that?' Siobhan felt she needed to bring it up with Emily.

'Leave it, please.'

'No, I'm serious.'

'He's a sweet guy. I'm just not prepared to be railroaded into some romance here.'

'You need to open up, girl.'

'My folks were friends and work colleagues for years before they got together.'

'That was a different generation, Emily.'

'Look, Siobhan, Mark's a nice guy, but I'm not moving in that direction right now.'

Siobhan put her arm around Emily's shoulder. 'You have to do what feels right; I just wish this once you'd stop being so cautious. You could seriously do with giving happiness a chance.'

'Enough for now, yeah? I have serious plans, and they take priority.' Emily was bringing the conversation to an end.

Oden sashayed into the kitchen full of excitement.

'How's Emily?'

'Set in her ways.' Siobhan stated, shaking her head as she smiled. 'At least she hasn't the temperament of a nun.' Siobhan bounced her hip against Emily's side.

Oden grinned as he broke into dance with some humorous moves.

In the living room, Lucile was deep in conversation with Elliot; he was enjoying her company. Brian and Mark were clinking bottles; throwing back their beers alongside them. Oden was still rocking the house as Siobhan and Emily watched on in amusement.

The chowder started to bubble before they lifted it off the cooker ring. 'Grubs up you lot!' Siobhan had managed to get everyone's attention.

'The dog track was great, eh?' Elliot asked as he lightly pinched Oden's chin.

'I won forty quid,' Oden laid claim loudly. 'It's a maths thing I reckon.'

'It's a guessing game!' Lucile called out as she squeezed her face in between Oden and his brother's arms; the boys were waiting hungrily for the food to be handed out. Lucile knew exactly how he'd tackled the game, backing second favourites at long odds.

'You were in luck.' She said wisely.

'I had a strategy. You always need to have a strategy.' Oden insisted.

She had her point of view. 'That may be, but the gambling thing... It's bloody opaque to me; I can't make it out.' Lucile was not alright with the idea of having a gambler for a boyfriend.

The seafood chowder was nourishing and well tasty. To thank Siobhan for her efforts, Brian, Elliot and Oden took to making Mississippi Mudslides. It took three measures of vodka, three baileys and three further measures of Tia Maria. They added full-fat milk and ice, then blitzed it in the machine. In the end, the drink had the consistency of a creamy mocha flavoured milkshake.

At one point, Emily and Mark found themselves alone in the kitchen. Mark suspected that the others had left them there deliberately, but either way, he didn't care.

'You're looking wonderful tonight.' Mark started out.

'I'm looking in a few different directions. Look closely, here,' Emily tilted her face in his direction. 'I have a permanent squint in that eye.' She had her own unique way of pulling the piss.

'You're rubbing me off again.' He insisted. Giggling, she pushed him back a step and gripping hold of his arm, they laughed. 'I'm not that big of a fool.' Yet again he insisted.

'Some would say naivety is a thing to be cherished, Mark?'

He was quick to respond. 'It wasn't me that blew my hard-earned money tonight?'

She was incensed. 'I'd hardly call twenty quid hard earned.'

'It's a score, girl, twenty quid is a score. You need to have the head for it, it's that type a scene; not everyone can lose gracefully on a regular basis.'

'So, you did well tonight then?' Emily enquired.

'I could think of a few ways I could have done better.'

Emily blushed though her return was nonchalant. 'Sure, isn't that always the case?'

'I could make sure you get home safe tonight. Should we join the others?'

He had a way of disarming her. 'For now!' She responded as he offered her the room to take the lead, she moved over to the gang quietly shocked by her own frankness and what it implied. He was a bit of a trickster, Mark, she reckoned. 'For now!' implying that she wanted him to take her home. How that had that happened, she had no clue.

The crew swept the pair of them in around the fireplace. The boys were amusing each other with more talk of the greyhound industry. Elliot was talking about the coursing tradition and the re-population of hares. He was quick to assure Emily that the track board of management had a retirement fund for greyhounds. They did a lot of stuff around greyhound welfare, more than the public knew for sure.

'These headbanging track protesters never get their facts straight, a waste of time trying put facts to dogmatic activists.'

It was fascinating to Emily though she was still distracted by the conversation her and Mark had just shared.

Siobhan decided to make sure that everyone knew about Emily's success.

'She made a right few quid, our Emily.' She'd let Mark assume that she hadn't succeeded and was now exposed; he had only witnessed her two losing races.

'How did it go with Arthur?' Elliot suddenly remembered. 'Did he make you an offer?'

'Not now, Elliot.' But Brian had overheard the question.

'Go on what did he offer?' Brian was keen to know. Mark hesitated not wanting to sound precocious in front of Emily.

'I didn't let him make an offer; he couldn't have matched what was on the table from the T&E crowd.'

'You're joking, Mark? I'm delighted.' Brian was over the moon.

'I think Arthur has plans of his own.'

Mark was forced to fill them in on the news, and naturally, Brian was the one with the most questions. He would have jumped at an opportunity like that, he told them. His friends were aware of that; they were privately outraged by the fact that there were no opportunities in this God forsaken country for him to hold onto, qualified or not.

Another batch of mudslides was thrown together, and the party went into full swing, all of them losing themselves to the music, lowering their potent mocha milkshakes and waving their arms in the air. It was a good half hour of madness before the first of them fell onto the sofa in a sweat, at which stage it was getting late, time for them to lower the sounds. Elliot was being vigilant.

Copious amounts of alcohol were demolished as they gathered on the sofa and floor in a semi-circle. Brian was chatting more about life in Australia and what might await him on his return. He told them about a favourite haunt of his, a cool cafe where they turned out new dishes every week; the staff gave out the recipes to anyone who was interested. It was niche in that way, besides they had live bands there on a Friday night, and it served the very best German beer. Australia had given Brian a real love of cookery, and he was sorry he hadn't cooked for the gang while he was at home, although under the circumstance he could be excused.

The gang were in high spirits; they were going to miss Brian all over again, they wanted to know everything about his new life. The park beside his apartment was teaming with wildlife. Watching critters come and go, it was a hobby of his now; they laughed hard at the idea of him watching birds. He had an extensive circle of friends there. They weren't supportive in the way that his Irish friends were, you had to be standing on your own two feet over there. There was very limited sharing of woes in Australia.

His mother and sister, Marian and Sarah, they were okay with his decision to return to Australia. If he was happy so were they. With the economic difficulties in Ireland, he just didn't have the luxury of staying. He had Melisa to fall back on though, and she could be a strong guiding force that way, he knew that she'd be looking out for him.

He was coming back for Sarah's wedding, and all of them, the whole gang were going to be invited to his sister's big day. He'd be bringing Melisa home with him, Alfie too, that was if he could drag him away from the mirror. Alfie was notorious for his love of all things Alfie.

As the night drew to a close, Oden and Lucile were the first to say their goodbyes. They both had assignments to work on tomorrow, they had enjoyed themselves, but it was time to call it a night. Brian asked if it was okay to crash in the spare room and Mark offered to see Emily home.

There was heartfelt emotion as Mark and Brian hugged. Mark brought up the point that it wouldn't be long before he was home for his sister's wedding. Besides, they would most definitely be on Skype before the week was out.

As Elliot closed the door after them, whispering goodnight, Mark turned to Emily. 'Looks as if we're back where we started out.'

'I don't know, we're friends now,' she elaborated.

'I appreciate that, but know that I want more...'

He wasn't sure where that came from, but it was out there now. The truth standing between them like a pair of old knickers on a washing line, waiting for a gust of wind. There was no point in holding back anymore, Emily knew as well as he did that his feelings were growing.

'I don't do more, Mark.'

'You could leave that up to me.'

'Again, I don't know how to.' Emily attempted to balance herself on the steps. 'I don't want a relationship with anyone, nor do I want something casual. I just want to work and be at peace. I want to be myself without having to try to second guess what's going on in someone else's head, Mark. Is that so wrong?'

Mark swept his hand along her arm and gently took her wrist.

Our Diligent Souls

'You know me long enough now to know that I'm respectful?'

They had barely reached the end of the steps when the lights in Elliot and Siobhan's went out.

'I can leave you home, and we can arrange to have dinner together during the week, we can do twenty dates before this has to go anywhere. In saying that, you're never off my mind. They know it, I know it... The sad truth is I want the world to know it too.'

'See that's what I don't want.'

He was nothing if not persistent. 'I can do restrained. Are you tired?'

'Yes and no? No, not yet!'

'Let's get a taxi back to mine.' He suggested, 'we can have tea and toast and talk. Unless. Do you want to go somewhere? I have wine in the flat.'

'I'll go back to your place, but only to talk; we can listen to music, maybe tea? We're friends, Mark. Tonight doesn't go any deeper. I'm not sure you get that, but you need to and sooner rather than later.

With their senses on high alert, it was as if a distant universe had answered their call. They both turned to the sound of a car splashing through a puddle; it was a taxi. They laughed and ran to catch it.

'To my place?'

'Yeah to yours, mine's in a right state.'

'That's no problem then.'

They didn't say a word on the way over. He paid for the taxi, and within minutes they were inside trying to get warm. He turned on the central heating to take the chill out of the room. Having lifted her coat, he threw her an enormous woolly jumper and put on the kettle, taking a pan of bread out to make toast. She sat on the chair, not the sofa, thinking that he might take the chair facing her. First, he made her a cup of tea, and a large stack of golden brown toast smothered with butter. He grabbed her a few cushions for her back and a throw to place over her knees. He was glad to note that she felt comfortable enough to slip off her shoes.

'I normally hold back.' He announced. 'I have never chased a woman; I'm not used to having to lay my emotions out in front of someone. I've never told anyone that I was keen on them before.'

'Manly hah?'

'Don't be at it.' He smiled; it was something she'd say alright.

'You weren't pushy; I understand you just want to make your feelings known but feelings are fleeting, Mark. When you let the notions pass you, you'll find that very few feelings have substance; life is fundamentally superficial.'

'What I'm feeling has substance, Emily; it has energy and a will of its own, it's not even close to what I've experienced with other women.'

'That's very romantic but to place that on me is hardly fair, one step at a time, Mark.'

On one level she wanted him, he could sense that, but there was something significant in the way. Tonight, she needed to talk, to explain herself to him and he was initially flattered.

As she spoke, he started to realise that this peculiar asexual ideology did exist. This asexual orientation that Elliot had described was deeply rooted. From what he could fathom it started and ended with Emily's parents. It wasn't that they were devout Christians or anything of the sort, agnostics was how Emily described them. Being without a family was not easy. She had loved both her parents when they were alive. Emily proudly recalled the pleasant memories of her childhood. She missed the closeness of her family and the quirky form of independence that they shared.

Emily relayed what that meant as a family in practical terms. She had found it nowhere else, then or since. Both parents worked separately in different countries and met up to collaborate as a married couple on Emily's development. They met up to spend time with her.

'How odd was it that they were driving somewhere in the same car when they were killed?' Emily asked. She had only ever known them to drive separate cars, except for the very odd occasion.

She had been supervised by nannies before she went to boarding school and had travelled the world with these women. She met with her parents once a fortnight, then once a month as time went on. It might have looked odd to other people, but it was exciting for her.

The time between visits grew longer, she admitted. It was just part of their relationship, creating a bond that was unique to her. She'd never seen her parents be physically affectionate with each other. Except when she had seen them dance together once at a wedding that she was invited too; she had gone with them to the event, rather than with her nanny.

The nannies changed every six months, a new nanny always capable, always kind. It was a terrific life they had given her, she never wanted for a single thing, even at boarding school; she only had to ask. In the summers when she was not at boarding school, her nannies were more like temporary confidants. They were there for companionship as they toured around Europe, meeting up with her parents at different events and locations.

When she was younger, Emily travelled where she pleased, and by times when she'd run out of places to visit, these nannies made a point of taking her to the most impressive locations they could find. They never took her home to meet their families, but that went without saying. They were on six-month contracts, never the same nanny twice but they were there at her disposal twenty-four seven. Her parents didn't want her sitting at home in a virtually empty house though she was never a handful.

When Emily was with her parents, she felt fulfilled and interesting. Those occasions went beyond her expectations; her parents were always insightful. Over dinner, her mother would talk about the countries she'd been to, her parents hadn't always been to these places together, but it was still in a sense a shared experience. 'My mother would let us know what show or opera she'd seen while she was away.'

There were musicians her mother had always respected, some of them she finally got to meet. She talked about books she had read books that had captured her imagination, and her father was the same, he loved to read. Vivid and relevant, they were just as interested in Emily's experiences. They wanted to know just about everything in respect of her friendships, the places she had been to, and the subjects she was studying. It was a life that she remembered very clearly, real and unwavering, a world that she very much missed.

'A lot of it sounds amazing Emily, but is it fair to say they were completely detached?' Mark responded, 'from each other and you.'

'I guess that was their lesson,' Emily replied.

'But what did it teach you... how to live alone for the rest of your life?'

'Mark? No. They taught me independence, how to follow my dreams.'

Mark felt sheer frustration, to him it all sounded repugnant and no way to bring up a child. 'Follow your dreams okay but to what end?'

'They died together.' There was a long silence as Emily stared into her cup, wanting to wipe away her last sentence. 'No,' she pulled him back. 'Look, they made good money, they bought a nice house, which they left to me and from the proceeds I bought my home in the city. They made good money touring and enjoyed spending it, on my care, on their lifestyles, on mine, why not?'

Mark was at once filled with empathy.

'What did they do, Emily?'

'My father was a foreign affairs journalist and my mother a classical musician; they were top of their profession.'

'But when were they there for you, was it enough to fit you into their schedule?'

'We had amazing adventures, they could afford these things, and they loved me, and they loved what they did. It worked for us.'

'You're not getting what I'm saying here, Emily.'

'No, I'm not sure that I am.' There was another dramatic pause. 'Go on?' She insisted.

'Where is your life going, is love just an afterthought to you? It's going to keep passing you by if that's what you've been reared for.'

'No. Don't you get it? I want to achieve as much as they did, out of my career as a songwriter. They would expect that of me. I want to make records with people. I want to travel the world and achieve the same standard of excellence.'

'But they sound so dispassionate? Do you want the same relationship that they had?'

'How do they sound dispassionate?'

'To allow you to love and be loved, it's worth so much more than any career.'

'I don't know about that?'

'No, I don't know that you do!' Mark retorted harshly.

From the stories that she told Mark, he came to realise that her parents were virtual strangers. Mark was bursting with sadness for her; he was overwhelmed. That was why she was so distant and reserved. He would be the very opposite in a relationship with her. He found it impossible to be reserved with the people he loved.

As he listened, it was transparent to him that there was a darker side to her parents' relationship. He was soon to realise that it was one that Emily had not even considered. The more she talked, the more he realised how impossible it was going to be for Emily and him to come together. The grief of it laid heavy on him. With Emily, he couldn't tell if she'd ever find someone to fill the vacuum of the void she had been left with, the missed adventures, the longing to arrive at the same plateau that her parents reached.

'Do you think that they were happy together as a couple or was it just show? Were they together as a couple?'

Emily was genuinely shocked. She unconsciously reached to protect her throat, appearing bereft. Mark moved in beside her and took her hand as she attempted to smile, but it didn't reach her eyes.

'That is a question I never thought or dared to ask myself, not even in the darkest corners of my mind,' her response was breathless, but her words were faithful.

He left her alone in the quiet of his room while he retreated to the kitchen. Returning moments later he put on some light music, she made easy work of the tea and toast, but she was barely able to keep her eyes open. He insisted that she stay the night, and she agreed. Taking clean sheets from the hot press, he made up his bed; he took a few minutes to process what she had just shared. By the time he got back, she was asleep in the armchair, the tips of her socks peeping out from under the blanket.

He listened to the music which had been on low since they arrived. He didn't want to stir Emily from her slumber, she looked to be out cold, it had been a long day for her from what she'd said, but the armchair was too uncomfortable to sleep on all night. He moved closer to her, got down on his hunkers and called her name twice, but she made no response. He sat back to weigh up the situation before eventually lifting her into his arms.

She was warm and malleable as her sleepy arm wrapping around his shoulder. He carried her to his room. Sweaty strands of hair were pressed against her cheek; she was more desirable than ever, more fragile than he had ever imagined. She appeared to accept his idea of him carrying her, her eyes remained closed, her body cocooned in his jumper and blanket.

As they rounded the bed, she moved her face up under his chin to kiss his neck with wanting. A coldness ran through him as he stood there, his eyes closed as he searched for the strength to hold back. The temptation to be with her was great; he leaned in and placed her gently on his sheets before covering her to her shoulders with his quilt. He bent over and kissed her on her forehead. She rustled under his quilt aware of his presence as he watched on, thinking for a moment before he made his way to the sitting room sofa. He closed the door behind him quietly. Her heart was racing as she opened her eyes, curling her hand round the top of the quilt as she stared into the darkness of his room.

    In the sitting room, he lay awake knowing the degree of healing that Emily would need. There was no immediate fix for the life she'd been left with, she had no family at all to adhere to, she was neither loved and received by a relative on a regular basis. He could take her out for wine and dinner but for the meantime, nothing more. She was searching for a way back to her folks, a way to connect on their level. That much she had made plain. He had never contemplated what it was to be entirely without family.

    The desperate longing for her parents, the broken shield that she hid behind, it was more significant than any love he could offer. The urgency in him, the gravitational pull to be with her, it was gone. A more in-depth understanding was starting to strengthen his resolve. He would become a more devoted friend. He needed to put her before his own selfish reasoning; already he could feel the shift.

Chapter 26

Mark and Emily grew close over the coming months. The relationship between them never matured into anything physical. To Emily, Mark was more like an amiable ex-boyfriend. She was comfortable with how he treated her, he never tried to change her ways but helped her to follow her passion for music. They laughed a great deal and never took themselves too seriously.

Mark had convinced himself that a romantic relationship between them was never going to be workable. He knew he could not do detached and distant with her if they were to get involved. He would have opted at one stage for something casual and light, but that was never her thing either. She needed a relationship that she could be a hundred percent with before she got involved, something that grew over an extended period through friendship.

In saying that, Emily's deep-seated dreams were of a committed long-distance relationship; she was steadfast in her ambitions; she was looking for a childless, career orientated future. Her goal was to reach the dizzy heights of her parent's success, from there pertaining the ability and freedom to work outside the conventional family constraints; for her, it was all she knew.

Understanding her deep-rooted family agenda had broken the spell, Mark's yearnings and dreams being based on something entirely more organic and down to earth. The night she had made advances by kissing him on the neck, he was wise not having reacted, he had for large part convinced himself of that.

She'd been stripped of a family under tragic circumstances and was still fearful of yet another loss. He enjoyed her company far and above anyone else's but her need for an unordinary life was understandable, in life he understood that there were no guarantees. She could not wipe clean the unique perspective that she'd developed through her childhood.

Having listened to her recordings, Mark convinced her to release equity in her home. It was time that she started to invest in herself. Emily gave up the waitressing job and cut back her hours in the law firm to focus in on her song-writing. She didn't hang around; booking extra studio time once she had musicians in place.

Our Diligent Souls

The Songdoor Songwriters Contest was an extraordinary opportunity that was coming up soon. She was entering as many song-writing competitions as possible. There were plenty of opportunities to make a go of things, but Songdoor stood out to her as the big one. There was money to be made in getting the finished song to the right musician, but first, she needed leverage. She required singers that could emulate her work.

She had quiet concerns when it came to her songs, writing the lyrics on one level though over time their meaning evolved, sometimes changing the essence of what she wanted to convey. In saying that, it was too easy to be overly concerned. Thinking too intensely had stifled her development as a songwriter on numerous occasions.

Work was going well for Mark. Joyce was back to form sooner than expected. Mark worked with him most mornings and then took to the sales room in the afternoon to hunt out new clients. The two men operated well together, allowing them to reap substantial rewards for the company. When Christmas arrived, Mark was only too delighted to fill his pockets with the fruits of his labour. He obtained a hefty sum in the end-of-year share of the company profits.

He had been out with Elliot on their regular Friday night venture to the pub and had attracted the attention of some beautiful women, but something had changed in him. He appeared to have completely lost interest in the opposite sex. He was quieter in himself, talking on a much deeper level about global atrocities and the fundamentals of family and friends. He had less to say about work and did not refer to the concerts he'd attended with Emily or the restaurants they had visited.

He had booked time off work from St. Stephen's Day to the second of January as Emily had agreed to let him travel with her over the holiday season. She spent Christmas day at Elliot and Siobhan's place while Mark returned home to his parents. The following morning, both met at Dublin airport and took a flight to Marrakech.

Emily and Mark were excited about the prospect of time away from the daily grind. While the two of them were abroad, they weren't aware that Arthur had died. Mark, not knowing that he had passed, missed the funeral. They were on their long-awaited adventure; the idea that someone might die in that space of time was so far-fetched in their minds.

Elliot was waiting at the airport when they got in, he had tried to call them during the week but couldn't connect, and no messages were received on Mark or Emily's phone. It was odd. After giving Mark the news, Elliot drove him over to Arthur's' house, dropping Emily off on the way. Mark was met by Arthur's bereft son; the son that both Arthur and he had talked about on previous occasions.

He was brutally hostile and sharp enough to let Mark know that in his opinion, his father had died heartbroken as a result of selling up his business. The onus of this was firmly placed on Mark's shoulders. Mark hadn't heard that Arthur had sold up shop and yet Arthur's son knew that he had refused to even look at Arthur's offer to return to the factory.

The depth of Mark's loss brought about a sense of guilt that set fast. It would later prove impossible for him to lift. It had been three months since he'd seen Arthur at the dog track and unbeknownst to him, Arthur had sold up that very week.

Arthur's son was bitter, near fuming as he vented his remaining strength onto Mark. It was envy that surged from the boy's lips though Mark didn't recognise it for what it was. Arthur had been close to Mark and barely been there for his son.

Something changed in Mark after that conversation. It weighed heavier than grief. As time went on, he was less confident in his relationships, shutting people out entirely as his work became his sole purpose in life. He was rarely available, Elliot and Siobhan, they felt the full force of it as did Emily. The man was hurting, but moreover, he was suffering profound remorse, the secret kind that is hard to flitter away.

In his eyes, he had put the weight of his wallet before his loyalties. He convinced himself that Arthur would still be alive if he had returned to the factory; the knowledge of this was eating away at him. He bore full responsibility for Arthur's death, revisiting their last conversations repeatedly. He could find no reason to let go of his anguish. Arthur had been a second father to him. He couldn't focus on relationships when he might just as quickly betray again.

His excuses for not showing up for dinner or drinks became plentiful, to a point where he became unreachable. Siobhan, Emily and Elliot were at odds about what do. Brian, they discovered was in the same boat, he couldn't get Mark on the phone, and when he did, Mark was distant.

There was one hopeful date in the future. Emily had been short-listed for the Songdoor competition. They were airing a few contestants on the Late Late Show, and she was given a slot. Managing to get her hands on three tickets for the event, she called into the shipping company in the hope that he could not refuse her face to face.

When he saw her walk through the door, it was all he could do but not fall to his knees. Instantly conflicted, he needed to send her packing when all he wanted was to cry openly in her arms.

'I'm way too busy, Emily. I have work.'

'You put me in this position. You got me to give up waitressing, did you not? You got me to release equity in my property and chase my dreams. Now, when I land this enormous opportunity, you're not going to be there to support me? I don't think so, Mark.'

'You have to understand...'

'What I understand is that you're closing us out, the people that care about you. You can't go on beating yourself up over what you think you should have done. When someone gives you the gift of friendship and then turns their back on you, it hurts. Honestly, Mark, you can't keep isolating yourself.'

Mark kept his eyes on the ground, unable to look at her. He wanted to tell her how deep the pain went, how hopeless he believed he was when it came to relationships now. How he was only capable of hurting people, especially those, he loved.

'This is a big opportunity for me. Hear me when I say, I've worked my backside off to make this song happen. Promise me you'll be there. Promise me, Mark? Elliot and Siobhan will pick you up on their way.'

'I'll do my best.'

'No Mark, I want you to swear. You have to do that much for me, do you not?'

'I can't; I cannot be there for you, Emily.'

'I'm not accepting that. Are you trying to crush me?'

'Okay then. Okay.'

Joyce was listening on the sidelines. He had suspected something was wrong, but he hadn't been aware that there were issues to that extent. Mark had mentioned that Arthur had died, and Joyce knew that they'd been close, but Mark's friendships had always been vital to him. He no longer took time out from work; he'd been obsessively driven, steadily raising the barometer.

Mark had taken to working late on a Friday night, where before Christmas he had always ventured to the pub with Elliot. When Emily left, she was visibly relieved, satisfied by Mark's agreement to join her and their friends on this night out. That much Joyce had over-heard. He moved in and stood beside Mark, their eyes following her steps as she quietly left the building.

'You've been going at this full throttle for I don't know how long, Mark. All work and no play, it's counterproductive.' It was then that Mark turned to look at him. 'It isn't good for you, Mark. There's something that's got into your head that you need to address, for your own sake.'

'I'm fine.' Mark shot back at him.

Joyce could see the state he was in just then.

'We need friends and family, Mark, you know this, come hell or high water you can't do this alone. It's a sad enough world as it is. You've got to put an end to this.'

Mark was frustrated, Joyce's remarks were compelling; he could raise no argument. He struggled to carry on working as the day wore on, the thought of having to attend this event made him increasingly anxious.

Mark called his parents and arranged to visit them on Friday evening. He let Joyce know he would be leaving early that day. At home, his father would try to assist. Mark knew he needed to at least weigh up the issue with somebody; the guilt was worsening. Maybe there he could find some relief.

On Friday evening, the family were sitting down to tea when Mark arrived in off the train. A foil covered plate was prepared for him, and a place at the table was laid where a fresh pot of tea was being poured. Mark was far from his regular, jovial self, his expression strained. His mum and dad, Breda and Andrew, they caught each other's eyes while he examined the food in front of him.

'How was your journey, son?'

'Yeah, it was fine.'

His mum was keeping the atmosphere light before slipping out to leave her husband and son to talk. 'I have to nip out. I'm going to leave the dishes as they are. See you in a half hour or so.' Mark's mum smiled, before kissing her husband on the forehead, she took off closing the door behind her.

'Work's okay then?'

Mark looked up at his old man. 'Yeah, that's going fine.'

'And the gang, are they doing okay?' Andrew asked.

Mark again went quiet. He finished up his apple tart and washed it down with the last of his tea. Although his appetite hadn't been up to much lately, there was nothing that would stop him eating his mum's apple tart, and she knew it.

'I haven't seen much of anyone dad, to be honest.'

'How come?'

'I'm not feeling the May West this past while.'

'It's been nearly four months since you visited son, and you've been hard to get on the phone. We're aware that there's a problem of sorts.'

'Arthur died.'

'You did tell us that. So what else is it?'

'I did what suited me. Arthur sold up his business. He was a worker, dad.'

'So, what is it? Do you think that giving up work finished him off health wise?'

'I wish I had gone back there.'

'Now hold on a minute, son. You can't hold yourself responsible for Arthur's death. I know he meant the world to you, but he had a heart condition in the end. That was what took him, son. I'm not wrong.'

'That job was what kept him ticking over, dad. That job alone. You didn't know Arthur in the way I did.'

'So, are you saying that you should have refused the pay rise with this other company and stuck with him for a lesser sum?'

'I am, dad.'

'Maybe, that's a mistake you made?'

'He had an offer for me that I didn't even hear out. I was too preoccupied with myself. I saw dollar signs and that was my only consideration. He sold the business the following week.'

'We're none of us without our flaws, Mark, none of us. If he finished up dying because of a shift of routine, you could hardly put that on yourself. You're not that important, son. There could have been a million other factors that ran into the mix, his heart condition for one.'

'His son was so angry with me.'

Our Diligent Souls

Andrew, his father, was stern but sincere. 'Maybe, he was angry with himself, Mark. People often experience regret when they lose a loved one. It looks to me like you've been suffering from a heavy case of guilt, unnecessary guilt. It might be time now to put that behind you and open your heart again.'

Mark choked back his tears. Since Arthur's death, he had fought hard against himself. Here now, he felt like a wounded young boy who was longing to be held.

'We love you, son, but taking responsibility for your actions is part of growing up. It appears to me that you've been doing a lot of that lately. You need to let yourself off the hook and start celebrating the man's life. He had a good life, and I know you have lots of happy memories of him. If the situation were reversed, he'd be celebrating your life. He was a wise man.'

'I think I've been letting grief take hold of me. I don't want to cause any more pain.'

'Have you spent time with Elliot, Siobhan and the crew?'

'Very little, I feel too guilty.'

'You may have hurt a few feelings in doing that. They're good friends, Mark?'

'They are...It's just, well. I've not been in the form to have too much fun lately. I've been angry with myself, moving on has been unthinkable.'

'See if you can lift yourself out of it, son. Otherwise, you might need to talk to a doctor. There are tablets they can give you. It might help distance you from these unnecessary regrets, help you get back on your feet.'

Mark listened to his dad talk. The sound of his father's voice had always been a comfort to him. It was good to be home, and Andrew was right, his son needed to pull up his socks and grow a pair. Otherwise, he could be looking at developing mental health issues down the line.

Mark stayed on for the weekend, helping Breda in the garden and the allotment. His mum had become more heavily involved in the idea of growing her fruit and vegetables, but Mark was just glad to find her in good spirits. His sister Moira dropped over, and the two of them talked while his parents took off with her kids. She had long since lacked the innate confidence to walk away from the issues that brought sadness to her life, but for once he could relate.

Our Diligent Souls

He went to the local with his father and relaxed over a few pints and a chat. It felt good. Monday meant work, so he took the train back Sunday night, refusing Andrew's offer of a lift. He felt stronger somehow and contacted Elliot when he got back to arrange that ride to the Late Late Show.

Elliot and Siobhan were only too happy to pick up their friend on the way to the studio. Mark still had his reservations, but this was a big night for Emily. He would do his best not to steal the limelight for the wrong reasons. The three managed to get backstage to wish her well before taking their seats in the audience.

There was a problem with the lead singer. Emily was too caught up in the argument to chat, so they slipped away. It was a big occasion for her, with her song being on the Late Late Show. It was way past halftime when they got the chance to hear the song.

There were two comedians on from the North. It was an insightful interview with the host Ryan Tubridy pulling no punches. He squeezed every ounce of entertainment from the pair and brought to life the fiasco that had been their personal lives. A representative for the Marie Keating cancer organisation was next. She talked about their recent achievements, the where and when of their next fundraising goal.

Another insightful interview but the three amigos were more concerned about the lead singer of Emily's song. In total darkness at the other side of the stage, the band members took their positions. They moved in behind the instruments without a sound. Tubridy then announced the tune.

He briefly mentioned that Emily's had been short-listed for the Songdoor award, praising her for having come this far. The lights went up as they began to play. To Siobhan, Elliot and Mark's complete surprise, it was Emily holding the microphone. The vocalist had backed out at the last minute, forcing Emily to sing the song she wrote.

Siobhan was delighted, but Mark and Elliot were in total shock and genuinely frightened for her as they had never heard her sing before, not ever. Emily's voice was spectacular; it was a whole different ball game with her on the microphone.

They had listened to the pre-recorded version on the way over in the car. Her voice completely lifted the song into another dimension. Finishing without a hitch, Emily basked in the enthusiastic round of applause without as much as a blush on her cheeks.

The host was seriously impressed and called her over to talk for a while, again not scheduled. He introduced her suitably to the audience. Siobhan was smiling ear to ear while Emily explained that she had an extensive portfolio of songs that she had written herself.

'Your voice is superb,' said Tubridy, 'One to watch out for, ladies and gentlemen'.

There was another thunderous round of applause. That was the confidence boost that Emily needed. Maybe now, her songs could be her own, sung by her as only she could sing them.

After the show, the four friends gathered backstage in a huddle. It was the first time in months that Mark had connected with them; he'd been more than missed.

'You were great, your voice is amazing.' Mark stated categorically. 'How did we not know?'

'I didn't want to go out on that stage, not easy folks.' Emily could now let her guard down; she had been undeniably shaken by the run of events.

'So, what happens, if you win the next round of the competition?' Elliot asked.

'I don't know how it works?' Emily was honest; the rules for the competition were complicated enough.

Mark was in complete awe after what he had just heard. 'You were powerful, an incredible song as it stood, but your voice, Emily. You're an even bigger mystery as time goes on.'

They smiled together all four in a circle. It was something else to be back as a team.

Chapter 27

Siobhan and Elliot had arranged to make dinner, and Mark had agreed without argument. Emily was thrilled. They arranged to dine a week from the day of the Late Late Show.

The next few days were busy for Siobhan. She had a dental appointment that she was not looking forward to and a prize-giving ceremony at work. At the event, an old buddy showed up from her boarding school days, a woman who Emily also knew well. Siobhan invited her to join them for dinner, but Elliot wasn't that impressed.

It had been months since he'd had the chance to connect with Mark on any level. She hadn't done him any favours by throwing someone new into the mix. Fortunately, the woman phoned ahead to say that she couldn't make it for dinner. She apologised but asked if she could join them later for drinks. That at least gave Elliot and the others time to help Mark get comfort again.

It was Siobhan's turn to cook this time, but Elliot took charge once the essential jobs were complete. She needed to steal off upstairs to get dressed. Elliot was extremely distracted, it was mid-April and Mark had been off with him since Christmas. They had met once in that time for drinks where before Arthur's passing, it had sometimes been a twice-weekly affair.

Elliot wasn't good with depression if that's what Mark had. He wasn't sure how to speak to him. He was stifled by the fear of saying the wrong thing. He wanted his friend back, but much had happened in the last year. Elliot was coming to terms with the fact that Mark had changed. He was no longer a carefree charmer who was hunting out his place in life. Elliot's life had changed too.

His thoughts on a move to Australia were gathering pace, and he knew something had to give. He had always loved Siobhan, but lately, he wondered more often if there wasn't more to life. He had done his homework in respect of doing a stint in the missions. It was something life-affirming that he needed, something that allowed him to stop feeling as if everything was pre-ordained. He sensed that Siobhan was going through the same, as she never talked about her work at the museum anymore.

Our Diligent Souls

Siobhan slipped into her dress and sat lost for words at the bottom of her bed. It had been a tough few months worrying about Mark, not knowing if he was ever coming back to them. He meant the world to Elliot, and he had been completely lost without his companionship. She needed tonight to work well as did Elliot. They wanted to see Mark back to his old self.

She had worried that Emily might never let someone into her life, but now, she was concerned for Mark too and the fact that he had faced a horrendous time letting go of Arthur. But what could she do, dress up and cook food for them that was it? She looked at herself long and hard in the mirror. It had been tough since Christmas when things were going well.

When Siobhan arrived downstairs, Elliot took her in his arms.

'Everything is done,' he whispered, as they sat back on the sofa. The fire was lit, and there was time to rest a while on his shoulder, time to relax and share a moment.

'Do you think we've changed recently?' She asked Elliot.

'I don't know, sweetheart. I think it's more that everyone is changing around us.'

'Are we at a standstill, Elliot?'

'Uhm...' Elliot kissed her on the forehead. 'You can't make an omelette without cracking an egg.'

'What eggs do you suggest we crack then?'

'Our two heads together might be a start.'

'You're too odd, you.'

'I'm with you years now. Does that not tell you something?'

Elliot and Siobhan hadn't been communicating very well over the past months, even the shortest of conversations sounded stilted. He was preoccupied with the fact that she had stopped consulting with him when she was making arrangements, this friend of hers that she'd invited, was one woman too many when he hadn't got the chance to talk to Mark in months. He missed the lads in Australia and the bonding that transpired when Alfie and Brian were around.

Emily wasn't long arriving. She was joyful when she came through the door. She had changed her mind; she was going be a singer-songwriter after all and give up on employing others to do the job for her, she'd solved a lot in that one decision.

'I never understood why you hid your voice in the first place.' Siobhan chuckled, as she watched her remove her coat.

'Who wanted to sing in that boarding school choir?'

'Fair enough, but you won't believe who is coming over after dinner.'

'Who?'

'Lu'

'Lu from the bike shed?' Emily asked.

The doorbell rang. Elliot left them and made his way to the front door.

'The very same, she hasn't changed a day, she married but never had kids, I'll fill you in later.'

It was Mark, and he looked much more relaxed.

'Mate,' Elliot mumbled, as he threw a bear hug straight at him. 'These two are going to be a handful tonight.' He whispered.

The men glance over at Siobhan and Emily laughing among themselves. They were busy recalling stunts they had pulled at boarding school.

'Hello there, ladies.'

'Hiya, Mark.' They called out in unison.

'Do you want a beer, mate?' Elliot asked, reached for the fridge.

'Sure, that would hit the spot.'

Mark handed over a large bag of allotment veg. It was the last of his father yield from the allotment this year.

'You talked with Andrew then; you saw your dad?'

'I did, and it helped.'

'Good, I'm glad for you, you've been missed.'

There was wine in his bag too and under his arm was a rug he'd brought back from Marrakech. He hadn't thought to drop it over before now.

'That's fantastic, mate. It's very much appreciated.'

'I'm sorry. I'm late bringing it over.'

'Don't even think of it. We'll get the dinner out shortly. The girls have a friend of theirs from boarding school coming over later. Be prepared; we're going to be outnumbered.'

The food was served, and the banter between the four of them was better than it had ever been. Elliot could see new ways in which Mark had changed. He was more settled in himself. Mark was a more sombre individual but content, they could be grateful for the fact that their friend was in reasonably good shape, it appeared that Mark was over the worst of it.

He and Emily talked as though they'd known each other their entire lives. She started in on stories from Marrakech, and their trip on camelback through the desert. They'd shared some great adventures on holidays, and Emily was finally free to relay a few choice situations that they found themselves in, while on tour. They had had a lot of fun.

'I could see the first oasis ahead of us, finally. I can't begin to tell you how I felt when we pass that oasis and then the next, with my legs splayed like a gymnast on this stinking camel.'

It might have been a painful experience, but they had gotten some great laughs out of it. Mark played along. 'Emily took the hump.' She was pleased that he had finally moved beyond Arthur's passing; he had a fresh set of eyes, but as with her losses his outlook on life had been altered.

'Aren't you very funny, Mark.'

Looking back to when she had first met him, he was a different person in so many ways. Even his looks had altered slightly; he held himself differently, his giddy demeanour had been replaced with an energy that was more refined.

Siobhan's food was as always delicious, wild salmon and fresh vegetables, with a Tarte Tatin to finish. Emily was glowing with excitement. Mark had made an impact in her life, her every expression was an acknowledgement of that.

There was no pretence, no masked emotions; they were in complete acceptance of each other. It was more than amicable, this love between them, Siobhan and Elliot touched hands beneath the linen cloth as their two friends operated in sync with one another.

Realising that the Christmas tradition of having Irish coffees had been missed, Elliot offered to make some up and no one refused. There was so much to catch up on that Emily feared it might justify the separation to him and allow Mark to keep them at arm's length again. But he picked up on her reservation and assured her that he was glad to back where he'd left off. He was looking forward to getting back into his regular Friday night out with Elliot and all the rest.

Our Diligent Souls

The logs were burning on the fire when they moved to the sofa. They were surprised when the bell rang, having forgotten entirely about their late-night visitor.

'It's Laura.' Siobhan whispered, headed for the door.

'Laura who?' Mark asked.

'Lu, Laura Turner.' Emily answered quietly. 'She was at the same boarding school as us. We were in the same year. She's a gas ticket.' Emily explained to the men.

Mark turned wild-eyed to Elliot, who looked puzzled by his reaction.

'You know her?' He interjected.

Mark nodded his head, laughing.

Laura arrived in her usual refinery, confident and cuddle-worthy at the same time, and boy did the girls cuddle. Mark waited for her eyes to catch his.

'Mark,' she uttered, as she fell back a step, 'I can't believe you're here. It's been a while.'

Siobhan and Emily were baffled. 'How do the two of you know each other, huh?' Siobhan insisted on knowing.

Mark needed to clarify the situation as both Emily and Siobhan were beyond curious. Laura shook her head in amusement.

'Work, we met at the restaurant where Emily worked. It was on that first night with Ralph Mournaghan.' He stated.

'But I was there that night?' Emily needed to decipher what he was saying.

Mark laughed as he tried to elaborate. 'Laura came later. I think you were gone.'

'Emily? You were waitressing there?' Laura stood aghast. 'Emily waitressing?' She asked as she turned to Laura.

Elliot stepped in to question, 'You were married?'

'I was... I'm widowed now.'

He gulped humorously as he stepped aside, alive with anticipation. 'Holy hell! Do you fancy an Irish coffee?'

'I'd love one.' Laura replied. She handed over a bottle of champagne that she had brought with her to celebrate the occasion.

'I happened to watch the Late Late show the other night; I nearly fell off the sofa. How did you keep that voice a secret, it took some doing in that boarding school I can tell you?'

'This is too weird for me?' Siobhan exclaimed. 'So how do you know Mark again?'

'Laura was dating my supervisor Ralph Mournaghan.'

'Never!' The words spat out of Laura's mouth. 'Who fed you that line?'

'Ralph.'

'And you believed him?'

'I'm confused now, Laura.' Siobhan knew enough to know that Ralph Mournaghan was one rotten egg.

Mark was not surprised. 'I met you at that charity event, remember? That's when Ralph told me you were going out with him.'

'I never went out with Ralph Mournaghan. Are we clear on that yet?'

'Steady on girl!' Mark was beside himself laughing.

'I'm not a girl, Mark. I'm a woman, and women have needs...'

Emily chuckled, Laura, holding out her hand as she watched Elliot approach from the kitchen, 'never needed a Ralph Mournaghan, thank you.'

'Your Irish coffee,' Elliot declared in good humour, carefully passed over the hot glass.

They shared some great laughs for the hour that followed. Emily was thrilled to see her old friend. It had been five years at least. There was so much news to get through, and the women were gobbling up every word, that same thrill of undiluted pleasure from years back was still there. It was a long way back to boarding school.

'I have to go, Laura.' Emily finally admitted. 'You won't believe it, but I have a nine o'clock doctor's appointment in the morning.' She didn't want to leave.

'Ah stay! You can't head off yet.' Siobhan pleaded so Emily stayed.

Laura sat next to Mark, and Emily kneeled at their feet. Elliot filled their glasses and made his way to the kitchen. He wanted to get ahead of the dishes, beckoning Siobhan over to join him.

'Leave them to it for a while.' He whispered.

Our Diligent Souls

The music was low, and they made sure not to clank any of the pots and pans, washing up carefully as if there was a baby in the next room. Emily and Laura continued to fill each other in on their adventures. There were a few witty remarks thrown in by Mark, though for the most part he was just spellbound by their summaries.

They talked about how Laura had met Stephen and how memorable the wedding was. Laura was brief in covering his passing as the conversation swiftly moved to the card business. Mark wanted to hear more of their girlish tales from boarding school. They were villains the three of them. Siobhan quickly joined them to give her end of the story. There came the point where Emily had to go, she made no fuss and went to the door once they'd swapped numbers.

Elliot sat down beside the two remaining guests on the sofa. Siobhan pulled up a chair, she wasn't long filling Laura in on the twists and turns that Emily's life had recently taken. She was making headway as a singer-songwriter now. They explained how the Late Late show circumstance had forced her to sing, giving her the confidence to continue down that road and thank goodness for that.

Mark couldn't help but interrupt the flow of their conversation. He needed to know how she'd fared out. 'So how did the business investment go? Did you sell the card business in the end?'

'You still don't know?' Laura replied.

'Know what?'

'How can I tell you this?'

'What? Laura, come on with yah!'

'I bought into another shipping company with my father?'

'Why worry, why be afraid of telling me that?'

'It was Arthur's business that we bought, Mark.'

'Okay. I didn't see that coming. I did see you at the dog track that night. I hadn't put that together.'

'Promise me you'll listen to me without going off the deep end?'

'Go on?'

'I'd better start at the beginning.' She stalled for a minute. 'The value of Arthur's business was primarily based on his list of clients. You never shared Arthur's client list to gain leverage or get results at T&E.'

'That would have been entirely unethical.'

'Many a man gets corrupted, Mark. Look, you got results in that place by working hard and pulling more out of your floor staff, that I discovered. Arthur knew you'd never sell him out. There was never any doubt of that.'

'We had a strong relationship; I was always a worker.' Mark returned.

'T&E is run by shareholders primarily, not my father, be aware of that in hearing this. The management at T&E wanted Arthur's client list which was why they were inclined to employ you in the first place. It was Ralph Mournaghan's idea to take you on. It was after meeting you that my father put two and two together.' Mark was intrigued.

'Mournaghan had realised that you weren't going to give them what they wanted. Another plan of Mournaghan's that fell foul. T&E tried to buy Arthur's place out from under him, but he was having none of it. He blankly refused to sell to them, but he knew my father, they were both self-starters in the industry at one point, and Arthur had long since respected him. He offered to sell it to my father and me as an independent concern. On his terms, mind you.'

'Which were?'

'He had planned to offer you forty-nine percent of his annual profit to run the business. He had investigated T&E profits and knew that they could afford to pay you the equivalent. If my father could make that happen for you at T&E, only then would Arthur consider selling him his business. You had already threatened to leave after that worker got injured.'

'Wow! You knew that.' Mark was shocked.

'But it didn't end there. Arthur made the proviso that his staff had to be kept on under the same wage conditions, and salary progressions that he had committed to with them.'

'Clever man. He was no dowser, Arthur.' Mark was excited to hear more.

'Uhm...' She still had lots to say.

'Arthur never let on,' Mark mumbled, stunned as he began to put together what she was saying.

'He knew that your accomplishments merited that scale of salary, being that they were a much bigger firm.'

'I need to take that in, Laura.' Mark was a little lost.

'He didn't want you to know of the agreement. He got what was considered an ambitious deal; later we learnt that he had a serious heart condition that was forcing him into retirement anyway. If you had gone back to work with him and he had died, his family may have been forced to foreclose. For a fraction of what he acquired.'

'His son hates me, I was away; I didn't even make it to the funeral.'

'Arthur loved you, Mark. He and his family would have got a fifty-one percent profit share at the end of each year if you had gone back. Not the lump sum he acquired, not a proper inheritance that he could watch them enjoy.'

'I knew he cared but to that extent, I don't know what to do with this information.'

'He worked with me for an hour or two every day, showing me the ropes. He was so keen to fill me with stories of how much humour you brought to the place. I understand that his son's not a business person. He told me that his son was envious in the way he spoke of you, that was Arthur's fault.'

'I didn't even know he had sold up the business.'

'He wanted it kept quiet, especially when it came to you. He wanted you to know that you had earned that pay raise off your own back, which you had. Arthur made the point that T&E should have been aware of your value in respect of the advances you'd made with your floor staff and that he was more than willing to take you on and pay more than a nominal rate. He made real the fact that they could lose you if they didn't up their game.'

'He was a shark, Arthur?'

'He was when he needed to be.' Laura quipped. 'T&E would never have paid you that salary had your work not have completely justified it. They'd taken advantage of you long enough to be scared.'

'So, you own Arthur's place now?' Mark asked.

'I do, but I'm still learning, and besides, I'm hanging out with your old mates. It's wild that we've met here of all places. We will most likely at a later stage become a subsidiary of T&E. We're at an early stage for that yet.'

'That's astonishing.'

'It sure is.' She agreed.

'You must feel better?' Siobhan whispered, 'about Arthur now.' She reached for Mark's shoulder.

'I guess I do,' he said when Siobhan stretched over and hugged him.

'What's been going on here?' Laura asked, but there was no comment.

As Mark climbed down the steps to their home that night, he had an actual bounce in his step, it was lashing rain, but he didn't care. He lifted his collar and turned to face his journey home when a voice called out from behind him.

'Here, you...' Mark looked back. 'Scumbag!'

There was a heavy-set man fast approaching with a malicious intention in his strides. It was the sum of what Mark could take in through the rain when he realised that it was Ralph Mournaghan. Out of nowhere, Mournaghan caught up, took a grip on his shoulder and turning him around, kneeing him full force in the groin. Mark gasped for air as he buckled over, trying to catch his breath. He could barely believe it; they were seconds from Elliot's house.

'I thought I was following you home. This was meant to happen at your place. Here is as good a place as any.'

'What now?' Mark groaned. The shock alone was enough to knock him off his feet. He hadn't seen Mournaghan since before the night at the greyhound track, month's back.

'What are you doing mixing with the likes of Laura Turner? What you're a hot-shot now? Look at you!'

Mark was still doubled over in pain.

Mark looked up, and his face immediately spat in it. Mournaghan had a crowbar jammed in his belt and was able to free it as Mark wiped the phlegm from his face.

'You're a nobody; you came from nothing in the first place. You will remain a nobody, you hear me, fool.'

'What the hell? What is this about, why?' Mark retorted.

'Cheeky!' Mournaghan quipped as he leant forward. He gripped Mark's face again with his left hand, steering the man's focus back to Elliot and Siobhan's front door. 'You don't want to put your little friends in jeopardy now, do you?'

Mark push him away before jumping to his feet to lash out with a robust blow to Ralph's chest. But the man could take it. It had been years since

Our Diligent Souls

Mark had been called to this. He was thoroughly emasculated, his punch falling short though he intended to do damage. A second jab knocked Mournaghan's head back, full force with a crack, yet he had returned unaffected.

He gripped Mark by the neck, twisted him and raised the crowbar to pound it across the back of his legs. Lifting the bar again to trash his right arm and then again on the same spot as Mark fell knees first onto the pavement. His body retched with pain as he landed on his hands and knees.

'What do you want, Ralph?' Mark cried out, barely capable of speech. He just couldn't take it in.

Mournaghan leant over and took a grip on Mark's jacket. Pulling him close as he slobbered into his ear, he was breathless himself.

'That young woman that left before you, she looked as if she could do with a right seeing to, I know I'd give her one.'

'Get off me.' Mark hollered, but Ralph had a tight grip. He was talking about Emily, Mark realised, dazed.

'That would give her a healthy perspective on the future, yeah?'

'You're pure fecking evil!' Mark yelled as he was straining to free himself.

Mournaghan let go of his grip as Mark swayed in disbelief; his head limp, his lungs gasping for air.

'What do you want?' Everything in Mark was crying out.

'I want you to stay away from Laura Turner for one.'

'You've changed your mind... on that count then?' Mark was breathless, but he managed to respond sarcastically.

Mournaghan brought the crowbar down full force on his back. Mark's spin curled like a bow, his head rising, his vision blurring as the blow shot blood from his mouth. With Mark again on the wet ground, Mournaghan pushed him over using his foot and waited for him to look up.

'Do you know what I want yet?'

Mark attempted a nod. Mournaghan kicked hard with yet another blow, this time Mark yelled out in agony.

'Stay out of my business, stay out of it and away from her, is that clear? Keep your nose out of my affairs period.' He raised the crowbar again. 'Yes?'

'Yes!' Mark shouted.

'We're good with that then?' Mournaghan mocked. There was silence. 'Do I have to repeat myself?'

'I hear you barking'.' Mark replied sharply.

Mournaghan lowered the crowbar and took off, tossing the crowbar as he went. Mark was left stumbling around attempting to get up on his feet. It was still pouring rain. In the corner of his eye, Mark watched on as Mournaghan got into a car and drove off, revving up his engine as he passed.

Mark pulled out a tissue that he had in his pocket and shook the blood from his hands, wiping his mouth. Minutes later a taxi drove by, Mark stuck out his arm in agony, and the cab drew into the curb. The driver was hesitant at first, but fortunately, he recognised Mark.

'Are you alright, son?'

'Just take me to the hospital will you, please.' The last thing Mark wanted was to bring trouble to his best friend's door. He rolled into the front passenger seat, and they set off on the road. It took twenty minutes to get him to accident and emergency. The driver pulled up and helped carry Mark to the door, then ran back before he got a parking ticket.

Mark was six hours waiting in casualty after a quick examination. He was finally taken in and told that he had two fractures and some severe bruising, but he would live. He was given painkillers and some sedatives to help him sleep when he got home. His knuckles and elbows were severely grazed, but it was the blow where he'd spouted blood from his mouth that they were concerned with.

It was two o'clock the next day when the doctors saw fit to release him. Mark didn't contact anyone but rang in sick for a few days. Leaving he realised that it would be a few days before he would be able for work, he was in a lot of pain, and there was no way to hide the results of a beating. When he rang in, he talked to Joyce.

'Are you okay, boss?'

'Don't ask Joyce; you don't need to know.'

'Are you sure? You sound as if you're in pain.'

'It's just a bang I took; I'll survive.'

'Mournaghan?'

'Where'd you pluck that out of?'

'He arrived in out of nowhere, he had a swagger on him, sneering gobshitte.'

'When I say it's not your business, I mean it.' There was silence on the phone. 'It's alright Joyce; I'm okay.'

Joyce was concerned but was not about to argue with the man. 'We're friends, yeah, but you're my boss, so what you say goes.'

'Then leave it at that.'

'Is there something I can do to help? Everything's fine here, but I can bring you whatever you need?'

'I have everything I need, Joyce.'

That afternoon a very broken Mark headed over to Arthur's old factory. He called the office first and checked in with Imelda, he knew there was a meeting of the shareholders, and she confirmed that Ralph Mournaghan was in attendance. 'He should be in the conference until three.' Imelda added. 'Are you ok? You don't sound great.'

'I'm fine Imelda, don't let on that I called, okay?'

'As you wish, Mark. You need to take care of yourself, yeah?'

When Mark arrived at Arthur's factory, he relayed the full story to Laura in a snapshot. Laura got straight on the phone to her father who had connections in the guards. She was exact and to the point in every detail that she shared. Laura's father knew that the guards had criminal evidence on Mournaghan. They were just biding their time, the nature of Mournaghan's offences her father could not disclose. After that meeting with Mark concerning the lifters, her father had made inquiries. He had contacted a retired superintendent that he knew.

He advised Laura to act normal around Mournaghan if he was to contact her. She could go ahead and meet up with him if she wanted, but she needed to be on high alert. Her father knew she could handle herself. He told her to tell Mark to rest up. She promised Mark that she'd be in touch with him to relay any plan of action. He could count on her to phone him later.

Mark headed home and took up their advice, falling asleep until the late evening.

Laura rang him at ten o'clock to bring him up to date. 'The guards lifted Mournaghan coming out of T&E at three o'clock with two squad cars parked up waiting. He was taken to the local barracks for questioning.'

The incident with Mark was not mentioned in the interviews as Mark himself had yet to make a statement. There were three detectives in with Ralph, and although they couldn't hold him, they did their best to disturb his peace of mind.

'Where does that leave me?'

'He'll not risk another attack.'

'You're sure of that?'

'The guards will be in contact, Mark, to tell you when they might be sending someone round to take a statement. You will need to collect and pay for a full medical report on your injuries. The detective inspector was the last to interview Mournaghan, he informed him that he was now being kept under close surveillance.'

'Let's hope that stops him.' Mark replied.

'The detective inspector asked where he was for the last two nights.'

'What did Ralph say?'

'Pure bullshit, the inspector went through Mournaghan's statement with him, recording every contradiction, he got himself into a right tizzy apparently and dug himself into a hole. It will all be used in a book of evidence against him; I'd imagine he was rightly shaken; they will get him eventually.'

Mark was relieved. 'I might never have gotten that response had I have gone to them on my own, Laura, you know that.'

'Are you still in a lot of pain?'

'It sounds like my mates are safe enough from here so yeah, I'm fine.'

'That was just Ralph mouthing off, Mark. You may put that out of your mind. I don't think you should mention it to any of them. You've nothing to fear from Mournaghan for now. He's being followed by the special branch, and they have given their assurances. If he does make any moves, they'll be there to lift him right away. '

'You're sure?'

'That was his first time in the Garda barracks, and he was rattled, he had no clue that they had a file on him.'

'Who'd ever have thought that the shipping industry could be so dangerous?' Mark said, still stunned. 'White collar crime I get, but this?'

'Companies don't necessarily do Garda checks on potential shareholders. Once these business heads are in, they can accumulate shares and go on to be partners. You don't know who you're getting into bed within business sometimes.'

'Well, I'm relieved if I can put this behind me.'

'Not completely, Mark.'

'Jesus... What now?'

'Mournaghan has weaselled his way back into working for the company; he'll be operating in a new capacity. It happened a few days ago, it makes sense when you think about it. Making a return, he wanted your nose out of his business. He had new contracts drawn up and signed before he jumped you. My father's word carries weight but it's not always sacrosanct, he couldn't admit much of what he knew.'

'But, the squad cars?' Mark asked.

'The company are within their rights to press Ralph for information on that, but he can come up with excuses.' Laura was sorry to say. 'He'll have worked out something irrelevant, something indisputable.'

'They've no way of checking.' He asked.

'No way of legitimately proving anything yet and Ralph can be convincing.'

'It's too bloody real.'

'Look...you might have to bump into the scoundrel or listen to the odd smart comment. The best part is that he has no clue that you know, you can surely create some humour at his expense.'

'I'm not going to egg the man on, Laura. The last thing I want is more trouble; he's unhinged. Do you hear yourself, he's way too easy to provoke.'

'Fair enough. You live life on the edge.' She said sarcastically.

'You need to wise up, Laura! You may be able to wrestle with these types of heads, but I haven't the stomach for it.'

'No, you're not wrong, I'd better get a move on... Do you have a takeaway menu?'

'I do.'

Our Diligent Souls

'Then you have everything you want, give work a miss for a few days until you heal.'

'I have no choice; it's been years since I was ruffed up this bad.'

'Boys will be boys... Okay, Mark, talk later.'

'I'm a thirty-year-old man, but... No. Thanks! I'm sorry if I've been a bit short with you, I've little or no energy right now.'

'No problem, Mark, just take care, yeah? You don't need milk or anything?'

'No, I can manage from here.'

'Night then, and sleep yeah?'

'I will.'

Chapter 28

Emily's nerves were playing havoc with her day. Tonight was going to be her first proper gig since becoming a singer-songwriter. According to her contacts at Songdoor, two talent scouts were planning to attend. The event was due to kick off in an hour or so, and her backing musicians were busy working through the sound checks.

Emily had downed hot water and lemon with several spoons of Manuka honey, something she had watched her mother do before a vocal performance. There were fifteen songs in her set, and only one song had been heard before, the song from her official debut on the Late Late Show.

The venue of choice was an intimate one that by day operated as a bistro. She had served as a waitress there some years back, and the owner had offered her the place for the night. He had hired the sound equipment and put someone behind the bar to serve drinks. The tables and chairs we carefully aligned with the stage to make the best use of the available space, the makeshift stage flooded with floor lighting. The band was in for a tight squeeze, having to perform in such a tiny corner. It was as much stage space as they could afford, the tickets had sold out.

Emily had just finished the first sound check when Mark walked through the door. He came with the gift of a fresh sandwich and a hot cup of coffee. The counter staff were yet to arrive, so the coffee was a welcome treat. Mark often made an issue of Emily's forgetfulness when it came to eating as she regularly skipped meals. The gig could run late, and she could faint if she didn't at least try to keep her strength up.

'You okay?' He asked.

'Yeah, I'm fine, nervous. I'll be fine once I get going.'

'I have complete confidence in you.'

'Did you think to invite Laura?' Emily asked.

'We're meeting her here. Now, I want you to eat that sandwich.'

Emily offered him a seat so, they could sit together at the table. She turned back the folds of crisp white paper to unveil her sandwich. It was oozing with cheese, beetroot and coleslaw, her favourite sandwich fillings.

She was usually a slow eater, Emily, but not tonight. Mark was pleased to note that even the crusts were devoured.

The musicians made small talk with him while she ate. It was commonplace now to see Mark at Emily's side. The guys were young, for the most part in their early twenties. That said they were seasoned musicians, having played in clubs and bars ever since their teens. It wasn't long before Siobhan and Elliot were at the door with Oden trailing behind them. There was no sign of Lucile. Come to think of it, thought Mark, it had been a while since there was any mention of Lucile at all.

Emily led them to a table at the front of the stage before responding to the call for one last sound check. There were twenty minutes left before the doors were due to open. The brother of a band member took his place to collect the tickets at the door and at ten past eight they opened to an orderly crowd.

Most of the audience claimed their seats with jackets before moving to the wine bar. The initial influx of people filled the space, but there were more sporadic arrivals to follow. The venue was full of chatter, and it appeared that everyone knew someone in the band. Only one talent scout was identified, there were a few unknown faces, any one of which could have been the second scout.

Emily was ready to get started, but the musicians held her back until the crowd had settled. Siobhan and Elliot watched her every move in unison. Sipping their wine, they were hypersensitive to every interaction on stage.

In her jeans and mohair jumper, Emily welcomed everyone as she stood behind the microphone. She introduced her first song with a dedication to Siobhan and Elliot. Laura took her seat and joined the gang as the first notes began to play.

The first song was called 'Tiny Times', and Siobhan was on top of every lyric. It captured the uniqueness of her and Siobhan's relationship. How Emily had managed to do that, to define what they shared, the way she had put the words together, it was way beyond Siobhan's skill set. As the night crusaded on, there was something haunting in the way she delivered song after song. The entire audience was entranced.

Mark was the one who understood the lyrics more than most as he had discussed with her the broader context of their meaning while on holidays at Christmas. Emily's asexual perspective unlined each song though it was subtle and understated. Only her closest friends could recognise the origin of those verses; her unusual relationship stance brought originality that no one outside her circle could pinpoint.

Her passionate ideals had a universal application. Three songs in and it was simple to say that she was searching for something in her songs, something that was very tangible to her. She gathered the crowd to her in an intimate display with total command of the stage. She was a natural; talking between songs about the where and why these tunes had been scribbled down. Mark was moved, transported back to their holiday together as he sat in the audience.

In Morocco, they had shared a room. They had not been out of each other's sight for more than moments the entire trip. The fixed ideas of where he had wanted his love life to go no longer mattered. The love he had felt for her, it had hoodwinked its way back into his life, he realised. Emily was rare and unordinary, even more so than the first time they'd met. What lay between them now was a deepening affection, and Mark again wanted more.

He had felt her need for him grow on the holiday, through glimmers of desire that were immediately disguised. But the morning they boarded the plane for the journey home, she spoke her mind. 'I feel panicked, Mark, look I'm trembling.' She had said; it was flooding back from some tired space in his mind. He could now remember her every word. He still had the picture of her stopping in the aisles as she made her way to the seat. 'What's wrong, girl?' He remembered asking. 'I don't want this to end. I want to be with you.' She had said.

Mark was choked by the recollection; his mind had been completely taken over by the news of Arthur's death. His recovery was still pending. He realised right there with her voice filling the room how consumed with the guilt he had been. He could barely contain himself on the plane. 'We should go out for dinner tonight and take it back to my place.' He now remembered saying that to her. He had kept a lid on the situation on the flight home to contain his joy, but his rapture was short lived on hearing the news of Arthur's death. Elliot had been waiting at the arrival gate when they returned.

That was twice it had happened, twice through grief that he had lost a vital part of the picture, still to this day he could not remember the conversation he shared with Jackie on his deathbed. Emily had said that she wanted to be with him and he had utterly lost sight of that fact.

Emily's voice felt distant and quiet as he was piecing together the events in his head. Elliot had dropped Emily home first from the airport that

Our Diligent Souls

evening. Mark was in shock, he'd forgotten his arrangement for dinner, he'd asked Elliot to drive him straight to Arthur's family home. Amidst the grief, the grand memory of Emily's declaration had been all but wiped. Only now, sitting in the audience, did he realise the full extent of what he'd blanked, what he was still going through since Arthur's departure.

The applause was deafening. The crowd whistled and whooped as if it was the audiences first encounter with music. The musicians smiled at Emily; she looked shell-shocked by the crowd's reaction; it made her even more endearing. Mark's face was burning up. The very last song of the first set was introduced as she cleared her throat.

'I wrote this when the illusion of my wonderful upbringing was torn to pieces. When you recognise the pure nonsense that has restricted your dreams, there is only one way to look, and that's inward. This song is my reflection on the concerns of a man who considered my direction, a man who held back on his desires, to focus on supporting something more meaningful I hope.'

When she sang not a sound was heard from the audience.

Mark was baffled; she had based the song on the night that Mark had held back, the night when she had boldly tried to kiss his neck. For Emily, it was the first time that she had expressed desire in any form. The fact that it was Mark that inspired her to sense such a surge, it meant something to her. The fact that he had held back on his own desires yet gone out of his way to make himself part of her life, it meant more to her than he initially reckoned. Mark understood these lyrics while everyone else seemed transfixed by the melody, tender and compelling as it was.

There was a rush towards her as she stepped off the stage. Everyone wanted to share their congratulations, but neither of the talent scouts approached. Mark understood her sideward glance as he made his way towards her. He craved to hold her in his arms, but a public display of affection was not appropriate.

'No one has left the building, these talent scouts, they want to hear more.' He stated.

Emily's chest felt heavy, the tears pressing against the back of her eyes. The waitress switched on the background music; so, there was no fear of them being overheard. People huddled around Emily momentarily separating her from Mark. More came forward to get their glasses of wine and return to their seats. Emily eyes filled with tearful laughter at the sight of Oden. In the distance, he was beating his chest with both hands. He never failed to bring a smile to her face, but truth be told she wanted to hear more from Mark, she had hoped that he would react to the song and recognise her declaration.

He slowly leant over and whispered in her ear. 'You'll get them, stay calm and down that honey drink, you'll be fine. I better get back to this lot.' She stood completely motionless.

Laura was waiting at the table with Siobhan and Elliot, the three watching Mark as he made his way over. Oden had started chatting with a guy beside him that he knew from college.

'Is she okay?' Laura asked, pushing over his seat.

'Yeah, spot on,' Mark replied.

'Her voice is so unique; I still can't believe that she'd kept it a secret, it took great cunning in that boarding school.' Laura needed to speak out. 'It's not that bizarre that she's so profoundly gifted. Her parents were notoriously talented.'

'We okay for drinks?' Elliot asked. He had made his way to the bar and back, with five glasses of house red, they weren't selling by the bottle.

'Cheers, mate.' Mark needed refreshment. He turned to Laura and asked. 'Are you good with this?'

Laura looked uncomfortable, but she smiled. 'I never get to gigs, and it's Emily, and she's great. I couldn't be happier.'

Emily was watching from a distance as she made her way back to the stage. She introduced her next song with a story about her grandmother's garden. It was something Emily had rehearsed; her voice was shaky. She mentioned that she'd always loved the sweetpea, watching it grew up the side of the garden shed. The comment caught Mark out, sweetpea reminding him of home more specifically the dreams of owning a home. She talked of the peach pearl china and the bracken cake that always sat in the middle of the table and the fun she had, just hanging out in the summer sun without a care in the world.

For those who didn't listen to folk music, Emily's offerings may not have amounted to much. But her voice was soulful, every song passionately laid out before the audience. She knew how to hold back and let her range tower and tumble, making it sound effortless all the while. When she finished her song, there was gentle banter from the audience most of which she was fit for; no one failed to be impressed. The night just seemed to fly in.

Our Diligent Souls

It was a tremendous finale, she had saved her Songdoor tune from Late Late Show until last. It guaranteed audience participation. She was relieved that her voice had held to the end and amazed by the response to her music. An encore was called for, and she delightfully obliged with another song. The crowd gathered around her with every form of congratulations as she stepped from the stage. She had forgotten that the talent scouts were watching until they presented themselves with cards. She agreed to get in contact with both as soon as possible.

As she watched the second scout leave, she began to search for the musicians. Mark appeared from nowhere and took hold of her arm. She felt broken, instantly reminded of his earlier lack of response, in writing her song to him she had visualised a radically different scenario. How foolish Emily felt right there; to have made such a declaration of love. She officiously told him the news about the scouts. He was startled by her tone, puzzled as he made his way back to the table to inform the others of her news.

The band was buzzing, elated by the possibilities and relieved to have successfully made it to the end of the night. They congratulated each other as they packed up their equipment. With the bistro still half full, they discreetly divided up the extra earnings from the door. They had squeezed in at least thirty additional admissions; no one seemed to mind paying to stand through the entire performance. The lad who had taken charge of the entry fee had done well. He refused to accept the few quid for performing his duties, so the lads arranged to bring him out for a late supper before heading to a club. They planned to meet up with Emily later in the week.

Emily was still full of nervous energy; she sat with the gang for a while to try and calm herself as they talked and talked about what had just happened. It would be a memorable event in her life for years to come although she was finding it hard to look Mark in the eye. He was quietly aware that something was amiss, but he was busy making plans in his head to ask her out to dinner later in the week. He needed her full attention if he was to revisit what was said on the plane from Morocco.

'We can't just leave here and go home, not tonight.' Siobhan announced whimsically. There was an eatery that they hadn't visited in ages. It was the perfect spot as the place was renowned for its late-night lock-in. 'Shall we go?' Elliot requested, watching as the gang were lit up by the suggestion. Emily made no protest though her heart wasn't in it.

Chapter 29

Siobhan couldn't take in the fact that Laura had never been to a market, not one craft market or car boot sale. Elliot knew rightly what Siobhan was scheming. She had made plans with him to go to St. Georges Market in Belfast the following morning. He was fit to explode, roping in Laura was yet another arrangement that Siobhan was making without consulting him. Mark quizzed him on the quiet, recognising that something was wrong.

'What is it, mate?' He asked.

'Women!' Elliot's response was sharp. 'Women and their scheming!'

'What?' Mark took him to the other side of the room with a glance. 'What's on your mind, pal?'

Laura and Siobhan were making their way upstairs by the time Mark and Elliot reached the couch.

'I miss the Friday session in the pub. I miss Brian and Alfie. I even miss hearing about the bullshit you're facing down at work. I don't want to talk to women every day; I miss our Friday nights.'

'We can amend that. It is Friday night, Elliot.'

'So, it is. Nice one!' Elliot whispered as his eyes widened in delight. He immediately stood up and went to get his coat.

'Slow down there. What's got into you? We can wait until the other two get back downstairs?'

Elliot looked upset; he wavered in his stance before slowly lowering himself back onto the sofa; he seemed stunned. 'Everything feels strained here at the minute, Mark. My fuse is getting shorter.'

'Go on.' Mark encouraged him.

'As much as I want things to be good with Siobhan, it's not working.'

'But you're still into her right?' Mark whispered as he checked for any signs of the two women.

'Yes! Absolutely! I'm still into her, were just pulling in different directions.'

'I'm confused here?' Mark stated.

'I need a challenge I think? We're stuck in this backwards routine, Mark, I'm head locked at the minute.'

'What's been happening at the pharmacy?'

'Nothing, I'm not good with change?'

'What kind of change?'

'There are decent challenges out there for me with my degree, opportunities. I don't have the will to chase a new career.'

'Come on Elliot, what are you at, mate? You need a swift kick up the arse.'

'It wasn't so long ago that you had your head in a teacup, mate.'

'Fair enough.'

Elliot looked away. 'I've thought of Africa, the missions but it's voluntary. It means abandoning Siobhan for an inordinate length of time. We have the mortgage too.'

'Woh! You're serious.' Mark was excited by the idea. 'Siobhan could always let out one of the rooms.'

'I'm not sure I'd be able for it.'

'This is unlike you, you're not pessimistic, Elliot.'

'Siobhan could be well pissed.'

'Siobhan will stand by you, Elliot, whatever you choose, she's not that tough.'

'We've been together for five years, Mark. We've been no more than the odd week apart at any given time.'

'You'd have that much to do in the preparation. If it's what you want, then you're making excuses.'

'The missions... Mark, are you for real, it's as far-fetched as moving to Australia.'

'Australia, not on your own?'

'I'd have the boys.'

'Have you tried talking to her?'

'You know what she's like, she'd just jump on an idea and run with it, organising everything as if she was the one in charge.'

'You need to calm down and talk to her, Elliot.'

Our Diligent Souls

'I need our Friday night in the pub, Mark?'

'Granted, I've been out of touch here. We'll sort this later.'

They could hear the two women coming down the stairs; they were still talking markets.

'We've decided to go to Belfast tomorrow.' Siobhan announced. 'Why don't you two go to the pub, we can catch the train first thing in the morning. Laura can take the spare room. You okay to join us, Mark?'

Mark glanced over at Elliot, but Elliot had his eyes firmly fixed on the reclaimed floorboards.

'That could be fun.' Mark decided, thinking that he wanted to stay close to Elliot.

Siobhan was excited. 'You can stay tonight too; you can take the couch, it will save time in the morning.'

'You're prepared to rough it then, Laura?' Mark jested, trying to ignite some humour.

Siobhan reacted sharply; she immediately took offence. 'Roughing it?'

'Jesus, Siobhan, I'm joking.'

Siobhan looked confused as she turned to Laura. 'You don't have a change of clothes for the morning.'

'I have make-up and stuff in my bag; I'll be fine.'

'In that case...' Mark answered, winking before he turned to Elliot. 'Are you okay with this, mate?'

'You're late asking me now,' Elliot responded.

She was not giving him the opportunity to air his views. 'Elliot's fine,' Siobhan announced. 'Don't mind him.' It was a defining moment for the pair of them, and Elliot knew it.

'Like I have a choice in the matter?' He stated. He put on his coat and turned to Mark. 'She's enough to drive any man to his wit's end.' Elliot wanted out of there. 'I've had enough. Can we get out of here now?' Siobhan and Laura looked on blankly.

It wasn't long before the two men were in the pub behind two pints of stout. They had walked in virtual silence to the venue and ordered pints without any ado. Where possible they always sat on the same stools, the barman was busy chatting with some bird on the sidelines.

'So, out with it?' Mark demanded, forcing the conversation.

Elliot took his cap off and turned to his friend. 'You know she used to be in the middle of everything, a real Dub, sharp and witty but full of compassion in the same hand. She had an impeccable sense of style, unique you know. She was always out there gathering attention with those eyelashes of hers and that bloody liquid eyeliner.'

'She's still a trendsetter. Siobhan hasn't changed, Elliot.' Mark needed to point that out. His back was up over Siobhan, but he could see his friend was struggling. 'You were short with each other tonight, but I'm guessing that's your new happy-go-lucky disposition.'

It was Siobhan that he was talking about; she was a woman who lit up lives, always intrigued, a great listener. She'd find the knack for raising souls, connecting happenings with astonishing empathy and good humour. That was her way.

'She's got comfortable, mate. Her edge has gone. There was a time where I oozed confidence having a woman as brilliant as Siobhan on my arm. You want to see her walk into a pub, command a conversation, the laughs we had. I had forgotten the ball of ill fortune I was before I'd met her, I was a bloody worry worm.'

'Ball of misfortune my ass!' Mark's response was genuine.

'There was my mother for one with her ear-bending, on top of having to watch over Oden for the best part of my life.'

'Jesus, he's not that big of a handful.'

'He's alright now, but Christ, he was one serious concern growing up. Kids on that spectrum are in a class of their own. I was brought up to look after him; it was up to me. They stood back from their responsibilities; they couldn't cope with Oden, not in the way I could.'

'Your parents?'

'It was me who took him to the head shrink. I was the one landed with him everywhere I went; they forgot about my childhood. I was at the playground when I should have been out at shopping centres with my age group; there was no room for girls.'

Mark laughed. 'He kept you from harm's way then?'

'I never rebelled. I could have been a punk me.'

Our Diligent Souls

Mark was busy busting his sides, but Elliot was not impressed.

'You're pissing me off! I had to lead the way and make it through college, straight into the pharmacy to set up making a shilling. I'm tired of it. I was groomed from the moment that they realised he was different.'

'You always wanted to be a pharmacist, Elliot.'

'Only because I reckoned it was an easy number when I visited with Oden. I had to collect the prescriptions every other week; I'm colourless me.'

'You have the craic?'

'I pick up stories. It keeps me from going off my nut! I need to have some bow to my string.'

'You mean apart from the painting, and the cookery, and that absolute hatred you have for music?'

'If I have to sit through any more amateur dramatic thing, I will be done for murder. It's just not enough, Mark. I'm biting the head of her lately.'

'Siobhan?'

'It feels as if I'm being groomed again.'

'Groomed?'

'Yeah! She wants that and all. I just want to break out, pack a bag and take off on my own. I need to see what it is to be out there taking care of myself with no one else for a change, breathing space.'

Mark was smiling. 'You're too into your fashion to jump on a freight train from New Jersey.'

'There's such a thing as a backpack.'

Mark shook his head, his body heaving with laughter. But looking over, Elliot was irritated again; he looked like he was fit to kill him. Mark sat up and took a sip of his pint. 'Seriously though, you mentioned the missions?'

'Is that what I'm looking for... something life-affirming?'

'Siobhan's not that then?'

'She's losing this precious part of herself; this raw vitality that she used to own. The spunky, passionate, sidestepping glance that use to put the hair standing on the back of my neck.'

'I get the picture, Elliot.'

'Seriously?' He barked back.

'Look, mate, to my way of thinking this may be something worth celebrating. You're just moving into a different phase in your relationship.'

'She's gone gooey-eyed around children. She sees this one-way ticket that's slipping away. We've been together now five years, and she's getting on in her head. She's surrounding herself with these thespian yuppies that are lining up playmates for the children that they're planning. Planning!'

'And you're not ready?'

'It appears not, look; maybe it's my ego. It's not that I have an issue being with one woman my entire life. I could have benefited from some female encounters in my youth, but I do love Siobhan, and I can take or leave kids.'

'You couldn't eat a whole one then?' Mark laughed.

'I've done the daddy thing with Oden. Heart above head I want to do something of serious value or put colour in my soul first. Am I talking crap?'

'I hear you barking, our fella but losing Siobhan is not something you want to do. What I'm taking from this is that you don't need to drag this indecision out. You'll leave her feeling guilty for wanting something you're not ready to give her.'

'What to do then?' Elliot asked, scratching his face, 'It's back to that again, what to do that works for both of us, mate, for Siobhan and me?'

'You need to find ways to remind her that you're both still young.'

'What rock concerts?'

'Maybe, but, talk to her. Let her know how you're feeling never having been out on your own? Or figure out what's missing? Tell her what you've set your heart on achieving once you've decided. What other options have you thought through, joking aside?'

Elliot rested for a moment. 'I've been thinking of Australia.'

'Okay!' Mark replied.

'I could do other stuff here and look for a more challenging job. That way I could give her the family she wants.'

'That's not what I'm saying. I'm not saying don't have your adventure. Prioritise here. The missions are an option, a journey on your own. Just discuss it with Siobhan. The problem rests with the fact that you're having this conversation with me and not with her. If you can commit to seriously looking at getting married, to starting a family when you get back?'

'Do you hear yourself? How can I sincerely forecast that?' Elliot was narked.

'Just tell her what's going on with you. What you are and are not prepared to do right now, just make sure she knows how much you love her, mate.'

They were silent. Elliot lowered his pint.

'The plan is coming together in my head; we'll let it rest for now. You're alright you.'

'I'll agree with that much.' Mark stated, lifting his glass.

'So, what's going on your end?' Elliot enquired.

Mark was smiling. 'Are we talking work or love life?'

'You have a love life? When did this happen?'

'When we were travelling back from Morocco on the plane, Emily suggested that we might have a chance.'

'Nice one; it's a long time coming.'

'The time to act was then but with Arthur dying... I don't know if her feelings still stand. I'm ready to find out though.'

'So, what's the plan?'

'That's my concern; say nothing until you hear more, Elliot.'

'And what's happening at work?'

'Yeah, it's all good. I know I have a knack for doing right by the company and the floor staff now. So that's better than where I started. The bullshit politics I can deal with, Ralph Mournaghan too, and there's room to advance, there are significant opportunities.'

'That's great stuff.'

'Elliot, I don't want to be funny here but have you thought of offering Siobhan the support to branch out herself. It could be something to think on. She's such a creative force, and I know that job in the museum was never her first choice.'

'It could give me breathing space babywise but what the hell, Mark. I have a lot on my plate right now. I'd not be on my own in Australia with the boys there.'

Elliot's response came as a surprise to Mark. He had never recognised a single selfish trait in his friend, but he was focused on himself tonight.

'I don't recognise you tonight, mate?' Mark responded. He was embarrassed for his friend.

'To hell with it, I've been groomed my whole life? Groomed? What else does she want from me?'

Mark was feeling a little unhinged. Elliot hadn't heard a word that he was saying, this was not the gentle soul he had loved and admired for so many years. There was a new viewpoint emerging that was somehow distasteful. Siobhan was being objectified. There was no disguising the fact that the couple was having problems. Going by Elliot's definition, Elliot was reverting to his bitter former self, a person that Mark had never known.

Mark had agreed to stay in theirs and travel to the market in the morning, but in truth, he wasn't nearly as interested as he had been earlier. When they finished their fourth pint, they made their way back to the house. Siobhan and Laura were ready for bed, and to them, Elliot seemed in better form.

'You cheered him up, Mark.' Siobhan whispered. 'I don't know what's been eating him lately, but he missed you.' She kissed Mark on the cheek. 'It's great to see you back to your old self.'

Siobhan's words had a grounding effect on Mark. Elliot had been his pal for five years; he'd been a dear friend to Mark as had Siobhan. It was in honour of her that Mark's defences had been set ablaze, but Elliot was a great pal too.

In the sitting room, he was left alone to get some rest. He began to wonder when he might get the chance to remind Emily of how deeply he loved her. When he had relaxed his interest in her and opted for the role of close friend, he found he was more himself that way. She treated him differently; she laughed and spoke her mind openly when it came to how she honestly felt about all form of things. She shared secrets, her neurotic fear of men with greasy hair for one. She had become more physical with him touching his shoulder or his arm freely.

He fantasised a lot about finally making it to their first real kiss. He toyed with the idea of her touching his face, playing with his hair; his anticipation was focused and unwavering, to dream beyond those simple pleasures was abhorrent to him. He tried to visualise the way Emily might entertain his family or how she might hold a paintbrush in her hand. These were the treasures that he waited to collect. He was becoming a man by virtue of a gentler kind of thinking.

Chapter 30

The alarm clock went off three times at five-minute intervals before Siobhan lifted her head from the pillow.

'It's a quarter to seven, sleepy head.' She spoke softly as she sought to rouse Elliot from his sleep. Sliding from the bed, she stepped into the garments that she'd laid out on the armchair the night before; they had no time to do showers.

'I'll get the kettle; we've twenty minutes before we have to leave, Elliot.'

'Siobhan?'

'Yeah?'

'I...'

'Emily and Oden are meeting us at the train station. I called them to see if they wanted to join us last night.'

'You did what?' Elliot was crushed, but he was too tired to argue. He was barely able to raise his head from to pillow.

'It's okay. It was Oden's idea to meet us at the station.'

'I wanted to drive to Belfast,' Elliot explained as he turned around and raised his head up, his elbows digging into the pillow.

'There's too many in the mix now.' She asserted.

Defeated, he attempted to get up, muttering to himself as he hoisted on his jeans. Siobhan was at the spare bedroom door; tapping to get Laura moving. Once she got the okay, she went downstairs to wake Mark. 'Coffee in five, guys,' she hollered up the stairs.

In minutes they were gathered at the Kitchen Island where hot coffee and toast was being prepared.

'Morning guys,' Mark whispered, trying to raise his enthusiasm as he folded away his blankets.

'Morning!' Laura retorted; she too was not yet fully awake.

'We'll have to leave shortly,' Elliot pointed out, turning to Mark, 'Emily and Oden were invited to join us last night while we were in the pub. They're meeting us at the train station.'

'Big day so.' Mark suggested before he bit into his toast.

With breakfast barely consumed, the dishes were lobbed into the sink, and the coats gathered at the front door as they made their way to the car. It was nippy outside. Their journey to the train station was faster than usual with just a few cars on the road at that hour.

Elliot managed to find a parking spot right beside the station. Mark being an obliging soul, ran off to get a ticket to cover the car until three o'clock. Oden and Emily were waiting at the main gate. The place was heaving with early morning commuters. They found the ticket machines before running to make it to the train on time.

On board, they managed to find two four-seat cubicles that were directly aligned. Helping to organise two estranged passengers to the window seat of one of the cubicles; the entire group were now an arm's length from one another. The excitement began to hit home as the train departed; it was going to be a unique caper to the north with six of them in tow.

Oden had been to St. George's Market the once and loved it. He needed no excuse to go there again. Emily relished the idea of Belfast itself. She had only been there twice, and both times she had spent too much money. They were all in the best of humour, including Elliot, now that he got a chance to relax.

The train rallied on while window framed images of the coastline were revealed. There were long stretches of beach as they reached the outskirts of the county Dublin border and a nostalgic flutter of voices at the sight of the once great Mosney Holiday Camp.

The old wrath iron bridge at Drogheda was welcomed with its dirty grey basin and its brightly coloured shipping containers positioned inches from the dirt bank.

Oden quibbled with Elliot over the song his father used to sing, 'Didn't we have a lovely time', but that was about Bangor. They had to go to Belfast and then get another train if they were to head to Bangor. The song was disallowed. Arriving at Dundalk train station and Mark's hometown, all eyes were on him in jest. It was the final stop before crossing the border; they were at the half-way point between Dublin and Belfast.

'So weird to be so near and yet so far, guys, life is at its natural pace in that wee town.' Mark insisted.

As the train moved on, the artwork for the railway signage changed; a solid confirmation that they had hit the north. It wasn't going to be long, the two hours and ten minutes journey time already approaching its end.

As the wheels ground to a halt, Laura was delighted to discover that St. George's Market was a five-minute walk from the station. A sharp turn to the left of the exit with a five-minute downhill jaunt and they were there.

The ornately detailed red-bricked building was purposely designed to house the market, decades back. Laura loved it. Once inside the door, the bustle of stallholders and clients, they fascinated her as she stared past row upon row of offerings. There were a few stallholders yet to set up shop, but trade was in full flow otherwise. The gang gathered around the fabric and ribbon stall where Emily had spotted something that was worthy of a price enquiry.

Elliot and Siobhan were the only ones with sterling where the others needed to get to a cash point. They could exchange euros for pounds in the deli shop at the Market's side entrance but the rate of exchange there was bloody awful. Elliot knew where to bring them.

Arranging to get sterling for Oden, he left with the others while Oden and Siobhan made their way to the coffee dock. He kissed Siobhan's forehead before leaving, the boisterous Dublin gang on a mission to find the nearest cash dispenser, the hole in the wall. 'We won't be long.'

Siobhan and Oden managed to find two seats in the central coffee dock surrounded on four sides by food stalls. They got themselves two Americanos and watched as a band set up on a small stage three tables from where they had parked themselves.

Siobhan got talking to a woman at a table to their left who explained that the bands played through the morning at intervals. 'They're outstanding musicians, but it was usually cover songs they play. That's how we rolled in the north; thirty-year-old chart success bands play with regularity, that and the odd soap opera star off Coronation Street or Eastenders. It's a little different in the south, right?' The woman was witty and cute enough to make the distinctions having recognised their southern voices. Siobhan admired the woman's accent and explained where they'd travelled from that morning. It wasn't long before she turned her attention back to Oden.

'So, where's Lucile these days? We haven't seen much of her.'

'What, I'm her mother now?' Oden replied.

'Are you still going out together?'

'Who said we were going out together, Siobhan?'

'What you weren't?'

'We were going out together, and we still might be. It's not that important.'

'But you're still friends?'

'Why wouldn't we be?'

'Jesus Oden…You're making me feel old.'

'Well, you are old.'

'I'll have you know, young man…'

Oden laughed as Siobhan clattered him with her hand. She loved the boy, but it wasn't to say he frustrated her at times, that would have been an understatement. She glanced at the market floor to see if she could see Elliot and the rest of the troop, not that they didn't have plenty of time.

'So, what's the craic with you, Siobhan?'

'White and hairy!' She replied.

'You're getting wise, girl.' He returned.

'I'm not falling for that one again, Oden darling.'

Oden wagged his finger as the two of them smiled at each other. He had a lovely face as had his older brother. Elliot's expressions were reserved and meaningful, where Oden was childish and full of mischief but he'd a knack of swelling her heart.

On the way to the cash point, Emily was lost in a daydream as she sauntered behind the gang. They were all too high energy for her at that time of the morning; the city moving at a much slower pace. Mark took note and fell back to join her.

'It's like another world here, yeah?' He asked.

'It's clean in comparison, people dress better, am I right?' Mark laughed as she stopped and pulled a funny face. 'It's good to get away; I'm just being odd.'

'I loved the song?'

'Which song?' Emily asked, but Mark gave no response.

'There's an excellent Indian restaurant in my hometown, I was thinking of heading home next week for a visit.

'Good for you.' She stated.

'I'd be honoured if you would come with me? I want us to spend some time together; you haven't met the clan.'

'Did you see the troubles when you were younger?'

'I grew up in a border town, so yeah.'

'What happened?'

'There are a lot of cross-border marriages up our way. Lots of things happened I guess, I suppose Newry was the crux of it for us, we never ventured that deep into the north, at least from what I remember.'

'No story then?'

'My dad, Andrew, he left my mum, my sister and me at the swimming pool one day. He was supposed to collect us. In the public pool, you just got a forty-five-minute swim, and you were out on your ear. Anyway, dad's car broke down the other side of Newry, and when he didn't show up, we waited outside I think, before we set out in the direction of the bus stop. There were no mobiles then. Moira, my sister, was not feeling well, so mum sent me into a supermarket to get her something to drink while they waited outside...'

He stopped talking for a minute. 'Go on, don't stop there.' Emily prompted.

'This I guess was a regular event when you lived in Newry then. The supermarket had a glass front; I was about seven. Anyway, there was a British soldier the other of the street. I knew he had to be at least sixteen but a lot of them didn't even look that age yet. It did feel criminal putting guns in the hands of ones so young.'

'Sixteen?'

'I was carrying my swimming trunks in a plastic bag. To a soldier back then I guess that was suspicious. I'll never forget his face. I could see him trembling even at that range, watching me. He cocked his rifle and placed his finger on the trigger.'

'Jesus!' Emily's eyes widened.

'I tried to make my way around the shelves, but he was moving at the same pace to make sure he had a clear shot at me. A woman screamed two aisles down, and I drop the glass bottle that I'd just picked up. I thought I was dead; he lunged at me from the other side of the street, ready to fire.'

'Holy shit!'

'Anyhow, someone stepped in to block his view, I could see this other soldier grab and hoist his rifle upwards. My legs went from under me, and when I looked up, mum was there looking especially cross. I remember her dusting me off and telling me to get a move on, shooting a glance at the young soldier as we passed.'

'It must have been terrifying at seven?'

'No one said a word on the way to the bus depot, Moira, my younger sister; she just took my hand. In thinking about it, when you look back, it can't have been plain sailing for the Newry contingent.' Emily smiled.

Elliot had just reached the cash point and was beckoning them on. 'Come on you lot; the others are waiting.'

Back at the market, Oden had a few questions for Siobhan. 'What going on with Mark and Emily?' He enquired.

'Nothing, they're in top form.'

'Then why has he not asked her out yet?'

'It's complicated with Emily, Oden.'

'How come?'

'She's a complicated woman, that's just the way she is.'

'He's obviously into her, and she likes the attention.'

'You think so?'

'I know so.'

'Things just aren't that simple as you get older, Oden.'

'You're not being condescending for the sake of it then, Siobhan?'

Siobhan dug him a scornful look and drew away, turning back sharply with a wicked glint in her eyes before they fell around laughing.

'How well do you know my brother?' Oden asked.

'What is going to come out of your mouth next, you're forever flipping from one subject to the next; it's impossible to hold your attention.'

'That's my ADHD.'

'Oden, you don't have ADHD. Is having Asperger's not enough for you, Oden?'

'I knew you didn't know, he still doesn't trust anyone enough to share that fact, Siobhan.'

'What?'

'When I went on the medication it was seriously frowned upon; they wouldn't let Ritalin into the country then, it's still a heavily controlled drug. The papers, neighbours, everyone said it was dysfunctional parenting that caused ADHD, most of the therapist too. I reckon it's still the same. Elliot read a ton of books on it before he decided it was a real condition and the tablets helped way beyond fish oils or any of that crap. I wondered if he'd told you.'

'Jesus, what is wrong with that man. We're together five years like. I have to say it to him, Oden.'

'You lot are full of secrets.'

'Oh, my good God, Oden.'

'My initial diagnoses was ADHD; it wasn't until the Ritalin kicked in that they discovered I'd Asperger's as well.'

'Elliot would have told me if that was the case.'

'He'd faced a few battles with it, especially with relatives. There were no therapies, just more Ritalin when Elliot asked for support. Nobody looks favourably on the families of children with ADHD.'

'That's sad.' Siobhan was shocked by the newsflash.

'Don't ever mention it to Elliot; he'll be upset that I told you, he probably hasn't thought of it in a very long time. I don't take medication anymore, just super strength fish oils.'

'How do I not talk to him about it, Oden?' Siobhan was concerned.

'Old people are so weird.'

'See you, me boyo.' The two of them laughed. 'Seriously though Oden, it not funny.'

'Ah now, Siobhan?'

Our Diligent Souls

The band opened with a Van Morrison number as Oden spotted the posse make their way through the crowds. They were all itching to have a good rummage through the stalls and spend their hard-earned cash, but Siobhan and Oden still needed time alone. When Elliot offered to join them, they ushered him away from the others, no explanation needed, they were just in a groove.

With such an array of stalls, it was hard to know where to begin. Laura and Emily made their way back to the fabric stall together. Emily made the occasional cushion when she found a piece of fabric that was out of the ordinary. She had a sewing machine that had once belonged to her grandmother; she took to sewing when she needed to feel connected to the old woman again. Laura spotted a button stall and brought Emily's attention to some matching buttons. In total, she bought two metres of fabric, one of each of her favourite patterns, four metres of ribbon and eight small patterned buttons.

Laura was attracted to an old brooch on another stall. Emily jumped in and haggled it down, getting five pounds sterling of the asking price. Laura was utterly mortified though she was delighted to have bought the clasp. A young man was selling potted plants, the pair of them watched for a while, they were interested in his banter. He passed care sheets out, giving detailed instruction on how to get the best foliage and bloom out of his seedlings.

There were cupcake stalls and an old-fashioned sweet shop stand that sold mixed bags of some old favourites by the quarter. There were crocheted stalls with bits and bobs for new-born babies. There were antique stalls, one with a spectacular chaise longue. If they'd had the means to transport it home, Laura might have bought it on the spot, and it wasn't cheap.

There were stalls with jumpers from Peru, rugs from Morocco and the likes, essential oils, fruit and vegetable stands, and fresh fish stalls to the back of the building. There were comics and games, vintage clothing and hats. They had first edition books, and the vinyl record stalls were to beat all vinyl stalls; the market had an exceptional selection of just about everything.

At every turn, they were hit by a lingering waft of hunger-inducing headiness; the fragrant Indian curries were setting their senses ablaze, that and the sizzle of juicy meat and fried onions. The oak smoked cheeses that melted on the toasting machines that were accompanied by the sweet blissful rush of melted chocolate and marshmallow covered crepes.

Our Diligent Souls

The hot steaming vapours flowed downstream like a temptress on a tailwind; the rich, crispy batters and the buttery goodness of mouth-watering herbs. The other-worldly array of dishes in reds and strong mustards; that held captive the imagination, seducing them closer as the public moved in for a non-committal glance. It was a food lover's euphoria.

Siobhan and Oden finally got to task and abandoned the music to go pick up some merchandise. Siobhan got new head-gear; a pink tartan hat in a Liam Clancy style. She had no idea what she'd wear it with, but as Siobhan rummaged through the vintage coat stall, she found its partner in crime. They could be worn together as both the coat and hat were a perfect fit.

'Now that is the kind of magic I was referring to,' she told Laura.

Siobhan and Laura were done spending and grabbed two chairs in the food arena. The music started up again as they moved over and back from their table to the coffee stalls. They acquired one chair at a time, shuffling the seats around a small table, draping their jackets over them to secure some seats for their friends. They had a brief chance to catch up before the others arrived.

Laura was not around when Siobhan first met Elliot; she had gone to a different college and done her degree in business there. She was up to her eyeballs in her love affair at that stage and regretted not having stayed in touch after graduating from boarding school. They had great memories from their days there, but nothing was as big a surprise as Emily.

Siobhan and Emily had been the closest of friends at boarding school; she was the only one who was invited back to Emily's family home for a visit. Laura remembered more of what had transpired the day her parents died than Siobhan did; she remembered scenes from the day that Emily got the news.

There was a group of five girls in Emily and Siobhan's circle up until that point, and Laura had been one of them. The headmistress had met them in the corridor and took Emily aside to tell her what had happened. It was Laura, not Siobhan that had been at Emily's side when the news arrived. Laura despised as much as Siobhan did, the endless and often false empathy that Emily had to suffer through, it went on right up until they left school.

The closer Emily and Siobhan became though; the more isolated Laura had felt. Laura was close to both girls before the tragedy, but she could find no way to remind them of that.

There was a wall separating Emily and Siobhan from everybody else and Laura had no idea how to break through that though she genuinely missed them both. There was this one incident where a girl from third-year had accused Emily's parents of drink driving; a rumour had circulated, Laura reminded her. Poor Emily had made a swing at the girl and Laura then dragged her to the bike sheds for a smoke.

'I hope I'm not to blame for her still smoking.'

'I didn't know that happened.   It's just the odd one Emily does have.'

Mark and Elliot had scoured through every piece of vinyl and had bought two albums apiece; Mark had gone mod with an old Blades and an Undertones record while Elliot stuck to the more soulful black jazz albums. They assembled in the central food court where the girls had acquired five seats.   They'd been taking turns to get to the various food stalls for their lunches.

Elliot and Mark went to the Cajun-Creole stall and decided to both choose a different dish, Laura had Spanish paella, and Oden had the home-made pie with mash. Siobhan and Emily were determined to try the venison stew. They were hungry, and everything looked and smelt delicious.

An extra chair was finally obtained in time for them all to sit together and have a taste of each other's food. The gang were fifty-fifty on the overall enjoyment of their choices, but the anticipation had been too high. The collective aromas had promised more than any one single caterer could deliver. The dishes were reasonably tasty, but the delight at trying something new was what had won their support.

The music was top spec as they sat facing the stage in the central hub of the food court, the seating area for coffee drinkers and foodies. The next singer was more engaged than the last as he called for requests. Though it was hard to hear him over the crowds, the singer told warm northern stories to bring tradition to the proceedings. The gang got the banter going with humorous quips, and all was taken in good spirits. They were having a whale of a time, drunk on the atmosphere alone.

The three women made their way over to the far side of the market to buy chutney, jams and pickles to take home; they got handcrafted cheeses too. Sadly, it felt as if they had just arrived when it was time to leave; the stalls were shutting up, and the train was due to depart very shortly.

Siobhan linked Laura's arm on the way up the hill to the train station.

'So, what did you make of it, your first market?'

'Great morning, I feel refreshed, heart and head now honestly.'

Our Diligent Souls

Siobhan's eyes glimmered with delight. 'Good for you,' she stated. 'We will do this again someday soon, I promise? There are a million markets, plenty scattered around Dublin, we don't have to go to Belfast to have a great day out, but it has been a great one to start off with.'

As Emily caught up with them, she burst into song. 'Didn't we have a lovely time, the day we went to Belfast...?'

Laura had no shame either at that point. No Dublin elites were looking on, no finger-wagging executives to hold her back. She opened her mouth and let every lost note out. 'Beautiful day we had lunch on the way and all for under a pound you know, sir.'

Siobhan laughed. 'Here, I'm not sure we spent under a pound. I'm afraid to look in my purse.'

Emily laughed too.

Mark called back. 'Come on you lot, we'll miss the train,' he was a good two metres ahead of the game. 'Get a move on.'

They piled down the stairs, the six of them rallied on by the ticket attendant. A second train representative smiled as they ran to make it to the train; he had a flag in his right hand.

Luckily, the train was half empty; they managed to find seats together. Mark made his way to the bar where he ordered six small bottles of red wine paying in sterling. The barman gave Mark six plastic glasses and Oden took three of the bottles out of his hand. A glass of mid-day wine was just what they needed to round off the day. On the way back to the seat, Oden made a point of taking Mark to one side.

'What is it, Oden?' The train was chugging on the track.

'Why haven't you asked Emily out yet?'

'She's not ready for a relationship, Oden.' Mark spoke on a gut reaction; he wasn't ready to tell the lad that he had plans afoot.

'Mark, you need to get wise.'

'It's not that; you think I haven't thought of it?'

'I think you've thought of nothing else to a point where you're now too chicken.'

Mark was caught off guard. He could feel the food rise in his throat as he watched Oden rush back to his seat. He edged his way in; nervous about what Oden might say next. Emily whipped out the cheese and chutney they had bought, and they made do without crackers, having obtained a plastic knife from the food trolley. The craic was wild, but Mark was not on form, he was still perplexed by the notion that Oden might put his foot in it with Emily. He needed to sort stuff out with her before Oden got the change to interfere.

'I can't believe I've to go to rehearsals at six,' she informed them, 'I want to stay and party with you guys, it's not fair.' Mark suggested that they go back to his, he had the makings of a decent dinner for the six of them, and Emily had three hours before she had to be anywhere.

Oden declined the offer admitting that he hadn't slept the night before, so his bed was calling, maybe if he hadn't had that bottle of wine, but he was exhausted now. With the journey being two hours long, Mark ordered and paid for another five small bottles of wine, Elliot excluded himself as he was driving; he ordered a coffee and helped Mark carry back the load.

By the time the train hit Connolly the crew were at high jinks again. Elliot couldn't relax until he could confirm that the car was still safe. It hadn't been tampered with. Oden insisted on taking the bus as there wasn't room for everyone in the car. Emily tagged along for fear that if she went home, she might sleep and not make it to band practice at all.

They were looking in all directions as the over-packed car chugged past a uniformed Garda Síochána.

Mark's place looked great; the rugs he'd bought in Morocco when he'd travelled with Emily, they brought new life to the apartment. Mark and Emily went to the kitchen to check out the contents of the fridge. It would have been easier to order in, but Mark knew what Elliot thought about takeaways. He had meat in the fridge and the makings of a healthy lamb tagine pot. Mark left Emily to it while he rooted out more wine and some proper glasses. Laura joined her in the kitchen.

Siobhan was already curled up on the sofa while Elliot flipped through Mark's record collection. Elliot knew that Mark would want to hear the records he'd just bought, so he went ahead and put them on, the Blades were on first. The second track on the album Elliot just loved; they were all forced to listen while he sang the lyrics.

'Does everyone eat lamb?' Emily called from the kitchen.

She had bought the same style of ceramic tagine in Morocco and had mastered the art of a great lamb dish that could be conjured up in less than two hours. The spices were there from the party. They had eaten their fill at the market, but with the travel and the wine and the prospect of the evening ahead, it would do them no harm to eat again before Emily went to rehearsals. No one had any complaints. Once the ingredients had been assembled in the dish, she could leave it to bubble away in the oven.

'So, when's the next gig?' Siobhan mused as Laura and Emily returned to Mark's sitting room.

'There's a good few gigs on the cards over the coming weeks as it goes. I'd love if you lot could come but I'm comfortable enough now. I can manage; I needed support that first night, but I'm fine.'

'Like we don't want to hear you!' Mark called her out on it.

'You'll be well sick of the same songs if you keep coming to the shows.'

'You're being ridiculous now.' Mark muttered, glaring right at her.

'And the talent scouts?' Elliot prompted.

'Yeah! I've been to see them both. One of them is keen to lay down tracks in their studios, but I need to tweak the songs first.'

'You'll be famous yet, girl!' Elliot added.

'Why do people always say that; it's not where I'm coming from, I just make music.'

'There will come a time when you'll want to make an income from it, that's part of the territory?'

'Well, so be it when it comes. I can cope with that, but it's not the point.' Emily turned her back and started tidying up Mark's magazines to avoid any further conversation on the topic.

'How's the shipping industry going, you two?' Elliot sparked again.

'I'm enjoying it.' Laura said. 'I love it there. I'd try to persuade Mark to come back and work for me, but I don't think he'd have it.'

'She couldn't afford me,' Mark stated though he was surprised by his confidence in that respect, after everything that had happened with Arthur.

'That's true.' Laura confirmed, laughing.

'What's so funny?' Emily asked as she sat with them again.

'It's just Mark and these grand notions he has of himself.'

'Don't start me!' Mark shot back.

Their stories were full of witty character assassinations; they went back and forward for the next two hours. There were a few deadly descriptions of Elliot's altercations with a girl he'd had a crush on when he was in his teens. There was a story of Mark having whitewashed an eccentric geriatric into buying a rare Patrick Kavanagh poem that he'd found in the local archives. It took him eight weeks to clinch the deal without proof of authenticity, and it was just a public record in the first place.

'I was sixteen and desperate lads, if you ever tell my mother. I sold it for a fiver like; you could hardly say I was wide.'

There was much debate on who bought the best vinyl, but it wasn't long before the tagine was ready. The Moroccan spices flooding the room as the clay dish was taken out of the oven. It was brought to the coffee table and placed on a tea towel alongside a stacked plate of couscous, and some bowls and spoons.

The taste of the couscous, the peppers and chillies, the soft, succulent meat, it was deliciously warming and at once allowed for more wine. The morning's visit to Belfast was utterly erased from their minds as they hunkered around the spread.

Emily was cleaning up in the kitchen when Mark followed her to take over the task. He came right out and said it. 'I should have kissed you that night you stayed over in mine.'

'Which night?'

'The night I carried you to bed... The night from the song you wrote?'

'You did the right thing.'

'No, I didn't. I should have manned up and made out with you.'

'There are people in the next room; we have guests.'

'We, have guests? Are we in a relationship or what?'

'I don't want to have this conversation, not just now, Mark.'

'When then?'

'Try never?'

Emily abandoned the dishes and went back to join the crew. Elliot and Laura were talking about Arthur and the way he had run the company. Emily joined them telling Elliot about the adventure Mark had proposed to take her on, to visit Laura at work in the old factory.

'He's taking you to the factory?' Elliot enquired, finding it odd.

Emily could only imagine his reaction if he discovered that Mark had invited her home to meet his folks, she was incensed.

'Yes! I am,' Mark confirmed as he re-entered the room.

Emily was reaching for her coat to make her way to rehearsals. It was as if their conversation in the kitchen had never taken place. The gang said their goodbyes as Mark accompanied her to the door.

'Emily, I'm sorry, I just...' He shook his head. 'It's just I loved the song you wrote for me, I...'

She took his shoulder. 'It's not as if I don't care, Mark, there are so many missed signals between us.'

'What about the things you said on the aeroplane. With Arthur's death and everything, it went clean out of my mind, and I know that doesn't sound right. I had the same weird shit going on at Brian's father's funeral. It's like missing blanks. I can't explain it, and it does not reflect a lack of care on my part. I absolutely love you.'

'Please, just leave well enough alone, yeah? It's been a marvellous day.'

'No, don't do this now, we need to resolve this. We need to be together end of, its time.'

She kissed his forehead and disappeared; she was out of sight before he lifted his head again to go back to his friends. Never could he have imagined being so cut up about a woman, his efforts just kept falling on deaf ears. She left hoping that he'd later remember that he'd invited her home to meet his family.

Chapter 31

Oden was on his way over to see Elliot and Siobhan; they had called and said they needed a chat. He was in a league of legends final that night, so he decided to head over early. It was a beautiful evening with summer again in full bloom. The gardens he passed along the way were blushing with vibrancy; the tiny plots of freshly cut grass were edged with rose bushes that leant across the fences.

The tricolour buntings were out on full display in celebration of the football; the flimsy fabrics were fluttering in the gentle breeze. Oden passed a near-derelict house with its wild, nettle thronged pathway, the sun streaming down the left-hand side of the street as two neighbours stood chatting from their respective doorways.

The college terms had ended well, his results were now in, and his third year of games development safely secured. He lifted his phoned to call Elliot as he turned onto the street where they lived. He had been left knocking the door too long on previous occasions when Elliot's music was at full blast.

Elliot answered the call straight away and was waiting for Oden on the front steps as he approached. Siobhan greeted him from the kitchen once he made it safely inside. She moved with great delicacy towards him as she balanced a cup of hot chocolate and a saucer of his favourite biscuits. Curling up beside him on the sofa once she'd passed on her offerings. Elliot pulled the chair in alongside them to talk.

'This must be serious?' Oden noted; they both had hot mugs in their hands.

'We need to talk to you, it's important, Oden.' Siobhan began.

'Go on then?'

Elliot spoke up. 'We're trying to make a decision, but it hems on whether it's okay with you or not?'

'What is it?' Oden was puzzled.

'We know we're not your guardians.' Elliot needed to get this across. 'But we did say we'd be here for you; we can wait until you finish your degree.'

'You're leaving; you're going somewhere?' Oden coped on.

'Mum and dad are only an hour away by car.'

'Where are you going?'

The couple looked at each other before Elliot started to explain. 'We're thinking of packing up and heading to Australia.'

'What will you do with the house?' Oden was confused.

'We'd hand the house over to an agent to rent it for us until we are settled,' Siobhan continued to talk as she moved over and sat on the arm of Elliot's chair.

'That's not our key concern... our key concern is you and whether you could manage.' Elliot informed him. 'You're independent we know, and your house share has worked out fine.' He added. 'But, if we left, you might not have anyone to fall back on; you know what they're like, Oden. It's a serious concern for us,' Elliot said again, 'and mum will be worried of course.'

'She's on the phone every other day as is and that's her holding back.' Oden responded. 'She'll be pure torture.'

Siobhan could see that Elliot was struggling. 'We don't have to go, Oden...It's just Elliot, and I have been in a right rut lately, and we thought a new venture might help.'

'Sounds great; it's just convincing mum.'

'If there are any problems they will be there for you, Oden. I can assure them that fussing won't help, you're doing fine on your own. If there's any risk of you dropping out of this college course, we're not going.'

'I'm not dropping out of college, you daft ape.'

'You're a tonic, Oden.' Siobhan smiled. 'I can barely remember my life before you came into it, you have me hooked, we'd miss you, big style.'

Elliot wished that he'd never said a word; it felt all wrong right there. He knew that the bare mention of Australia would quickly turn into a new reality. Oden had his fair share of problems, he was more than socially awkward, and though he'd found a close niche of friends, he could be wildly misinterpreted with new people around.

Oden could cause offence without meaning to. It scared Elliot maybe not as much as it scared his mother, but people sometimes took the hump, they got nasty. Oden could never recognise danger; he found it challenging to read responses, especially emotional ones.

'When were you thinking of going?' Oden asked.

Our Diligent Souls

'The week the boys go back, Brian and Alfie are coming home at the end of the summer for the wedding. You're invited to that by the way. We thought we'd go shortly after they leave. We'll both be applying for jobs there.'

'Right!' For Oden, the idea was just starting to reach home.

'We should be set up nice and easy with our qualifications. Apparently, there's a shortage of pharmacists and experienced curators. We've talked to potential employers online, and they were ready to offer us jobs.'

'You're serious?' Oden asked.

Siobhan's face lit up. 'I know right. We'd earn a higher wage too, not that money is the motivator.'

'You both should go, it will be good for you, and I can Skype you once I get the time differences down. That's been tricky before; I have a friend who talks to this guy in Japan on Skype, they're into League of Legends stuff, then there's this final tonight. He's in games development this guy. He can stream conference three people at a time, with no problem. This guy that's in Japan, he's top of the league table.'

Siobhan got up from the chair feeling tearful. It had always been difficult for Oden and the people that loved him. He was such an odd individual, too intense for your average football loving male; driving home information that people had no interest in hearing. He found it hard to judge.

When Oden received news that would affect his life, it barely registered, and yet he was far from bulletproof. Occasionally, you got a window into this strange inner world where he lived, unaffected by emotion. The guy was not only relatable but witty and charming by times, then bang there it was this paradigm shift where he was blindsided to people's mood or emotional states, this other side of him was as fixed and unreachable as one can imagine.

'So, you'll be living with Brian and Alfie?' Oden asked.

'At first, we might be but yeah? Probably!' Siobhan just wasn't sure.

'I could be finished my degree the next time I see you. Comic-con is here next week; there's a one-day symposium on...'

'Oden!'

Oden's detachment was something that always hit Elliot hard; he felt that he'd earned the right to be by Oden's side forever having been made to play the role of stand-in parent. The reality of Australia was hitting home.

'You could join us when you're finished your degree and get work over there.' Siobhan suggested.

'In Australia?'

'We'll be raising the money to bring you over in the meanwhile, every summer,' Elliot insisted. 'I won't fail to do that.'

Siobhan leaned over and took Oden's hand. 'Beaches... long evenings with endless sunshine, surfing, Oden, and meat on the barbeque.' Poor Oden was perplexed; he couldn't understand why she was touching his hand. Elliot took his cup and plate and headed for the kitchen.

'Sounds great, but maybe I'll get a job with a games company here. It's a tax haven; you knew that right?'

'We could be back next year and to hell with Australia, Oden,' Elliot called out from the sink; the whole idea of being separated from his brother was becoming unthinkable.

Siobhan was trying to cover every scenario. 'That could happen, Elliot but if we were to settle there, we'd be over and back anyway.'

'I can work here,' Oden announced, 'and save up and get a team together so that we can make our own games, I can make money debugging code for companies, it is just discovering their system flaws and keeping dated copies of my findings. You do need to dig really deep to find the chinks in their armour, but then they're throwing money at you for it, you need to be shrewd mind you. Coding is logical to any basic understanding.'

Siobhan smiled. 'I can see you in Silicon Valley.'

Elliot was roiled. He liked the fact that Oden came up with his own ideas. 'Where is Silicon Valley seen as you're so smart, Siobhan?'

Oden stepped in. 'It's in San Francisco Bay, North California. Geographically, it encompasses Santa Clara Valley, the southern half of the San Francisco Peninsula and southern portions of the east bay. San Jose is the capital.'

'If you say so...' Elliot stated, looking over to snatch a smile from Oden with an Indian head wobble that he used on occasion.

'It's only a consideration,' Siobhan suggested. 'The key thing is achieving your degree. You'll have endless prospects from there on in Oden, and I think you'll be fine. If we're in Australia, we could do the research that end, and see what options you have over there. What do you say?' Siobhan was curious.

Oden hadn't taken in a word she said, 'San Jose is the capital, Elliot.'

'About us going to Australia? What do you say?' Siobhan was starting to lose the plot.

'Yeah, it sounds good. I'll miss Elliot's cooking... And yours, you can cook. I don't envy you telling mum and dad though.'

'They'll get over it.' Siobhan stated.

Elliot returned to them to wade in on that. 'Are we talking about the same people? Mum stays off his back because she thinks his big brother Elliot's watching out for him, we're talking nightmare here in truth Siobhan when it comes to my mother.'

'I'll make sure she stays off your case.' Siobhan swore it.

'So, what's the plan? How do you start to organise this? I will help if I can?' Oden was always keen to lend a hand. Siobhan had the whole thing plotted out in her head.

'We'll secure jobs first, that's the most straightforward way to arrange things, visas, and then tickets. Pack up our stuff here, organise an agent to collect the rent, find accommodation for when we get there.'

'We'd have a load to do.' Elliot stated being for and against any agreement on the matter; he was in two minds.

Siobhan cut short the conversation, realising the time. 'Mark's on his way over; we wanted to talk to you first before we made any announcements. We're planning to see your parents the weekend, and mine.'

'So, I can go now, I have League of Legends stuff on in a mate's house. Can I go?'

Elliot was rummaging through his jacket pockets. 'Go, buddy, no problem there.'

'We'll talk again soon,' Siobhan suggested, 'just keep us posted, and yeah that wedding reception invite, I have it here somewhere?'

'Brian's sister's wedding?' Oden asked.

Siobhan went to the drawer and pulled out his invite.

'Yes,' she was reading it, 'Oden, plus one.'

'That's good. I'll have to give thought to that. What are you doing for a present?'

'I think we're putting in fifty euro each, saves us from getting her the same present,' Siobhan informed him.

'Fifty euro,' Oden replied.

Elliot was appalled by Siobhan. 'Just put twenty in a card, mate.'

'No. I can stretch to fifty.'

'You'll have to stay in the hotel overnight. I'll pay for that; you can see me right when you're making millions in Silicon Valley.'

'If you're sure, Elliot?'

'A hundred percent.'

'Okay then, I guess that's it? I'll talk to you soon, guys.'

'Be happy, Oden.' Elliot re-checked his pockets.

'I'm always happy.'

'Fair enough. I can't contradict you on that one; we'll talk soon.'

Elliot slipped him twenty Euros.

'Thanks, bro!'

After a short embrace, Oden was gone. Elliot turned to Siobhan. There was a nervousness separating the couple now that he was gone. Ever since Christmas, she had noticed a shift in Elliot's affections; he was restless and uptight with her all the bloody time.

She had discovered pamphlets that he'd brought home about the missions, she never mentioned it to him for fear that he might genuinely want to go. She knew if he went, he'd not come back the same man, hard news stories left him resentful and angry, especially when it came to children and bomb attacks.

Elliot was innately empathic and bewildered by atrocity; he struggled more than most about the state of the world. A stint in the missions could profoundly affect him, that much she knew instinctively. Siobhan had been waiting for him to broach the topic when he turned around and started talking about a move to Australia. In truth, she was a happy passenger for his sake as much as hers, knowing that he'd decided not to go that road.

'How do you think he took it?' Siobhan asked.

'Yeah, he was fine, but he's right my mother won't take the news lightly. You may be prepared for a battle when we go to see them at the weekend.'

Our Diligent Souls

Elliot was off again, leaving her standing in the kitchen half stunned. As much as she loved him, he was pushing her beyond her limits, keeping Mark to himself was the latest thing and he had less time for Emily. She couldn't reach him, even now with these big plans for Australia. He kept taking off on his own, pulling out of arrangements without any explanation. He'd avoided all phone conversations with the Wicklow couples they'd become acquainted with and the country village thespian scene.

'We won't be long; I'm just going to take Mark for a kick about in the park...I want to tell him the news.' He didn't wait for a response. She knew as he shut the door that he wasn't going to bring Mark back when he returned.

As Mark watched Elliot come down the steps with a football and his jacket in hand, he knew something was going on, something significant.

'What is it, mate, you're not yourself?' Mark inquired.

Elliot paused. 'I've got news.'

'Go on.'

'We're moving to Australia.' Elliot announced.

'Why?'

Elliot pointed in the direction of the park as they started to walk. 'Why not, beaches, long summer days, better pay?'

'Higher cost of living.'

The two men stopped in their tracks.

'When?' Mark asked.

'Just after the wedding, end of the summer.'

'I don't know what to say, I'll miss you both, as will Emily and Oden, especially Oden. What prompted this?'

'We just need a change of scenery. I told you that we haven't been great.'

'It such a drastic thing to do...and the house?'

'We'll rent it, our jobs will sort the rent in Australia, and the rent we get here will cover the mortgage this end, so we've something to fall back on for now anyhow. We need to get a fresh start.'

'At least you're holding onto the house. You can always come back to that if it doesn't work out. You put so much into that place. I'm glad you're not selling it?'

'Not yet.'

'Look, I'm sure I don't have to say this, but if you have gripes with Siobhan, Australia won't automatically fix that Elliot.' Mark was sincere.

'I have no gripes with Siobhan; I love her. It's me. I just need a change of pace.'

'And Siobhan?'

'She's excited by the idea. How could she not be happy, it's Australia?'

'Have you taken her into account though?' Mark spoke calmly but under his soft exterior lay something more volatile.

'What's with you, of course, I have!'

Mark walked on in silence; he needed to process the news. Siobhan was a strong woman capable of making up her own mind, he knew this, and it was not for him to interfere. The last thing he wanted to do was have a bust-up with Elliot, but his friend's propensity towards Siobhan had altered in recent times. Instinctively, Mark knew the plan wasn't thought through enough. Elliot was just jumping on any old idea.

'If your mind is made up?'

'It is, Mark.'

'Then, know that I will miss you and Siobhan.'

'Can you look after Oden?' Elliot asked.

'Of course, I'll be there for Oden… you don't have to worry on that front. I can involve him in as much as possible, Emily and Laura will still be here too.'

'I'd appreciate that. My brother needs to be able to stand on his own two feet anyway, without his brother having his back all the time.'

'You have a few weeks to think it through fully. Maybe you'll change your mind, Elliot?'

'I won't change my mind.' Elliot snarled.

Mark was not convinced by his friend's reaction. 'Woh Tiger! Keep your boxers on,' he retorted, he was hoping to defuse Elliot's anger.

'Have you been talking to Brian and Alfie?' Elliot asked.

'You're going over to them then?'

'No, but we're going to the same region, so we have a place from where we can establish ourselves.' That wasn't entirely true to the plan, but Elliot was feeling defensive.

'It might be good to have someone there. The boys could organise temporary accommodation for you until you find somewhere more suitable.'

There was a silence between the men as they entered the park both avoiding confrontation. The grass was freshly cut, and the flower beds had just been watered. The dog walkers were as always apologising as their pets came up close for a sniff. The two lads sat on the green.

'So how are things with you?' Elliot asked.

'Yeah! I'm doing fine.'

'Are you bringing anyone to the wedding?'

'No, Emily's going.'

'And you've no interest beyond that.' Again, Elliot was snarly. 'And Emily, how is she?'

'Yeah! I bumped into her briefly yesterday.'

'If you see her don't mention the Australia thing, Siobhan will want to tell her herself.'

Again, there was a long silence. 'I'm going to miss you, mate; you have no clue, I'm stunned here.' Mark had no idea how to process the news.

'Will we do a lap of the park? We might get in on a match.' Elliot had the ball in his hands that he'd carried from the house. 'There's a crowd over there, looks like a kick about.'

Mark's eyes scanned the area. 'There are only four of them.' Elliot looked away, but Mark needed to say what he thought. 'We're not going to talk about this are we?'

'No.' Elliot responded bluntly.

'You had me worried after the conversation we had in the pub the other night, I...'

'Enough, we're going, and that's it; end of story.'

'You're my best friend, Elliot.'

'And I need to get the hell out of here, so what are you going to do?'

'That's rough man.'

'Look an extra two.' Elliot was pointing to the gang of lads mucking about with their own ball. 'That will make eight of us... Come on we can give it a shot. Elliot got up and started towards them.

'Alright, alright then, let's hope they're obliging.' Mark warned, trailing behind him. He knew he was getting nowhere fast; there was no point in even trying to talk about it today. There was still time yet to get to the core of what was going on.

Chapter 32

The river bank was the best place to take someone on a picnic, but that was to be a surprise. Lucile had agreed to go with Oden at the last minute when he had shown up at her door with a rucksack full of hidden treats.

'Where have you been? I tried to call you.' Lucile quizzed.

'My phone broke earlier this week; I need a replacement. On the upside, you have my full attention now.'

'I'm not sure I want your attentions?'

'That's attention if you ever feel the need to be grammatically correct. Come on it's a lovely day; it might be fun.'

'My internet is down.'

'We may as well revisit the eighties in that case, you know when people had to find things to do,' Oden added sarcastically. 'I've read all about it online.'

'Hold on until I get my phone.'

Oden was left standing at the door until she returned.

'Are we right then? Where are you taking me?' She enquired.

'It's a short walk away.'

'What, Aldi? If I ever see Aldi again, I hope it's the last time. I do honestly. I'm never out of there.'

'What's wrong with Aldi?'

'I'm just never out of the place. Do I have to repeat myself? Are you bringing me to Aldi or what, Oden?'

'No... not today.'

Lucile wanted to let him know how much he frustrated her, but she fancied him in the same hand, so she calmed herself.

'You are daft,' she proclaimed, though it was affectionately said.

The sky was a wondrous coral blue. The buzz of summer was in the air however long that might last. The sounds of tiny creatures were worth a listen; bees and butterflies, blue flies and midgets that were autographing the sky. These creatures keep their distance so as not to be a nuisance, she figured.

The fragrant flowers were pungent though neither Oden nor Lucile could put a name to a single flower. It didn't stop them from admiring Dublin Corporation's efforts to bring a little brightness into their lives.

'Winter seems so far away on days like this.' Lucile uttered wistfully.

'Yeah... The sunshine is out to trick you, remember the mind-numbing winter weather, so you are at no stage deceived. Hold that picture in the darkest corner of your mind.'

'Will you stop taking the piss out of me, please or I'm going home. I'm not in the form for this. Where are we going? I'm not into mystery tours.' Oden could wind her up when he wanted. 'We're twelve minutes away now.'

'You said fifteen minutes, ten minutes ago.'

'No, I didn't.'

Lucile looked frustrated.

'You're in a heightened state, Lucile.' He swore to her, you perceive time to move slower when your thoughts are suspended in doubt.'

'I wasn't born to be guided the wrong way into deserted wastelands. I insist on knowing where you are taking me?'

'Have you any patience?'

'Just the ones I've left in the hospital.'

'Come on.'

'How far are we now?'

'Another seven minutes by foot no more.'

'So where are we going?'

Oden knew then that she had never seen the old harbour. He was glad that he'd hidden the contents of his rucksack; the surprise picnic safely tucked away inside. Oden took her by the hand as she rounded the corner, but she said very little. He watched her expression change from flustered to a kind of curious delight.

From where they stood, they could see sailing vessels dotted along the harbour wall and the odd dishevelled boat that was port bound thanks to the new restrictions in EU fishing laws. These restrictions left many an ancient mariner without a quest or viable adventure. There were a couple of herrings to the left of the little tugboats as they moved closer to the quay's edge. It was a picture to behold. In the middle of a bustling city it was hard to believe such places still existed, and this one more or less on her doorstep.

Oden took out his rug and the two cold cans of cider that were safely tucked away in his rucksack, he placed the cider on an old anchoring stone and spread out a blanket so that they could sit down and throw their legs over the edge.

He removed the ham sandwiches that he'd wrapped in tin foil and the pack of two shop-bought cupcakes which he hoped would be right up her street. It was hard to predict her mood, one minute she was singing from the rafters, the next she was biting his head off; he'd a limited understanding of the opposite sex.

'Nice here...Eh?'

'I suppose I can give you that. It's not like you to be romantic.'

'Romantic, you'd call it romantic?'

'I would.'

'Well that's good, mission accomplished I guess.'

'That depends on why you have brought me here. I still want to know why you've been avoiding my calls.'

'I wasn't avoiding anything; I told you my phone is broke. Just enjoy your cider, eh?' He had needed time to gauge his level of interest in her, but his phone was broken.

He passed her a can, amazed by the fact that they were still cold.

'Cider is a perfect summer drink.' Unlike most in his age bracket; Oden enjoyed a glass of wine but today was about Lucile, and he knew the cider was the way to go on a warm summer's day.

The sky was teeming with wildlife. A large flock of tiny birds were dancing and swooping in and out of the shade. The seagulls were dotted from pillar to post; they seemed oblivious to their surroundings, unmoved by the two herring that were standing tall with their long pencil width legs.

'I'm completely relieved that the exams are behind us.' Lucile mentioned. 'I'm going to stick with computing, I've come too far to turn back now, and gaming seems ridiculously hard.'

'They're much the same! You can still play games; you might even have more time.'

'You're contradicting yourself there.'

'So, I am...'

'Gaming is a level eight, right?'

'It is.'

'Computing is level seven.'

'So, you're not decided?'

'Not fully, not yet. I'd have to get a job... I'd have no grant if I changed over to a different course.'

'Not if you go up a level.' Oden told her.

'Really? Are you sure?'

'As far as I know, if you move from a level seven to a level eight your grant stays unaffected.' Oden replied.

'I'll have to check that out. I'm a gamer at heart. Hey, did you see Bjergsen from Team solo mid at the LCS last night?'

'It was great,' Oden responded enthusiastically. He was delighted that she'd caught the game online.

'Mind-blowing,' Lucile continued. 'But don't start analysing it, not now please, it's lovely here.'

'If I stick with you I know I won't miss the champion series.' Oden said, smiling ear to ear.

'And if you do stick with me you won't end up with a 'gaming widow'.' Lucile blushed at her comment, it sounded way too childish, but she'd heard the term used at college a lot. Girls who weren't into gaming, they tired quickly of boys who were obsessed with the sport.

'Elliot and Siobhan are moving to Australia.'

'Nice one!'

'Well they're not selling up their place yet, they're going to rent it out and put their stuff into storage at my mum's house. They'll rent over there and check out the run of things before they make the full move.'

'How do you feel about that?'

He shrugged his shoulders.

'You'll miss them.'

'I'm happy for them, I guess.'

'But you're always round there?'

'I'll still see Mark and Emily.'

'Are they together yet?'

'Mark and Emily? No. I don't think so anyway. They were asking for you, well, Siobhan was more specifically.'

'I must have made an impression so?'

Oden went quiet, he passed along a ham sandwich, and they dug in.

'I didn't think I was hungry.' Lucile mumbled between bites. 'Ham sandwiches are the best when you're hungry.'

'I like salty tomatoes ones too, salty, not soggy.' Oden mentioned.

'Good to know.'

Lucile looked embarrassed; she kept turning away, trying to eat in private. They sat there for ages. At one point she took out her phone and put some music on; it had a decent speaker. They stayed perfectly still for the first few songs, both joined in on the chorus of a tune, drowning out the music when they laughed. Neither of them would win a medal for vocals, but it was a pleasant change and better than talking all the time. It was such a quiet spot; they'd seen no more than two people come and go in the hour and a half that they spent there.

Oden tried to fill her in on his college exams and told her about the day that Elliot and the crew went to St. George's market in Belfast. He'd seen her a few times since then, but he'd forgotten to mention it. Lucile had been to the market herself and bought a vintage jacket there, but it was some time back. She still had the jacket she told him, though it was well worn by now.

Her exams were a bit more touch and go than his, but she'd managed them alright. In truth, he never got stressed out about exams where she was the complete opposite. There were a couple of fights over cleaning and food bills in the house she shared, but that had worked itself out. Outside of her nearly losing her marbles when he hadn't called, all had gone well.

She had been to an end of term party and had felt way out of her depth as it was mostly fourth years at the gig; there was a lot of alcohol and pot flying around, more than she was comfortable with for sure. She said nothing to Oden, but she had met someone he knew there. The guy thought Oden was a bit pushy, but she had jumped to his defence. She hadn't liked this guy much anyway; like a lot of students heading into fourth year, he was a bit into himself, she thought.

It was a rare kind of day, and it seemed like they had a lot of things to talk about in the sunshine. Up until that point, she'd only ever talked about her feelings, her family life, and the highlights and fall outs in her other relationships.

She recognised that he liked to analyse the issues. Otherwise, he'd just rattled on about some new technology, but this was much more personable than usual, he shared some truths about his upbringing and dreams he'd had as a kid. He had missed her.

They decided with a heavy heart that it was time to go, too much sun was plain dangerous for their very Irish skin. Their backsides felt like they were fixed to the concrete pier, they brushed themselves off, folded away the rug and headed out in the direction of her house. It had been a nice change from sitting in front of a computer screen. On the way back, he dared to ask her what he set out to ask her in the first place.

'Do you remember Brian?'

'He returned from Australia for his dad's funeral, right?'

'That's the one.'

'Are Elliot and Siobhan going over to be with them then?' She asked.

'Yes, well kind of, that's not the point.'

'Go on?'

'Well... Brian's sister is getting married at the end of the month. Three weeks from today to be precise.'

'Yeah?'

'Well...I've been invited to the wedding, and I was just wondering if you'd like to be my plus one.'

Poor Lucile was gobsmacked; her head was already working overtime in respect of finances.

'If you want to come with me, it's down the country so, we'd have to stay the night; we could stay in the hotel. The cost of the hotel is covered. I can get a twin room or a separate room for you if you like. I mean if you want to come with me.'

'I'm flattered.' She insisted.

'But you don't want to come?'

'I'd love to go.'

'Wow! It's the last Saturday of the month. You don't have to go, Lucile. I can go alone; I just thought that maybe... I don't know.'

'Yes Oden, yes please and thank you.'

'You'll go?'

'Yes, I'll go, of course, I'll go, and we can share a room, it's fine. We're friends, right? We can do a twin room. How much are the rooms I can raise some funds, I think?'

'No, absolutely not, Elliot is covering the cost of the hotel, and I'm buying the present. Well, I'm putting fifty quid into a card.'

'I can help with that!'

'No, I got advice on it.'

'Advice?'

'Yes, like what's normal practice, I asked my mum.'

'Your mum?'

They had reached the front gate to her house.

'Just advice, she won't be there.'

'That's a relief.'

'Elliot's paying for the hotel and I'm buying the present, all you have to worry about is having a few quid in your pocket for drinks, and I can buy you a few.'

They had by then reached her front door.

'I'll be in contact with you today or tomorrow... Okay? I'm buying a new phone today if they have it in stock. I need to go to the phone shop. I'll ring you.'

'That'll be great. Can I rely on that though?'

'Give me some leeway in case there's a problem in the shop, but with a bit of luck I should be sorted by this evening.'

'I'll talk to you then.' She stated.

'Great.'

As Lucile was about to retreat inside, she turned on her heels. 'You can come in for tea if you want? The house is a mess, but...'

'No, I'd better get going, collect my phone and that. I'm glad you're going.'

'I'm glad too.'

'Bye so.'

'Bye...'

Lucile shut the door behind her and pressed her back against the frame, her knees bent as she slid to the floor in a combination of relief and excitement. 'Well, what do you know?' She whispered.

Her flatmate was on her way down the stairs. 'Was that the infamous Oden then?'

'That was him.'

'Thank Christ!' The flatmate flopped onto the second last step in great cheer. Lucile had been a pain in the butt for a solid week, not having heard from him.

Oden, on the other hand, was happily making his way home via the telephone shop.

'A bit of a turnaround,' Lucile uttered. 'A bit of a turnaround.'

Chapter 33

Mark was ready to finish up in the salesroom; he'd been working upstairs since early morning but had secured two new clients who were willing to commit to using the company for their deliveries on a regular basis. He had spent the day before sitting in with the customer care workers to see if he could figure through any issues or pick up on any mention of difficulties that their new clients had, with their previous shipping contractors.

The management team were wearing the floorboards thin. One of them had mentioned that there was a restructuring of staff taking place in the upper levels of management.

The decision to have Joyce manage the floor had worked out well while Mark intermittently took off to the salesroom. Joyce had kept the staff on their toes; no man stood still on his watch. He was never a ball breaker, but the men took him seriously. Joyce had built up the confidence to make a proper stab at it; there was no denying he'd a way with the men. Mark made his way to the floor and joined Joyce.

'So where are we now?' He asked, waiting on Joyce to bring him up to date.

'Those three sections are completed, hold on there...' Joyce tapped Mark on the shoulder and nodded in Mournaghan direction. The man was pounding out every step across the floor as he approached.

Laura's father had been right in saying that Mournaghan had persuaded his way back into the company, even after the incident with Joyce's hand. The squad cars rolling up at the gates hadn't changed much either. There was no such thing as a criminal clause in a business contract, as far as Mark knew. Still and all, Mournaghan was showing tremendous bottle; he seemed unaltered by his predicament.

'Right, I want this place moving, too much chatter and not enough action,' Ralph was already making demands. 'It's time you stepped back and watch a professional do the job.'

Mark stood tall, fully conscious of the assault he had suffered at Mournaghan's hands. 'Just let me confirm, Ralph?' Mark asked fearlessly. 'You were relocated here for the day?' It was their first face to face meeting since the assault.

Our Diligent Souls

One of the workers skidded by on a wheelie trolley. 'Nee-naw, nee-naw.' He sounded out making a childlike police siren noise as he passed. Joyce and Mark showed no reaction as Ralph looked past them to put a face on the culprit. Their blank expressions provided no support as they followed his beady little eyes.

'I will be taking charge here today. I am your senior am I not? I'll want you to...'

'Hold it right there.' Mark interrupted, raising his hand just below Mournaghan's face.

'If you could allow me a minute to talk to my colleague?' Ralph was somewhat taken back as Mark turned Joyce around to have a quick word.

He whispered. 'How long to finish up today at a push?'

'Two hours, but that's a serious push. We're in good time today, and the boys know it.'

'Lovely,' Mark responded.

Mark had a plan as he turned to Ralph again.

'With the present schedule as is,' he started, 'we only need one man on the floor. Joyce and I would be delighted to have you on board. We can head upstairs and push forward with the client list while you take control here if that's okay with you?'

'Not a problem, I can put these boys through their paces.' Ralph was acting like the assault had never taken place though both Mark and Joyce were fully aware of the damage he'd done.

Two of the workers were standing behind Mournaghan with their arms folded, one of them winking at Mark.

'Hold on a minute, lads!' Mark called out. Mournaghan instantly glanced back at them.

'Okay Ralph, it's one o'clock now, and we're to be out of here by five, do you think you can manage? If need be, we can stay and show you the ropes.'

'Are you daring to question my ability?' Mournaghan spouted aggressively.

Mark had anticipated his response. Two lads were listening from the side aisle where they were having a great laugh. When Mournaghan turned his back again to check on them, Mark winked over smiling.

'Here you go then,' Mark stated, raising his eyebrows as he handed Ralph the clipboard.

'So, fill me in, what's been done to date?'

'It's on the clipboard, Ralph. You do know how to read the clipboard?'

Mournaghan frantically started flipping through the sheets as Joyce and Mark turned and headed for the stair. When they turned back, Mournaghan was already shouting.

'Get out here!' He called.

But there was not one worker to be seen.

'Hide and go seek!' Joyce whispered.

'They'll have more up their sleeves than that,' Mark returned. 'And rightly so.'

At twenty past three, Davin Turlock came running into the upstairs office, where Mark and Joyce were hard at it, they were going over schedules and new even better layouts. Davin was frantic.

'He's ready to explode downstairs. The board of management are on the floor trying to rescue the situation, please. You have to get down there.'

''That's terrible.' Mark responded as the two men quickly moved from their seats.

'It's like a scene from a Monty Python show.' Davin explained. As Mark and Joyce reached the bottom of the stair, their ears were caught by the absolute silence that was broken by Mournaghan and Mournaghan alone.

'Do you see the fools that this dim wit is in charge of, guys? In one and a half hours, they got less than one shelf cleared?'

Mark's team of workers came parading out; their heads lowered to the ground.

'And you call this effective?'

Six management officials were watching on as Mournaghan flinched like a caged animal. They waited for Mark to approach, one executive, moving forward to question Mark at once.

'Why was Ralph Mournaghan left in charge here, and on his own?'

Our Diligent Souls

'His authority supersedes mine. He came down here giving orders, he said that he was in charge. He insisted that he had been relocated here for the afternoon, he was not taking no for an answer.'

'What is going on with the men?'

'It's the way he addresses people, my men won't respond to that, and I cannot blame them.'

The executive nodded at Mark and turned again to look at his colleague. 'Ralph, can you come back upstairs please.' He called out.

'Not until I give these a piece of my mind. You see that fool?' Mournaghan shouted, pointing to the worker at the end of the line. 'He made me chase up the aisles after him; I want him fired. If I have the authority and I assure you I have...You...' He said pointing his finger, 'are finished today.'

'Ralph, now!' The executive pressed him.

Ralph bent over and lifted his jacket which was by now on the floor gathering dust.

'What?' Mournaghan growled, retrieving his jacket.

'Can we talk about this upstairs?' The same executive said calmly. They beckoned Ralph to join them, patting him on the back as they checked to confirm that he was alright.

'I am better than this.' He spat out, and again in a lower tone, he repeated himself. 'I am better than this.'

Mark and Joyce lowered their eyes as the executives passed, Mournaghan making his way back up the stairs with them.

'Right, guys, back to work.' Mark called out.

'Don't imagine we'll hear any more on that matter.' Joyce commented.

'Me neither.' Mark said, smiling.

It was a long, arduous afternoon, but they had great laughs, laughs the men deserved. Joyce and Mark had the work sown up smoothly by the end of the day; they were back ahead of themselves and could take it easy for the last fifteen minutes. Mark asked Joyce if he could close up for him so he could make his way over to Emily's on time. He was taking her over to visit Laura in Arthur's factory; he was keen to show her around.

Emily was waiting at the entrance to the solicitors when he arrived. There was no messing; she jumped straight into the taxi as they took off in the direction of the old factory.

'So how was your day at the office?' She asked.

'Not too bad as it goes, not too bad.' Mark smiled. 'Have you a gig tonight?'

'No, but I have the recording studio.'

'Good, how's the album going?'

'We're planning to finish it up tonight.'

The conversation was back to business with them ever since his outburst on the day of St George's Street market. It wasn't long before they were at the factory gate.

'God, it's very different to T&E.' Emily observed as they drove through the gates.

'I think it's atmospheric.'

'Me too, sorry, it has a lovely old school feel to the place.'

When the two arrived through the door, Laura was the first to greet them.

'I'm very honoured that you guys could make it. It's time Emily got to meet the brigade.' The men were readying to go home but not without a word for their champion. Emily had heard so much about them; she felt as if she knew them intimately.

'So, when are you coming back to work with us, Mark, or are you too high and mighty for that now, eh?'

'I'm tied up in contracts at the minute, lads. There's all of no chance of getting out of them right now.'

'We miss Arthur, Mark; it would be great to have you back.'

'I appreciate that lads, sincerely. Arthur would be happy to see you working like Trojans for Laura; you do him proud.'

There were pats on the back and the odd hug. Mark never lost that closeness that he'd shared with his men.

'Introduce us then, is this your new lady friend?'

'This is my friend Emily, lads!'

'Pleased to meet you, love. We won't shake your hand. We're filthy buggers, dusty too.' She laughed.

'Here, do the three of you want to go for a drink, we're heading over to Mulligan's pub. Laura never comes with us; she's afraid we might drink her under the table, right Laura?'

'I don't think it, I know it.'

'Come just this once, boss, we need a catch up with Mark too.'

Mark looked at Laura.

'I'm exhausted, Mark.' She whispered. 'I've paperwork to get through later tonight. What do you think Emily?'

'I have to be in the studio in an hour.' The boys had got the message and were fading into the background to collect their things.

'We'll leave it, Laura,' Mark said, 'but next time, yeah? Are we getting the full tour then?'

'Come with me so.' Laura suggested. Mark had a thought and stopped the two women in their tracks before he turned to Laura, 'Can I stay here if you don't mind, re-acquaint myself with Arthur's desk. Am I asking too much?'

'Not at all, not a problem,' she said. 'Please, make yourself at home.' Her paperwork had already been tidied and was safe under lock and key.

The two women watched the last of the workers leave as Mark sat firmly in Arthur's old chair. They looked back at him as they took off; he was already lost in nostalgia.

'Night, lads!' He called out.

He had never sat in Arthur's chair, nor ever felt the leather of his desk. It had been a while since he had thought of Arthur, but he was at the centre of the man's universe here, and boy did it feel good. He felt no grief just a oneness with his old friend. A short duration of time was enough to put him at ease, and he stayed there until Laura and Emily finally returned. Emily went straight up to use the toilets.

'There are a few things that have slipped since my days here when Arthur and I managed, do you mind if I point them out, Laura? It will put something else on your to-do list.'

'I'm glad of your input, Mark.'

'There are minor bits and bobs that I noticed on my way in.'

There were fire extinguishers in the wrong place, enough for them to be a trip hazard. The second shelf to the left has seen better days and needs replacing. If a man was to lean heavily on it, the shelf might collapse causing possible injury or parcel damage. He was right of course, and she was glad he was bringing her attention to the problems as they did a full inspection of the place.

He went through the number alignment with her and showed how a simple re-jigging of the shelving units could cut ten to twenty minutes off their work schedule. She took his advice as it was intended not as a criticism but an accurate evaluation.

'There is so much to do on your own. I'm not saying you're not capable, you are. You need to think about getting someone to act as back up to take the pressure off yourself. It's a tough job; you only have one life, Laura.'

'I love it here, and I can give the guys a few extra, time and a half hours to sort out these problems, I'll need to get a carpenter in to do a few jobs too.'

'That young fella, Conor, he's a fine carpenter among other things.'

'I'll get him straight onto it.'

'Do you want to call over to Elliot's on the way home?' Mark asked.

'Maybe, sure. I could do with a change of scene.'

'They're in good form, Elliot and Siobhan.'

'How are their plans coming on for Australia?'

'Fine. I meant to say to you; we're going to a wedding in the country Saturday fortnight. If you want to head over with us; I have a plus one as does Emily and neither of us is bringing anyone so, you could invite someone to join you.'

'That sounds amazing.'

'Oden's bringing Lucile.'

'Who is Lucile? Oden's Elliot's brother, right?'

'He's adorable. She's quirky, Lucile that is, very entertaining character to watch. We'll be keeping an eye out for Oden while Elliot is away, so maybe you could tag along with us on a night out at a later stage. We've grown accustomed to having him around, he's irreplaceable Oden, never a dull moment with that fella.'

'I love the way you bring people into the fold; my life has changed drastically in the last few months thanks to you lot. I'll be wearing ripped jeans next.'

'Well now, you don't have to go that far.' Mark smiled, pleased by Laura's assertion.

'So, you want to help me shut this place down for the night or what?'

'I'd be more than honoured,' Mark declared. 'This duty had been conducted by Arthur in his day. He always stayed a full hour after closing. He'd leave at six o'clock on the dot, not a minute before.'

'He was a creature of habit, look here...' Laura brought Mark over to the photo the men had mounted, a picture of Arthur on the wall; it was in a simple old wooden frame. Arthur had meant a lot to them both, they stood looking at his image together for a while.

'They're big boots to fill, Laura.'

'You're telling me, but I'm getting there.'

With that Emily re-joined them. 'Jesus, those toilets are nasty.' Laura and Mark laughed.

'I'm having a toilet put in on the bottom floor next week, just for me. It's a necessity.'

'They're men.' Mark stated.

Laura smiled, 'shall we go?'

'We can do that.' Mark bowed, leaning over to one side and rolling out his arms in jest. 'After you, ladies.'

With that, Laura moved towards the alarm, Mark ran over and checked the lifters while she turned off the power; they were out of there in less than ten minutes.

Chapter 34

'Mark... It's Emily here. Can you get away from work for a while, it's Elliot.'

'What's up?'

'He's gone.'

'Gone?'

'To a mission in Africa, the whole Australia thing is off for six months, a year, indefinitely, I don't know. He left Siobhan a note.'

'What? He just took off?'

'He didn't say a word, not to Siobhan or me, or anyone for that matter if he didn't mention it to you?'

'What is going through his head? I always said that I'd send him to the missions if he were to break up with Siobhan.'

'You said what?'

'It was a running joke at one stage, relax.' Mark held his breath for a minute. He had picked up on Emily's defensiveness.

She needed to fill in the gaps. 'Look, this is bad news for Siobhan... She's not in a good way. She was staying with her folks for the past two days and arrived back to this. All he left was a note; his clothes were gone too.'

'He mentioned the missions a few weeks ago, he wasn't himself that night. Why just up and leave? What was in the note?'

'It was three and a half pages of horseshit from what she read to me on the phone. It's not the Elliot I ever knew, Mark. Since when has Elliot ever been impulsive? Her world's been turned upside down. He's run off on some romantic notion of the missions, the missions like.'

'I knew things weren't right with him. I genuinely didn't recognise the person that was in front of me, in the pub that night, Emily; he was in a bad way.'

'Where did he get the idea from, Mark? What bubble has he been living in, and to keep her so completely in the dark, it's insane?'

Our Diligent Souls

'He was planning it for a while.' Mark realised out loud. 'He had to be and the Australia thing at the same time. He wasn't getting on with Siobhan, Emily. I warned him that Australia wouldn't fix that. I pleaded with him to talk to her about his feelings... She'll think me disloyal for not having gone to her and kept her abreast.'

'What do you mean he said it to you? Jesus, but this had better be good.'

'He's not been happy with their relationship for a while, just the whole couple's thing, I promise you, it wasn't any reflection on Siobhan.'

Emily made a noise that sounded wounded. 'And how could it possibly not have been any reflection on Siobhan? Tell me that!'

'He felt they were stagnating. He was bored with his job, bored with the routine of his life, he needed to feel challenged.'

'I'll tell you something, Mark. He'd know the meaning of the word challenged if he came up against me right now.'

'Calm the head, Emily. You're not going to help Siobhan by being defensive.'

'My best friend is in a heap, I've never known her to be floored by anything. I have no idea how she's going to pick up the pieces.'

'She's a strong woman, Emily.'

There was silence on the phone.

'It's a week to the wedding, Brian and Alfie will be home soon.'

Mark needed Emily to focus. 'We'll get her through the wedding. We don't know what's happened yet and besides time will heal what he's gone and done.'

'They were supposed to be buying their flight tickets today for Australia. They were supposed to start work in Australia in three weeks. They made oral agreements on jobs there last week, while he was busy avoiding going to the travel agents to get the tickets.'

'Pressure!'

'It must have been, but he had her blindsided.'

'Because he cared, Emily. I know he loves her.' Mark was sure of that.

'Then what was he thinking?' Mark failed to give a response. 'Look, we've talked enough, Mark. Siobhan is in shock. I'm on my way over to her now, can you see if you can slip out? She needs to be surrounded by friends.' Emily was adamant.

'Maybe she needs to talk with a girlfriend first.'

'Feck you!'

'It's as big a shock to me as it is to you, Emily. Siobhan doesn't need to find out that he was in two minds about their relationship, not yet, not right now.'

'What is it that you have to hide from her?'

'Nothing! Did you tell Siobhan that you'd contact me?'

'Yes.'

'She might think I have some idea why he left when I have no clue. He wasn't himself but this, I didn't see this coming either.'

'You should be there, Mark. She needs to know we have her back. I think! Personally...'

'Okay then, I'll leave at lunch. I'll be there before one o'clock, keep me posted if Siobhan needs to rest, let me know. We're assuming that she's taken a day off work?'

'She has, and she's supposed to be working her last week of notice.' Emily informed him.

'Wow!' There was a silence between the two as they both gathered their thoughts.

'She'll not go to Australia on her own now?' He asked.

'I don't know, Mark, I just don't know.'

'Look Emily... I'll see you at lunchtime, one way or the other. I'd better get back to work, what time are we?'

'Ten past eleven.'

'We'll talk later. One o'clock, yeah?'

Joyce was already at Mark's side. 'Something's come up?' He asked.

'What is it, Joyce?'

'No, with you, did something happen?'

'You could say that. Can I leave you to manage after lunch?'

'No problem, we're well ahead of the game today.'

"Let's get a push on then, I at least can console myself with the fact that you're not going to be under any pressure through the afternoon. It might only take an hour but just in case.'

'Suits me!'

The next hour flew by, and soon everyone was off to lunch. Mark's mind was flashing back to the last few conversations he'd had with Elliot. His friend loved Siobhan, there was no other woman for him, but he did get frustrated with her. She needed a broader commitment from him then he could give, and he'd had it, being groomed as he put it.

As Mark jumped in a taxi, his immediate thought was of Oden. Elliot was not going to leave without saying goodbye to his brother. It was Oden that Emily should have been calling; he would know what the score was more so than anyone. On the way over, Mark gave the lad a call.

'What's up, Mark?'

'Elliot, Oden? Have you seen him in the past few days?'

'Yeah, he was over yesterday morning. Why?'

'Did he talk to you about going away?'

'Yeah, to Australia?'

'No Oden, did he mention anywhere else?'

'No.' There was a long pause. 'Thinking about it he was acting strangely; he just kept going on about responsibilities. He said he couldn't cope with the pressure of never being able to do what he wanted. He was in a weird mood. I didn't get it... I thought leaving for Australia was his big thing. Are they not going now?'

'Oden, can you make your way over to Elliot and Siobhan's?'

'What now?'

'It's important.'

'Okay, fair enough, I've no more lectures until three o'clock. I'll meet you there in half an hour.'

Mark stood outside the door wondering if he should ring Laura before he went inside, but there was no point in worrying her, he didn't even know if Elliot had left the country yet. He knocked three times and when Siobhan arrived at the door her face was drained from crying.

'You better come into the house.' He wasn't sure at first if he was welcome. Emily was watching from behind the kitchen island as Siobhan helped him off with his jacket; she was rough and unaware of what she was doing. He was old and ugly enough to take his own jacket off. It wasn't the typical procedure with Siobhan, quite the reverse.

'Do you want coffee?'

'Yes, please. It's too awful Siobhan; I had no idea he was contemplating any of this?'

'No idea?' Emily quipped.

'None!' Mark confirmed. He could see that Emily was shaken by the notion that a life partner could leave in such a callous way. For some reason, her anger was directed at him.

'I knew it, Mark. It's my own stupid fault.' Siobhan came straight out with it.

'You knew?' Emily quizzed her.

Siobhan lowered her head and sobbed.

'I've just arrived myself.' Emily explained to Mark as she stepped in to hold her friend. Siobhan soon snapped out of it.

'He had an information leaflet on the missions, but I just ignored it and never brought up the conversation.'

'Why?' Emily asked.

'Why? What?' Siobhan snapped. She was wrenched by what had happened.

'Why didn't you bring it up?'

'I didn't want him to go.' She sobbed again as she spoke. 'I was surprised when he put the idea of Australia on the table; I was so relieved I didn't give him the chance to back out. If you go to the missions, you come back a different person, yeah? I've seen it before, in a good way too but nothing is ever the same? I've listened to stories about what goes on in some of these places, and for most, they have a positive effect, but I knew how he would operate in those circumstances, I knew he wouldn't cope, not initially anyway.'

'Are we sure he's physically left the country?' Mark asked.

'I rang the mission's head office this morning... they flew out at ten o'clock last night.'

'He didn't even tell Oden.' Mark informed them.

'You talked to Oden? Siobhan was miffed.

'He's on his way.' Mark replied. 'He doesn't know what's happened yet, he still thinks you're both going to Australia.'

'Why did you do that?' Siobhan barked at him. 'What gave you the right?'

'I thought if anyone knew what was going on, I still can't believe that he left without squaring it with Oden.'

'What?' Siobhan was severely ruffled. 'How do I face this kid? What have you done, Mark? What do I say?' Siobhan was again drawn to tears.

Emily took hold of the steering wheel before they hit a ditch. 'Go; pull yourself together and put on some make-up.' Emily was being practical.

Siobhan looked shocked but made her way towards the stairs, turning around before she disappeared. 'This is not what this kid needs right now.'

'He wrote a letter?' Mark inquired after her.

'Yes, it's there on the table. I won't be long.'

'How long did Oden say he'd be?' Emily asked.

'I'm sorry... he'll be here in the next ten, fifteen minutes.'

Mark sat and read through the letter of three and a half pages. Elliot said straight off that he loved Siobhan though he insisted that she deserved better. It was itchy feet on his part, and he was done pretending that he didn't want just to take off and leave his life in the rear-view mirror. Again, Mark could see glimpses of the contempt that Elliot had displayed in the pub that night. Reading on wasn't easy, Elliot was so far gone in his need to escape that he couldn't even soften the blow.

He wrote that he had to do something more meaningful and not her idea of meaningful. Elliot needed to be somewhere else, a place where he could make a difference. He was sick of his comic antidotes from work, he was sick of doing the same old, repeatedly. Australia could be much of the same; Elliot had reached that conclusion. There was no easy way to tell her, and if he had tried face to face, he'd have backed down and stayed.

He mentioned that he had written to Oden and his parents, he'd dropped the letters in the post. He let her know that he had seen Oden but hadn't had the guts to tell him face to face either. He insisted that the house was Siobhan's, he'd requested that the deeds be transferred into her name; they were with their solicitor ready to sign. He felt that it was up to her to follow her heart, adding that he wasn't convinced that Australia was where she wanted to go in the first place.

Emily handed over a cup of coffee to Mark and sat beside him.

'Tough love, Mark...'

'He sounds sharp and self-determined to me and well organised. No one can force his arm and make him be what he doesn't want to be anymore, sad as that is for his family, and his friends, not just Siobhan.'

'She's the one in the firing line here. It's her heart that's been torn in two.' Emily was defensive of her friend.

'It's tough, and it's nothing short of cutting at the minute, but that will settle.' Mark knew that. 'Have you considered what's at play for her, what decisions does she have to make?'

'The biggest question right now; does she leave for Australia on her own, and if not, can she get her old job back, and then there's Oden of course. There's the wedding too.'

'Better Oden hears it from her than via a letter, don't you think?'

'Possibly...' Emily couldn't completely agree. 'He'll be here shortly, and we'll know then right?'

Siobhan arrived back downstairs and went directly to the kitchen where she reached for her fourth coffee. There was a shake in her hand.

'So, what do you think, will you go to Australia, Siobhan?' Mark asked her.

'On my own, I don't think so. I'm not sure what I'm going to do anymore, Mark. My first thought was to fly to Africa and find out what he was thinking, but I guess I could be setting myself up for a fall there. I've been holding on too tight to the reigns, you know I've been four years in my job, and there wasn't a week that went by that I didn't worry about losing the fecking position. I never told him that. What is wrong with me, eh?'

'Holding life and soul together, Siobhan, that's what you've been doing.' Emily was cut up into ribbons over her friend.

'But have I been gripping so tight that I've strangled everyone around me?'

'You have no reason to be so hard on yourself, Siobhan.' Emily was adamant.

'The man I love has just walked out that door for God knows how long, six months, for a year, forever, I don't know. He went without a bye or leave, and I haven't got the chance to give him my blessing or get on my knees and beg him not to do it this way, not in this fashion.'

The bell rang, it was Oden most likely. 'What do I say to this guy? Why did you phone him?' Mark lowered his eyes at her criticism.

It was Oden; he had caught the sun on his face and looked as always, unphased.

'Come in, Mark and Emily are here.'

Emily jumped up to give her favourite guy a hug while Mark stepped in to shake his hand.

'What's the craic, Oden?' Mark tried to smile.

'White and hairy. Where's Elliot?'

The three stood in silence for a moment.

'He's in Africa.' Emily stated. 'He's gone to join the missions.'

Oden laughed out loud. 'You're joking. He was over with me yesterday morning.'

Siobhan moved over and touched his top arm with her hand. 'He left last night, Oden.'

'Why did nobody tell me?' He pleaded.

'None of us knew until this morning, he left last night, Oden.' Emily answered.

Siobhan was barely able to speak.

'Have you tried to call him?' Oden asked.

Siobhan put up her hand. 'I tried earlier... It was a foreign tone with no pickup.'

'What about Australia. Is that still going ahead?'

'No, Oden.' Siobhan replied. 'He's signed up for six months, with the choice of a full year; that was the total of what they could tell me at the mission when I called, we don't know when he'll be back.'

'Do mum and dad know?'

'No,' Mark stated, 'he posted you and your folks out letters that should arrive tomorrow at this stage. How did he appear to you yesterday?' Mark asked again.

'Same, I suppose. Elliot just kept saying that he didn't want the responsibilities that he had in his life and that he yearned to make a difference. He was just rambling to himself; I didn't pay much attention to him. He said the pressure of everything was too much; I guess I just wasn't listening.'

'That's okay, Oden. Who was to know?'

'Well, it's not okay if he didn't tell you or me, or any of you that he was going. My mother will be so angry, and I don't care what he was going through. Elliot told me he loved you, Siobhan, but if my brother loved you, how could he leave you like this? You keep saying things are different when you're older, but are they? Cruel is cruel right, how can that be love, I don't get it.' Oden sounded vaguely poetic. There was complete silence in the room.

'I'm not supposed to be able to empathise, Siobhan, but I'm hurt for you. You can't believe in him if he says one thing and does another. What's going to happen with Brian's sister's wedding, can I still go?'

'Of course, you can. We're still going.' Mark responded.

'But there will be no Elliot.' Siobhan stuttered.

'No, that's not going to happen. But it will be fine, Siobhan, yeah? We will all be there to help each other through. It will be fine, Oden.' Mark tried to speak in a soothing voice.

'Will Brian and Alfie still be coming back?'

'They will Oden, no worries on that count.'

'I'm bringing Lucile. He said yesterday that he'd paid for a twin room for us, we're friends Lucile and me, I think we're just friends.'

'Do you want something to eat, Oden? I can whip you up an omelette.' Siobhan just wanted to escape through the back window of her own home.

'No, I need to get going soon. It won't be the same without Elliot at the wedding, but you were both going to leave for Australia anyway. Are you still going to Australia, Siobhan? I hope not.'

'I don't know, love. I've thinking to do and a very short space of time to make these choices, such as they are.'

'I would never get in your way, Siobhan, but I don't want you to go alone. I couldn't bear to think of you so far away without Elliot.' She could feel a lump rise in her throat. 'I best get going. Oh! I meant to show you I got a new phone.'

Our Diligent Souls

He pulled the new phone out of his pocket and went on to explain its primary functions to Mark. The two women turned away to chat with each other.

'Alright, guys.' Oden called out again, shyly readying himself for their embrace. They stood up and gathered him in their arms.

'Love you.' Siobhan whispered, sounding more cheerful. The others didn't need to say another word as Oden let himself out.

'The poor fella.' Siobhan cried, turning her back on her two best friends.

'He'll be fine.' Emily was trying too hard to be reassuring.

Mark made himself clear. 'Look, Siobhan, if you decide that you're going to go to Australia, we're here for you, and we can help you to get organised. We're still behind you if you want to go; you'd not be on your own. Alfie and Brian will be there to do your nut in, and maybe a fresh start is what you need.'

'This is her decision, Mark.' Emily lit on him, but Mark dismissed her comment.

'Give yourself until the weekend to decide, but talk to your managers at work first, tell them what's going on and see if your job is still a workable option. You should talk to them tomorrow. That might give you time to decide. You can go to Australia at any stage, better to go when you're in the right frame of mind.'

Siobhan was too scattered to agree to anything.

'I can't believe he's left, we went ahead and agreed to these jobs in Australia. Until the very last minute, it must have all hung in the balance?'

'He's done what he's done, there is no reversing the decision he made, but it's going to be okay. Maybe even an opportunity, you don't know what the next few days or weeks are going to bring.' Mark was a big fan of Siobhan. She knew he believed in her and her ability to come to terms with this.

'I need to get back to work, Siobhan, I'm just the other end of the phone and ready to jump into action, I'm here to help with anything you need given an hour or two's notice. I'll be in touch.'

Mark didn't have to be back at work yet, but there was little else he could do there. On their own, the two women would talk things through and get the ball moving.

'Thanks, Mark.'

'You're okay to stay, Emily?' He needed to make sure.

'I am. We're grand here for now.'

'I'll let myself out, don't move a muscle.' Mark kissed Siobhan on the forehead. He nodded at Emily and smiled sadly. Closing the door tight behind him to leave the two women alone.

Over the coming hours, Siobhan talked through the events of the last few days that herself and Elliot had spent together, the past few months. She had known that they had grown apart, she had lied to herself. Elliot knew that Siobhan didn't want to talk through all this with him, she had on so many occasions avoided the conversations that they needed to have.

The missions and Elliot were a bad fit, she knew he'd never recognise that, and she didn't want to be the one to play devil's advocate with his dreams. She understood what made him click and what he couldn't take sitting down. The missions would damage him as sure as this abandonment would undermine her trust in men.

They had always prided themselves on being honest with each other, and she knew that he wanted to go to the missions. In truth, she was trying to hold onto something floating in the opposite direction with Australia. At least there, they would have been together.

She loved Elliot and could never see past him to another man, nor had she ever wanted to. She wept, and they laughed, and then she wept some more. Emily was giving her time to experience the full range of emotions; the woman was grieving heavily.

Emily cancelled her band practice and decided to stay the night. When she finally got her to bed after a bottle of wine, she rang Mark to let him know that Siobhan had made an appointment to see the manager at the museum in the morning.

The less extreme, more business-like version of the truth was the best way forward they reckoned. She and her partner had decided to go their separate ways, and her decision to go to Australia was now hanging in the balance. She'd get a straight up answer on the spot, to the best of her knowledge no one had been hired to fill her position yet.

In the middle of the night, Emily was awoken by the sound of gentle sobbing. She went into Siobhan's room and cuddled up alongside her, pulling back the hair from her face as she sang her to sleep, she knew too well the tune that would calm her. The song that she had written to spell out the enormous strength that lay between them.

In the morning things looked better, Siobhan was dressed in full combat gear, she was in her best daytime clothes with her face thoroughly made up.

'Thank you for last night' she whispered.

'Sweetheart, it was no bother.' Emily was still in her nightshirt, sipping on her coffee.

'I'm going to be grand from here on in, just a lot of choices and busy days ahead.' Siobhan was brighter today.

'If you're not okay, that's fine too, honey... I'm here for you, for as long as it takes.' Emily knew that she was a long way from repaired. 'I thought I could move in for a week or so, keep you company.' Emily suggested. 'I have practices and stuff, but most of the time I'd be here. We might even get a laugh out of it.'

'It's been a while since I lived alone.' Siobhan admitted, raising a smile.

'We never did share a flat together.' Emily was delighted.

'You're so good.'

'As are you, my friend, it's just getting through this tough stuff for the next week or two, and I'm here for you, no matter what decision you make.' That was how it started.

Chapter 35

Of all days to be late, this was not the one. Still stunned by the news on Elliot's flight of fancy, Mark had forgotten the meeting. He had found it hard to sleep as he ran over his last conversations with Elliot. He'd ended up sleeping late and arrived to work ten minutes after the men.

The board of management were said to be working on the reconstruction of the company divisions a few days before, and they had specifically asked to talk to him. It had been the last thing on his mind, but now he was apprehensive, running late didn't help. He knew that his team were doing a great job, and he had nothing stirring in his conscience work wise.

'You can go on through; they're waiting for you.' Imelda advised as he passed where she sat at the reception.

He smiled, and Imelda left him to knock on the heavy wood chamber door before pushing it open.

There were three executives behind the table, but no sign of Turner, Laura's father. Laurence Wittiger was the management head at the centre of the three men. He was the top man internationally; the companies CEO, so Mark at once knew that this meeting was of more importance than he had initially anticipated.

'Sorry, I was delayed, gentlemen.' He stated as he checked his watch. He walked to the table and put his hand on the top of the chair that was facing them.

'Please, sit.' Mr Wittiger insisted, gesturing.

'Thank you.' He replied as he sat down. 'How can I help you, gentlemen?' He spoke firmly, getting straight to the point.

There was an awkward moment as papers were passed to Mr Wittiger. He lifted his pen in his right hand and peered at Mark from behind his thin-framed glasses.

'I hear you're doing sterling work and that your division downstairs is a tightly run ship. Do you agree?'

'Yes, yes, sir. I do.'

'Is there anything that you might like to say about the team itself? Is there something you can put forward, ideas to greater improve the activities on the floor?'

'No, as you say, it's a tightly run ship.'

'And Joyce?'

'He's a great man; I couldn't ask more of him; he commands great respect from the men and has not once let me down, gentlemen.'

'That's good to know. You've achieved much in the past few months, Mark. You have as well brought in new clients; this is more than can be said for some members of our sales team who are specifically trained for the task.'

'It is a decent service. It's never hard to sell a decent service. It's getting potential clients on board with you, so you get the opportunity to convey the benefits of the package. It's not a mystical feat.'

'Very good, I have a question to put to you, Mark. You don't mind if I call you Mark?'

'No, not at all.'

'Do you think Joyce might be capable of commanding these types of sales figures?'

Mark hesitated for a moment. 'Joyce's abilities are floor bound at the minute. I've taken him up once or twice to get a handle on how it's done, but I'm not sure how he'd fare out in that respect.'

'Could he be trained?'

'Joyce, I'm not sure if I'm to be honest. It's difficult to say; I genuinely couldn't tell you how he'd adapt. He does a fantastic job on the floor but gathering clients is a completely different exercise and Joyce is not that vocal.'

'Is there any other man on the team that stands out at the minute?'

'In respect of sales or the groundwork?'

'The groundwork.'

Mark again drew a blank, hesitating before he spoke. 'I'm not sure I follow where this is going? What do you have in mind, gentlemen?'

The three executives looked at each other, but Laurence Wittiger brought back the point.

'I'll repeat the question, Mark, is there any other man on your team that stands out from the crowd?'

'No, not particularly. Well maybe. I'd have to think hard about that one. The team are pretty evenly spread in respect of responsiveness and work ethic, Joyce always stood out to me.'

'Mark...we're looking at taking you completely off the floor in a month or so.'

Mark paused. 'To do?' He was mildly curious, but also slightly panicked.

'The idea is to have you train Joyce in sales, and allow him to slip into your position, training up who you both see as the next in line, to fill his shoes as he moves into sales. Between the two of you, I'm sure you could figure out who has the most potential.'

'That could cause rifts with the men from where I stand.'

'Are you sure of that?' Wittiger inquired. 'You need to give this thought.'

'I'm not sure that Joyce is interested in working in sales, he's very much hands-on and likes to be central to his floor team. He has a natural bent when it comes to managing the men and getting the best out of them. I don't know if he could be trained in sales to a point where he could acquire any decent number of clients for the company... maybe?'

'We want you to spend time with the sales team here, coach them to a degree. You're generally on the floor in the morning, and the latter part of your day is spent in sales, correct?'

'More or less.'

'Good.' Mr Wittiger sat back waiting for Mark to speak.

'I don't know that I have much to offer in respect of coaching, but I could certainly give it my best shot.'

'We have bigger plans for you beyond that?'

'Go on?' Mark was curious.

'Our American depots. We believe you could bring improvement to our depots in America. You're a charismatic character, and you've worked diligently thus far.'

'America?'

'We have eight depots there as you know; the idea is that you would spend six weeks in the first depot and then return here to bring back your development. You'd be working with the floor and sales team here for another six weeks, then back to the states to another depot. You could coach their sales team as well as their floor managers, sorting out any tweaks in their armour in respect of the ground works. You'd be working to create a documented system of work practices, working methods in sales; set up standards practices and so forth.'

'This is a lot to take in; I'm not sure that I might want to be away from Ireland for such extended periods of time. I have friends and family to consider.'

'There is a substantial benefit, salary wise.'

'How substantial?'

'We haven't worked out the final details yet, but you're looking at two and a half times your present salary, extra shares in the company and expenses. You do want to climb in this industry?' Mark flattened his lips, pressing them together as he considered the idea.

Finally, he spoke. 'That is a serious difference in salary, and a challenging opportunity to boot but as I said, it's not something that I'd take on lightly.'

'We respect that, we can set up another meeting for this day next week and give you time to mull it over, talk to your family and friend and your partner of course.'

'I don't have a partner.'

'That may be for the better this would be an ongoing contract, depot to depot that could later shift to one-year contracts in New York. The New York depot is the pivotal cog; you'd be operating from there, that's what we anticipate, all going well.'

Mark at that moment slowly realised that taking on a job of that calibre would render him unable to lay the foundations of a relationship with Emily, for possibly years to come. Emily was the first thing that struck his mind.

'Can I ask do I have the chance to move up here if I stay, gentlemen?'

'You have, of course, Mark and though we have room for you to grow, the executive ladder here will never offer you this level of financial security, turning away this opportunity will certainly inhibit the extent to which you can climb.'

'I see.'

Our Diligent Souls

'We appreciate that you will have considerations to take into account. As we said, a week from today we can meet again, and get a better understanding of the extent of your ambition.'

'I'll leave now if that's the end of our discussion, gentlemen.'

'That's it for now.' Mr Wittiger replied.

'Thank you for the opportunity; I'm relieved to hear that you appreciate the work I'm putting in here.'

'We do indeed, Mark, you are a bright newcomer and an asset to the company.'

As Mark headed to the stairs, he stopped for a moment to take a breath. He didn't feel cornered or trapped; they were offering him an enormous opportunity though it might not be where he wants to go. Everyone else seemed to be heading off in different directions, but alone in America for six weeks at a time. He wasn't sure if that appealed to him or not, let alone the one-year contracts beyond that.

He would talk to Joyce and Laura as they might be better able to measure the challenge. Besides, everyone else had too much on their plate at the minute to hear him out, especially since Elliot had just disappeared.

Joyce came marching over to where Mark was standing. 'Well, what did they want?'

'I need to digest it first. Will you give me a day or two?'

'Sounds serious?'

'It is. Just out of curiosity, where are you regarding sales? What's your thinking on what I've already shown you?'

'Sales aren't me, Mark. You know me, I'm more of a hands-on guy myself. Why what's up now?'

'I'm wondering if I gave you a few further pointers, maybe you could manage it?'

'My confidence has grown for a fact since I was moved up in the scheme of things, Mark, but I'm not the best speaker, and I can't see that I have it in me to push something on somebody.'

'We're not talking about pushing our services on people. We're talking about letting corporate companies getting the measure of us in respect of how we can lower their costs or strengthen their operations.'

'Uhm, I'm curious.'

Our Diligent Souls

'You have a very likeable demeanour. I wonder how that might translate on the phone.'

'Jesus Mark, are you trying to keep me up at night? We're going to lunch together today, okay? I want to hear blow by blow what they said to you up there. You're not getting out of it. How am I going to concentrate on work?'

'Just follow my lead. Organise the team in aisle three, the harder we work, the sooner we get to lunchtime.'

'We are running behind, not by much but we've two men sent home this morning, flu bug, they had it bad, Mark. We don't need the whole place going down sick. Hopefully, though it's a twenty-four-hour thing.'

'Come on we should get going.' Mark stated.

The men were taken back when they saw the shapes that Mark and Joyce were pulling as they approached, there was to be no messing with these fellas this morning. By lunchtime, there wasn't one man that hadn't broken a sweat.

'Molly's!' Joyce suggested as he grabbed his jacket. Mark nodded without a word and followed behind him. That was the first time he'd seen Joyce swagger; he was sincerely interested.

Molly's was your bacon butte cafe, just a five-minute walk from the warehouse. They both sat over mugs of strong tea as Mark lead Joyce through what management had suggested.

'Feck me!' Joyce exclaimed. 'You can't do too much it seems? What a position though?'

'You could negotiate a much better wage for yourself Joyce, a serious wage if you could manage to get clients. It will be the same hours, company shares, maybe...'

'I can see it, Mark. I know you believe I can turn my hand to anything, that sort of recognition I've never known. I'll put my best foot forward.'

'I don't know if I want to leave here to travel over and back to America, it could get isolated over there?'

'Are you joking me every six weeks in a new city?'

'And then home for six weeks.' Mark added; he was still trying to convince himself.

'And then another city.' Joyce added.

'It's still up in the air in respect of this happening until I see if I can get you into shape sales wise. The team can be mediocre up there, one or two of them make a sale I noticed and skip off home, others are just unorganised and poorly focused, but I will be coaching the full team. They work on a commission basis, but you should have a ground salary as floor manager which would mean you'd get the same wages as I'm getting now or something near to that figure.'

'And how much is that?'

'That's still my business for now, but it's a fair bit more than you're getting at the minute. You need to be warned, trying to get a pay raise for the ground staff will have you hitting a brick wall; I've been there. If you're to take over my station, then you should know that in advance. I have put a solid case forward to get a better salary for the lads; they deserve it having upped their game for me, but I was met with contempt, sheer contempt.'

'I wouldn't know how to argue a better salary for myself, let alone the guys.' Joyce replied.

'I could aim to negotiate the same wage for you Joyce and get somewhere close to that, but in all honesty, it will be down to you to make that happen, you can build into that.'

'You know the change that this could make to our lives? My family I mean.'

'Joyce, don't get your hopes up too high. I'm not even a hundred percent that I'm going to take the offer.'

'Mark, you've definitely helped me create a better life for myself as is, and that's fair enough. If there comes a time where there's an opportunity to up my game, either now or in the future, great, but we're doing just fine where we are. The wife doesn't know herself with the money that's coming into the house lately.'

'So, who might be the right candidate to take over your position in the long run? Mark asked.

'Murtagh?' Joyce caste his sail for what it was worth.

'I would have thought Mulligan.' Mark replied.

'Yeah, Mulligan's not bad. I'm starting to get into this now. I'll end up driving the Mrs to drink; she'll have solid ground to divorce me.' Joyce chuckled. 'It's not what she signed up for when we got married.'

Our Diligent Souls

'I could be busy this week, with a friend that I might need to help out. If not, I'll arrange for you to come over to my place for a few nights in a row, and we'll go through how the whole sales thing works. I'll bring notes, research stuff and we'll start at the very beginning. Three nights and we should have you up to speed. You got to be open to it mind you.'

'Where should I tell the Mrs I'm going? Hiding stuff leaves me jumpy; she can read me like a book. There's no point in hiding what's going on; she'll figure me out, and if I tell her the truth she'll panic.'

'One step at a time... tell her that you're coming over to my house to learn sales. That is where we're at, at the minute. It is just part of the job. We can talk like this now, but if I leave for America you'd be on your own, mate, that's not always easy.'

The afternoon flew in, and after a quick chat with Joyce, Mark was gone. The next few days were pandemonium at work and on top of that Mark had to travel home as his mother was unwell. It was two days before he lifted the phone to ring Emily. She had some news. Siobhan was told her job was still open for her, they advised her to take the week off and think it over. If she wanted to, she could return the following Monday.

Emily thought she was doing much better, her panic was beginning to fade, but she was still disillusioned and bound to be lonely for some time to come, that was only to be expected. She mentioned that Siobhan was sleeping for much of the day. 'It's best to leave her be for now.' He followed her instructions. Emily was staying there this week so she would be popping in and out when she could; she had the key so she wouldn't disturb her.

Two days later, Mark phoned, not wanting Siobhan to think he'd abandoned her.

'Siobhan.'

'Is that you, Mark?'

'It's me. Did you decide on work then?'

'Yeah, I'm keeping my job for now. I'm going to put Australia on the back burner for the minute. Emily has decided to rent out her flat to a musician that she knows; she's going to move in here for a while. I'm packing up Elliot's stuff to store it in his mum's house for now. They're going to collect it in the coming weeks. There is no rush on that though.'

'She didn't say...'

'Who Emily, you have talked to her then?'

'Yeah, a day or two ago now, she said you were sleeping so I didn't want to disturb you. She didn't mention that she was moving in with you. I could leave Elliot's things over with his parent's next week sometime; my dad's down for a check-up so I can get him to lend me the car to save you having to face them. I'll give him a ring and arrange something.'

'That's helpful, that's very good of you.'

'Are you feeling any better?'

'Yeah and no, the initial shock has passed, but I'm still tearful. I'm planning to be spending a lot of time with Emily. I'm looking forward to that. She will be paying rent here and renting out her place. So we can both meet our mortgage; at least that much is in order. It might be nice having female company here for a change. It's all moving very fast.'

'Good on you!'

'I never had a flatmate. I went from home into a flat with Elliot so it might make a pleasant change.'

'Well, that's good news.'

'I guess I'll be going to her gigs. I'd imagine I will anyhow?'

'We'll do something before the wedding, even if it's only a coffee.' Mark insisted.

'I can't believe it's only a few days away.' She said nervously.

'Are you going to be okay with that?' Mark inquired.

'Yeah, I'll be fine. I still can't believe Elliot's gone, but I'm fine. Oden's looking forward to the wedding; he was here with Lucile last night. They're as cute the pair of them... I'm kind of in and out of my skin at the minute, you caught me at a good moment, and I'm glad. Look, it's tough. Anyway, Oden seems fine.'

'I can't wait to see him, Siobhan.'

'His mum got Elliot's car keys in the post. They have a double garage so...'

'We could pack up his car, and I could drive the stuff over to them if you can organise a key. I could get the bus back, that way I don't need the use of my father's car.'

'Sounds good.' Siobhan agreed. 'It's a bit awkward with his folks, I want to see them, and then I don't. I've known them for what seems like forever but yeah, getting the keys is a good idea. Oden can sort that for me.'

'That's it then, another thing off the list.'

'That's it, Mark.'

He sensed that she was unnaturally upbeat. A lot had happened in a short space of time, but she was adjusting. He promised that he'd make a point of calling around to see her before the wedding, but he had stuff of his own to figure out for now.

'Okay, I'll leave you and ring you in a day or two.'

'Thanks, Mark.'

'You take care, Siobhan, and relax this week as much as you can. Later, yeah?'

Mark was relieved by Siobhan's decision to stay at work, for now, all that was to be done was to hot foot it over to his apartment, he needed a shower and a change clothes. He was then heading to Emily's gig where he was showing up unannounced; he had to talk to her about the job offer.

Things were going to change now that she was planning on moving in with Siobhan. He didn't know if he'd be spending less time with her once she moved, or if he'd just be seeing more of Siobhan.

Emily hadn't spotted him in the crowd as the stage lights were making it difficult for her to see the audience. He felt distant as he watched her. The venues were getting more prominent, and her popularity was growing. As it was she'd always been able to single him out in a crowd, but not here, not tonight, it was the first time that had happened.

He was no longer the only person that knew her songs. Standing behind her army of fans as they sang along, he was beginning to realise that if he went to America, it would put an even wider gap between them; the extent of which was hard to fathom.

It felt as if he'd only been hanging on her every word for days when in effect, it was the best part of a year now. She was surrounded by attractive young musical types who were enchanted by her every note, you could see it on their faces, in the way they moved around her, in every morsel of their being.

As soon as the concert finished, she was surrounded by admirers from every corner. She was receptive, grateful and charming, checking back with the band as the audience departed. He watched on as she was invited to different places; she was refusing as she physically checked her watch and shook her head each time.

The place was nearly empty when she finally became aware of Mark. He was still seated at the back of the venue; she looked twice before coming closer.

'My goodness, have you been here the whole night?' Mark nodded. 'I had no idea, how could I have missed you, you always stand out.'

'You tired?' Mark asked.

'I'm as flat as a pancake energy-wise, but I could do with a brew and a few slices of toast. What a week, Mark, you have no idea.'

'Are you ready to leave?'

'I just have to get my coat.' She disappeared off to say goodnight to the band.

'We'll hail a taxi and head back to mine.' He suggested on her return.

'Sounds good to me!'

They were a few minutes waiting. It must have felt strange for Emily, though you could never tell, going from being the centre of attention to just an ordinary Mary Jane on the street.

'It's a nippy one.' She said though she was well wrapped up, bouncing gently on her toes at the edge of the footpath. It was mid-week, and the city didn't have an off button, it was early in the night yet. A few passers-by called Emily by name. 'Hi, guy's!' Mark had rarely felt that invisible, especially with work.

Back at the flat, it was colder inside than out on the street, he threw on the heating and went to grab the quilt from his bed to throw over her, by now it was a force of habit. He put some music on and headed straight for the kettle. 'Tea, coffee?'

'Tea, please.'

He had the thick white toast bread that she was fond of, and the butter was left out, so it was easy to spread. He placed the cup on the side table with the plate of toast and landed himself in the opposite seat. She curled up under the quilt before she took her mug of tea in hand.

'So, Mrs Rock and Roll, what's your news?'

'You heard that I'm moving in with Siobhan?'

'I did.'

'I'm looking forward to it, I don't imagine I'll get quite as much work done, but I have felt isolated over the past few months so... I do need a break from writing and the work will still go on with Siobhan around.'

'Where are you with the contracts for the record label?'

'I will email them to you tomorrow.'

'Good woman, I'll check those out. I'll be able to get back to you on that before the wedding.'

'I'm not due to sign until the week after so there's no rush. What's been happening with you?'

Mark hesitated for a minute, shuffling in his seat.

'Big news!'

'Go ahead, spit it out?'

Mark went on to share what had happened at the board meeting where the offer had been made. Their first idea was to train Joyce in sales if that was even possible? In respect of the time frame and when this would happen, he was still unsure, but it was sometime in the very near future, not six months down the line. He had to return with an answer to their proposal in two days.'

'You're their brightest star sales and floor wise across the company when they want to send you to the states.'

'I guess.' He was proud of himself though that hadn't dawned on him until then.

'There is no point in staying stagnant for the sake of it. You've seen what that did to Elliot, Mark.'

'I still have our relationship to consider and my other friends and family.'

'It's you that you have to consider first and foremost, your family, they'll just say go for it, Mark. You know that.'

'What do you think? I want to know what you think?' He hesitated again. 'Above the lot of them in truth.'

'I think it's a great opportunity.'

'But I'll be so far away from you. It's the other side of the world.'

Emily went quiet, but her silence left him rambling verbally.

'It could get lonely in America, it's unlikely that the staff will want to mix with me, coming in like the big chef re-organising stuff, and work is only nine to five.'

'You'll have cities to explore.'

'I'd miss you, Emily. We're still close right?'

Mark's softer side was coming out.

'I'll find some interesting books for you.'

'I'm not a reader nowadays, Emily.'

'Then become one, it's a healthy endeavour.'

Mark dropped his eyes. He just wanted to hold her, to tell her that he wasn't going anywhere at that moment, the weight of his feelings pressing hard on his chest.

'You could meet loads of people and have a whale of a time, your outgoing, full of banter, come on. You can't refuse this, imagine the kitty you could save up in two or three years, you could have your property bought outright before you know it, Mark. You will be set up for the rest of your life, do you know how many people get that chance?'

'You're right of course.' He stated bashfully, recognising a brand-new level of expectations.

'More tea, I'll make it?' She knew her way around his cupboards by now.

'No, I'm fine, Emily.'

'This is something to be celebrated. I'm going to be high-tailing it to gigs across the country with this record company. Do you think that doesn't scare me? You just got to be your natural self and let the good times roll, Mark.'

'We can talk on Skype.'

'We can email, and hand write letters to save up for when we're old and decrepit. Cheer the hell up, will you?'

'No, I'm good.' He said.

'Then you're going to go for it?'

'I knew it was likely to happen the minute they told me; it's just coming to terms with what I'm letting myself in for if I take this dive.'

'Can I get a cuddle?'

Mark was flabbergasted. 'Sure, why not?'

He mooched up in the chair and made room for her; she had completely forgotten about the tea. It was an almighty squeeze, but they held each other for a couple of minutes, putting the cups to one side. She was welling up inside and struggling to keep it all in; the emotion had taken her by surprise.

Putting a brave face on the matter was crucial, her heart was struggling with the thought that he'd no longer be around to the same extent. 'This is too uncomfortable.' She said jumping out of the chair.

'I'd better get home.' She said, smiling. 'You've work in the morning, and we have this wedding to prepare for at the weekend. It will be good to see Alfie and Brian again,' her voice was shaking. 'We'll finally get to meet their partners in crime.'

He responded gently. 'Alfie's coming alone, and there's talk that Melisa won't make it either.' Mark had forgotten to mention it until now.

'I hope Elliot's okay in the missions; I imagine he's going through a lot of readjusting at this given moment in time.' Emily seemed to be coming to terms with his abrupt departure to an extent; she wanted Mark to know.

It was not until that moment that she realised that she had forgiven Elliot for abandoning her friend. Emily had to if she was going to forgive Mark for leaving her. Not that Emily had any claim on him, but she had almost felt it coming. She needed to be a guiding hand to Siobhan and wanted him to be aware of that; she was keeping an open mind in respect of Elliot for her friend's sake.

'He'll have the mission work to distract him. Siobhan will be okay, what is it they say, it's rare an ill wind that doesn't blow some good.' Mark paused for a moment. 'You're a sweetheart, you.' He was going to miss her.

'Before you say it, I'm aware you know, that the world is full of sharks.' She was childishly triumphant in what she was saying. She wasn't going to let her emotions get the better of her. She was starting to feel angry at him and couldn't understand why at that point; it was confusing.

'Where did that come from?' He responded partly concerned, he had no idea of how cut up she was. In her mind's eye, she had only to hold it together for another few minutes.

'I have to go. I won't see you until the wedding.' She dropped the dishes in the sink and gathered her things.

He jumped up to see her to the door. 'I thought you'd stay a while.'

'Enough yeah, I'm tired after the gig.' She was flustered by what she was feeling. He stood quivering in a cold breeze before he shut the door behind her. He had expected some comment, something that would make him think twice about his situation, but there was nothing.

Chapter 36

The family belonged to the church of St. Josephs, so there was never any doubt as to where the wedding was going to be held. It was drawing close to the end of the summer, time yet to cherish the last of the late evening sunshine.

The flowering bee balms were the predominant churchyard's perennials; their heads were like firework displays that were fragrantly wafting in the heat. The elegant globes of purple blossoms were also attracting attention, the alliums standing on stalks that were eighteen inches tall.

It was the perfect day for a wedding, tainted or not by the recent loss of the bride's father. The tiny chapel was full; the guests had arrived a good twenty minutes before the service was due to begin. Brian's sister would soon be standing at the top of the church with her fiancé, her excited soul mate and his best man dressed in tuxes, smiling and sharing banter with the guests that were sitting in the first few pews.

Mark and Alfie were at the old oak church door entrance, waiting for Brian and his sister to arrive in the car. They could spectate on the entire congregation from where they stood, and on the arched gateway through which Sarah and her brother would soon arrive. It was a momentous occasion for Brian, stepping into his father's shoes.

The bridesmaids were a flutter as they waited alongside Mark and Alfie, clapping their hands with excitement as the car drove up. Word was sent up to the eaves to let the organ player know that they had arrived. Sarah seemed to shimmer as she was lead across the path by her brother, Mark and Alfie were knocked back by her beauty. The boys had grown up with her running around in jeans only now were they forced to sit up and take notice.

Sarah's dress was tight, her figure shapely, the gown softened by lace and sparkling with beaded inlay, her hair curled to one side and pinned with delicate flowers. Brian was wearing the same suit as the groom and best man, a sharp grey tux with a white shirt and light blue tie.

'You look amazing, Sarah.' The choir of bridesmaids cooed at their bride in waiting. 'Are we ready?' Brian's whisper was met with a deep smile. Sarah loved her brother. He signalled to the bridesmaids as they fell into line. The little flower girl was followed by Sarah and Raymond's seven-year-old son, again in matching tiny tuxes; he'd travelled over in the car with his mammy and Uncle Brian.

Their boy steered the little flower girl and her only three, to the front of the procession where she scattered white petals on the church floor. The bride beamed with delight as the entire troop paraded elegantly past rows of wooing onlookers. Alfie and Mark slipped into their seats at the back, onto a bench reserved by Oden, Emily, Laura, Lucile and Siobhan.

Brian took the seat beside his mother, once he had delivered his sister safely to her groom, positioning Sarah's son in the very first seat with the bridesmaids and flower girl. Sarah was glowing as her young partner took her in, the love in his eyes. Brian was at his mother's side at that moment to put his arm around her waist and press her close from her half kneeling position. There were no tears from Marian as she was in full makeup. It had always been her husband's place to shed a tear.

'We would like to welcome you here today to the joining in Marriage of Sarah Byrne and Raymond Smith.' The priest began. He wasn't long in mentioning Sarah's dad who had recently passed on into the warm embrace of the lord and reassured the congregation that Sarah's father was with them now in spirit, both on this extraordinary day and through the rest of their married life. Sarah turned around to look at her mum.

Mark's thoughts were with his sister Moira and the stupid mistake she had made having two kids with the wrong man. Sarah, and Raymond, her groom, were the polar opposite of Mark's sister and partner, they made a solid match. The ceremony was kept light and cheerful. The couple openly adored one another and the child they had brought into the world together.

The brothers and sisters on Raymond's side did the prayers of the faithful, while Sarah's cousins were the backbone of the folk choir, that was seated to the right-hand side of the altar. The guests had been asked to mix and sit where they liked; the idea of his family on one side and hers on the other was a tradition too far for Sarah and Raymond.

The couple's vows were simple and entertaining and said much about the pair. Raymond was promising to love, honour and negotiate, while Sarah swore never to shut him out when she got angry but talk frankly and from the heart.

A choir of angels sung 'The Dimming of The Day' as the hairs stood on the necks of every person in that church. The couple share from the same silver cup, they lit their sizeable central candle together and extinguished the flames of the smaller candles at either side, there was a look of love that passed between them that was cherished by parishioners, it was a genuine expression of how deeply interconnected they were.

It wasn't long before the service came to an end, but the priest was not letting them go without a few words. He thought they were a unique couple in many ways, they were trusting and open and shared heartfelt values which was to be admired in people of their age.

From the perspective of the congregation, the couple were in awe of each other, attuned to the importance of ceremony and the utterance of their vows. The priest believed theirs was a good match, with more chance of success than most, with a little work and persistence. He wished them the very best in the future and hoped they would not encounter too many obstacles along the way.

With that, there was a round of applause as the couple, accompanied by their photographer, followed the priest to a side room to register their marriage. The congregation chatted among themselves, defining the event while they waited. There was yet another round of applause as the couple re-entered the church.

Sarah and Raymond gracefully made their way to the church door where a handful of the guests were already gathered, primarily to fill their lungs with cigarette smoke. There were lots of congratulations before the couple and family lined up for photographs.

The sun was splitting the trees as the lack of road noise gave way to the twittering of birds. The entire crowd were in joyous form, looking forward to the reception and a day off from everything else in their lives.

Brian was too busy with the photographers for the moment to stop and chat with the gang. They had seen him at his father's funeral, whereas Alfie, they hadn't seen in two years. Alfie had hugged and shook hands with everyone earlier when he arrived at the church, but now it was time for the endless barrage of questions as old friends shuffled in to hear his news. He was tanned, he had grown his hair out long; the guy looked handsome with it.

The local girls didn't recognise him straight away. He was much cooler than before he left, not as likeable or open the girls thought, but that was only the initial impression. It wouldn't be long into the reception when he would go back to being his old self but perhaps, with a touch more confidence.

Our Diligent Souls

Alfie genuinely loved his work in Australia. He loved Australia full stop and even had a slight Australian twang when he spoke. He was sincere as he relayed the news that Brian had good and bad days since his father died. Alfie reckoned that he was going to go through that, regardless of what side of the water he set up camp.

Brian was still with Melisa, but she couldn't make it over to the wedding as her mum was unwell and needed the support. Alfie thought the world of her and said they were very well suited. He enquired after Elliot, anxious to be brought up to date but no one wanted to talk about Elliot today. The very mention of him put Oden on edge until Siobhan stepped in and started arranging lifts to the reception.

Mark finished up with his end of things and headed over to Siobhan for his first sweeping cuddle. 'You okay, sweetheart?' He asked once her feet were firmly back on the ground.

'A hundred and ten percent.' She retorted.

'Well, you look great.' Mark assured her.

One by one, everyone had an embracing 'welcome back' for Brian. He was introduced to Laura and wasn't long pulling the piss out of Mark and his talent for mooching out good looking women. Both Laura and Mark corrected him at once. 'We are not an item.' Brian laughed, he was only checking to see where the land lay.

Brian soon picked up on Alfie's body language, noticing that the man had spotted Emily. The last time Brian was home, Mark had told him that he was infatuated by her and from what Brian could make out that still stood, so he was on to Alfie in a flash, steering him in another direction.

'I want you to meet Jane and Miriam, over here Alfie.' Brian requested.

'I know Jane and Miriam; they're your cousins, I've met them a load of times.'

The two cousins were delighted to see him. 'Alfie, you look a million dollars, mate. Bet you have loads of stories to tell us, what's new in Australia then? We hear you're a bartender now, in a Bondi beach bar...'

'Well now,' says Alfie, 'that's what's keeping the money coming in, but you know me girls, not one to sit on my laurels.'

'You haven't lost your charm then?'

'Not for a minute, ladies, I was breed to have grace and good manners.'

'We're grateful for that Alfie, and Brian's doing well?'

'He's keeping his good side out, but he misses Jackie, sure who doesn't have their moments.'

'You're a great bit of stuff, Alfie; they broke the mould when they made you, no two ways about it.' They were young to be speaking that way, but they were the walk of their mother.

Oden and Lucile were also making an impression with their new and unforgettably funky outfits, everyone remarked on their style. Oden was still uncomfortable around the whole Elliot thing and could barely take his eyes off Siobhan. He was anxious about her, while Lucile was busy taking everyone in; waving cheerfully at people as they made their way to the reception.

The crowd soon disbanded to their cars, the gang were staying over at the hotel and had yet to check in, but they expected it would be at least another hour before the happy couple were welcomed into the wedding reception. There was plenty of time for everyone to collect their keys at reception and drop their hand luggage in the rooms.

Brian and Alfie travelled with Mark in Laura's car.

'So how have you been, mate? It's so good to see you in the flesh Brian, and you too Alfie, what a transformation. Skype doesn't give you any real picture, man. You've toned up and look at the colour of you.'

'Please gentlemen,' Laura scoffed. 'At least wait until you have a room. He tells me you lot grew up together?'

'We did, we went to the same schools; we even shared the same girlfriends.' Brian returned, laughing out loud.

'When girls were yours for a slow dance, and you got in on the way home on the bus.' Alfie remarked flopping back into his seat in hysterics.

'That's too much detail for me, lads!'

'We had good times, Laura. He's making it sound way murkier than it was.' Mark redefined it for her when he explained that 'getting in' was never more than a quick snog and a fumble. 'He makes it sound murkier than it was.'

'That's a serious mouthful.' Laura replied.

'Murkier!' quizzed Mark.

'Yeah! Murkier!' She struggled to reiterate the word.

'It might even be a made-up word,' Mark admitted, 'who's got Google on their phones?'

Alfie and Brian were in the back seat, but they were acting like young boys; sticking their heads in through the gap between the driver and front passenger's seat.

'Seatbelts lads!' Mark was on to it.

'Jesus, would you live a little.' Brian was crying he was laughing that hard.

'So, you own and run the shipping company where Mark used to work, Arthur's old place?' Alfie asked while attempting to ignore his buddy.

'I do, Alfie.' She replied.

'How do you control the men there? I've met that bunch.'

'Easy, I rule with an iron fist.'

'As did Thatcher?' Alfie still remembered his British politics.

'Yes, but she had a tight perm.'

'Don't mind her; she's great with them.' Mark was putting a stop to where this was going. He knew Alfie and Brian too well; they regularly entertained themselves by winding people up and too often crossed the line when they got going.

'I have to pull over for a minute.' Laura said suddenly.

'What's up?' Mark was concerned.

'I don't know. I just feel dizzy.' She pulled the car in; taking up a section of the adjacent path to a busy road.

'Do you want me to drive?' Mark asked.

'Hold on a minute.' Laura took deep breaths over the wheel.

'Can I drive?' He asked again.

'Yes...Please.' She struggled to answer.

Brian butted in, poking his head between the front two seats again. 'It's not even five minutes away.'

'Still, I feel dizzy.' Laura wasn't well.

'Okay!' Brian whispered before they both went as quiet as two field mice in the back seat. Laura and Mark got out the front and swapped roles. Nobody said a word for the rest of the journey.

'You okay?' Mark whispered as they drove into the hotel parking lot, she released a sigh, she was feeling less overwhelmed.

Mark went to the reception with the bags, got their room keys and then headed straight upstairs with Laura to her room. The first thing she did was lower a glass of water and sit on the bed. They had a good half hour to kill before the wedding reception took off and she just wanted to be left alone in the quiet for now.

The room was breath-taking; the bed was a four-poster, with golden yellow taffeta curtains on either side. Beside the bed was an elegant Edwardian chair covered in the same golden yellow but this time in velvet. The sash windows were original with their white shutters. There was a claw foot bath in the washing room, Egyptian cotton on the bed and fluffy white towels in two stacks waiting to be put to good use. She was looking forward to not one, but two nights of peace and tranquillity in this venue.

'They picked a great spot; it's nothing short of beautiful.'

'I know.' Mark whispered, 'I hope my room's as nice.'

They took their time but said very little in the interim. Laura fixed her hair and make-up while Mark left to check out his room, he was back in a flash. She had another glass of water and again straightened herself in the mirror before going down to the party.

'Are you sure you're okay?'

'Yeah! Better I think.'

They had lost Brian and Alfie at the reception desk, but they weren't too far away. She imagined it was the talk in the car that had her head spinning, but so be it, they had just caught her at a weak moment when she hadn't had much rest the night before. She ordered tea and toast at the reception; it would be another hour or so before the dinner was served, and she needed to steady herself.

Mark left her alone for a moment to gather herself. He had helped her move on from her sadness, but her grief was an addiction so unbeatable; the memories of Stephen freewheeling through her mind when she gave into it. It said the same thing over and over in the end; that she would only ever know that one true love.

When Stephen came back into her thoughts, it was like chugging from a bottle, having been deprived of drink for an unordinary length of time. The shakes, the jitters, the relief, it was all part of it. Then the self-scolding started; Laura would criticise herself for her lack of discipline and will, for wanting just to be left alone with all the things they shared that were forgotten and remembered. Weddings were never easy. She knew that dwelling was unhealthy but living with one foot in the past was what kept her alive for now.

    Lately, she hadn't been feeling herself. In ways, she was more fun-loving, but she had a much shorter attention span, a shorter fuse and a preference for all things droll, that way she didn't have to feel present. She wasn't as physically fit as she been the year before, tiring quickly but that could easily be her workload. She took a bite of her toast and a sip of tea before joined the crew.

Chapter 37

The reception room was spectacular; the seats were covered in a silky cream fabric, each table presented with a matching tablecloth and an ornate bouquet of garden flowers. There was a top table for the bride and groom, the parents, the best man and chief bridesmaids, while the guest's circular tables were positioned either side of the dance floor.

The table names were well mapped out and easy to follow. Mark and the crew were spread across two tables and mixed in with two of Sarah's best friends, both of whom Alfie and Mark knew from their youth. The majority of the eighty guests were seated, their flutes filled with champagne to sit neatly beside the other assortment of drinks that filled the tables. The music could barely be heard above the laughter and goodwill.

The bride and groom's arrival were soon to be announced. The happy couple were the other side of the large window that lit up the dance floor as each alternating family member joined them for their final photos.

Moments later, everyone was asked to stand for the couple's entrance with the music going up a notch as the pair were greeted by an enthusiastic round of applause. The pair of lovebirds scrambled to make their way through the tables unceremoniously. The bridesmaids and flower girl moved in a flutter, surrounding Sarah while people rose to shake the hand of her groom.

It wasn't long before the waitresses started to appear with the first course and everybody took their seats, Oden, Lucile, Alfie and Emily were at a table of four. At the adjacent table, Siobhan was in the throes of conversation with Laura, and Sarah's two mates while Mark sat on looking confined to the one position; wondering why he's been made to sit with four women.

Alfie had turned his back on Oden and Lucile; he was busy wanting to know everything there was to know about Emily's singing career to date. Mark had sent a copy of her album to him, and he had listened to it on several occasions. It was an astounding piece of work, on that count, there was no dispute.

'We managed to get a copy of your album.'

'You did?'

'Yeah, Mark sent us over a copy in Australia. I was very impressed. I hope you don't mind, I made a few copies and passed them out. Everyone loved it. It's a great first album.'

'Thank you; it's nice to hear after putting so much work into the thing. So, I have a following in Australia, then?'

'I know a radio DJ in one of Sydney's biggest stations. I didn't want to give it to him just yet.' Alfie said in a very smug tone.

He aspired to promote her on the music scene in Sydney from the moment he heard her voice; there was nothing of that calibre in Australia to his mind. Alfie could see enterprise in an empty crisp packet; she recalled Mark having said as much. Alfie was always the same. He had met Emily just the once before he left for Australia, but he certainly couldn't remember finding her this attractive.

'I'd love to get you over to do a tour, rally up support for your new album.'

'There are five of us in the band, so it's not a cheap exercise nor would it be easy to manage in any way.' She didn't mention the record deal or get into how that might not work with her label.

'If I could get a few venues booked that should be no trouble if I have your say so I can afford the time to go and enquire. I've made contacts at the beach bar, and I know I could make it happen.'

'I'll think about it, Alfie.' Emily had no interest in organising a tour of Australia, but it was a wedding, and she was expected to be polite.

'I heard you got talent scouts that were ready to work with you. It's the sound of your voice that gets people going, and your lyrics are sharp, you have a distinctive voice.'

Oden and Lucile were in their own bubble by then, having tried to involve Emily and Alfie in their conversation without success.

People wanted to get to know Lucile for some peculiar reason. There were introductions and explanations as to who knew who and from where. She was in her element, and Oden was surprised to discover that people were intrigued by her, enamoured in effect. He was nervous earlier when she abandoned him to roam the reception chatting to guests, but he was glad now to have her anchored to one spot, at least for the meal.

Brian was seated next to his mother at the top table; she was serene though happy to see her children in such great form. Brian could sense the quiet part of her that was missing his dad.

Our Diligent Souls

The food was excellent, soup or shrimp cocktail for starters as always. There was the option of beef or turkey and ham, the same wedding staple with its crispy roast potatoes and platters of mash and veg. The dessert choice was fruit salad or Pavlova. Brian couldn't think of a wedding that ever served anything else. The vegetarian option was pasta bake; veggies never did well at weddings.

The atmosphere was pure electric as people called over from one table to the next or squatted for a natter with cousins on their way to and from the bar. In the mix, there were speeches from the best man and Brian as well as he stood in as the father of the bride. Their stories were light-hearted in their approach with absolutely no animosity or crudeness in their accounts of the couple. 'Sweet as a nut,' was the repeated comment that Brian shared. He was glad to be home.

As the plates were cleared the bride and groom were asked to lead the first dance, and within moments, the dance floor was filled, hats were off, and every form of shape was being thrown.

Alfie had been knee-deep in a conversation with Emily for the entire meal and Oden was not impressed by his manners. He was out to catch the girl, and Oden was having none of it; the guy was too smooth to be sugar. Lucile also found the guy controlling, poor Emily had not been given the opportunity to as much as turn around to them and say hi, not even once. Lucile insisted that her and Oden dance. It was her attempt to shake off his growing aggravation in respect of his fellow table guest.

'Get up and don't embarrass me!' Lucile insisted.

'Do I have to, no please?' He pleaded.

'Yes, you have to, and now, I've not come the whole way to a wedding reception with you to sit on my arse.'

'Fair enough, keep your hat on.'

Lucile giggled softly. She was the only female in the place who hadn't come in a fancy hat. It was odd for her as she was known for wearing extravagant hats; Lucile rarely ventured out without some fitting bonnet.

Siobhan and Laura were busy observing everything from afar. Laura's own wedding had been a similar affair with a hundred or so guests and then came the weddings that she and Stephen were invited to, the invitations stopped coming after he died.

At least here she was not seen as the bereft widow, the kids that were invited were flocking to her with their spittle-prattling stories. If there was one thing she regretted it was not having a child with Stephen before he died, it might have filled her life in a way that was more vital, more present.

'I'm not feeling a hundred percent, Siobhan.' Laura said out of the blue. Mark had just sat down to join them.

'What is it?' He asked.

'Just that dizzy thing again, a headache, I don't know.'

'I'll bring you up to the room to get some peace?' Mark was as ever the gentleman. Siobhan took hold of Laura's arm and pressed it gently. Laura was in two minds knowing that Siobhan wanted her to stay by her side.

'No, I'm okay, but could you see if you can locate two painkillers?'

'Sure.' Mark stood up again. 'Just hold on there.'

There was a call for another round of drinks from the newlyweds as Mark slipped out to the reception desk to see if they could help. He met Brian on the way and filled him in on the urgent need for painkillers.

'Not to worry.' Brian told him, his mother always carried that stuff in her bag.

'I'll check reception just in case.' Mark said as he left him.

By the time Mark made his way back to Laura, Brian's mum was at her side with a glass of water in hand. Mark asked again if she wanted to go to her room, but this time she agreed, at least until her headache and dizziness subsided. He went with her just to be sure that she made it there safely, leaving once she was horizontal on the bed.

'Just give me an hour, yeah? Then come wake me up, promise?'

'You sure you don't want me to stay, its fine if you're not well?'

'No, I want to be alone if you don't mind.'

'You sure you want me to wake you in an hour then?'

'It's just a headache, Mark. I'll be fine. An hour is perfect.'

'Okay then.'

'Please go and wake me. I don't want to miss the band.'

Mark headed off to leave her to recover. He was only out the door when she jumped up and made her way to the bathroom to be sick, she had vomited twice or three times in the past week.

She wondered for a moment if she could be pregnant but dismissed the thought at once. She had made herself sick with the guilt she was feeling for getting on with her life; she'd had a night with one of the guys from work. Her eyes began to swell up; truth be told, she was happier on her own.

What was more upsetting was the fact that no one understood, no one allowed her to have her grief, much of which she kept under wraps. She was good at keeping things under wraps. Her parents wanted more for her, and until she could say that she was in a relationship, they would be on her case in the interim. They were afraid of what end she might come to; having not yet let go of Stephen.

Siobhan was standing at the bar when Mark strolled back into the reception room; she was on her own, her head shifted to avert his gaze. He made his way over to check that everything was okay. As brave a face as Siobhan was putting on it; she was finding the whole day overwhelming.

'Come on; we'll take a walk on the grounds.' Mark suggested casually. 'Come on.'

'I could do that to be fair.' She eventually admitted. The last thing that Siobhan wanted was to be identified as lonely at this grand event.

With that the pair went outside, the night was just on the verge of setting in, so he took his jacket off and placed it around her shoulders.

'Thanks, Mark.'

'You're holding up okay?'

'It's weird Elliot not being here; I can't deny it. I understand his reasoning and everything, but it makes me physically ill to think of it.'

'I'd be angry myself, Siobhan.'

'Mark, if he was in front of me right now, I might stick a knife in the fucker.'

She welled up, her eyes pleading for mercy. Mark smiled at her. 'He always said you were a lover, not a fighter!'

'I'm not in a position where I can allow myself to love or miss him. I have to shut that part of me down to get through this.'

'Someday, maybe you might yet be able to rebuild that trust with him again. You were together for five years, pet.'

'I think I'd scream at any man who came near me or worse again, lash out in the company of friends. I'm afraid of myself at the minute.' She paused. 'I'm afraid of losing control. Have you ever felt as if you were standing on the edge of a precipice waiting for someone to push you off the edge? I keep seeing myself there; it's not a helpful visual.'

Mark again smiled at her, and they laughed at each other.

'Have you heard from him, through his family, maybe?'

'No, besides what can he say to make this any better?'

'Sorry might be a start.' Mark reasoned.

'He knows that sorry won't cut it, Mark. I honestly don't think he thought through what this might do to me. If I thought him capable of that, I would never have been with him in the first place. He's busy getting on with his new life now.'

'I think you're wrong; he'll be stunned, struggling to come to term with what he's potentially lost.'

'He always looked out for his brother, Mark, to a point where he felt a heavy burden of responsibility, Elliot felt he had to compromise his dreams, you know that?' Mark nodded. She walked on with him a while but kept talking. 'It was cowardly the decision that he made; to leave the way he did. That doesn't change.'

'I'm sure he knows he was wrong in doing that by now.'

'Even if he does, how to repair the damage, how does he make it right?'

'Time will heal things between you two.'

'And what am I to do in the meantime, Mark? I'm not a widow. I'm just someone who was unceremoniously left behind.'

'But things are okay with you and Emily?'

'Things are great between Emily and me; if I didn't have her, I don't know where I'd be. We don't talk much about Elliot because there's nothing to say.'

'You're still hurting. It was a blow to the head.'

'I have low moments, Mark, but my focus isn't on Elliot most of the time, and Emily and I are enjoying sharing the house. I'm going to save to buy out his share of the place. It's half his no matter what he says. I'm having none of that.'

'Guilt money.'

'Uhm! I'm holding on to my job, but I'll try a few things out on the weekends when I'm not at work.'

'Money-making ventures?'

'Something like that. As busy as I can make myself is where I want to be. The weekends are odd now. Couples don't get involved in breakups, and those friends are as good as gone.'

'The couples that were lining up playmates, for the children that they intended having?'

'Elliot told you that?' She stalled for a second. 'Jesus, it sounds awful when you put it like that. What was I thinking?'

'Oden's been round to visit; Emily mentioned that he'd called.'

'Oden's a star, but he worries too much about how it's affecting me. He doesn't want to lose me; it's sweetly fearful where there's no need. I couldn't be without Oden in my life.'

'I still don't know what to say to you, Siobhan. I miss Elliot myself; it's still a shock to me. I hope Brian or Alfie weren't asking any stupid questions. I had to fill them in briefly before they came home.'

'No, they were both fine, it's just hard for them to see me as anything other than Elliot's girlfriend. Australia wouldn't work, its fine though, I can see they're uncomfortable with what happened, but it's fine. I'd already decided not to go to Australia on my own.'

'You're sure.' He stretched his arms out to cuddle her.

'I'm sure. Will we go back?' They smiled and turned to face the hotel in its full glory. 'I'm ok. It's good that we've linked up with Laura again, yeah?'

'Shit!' Mark muttered, checking his watch. 'We're okay; I have to wake her soon though I promised... She's still hung up on Stephen. She's still grieving in her own way, Siobhan, though she hides it well.'

'It's a long time to be grieving but each to their own. Laura's was a very passionate romance not as sombre as mine and Elliot's relationship. I get her, he was her whole world, and that's only beginning to change now that we're on the scene. We should give her time.'

'For sure...' Mark agreed. 'That sounds like the band starting up?'

There was a nip in the air. The night sky was without a single star as they stared up into its darkness. He took Siobhan by the shoulder and wrapped his arm around her. They started walking back; both privately hoping to find the gang on the dance floor.

'You okay with these guys?' Mark asked as Brian, Alfie and Emily looked up at once from a table of drink, the two emigrants singing along to some ancient song they'd forgotten.

'I'm fine.' Siobhan whispered. 'Go, get Laura before this party kicks off, big style.'

He made his way through the crowds, past the reception and went straight to the lift.

As he entered the room, Laura sat up in the bed.

'How are you feeling?'

'Much better, think I might be ready to rock-and-roll.' Laura let out a yawn.

'You sure?'

'I am...' Laura admitted.

'Glad to hear it. So, can we get our mojo on then? The band's going full kilter.'

'Yeah, I can hear that.'

'I was talking to Siobhan,' he shared, 'she's one tough cookie, that's not easy stuff she's going through with Elliot gone.'

'I should call her next week and see if we can meet up for a few drinks.'

'Sounds like a good idea.' He agreed.

'Ideally, I'd love to do a night in with her and Emily, share a bottle of good wine, get a takeaway.'

'They might be up for that. You should try to arrange that tonight or maybe tomorrow. I don't know if the girls are staying for two days but one way or the other, they'll be around until after breakfast.'

'I have drinking to catch up on.' She realised.

'I believe you do my dear. You ready?' He had sobered up somewhat between one thing and another, the rest of the gang were all well-oiled by now.

Laura was nearly ready: a last check of her lipstick in the mirror before measuring up her clutch bag as they left.

'You're looking good, Miss Laura.' Mark said in a thick Southern American accent that he got right.

'Jesus, are you all there?'

'I have a hankering, Miss Laura.'

'Get away you. I'm immune to your charms.'

'I'm hankering for a drink, you're a header, you.'

'Oh, okay!' Laura replied as she made her way through the door. Neither Mark nor Laura had a thing for each other. They both knew where each other stood without it ever being an issue; they were friends by now, friends in the same line of business that watched out for each other, that was plenty.

In the lift on the way to the reception, they bumped into a few stray guests making their way back downstairs. They were giggling and laughing mostly from the drink and only some of what they said was coherent. Mark and Laura played along in good spirits; the pair of strays had snuck off for a quick fumble on the bed sheets. The woman knew they were rumbled; she licked her hand and attempted to flatten her fella's hair; it was shooting off in the wrong direction.

As they reached the reception, the bride was waiting to throw her bouquet. The newlyweds were staying in the hotel that night, but most of the guests would be gone if she wanted to throw it the following day. Laura got Siobhan and Emily to their feet under protest; they didn't want to catch the thing.

It was fun and over within minutes, the bouquet landing in Siobhan's hands first when without hesitation she flung it in Emily's direction. Laura found the whole thing very amusing where Siobhan and Emily did not.

Oden was drunk and insisted on having a word in Mark's ear. Lucile was busy on the dance floor entertaining a mob of senior citizens who wanted to adopt her at that stage of the night.

Oden was adamant, this needed to be said. 'See that Alfie fella; watch your back, mate.'

'What do you mean, you nutter?'

'He's all over Emily like a rash in a heat wave.'

'Emily can handle herself, Oden. She is well able for him.'

'But you love her... I know you love her.'

'Of course, I do, Oden, but what to do, mate. There's no reaching her.'

'You're never for real, Mark. Diplomacy is a large heap load of horseshit when it comes to romance.'

'Oden, you're drunk.'

'But I'm not a fool, and I know that she's into you. This Alfie fella... don't let her go there, Mark. We've all had one too many.'

'Her life is her own pal; you have this wrong.'

'Do I?'

'Lord yes. Now please, go, enjoy yourself and let the night take its course. Do you think he's annoying her?'

'Yes.'

'I'll check on them if you'll relax the head for me?'

'Finally!' Oden yelped as he caved back into his seat, Mark was left standing there looking as if he needed directions, checking both sides of the room.

'Ok then,' he was a little frantic, 'but it's just to put your mind at rest.'

'You're supposed to be with her.'

'That's enough now just give it a rest.'

Laura was sharing a laugh with Brian and Siobhan, so Mark slipped away and headed over to where Alfie and Emily were leaning against a wall like teenage sweethearts.

'Alfie, Brian's looking for you. Can I have a quick word with Emily?'

Alfie looked discommoded, but he agreed none the less and went over to look for Brian, checking back as he moved away.

'Are you okay, Emily?'

'You're concerned, are you?' Mark pulled his head back in confusion. 'Are you okay?' He asked again.

'Yeah, sure I am! Her eyes glazed over. 'Why, what's up?'

'Oden is worried about you; he thinks you're being cornered by Alfie, to put it mildly.'

'To put it mildly, I guess I am. The guy's overbearing, but it's not as if I have a spectrum of choice when it comes to men that care?'

'What?'

'You've spent the entire day faffing around Laura and Siobhan; you're so bloody chivalrous.'

'What are you talking about?' Mark's head was ready to explode.

'I've been stuck with Alfie the entire bloody day.'

'Fair enough, here's the plan, you come with me, you latch on to Laura, and I'll move it up a notch with the lads, I'll keep Alfie busy... and Oden happy.'

'Mark?'

'Yeah!'

Emily lowered her head and stood in silence swaying.

'What is it?' He demanded, attempting to calm himself.

'You're not exactly ambidextrous, are you? At least, not with me.'

'What are you on?' Her eyes were bloodshot.

'You were gabbing with Brian the whole way through the slow set. I could have stood on my head, Mark, on my bloody head.' She took a deep breath. 'And then you go babysit Laura and Siobhan.'

'Emily?'

'Don't Emily me. You're going to America.' Mark was in shock.

'Look, Emily, if you want me to stay, I need you to speak up, I need you to let me know. I...'

'You're a sad fool.'

'What?'

'Look... I just meant that I'll miss you, sorry that I opened my mouth now.'

'I never know where I am with you, but I'm not going to have this out tonight. Not when you can barely stand. You had too much to drink.'

She stood there, biting her lip near tears when she just wanted to kick him.

Mark was vexed. 'Jesus! Are you deliberately trying to destroy me?'

It was a case of laugh or cry, so she laughed. 'You just don't get it.'

'You're drunk, you silly woman, you know rightly that you're all that I want.'

'Why are you not drunk?' She asked.

'Jesus tonight,' he whispered, 'you drive me to distraction, but if you want me I am going nowhere, Emily, you understand?'

'Yeah, you getting nowhere with your life, you think I want that responsibility?'

'This is mental.' He stated categorically, 'we need to join the others, that or I'm putting you to bed, you need to sleep this off right now.'

Mark glanced over at the gang; he needed support. Poor Alfie looked as if he'd been left at the altar. Oden sauntered over to give Mark a hand.

'She's drunk.' Mark stated.

'I am in full possession of who I am.' She declared unwilling to accept support. She moved off walking towards the others with Oden and Mark following suit; they were baffled.

Emily was dancing comfortably in the crowd within minutes, turning her back every time Alfie attempted to look over. Brian warned him to stay put as Lucile fell in at Emily's side to dance her socks off.

'What happened there?' Oden asked Mark.

'Don't quite understand it myself.' He replied.

'She's not any drunker than the rest of them, Mark.'

'So, it appears, Oden, you're not far wrong.'

The two lads stood back as the rest of the gang danced and sang their hearts out. The band played through those ageless classics that everyone knew and associated with a wedding, the bride and groom joined in, more drink was partaken of and more still.

Mark sat on the sidelines waiting for an opportunity, Emily hadn't moved off the floor or touched a drink in an hour; she was adamantly avoiding him. The band finished up at two in the morning, but that only started up a crowd of voices, every song in the book was covered, mostly traditional, but no one gave a toss as long as the booze kept coming.

Mark stayed on the outskirts of it all, looking in on the antics. Emily had noticed as he'd caught her glancing over. She stood up and was handed a glass of wine. 'Shush,' she called for with her finger on her lip. They gave her a chance, and soon she began to sing...'Some say love it is a river that drowns the tender reef. Some say love it is a razor that leads the soul to bleed. Some say, love, it is a hunger, an endless aching need.'

The whole room sat as her voice filled every note, awful and all as the song was. What had inspired her random choice of melody was beyond Mark. She was wide open to receiving backlash. As with many an odd song that people added a verse to in the 80's, the audience sang back in unison. Their fresh rhetorical melody knocked Emily out of her stride; the arrangement was familiar only to the senior section from Dublin as they naturally made their response in song. 'For its only love, yeah, it's only love that can take a foolish heart and turn it inside out.'

The melody rose and fell as Emily stood in silence, lost in the well-tested harmonies and pointed lyrics that were aimed directly at her. 'Yeah, it's only loving, yeah, it's only love that can take a foolish heart and turn it inside out.' Mark watched as Emily filled up and then, was cradled by the guests.

It was soon that time of night, the moment where the music hits an infinite note with everybody. Souls satisfied; one by one the crowd dwindled.

Brian and his motley crew were the last left standing. Emily had slipped away without being seen. Mark noticed at once turning in on himself with regret; he wondered too late if he should follow her to her room. He would have, but that entailed knowing what room she was in and there was no point asking at reception. She'd arrived with Siobhan, and Siobhan had left straight after that God-awful song.

It was five in the morning when the last of them crawled out of the reception room and headed for their beds, he waited to the very end in the hope that Emily might make a re-appearance, but it wasn't to be. What a day to remember, the man thought as he sat alone gazing through the reception window, but the event was not what he had hoped it would be. He'd got side-tracked and had messed it up between them so many times; he'd let it go on way too long and now all that was left were these clashes of emotions, and choices, hard choices where he had everything to gain and everything to lose.

For one couple though, the night was just beginning. Room 212 was shared by Oden and Lucile, and they were both in their separate twin beds, dressed in their pyjamas.

'Lucile?'

'Yes, Oden?'

'Do you want to join me over here?'

'For what exactly, Oden?'

Oden lay perfectly still.

'Is there room for me?' Lucile asked.

'Yes! Of course, there's room.'

'If I get into the bed beside you, does that mean that we're an item now?'

'It can do if you want, Lucile?'

'Do you want it, Oden?'

'Do I want what?'

'Oden?'

'Yes! I want to be your boyfriend.'

'Exclusively?'

He delayed his answer.

'Exclusively...'

He hoisted himself up on the bed. Lucile turned to look at him but didn't move beyond that.

'Are you okay?' Oden asked as he wasn't sure.

'I'm just nervous.' she replied she put her face on the pillow for a minute before coming up for air.

'There's no need to be nervous, we can just cuddle, and we've done that before, right? I swear I don't want to do anything that makes you feel uncomfortable, Lucile, and we've both had a lot to drink. If you want to stay in separate beds, I'm fine with that too.'

'Can I climb in with you then?' She asked.

He nodded and made room for her on the mattress. She moved without a sound from her bed into his. He wrapped her in his arms, her head resting neatly on his shoulder as they fell back into the pillow.

'You okay, now?'

'I'm comfortable, thank you.'

She carefully moved her hand unto his chest.

'You do realise you're the love of my life thus far.' She was blushing as the words came out of her mouth.

'Well, you're the only female I've had so...' She lifted her head and thumped him lightly on the chest as he laughed. 'We haven't yet exchanged bodily fluids. This is our first night sharing a bed together.' He went on to say. She lifted herself up off his chest again and raised an eyebrow.

'No pressure then, no pressure like.'

He smiled, his eyes filled with love. 'I care about you Lucile, I dwell on you too.'

'What do you be thinking?'

'I don't know. How much trouble you're going to get me into?'

'Stop that.'

'What you're going to get up to next?'

'You do, do you?'

'Sometimes.'

He was expecting another thump on the chest, but this time she turned and kissed him. She pulled away to look at his face.

'You're just alright, Oden.'

'Is this the prelude to something sexy?' He enquired. 'Because I'm not sure I'm ready for that.'

They smiled.

'Do you think we could get take away?'

He looked at her sternly.

'I associate all things primal with a bag of chips me.' She looked at him, searching his face. He pulled her up tighter and kissed her again. Within moments they were spellbound by each other, organically discovering each other's fears and inhibitions as they gently explored a road that neither had ever been down before that night.

They woke the next morning as the sunshine poured through the windows to make its way across their naked bodies, unashamed they lay safely tucked within each other's arms.

Chapter 38

Siobhan was in the thick of it when Mark arrived; she was busy in preparation for a market that she was due to attend. Emily was having a duvet day and was crashed out on the couch in her pyjamas.

'Come in.' Siobhan hollered as he poked his head around the door and made his way to the kitchen. 'If you're looking for Laura, she left an hour ago. You two are on for a business lunch, right?'

'Did you all have a good night?' Mark inquired. Siobhan directed her gaze to the five empty wine bottles on the kitchen island. 'We had Chinese again.' She admitted.

'She's a rebel.' Emily hollered from under her duvet, her left leg sticking out one side of the sofa, her head still covered. 'We went wild.' Emily cried out again.

'Is she still drunk?'

Siobhan just raised her hands, shrugging her shoulders at the same time.

'I'm giddy.' Emily insisted steadily rising to her feet. 'Am I not allowed to be giddy?'

Siobhan was smiling. 'That person over there scoffed the last of the fifth bottle of wine this morning with her new soul mate Laura.'

'You what?' Mark quipped.

'Don't worry,' she advised him, 'Laura got a taxi home.'

Emily poked her head up from under the duvet; she fanned out her arms like a peacock displaying its ruffles, her hair full of static throwing shapes at the back of her head. 'That woman has been clattering jam jars for the past hour.' She pontificated.

Siobhan held her hands up. 'It's my new chutney and preserves business. I have a market day tomorrow.' There were three large pots on the stove and one on the draining board cooling.

'Can I try?' Mark asked as he moved towards a pot.

'No, it's boiling, it's boiling hot, don't!'

Emily stood up and gathered the quilt around her as she headed for the stairs. 'I've heard enough; I'm going to bed.'

Siobhan sniggered. 'See these musician types...'

There was huffing and moaning as Emily made her way across the floor. 'Mark, nice to see you again, honoured to be in your company. I'll leave it at that. My bed needs me.'

'What is she saying?' Mark looked at Siobhan for answers.

'Don't ask me. Lightweight.' Siobhan mumbled. 'As you can see we're descending into chaos.'

'I'm lost for words, Siobhan.'

'Chaos, it's just the one word. A cup of tea?'

'Coffee, please.'

'Night, guys.' Emily hollered from the top of the stairs.

'Night?' Mark called out sarcastically.

'Don't encourage her, please.' Siobhan pleaded.

'So, you'd a good night last night, the three of you?'

'Lots of girly laughs if that's what you mean?'

'Good. I'm glad.' He whispered.

'Are you okay?' Siobhan enquired.

'Well, yeah! it's just...'

'What is it now? My head can't take much more.'

'I've come over to share my news.'

'Go on.' Siobhan put her wooden spoon on the table.

'The shipping company want me to travel to America for six weeks, then come back for six and return to America again for six indefinitely.'

'When did this happen?'

'A week or two ago, I've been holding off a decision with the management. I didn't get the chance to tell you.'

'You'll want to tell Emily too.'

'I have.'

Siobhan stuck her hands on her hips. 'Okay, sneaky cow, she could have said.' She relaxed again. 'It sounds like a wonderful opportunity though, what will you be doing?'

'The same as I do here. I'll be working with the sales team too, it will be more or less the same.'

'But, you'll be away a lot?'

'Yeah.'

'How does that sit with you, Mark darling?'

'I'd miss you guys. To be honest, I'm not sure where I am with it or with Emily for that matter. I don't know how it's going to work until I get over there and have a lash. I'm not itching to get away; Dublin suits me as you know. I'm not just sold on the idea yet.'

'Have you another option?'

'Not if I want to move up in the company, it will mean a serious increase in salary; I could buy a place here instead of renting.'

'Owning a place isn't all that it's made out to be, but yeah I see where you're coming from alright.'

'Dealing with my staff here, it might be a whole different ball game tackling an American crew, I'll be on a mission to see what improvements can be made and it could be isolating, or not.'

'I see your point.'

'On the other hand, it's only six weeks at a time, and I'd be back home. I'm working with the sales team here as is and training up Joyce to lead the way there. I need to see if I can make improvements before I agree to head to the States.'

'Where in the States?'

'They have eight depots there; the first depot is in New York.'

'We must know a few people in New York?'

'I don't, and I don't want to lose touch with Emily, or Laura or you for that matter.'

'You don't ever have to worry about losing touch with us. You hear me, Mark.'

'I don't know, Siobhan; this is a long-term thing that will progress on to one-year contracts over there.'

'You don't have to worry; there's nothing that will separate our tidy collective, dude.' There was a long pause in their conversation as they were both reminded of Elliot. Eventually, Mark spoke up.

'Laura's a strong woman, and I know she can manage a team of men, but she doesn't have a switch off button, and Emily, well she'll be on tour soon.'

'They had lots of fun here last night, no talk of work, other than my new chutney business.'

'When I get home for those six-week stretches, she could easily be on tour. I could lose touch with her. I could lose Emily.'

'I know you're into her in a big way, Mark.' Their conversation had turned to more of a whisper.

'So, what do I do, Siobhan?'

'It will work itself out.'

The two sat back for a minute to think. 'Where's that coffee?'

'See what a night on the booze does to me.' Siobhan reached for the coffee jug and got him a mug and some milk.

'So, what's this market thing?' He asked.

'The chutney business? I'm selling a copious amount of the stuff at a Sunday market in Blessington. There's a healthy stream of repeat purchases already. It's been two weeks since I started, and I have a catering company and restaurant buying in bulk.'

'Well done, you!'

'I'm cooking up batches through the week. The Saturday markets are the first and third Saturday of every month, and there's a weekly Sunday market in the city. Sales are good, but I'll need to expand on the restaurant and catering front. I've cleared a good wage from each of the events which is surprising, I'm told.'

'How long are you at it, two weeks?'

'It's the secret chutney recipes, I've held onto them for a while. I knew they were gold the first time I tried them out. So, I guess the product is good.'

'Then trade will only grow.'

'I'm a long way away from quitting my day job yet, but my savings are going up already, so I can't complain. I love that it's tax-free.'

'Is it fun at all out there?'

'I'm enjoying the craic. At a later stage, I might make sample pots and leave those around the restaurants, see if I can find anyone that might be interested in regular purchasing, that's where the money is, but look, there's ground to cover yet. I'm still trying to find my sea legs at the markets.'

'Are you not freezing on the stalls?'

'The Blessington market is indoors but the others yeah, I've picked up a few tricks, tights and thermals, you don't want to know.'

'I guess not.'

Siobhan poured herself a coffee.

'Don't say a word to Emily, Siobhan. I'm struggling with the idea of leaving and where that might leave us. I've been able to postpone the decision but not for much longer. It's not worth leaving if I lose her.'

'You're that serious about her?'

'Yes, Siobhan.'

'I had no idea. Emily will be globe-trotting as well.'

'I'd stay and hold on to what I had here if I thought that we had a chance, but I can't ignore the fact that her new life is taking off here with the tour.'

'You wouldn't fit the bill as a roadie. I'm only joking mind. Mark. Look, you need to sit down and work this thing out between you; it won't help if I get involved. It has to come from you, mate. It's a tough call with your job offer, and then her record company gig. The price of love, ah, it's a head-scratcher.'

'Right?' Mark one hundred percent agreed.

'I can't even think about that too much; my mind is already over-crowded with my own bullshit, Mark.'

'Not a word though, yeah? It was just advice I wanted. So, how are you two getting on together?'

'Emily and me? We're getting on a treat, I love her too you know, her living here is the upside of Elliot leaving, and it's a great upside.'

'In what way?'

'I'm getting back into going to gigs. There are so many wonderful bands out there. Emily has tough competition. I've made friends too and not your garden variety type, odd cookies, and I don't mean that in a shambolic way, it takes all sorts, right?'

'I'm glad to hear it.'

'It's freer than being in a relationship. If Emily wants to stay on late somewhere, I just make my own way home in a taxi. I worried leaving her at first, but it was unfounded, she always surrounds herself with good people.'

With that Mark's phone rang, he took the call to one side while Siobhan put on fresh coffee and fixed up another jar of chutney. It was Laura. She wasn't feeling the best and had taken to her bed. It wasn't a regular thing for her to have a day off; she'd appointed her best worker and was letting him take the reins for once.

She was cancelling their lunch appointment. Mark had a few choice words for her, most of which were humorous. Red wine for breakfast was not the way to go, but as it was a once off, he'd see her later in the week.

'What's up now?' Siobhan asked.

'She has taken to her bed for the afternoon.'

'Laura.' Siobhan nodded along as she quietly chuckled. 'Well, it was off the wall them polishing off that half bottle of wine this morning, the hair of the dog and all that.'

'She's fine, but I need to get her to go for a check-up with the doctor, she's been getting headaches and the odd dizzy spell again.'

'She didn't mention it!'

'It's the work as well, she could do with a supporting floor manager, but I may as well be talking to a wall.'

'Have you met her parents yet?' Siobhan had and wondered what he'd made of them.

'Yeah, I have dealings with her father at work on the rare occasion. Her mother, I met once at Arthur's factory. She's convinced that Laura will never move on from her ex-husband. Has her mother moved on from the fact that it happened to her daughter? That was my thinking on the matter.'

'I found her mother overbearing myself.'

'If Laura let go of the house and found somewhere new to live, she'd feel so much better. What does a single woman need with a big four-bedroom house?'

'Don't rock the boat, Mark, they bought and furnished that place together, Stephen and Laura.'

'That's my point. A fresh start is needed there.'

'Have you been to her house?'

'Laura's, no.' He admitted.

'It's just... I agree that place is strangling her emotionally. It's for part a shrine, photographs of him everywhere. It freaked me out.'

'So what time do you reckon Emily will be back on her feet?'

'I don't know, she has band practice at seven o'clock. I'm away out this afternoon. I won't be back until eight if you want to call again at five. My guess is that's a good time.'

'Sounds good to me.'

'When Emily says a duvet day, she means a duvet day; she could be up to watch a film, but she won't leave before then.'

'I have a few messages to do myself in town, Siobhan. I'll call back. Maybe, we can do drinks next week, Wednesday okay with you?'

'Oden's normally here on a Wednesday, but there's no reason why he can't join us, is there?'

'No, that sounds great. It will be good to see Oden.'

'Okay, Siobhan, I'll catch you later.'

She handed Mark a jar of her now cooled chutney. The fresh pot of coffee was going down the sink; she was reforming her intake.

'It's lovely with brown bread and cheese. You're paying for the next one.'

'Getting me hooked, ah?'

'That's the general idea.'

'Thank you, my friend.'

'Be safe now.' Siobhan whispered, opening the door. 'The best of luck catching Emily this evening, you'll be fine.'

Siobhan had missed what happened between them at the wedding, but the likelihood of Emily and Mark finally getting together under the circumstances seemed farfetched.

Mark hadn't got the chance to talk to Emily when they were at the hotel. He had attempted to have it out with her on a number of occasions since then, but she was endlessly busy; she was always on her way out when he called.

Sober or not she had made some telling remarks at the wedding, and a part of him was ready to abandon the idea of American altogether. He had postponed his decision temporarily, but he had to get back to the board of management soon. Emily needed to be frank; they had to be honest with each other and work out where they stood before he could commit himself to any contract.

'I'll ring her at half four, see how she's fixed.'

'Alright, love.' Siobhan's mind was already calculating the number of jars she needed.

'Take care, you.' He whispered.

Mark stood on the step for a moment wondering what kind of proposal he might make, what kind of commitment would he need to abandon this contract in America.

His eyes were drawn to the front spare bedroom window; he imagined her struggling with the same question. What to do? He zipped up his jacket and started off; the bus was a short walk away and would take him as far as the city centre.

Chapter 39

It had been a long day at the shipping company, but as the crew got ready to leave, Mark stepped in to talk to a member of his team with Joyce at his side.

'Mulligan, can you stay back a few minutes, please?'

Mulligan was not the nervous sort, he agreed without hesitation. The others gathered their belongings, and quickly dispersed, leaving the three men alone. Mark was ready to pass on the news with Joyce anchored directly behind him, Joyce staring over Mark's shoulder.

'We have a favour to ask you, Mulligan?'

'And what's that when you're not at home?'

'We want you to step in as second in command when there's only one of us on the floor. It's just for the next week or two until we see how well you can hold the ropes.'

Joyce rounded Mark's left side before moving into full view to speak his mind. 'After which point, Mulligan, work going well, we'll be leaving you to manage the floor on your own for an hour or two at a time. I'll be going upstairs with Mark to join the sales team.'

'Is there an increase in salary?'

Mark stepped in. 'That depends on how things work out over the next couple of weeks. If Joyce can manage to reach a credible level of sales, then he may be taking over my position and alternating between here and upstairs. His position will need to be filled, and yes there will be an increase in salary that comes with this new post if you're up for the challenge?'

'What kind of increase?'

'You'll have to prove you're able to step into his shoes before we get to that. If you're not interested, we have another man in mind that we may turn to; it was a close call between the pair of you. The opportunity will be passed over to him if it's not working out between you and the crew, so do not take this lightly.'

'No, I'm interested.' Mulligan recognised the opportunity.

Our Diligent Souls

'You'll need to be able to push the men on constantly to meet the deadlines, and you know from what you've seen through us that this means you working harder than any of them to get their respect.'

'I have their respect.'

'Not as their floor manager you don't.' Joyce advised.

'Point taken...' Mulligan knew he was right.

'So, we'll start tomorrow, at no time will the two of us be on the floor from now on and you will be called to manage by either myself or Joyce at any given point in the day. We expect that by the end of the week if things are going well, you should be able to take over for both of us at two-hour intervals when Joyce and I are in the salesroom together.'

Joyce nodded. 'It will be worth it for you if you stick with it.'

'I will!' Mulligan was enthusiastic.

'You can head off now if you have no questions?' Joyce concluded.

'Grand so, see you both tomorrow.' Mulligan was gone before they'd time to say another word.

'We'll have to watch that he ties up the details before he lets people go in the evenings, the man gets itchy feet at a quarter to the hour, that he has to conquer.' Mark insisted. 'So, let's head upstairs and work on this sales pitch of yours, I can be the potential customer while you're the other end of the line.' They headed for the stairs.

'I'm ready for this.' Joyce admitted with confidence as they nodded at each other. The two men walked across the floor, they weren't far from the stairwell. Mark was readying his apprentice for the challenge that lay ahead; they had gone over much of the technique in his apartment where they had been practising during the week.

'It's a dry run now. It's just you and me.'

'I hear you, boss.'

'Just remember you can save these companies money.'

'But they don't want to hear that.' Joyce added.

'Correct, they've heard that time over, don't make it complicated, you've done your research; you know what they're paying. Just deliver the bottom line.'

Only then did they realise that Mournaghan was standing just left of the stairwell. They were so caught up in their conversation, they hadn't noticed him. He rarely appeared when there were other executives on the scene, only ever speaking to Mark the way he did when there was no one to act as a witness.

'What's this with Mulligan then?'

The two men had no idea he'd been listening.

'Ralph, how are you? We didn't see you there.'

'I gathered that much. What plans are you two hatching? Is your memory short, Mark?'

'Actually,' Mark stated, 'I'm not going to be working here much longer, at least not full time anyway.'

Mournaghan smiled. 'You have to know when you're beaten.'

Joyce lowered his head briefly.

'Indeed.' Mark continued as he smiled falsely. 'Joyce will be taking over my position and Mulligan his.'

Joyce stepped in and spoke out to Mark's surprise. 'I will be working directly with the board of management, so I'm sorry to say we won't have reason to get deeply acquainted.'

'You'll be no different.'

'Yeah?' Mark quipped, as he nodded a farewell to Mournaghan and moved Joyce towards the stairs to continue the conversation they'd been having. 'So, clients... You can fax them the cost breakdowns or email them out, or you can offer to bring them through it in their offices if it suits them. Keep it personable, remember your tone and pace.'

For the following three hours they slogged away until Joyce could take no more. He was getting the gist of it, in fact, they were both learning from each other. Mark hadn't expected to gain extra insight, but that was one of Joyce's greatest attributes. He was indirectly insightful by times, humbling and never recognised these qualities in himself. He had practised the opening lines that Mark had given him, and with Mark coming up with a variety of unexpected responses, he was starting to form his own working dialogue.

The truth was that they had a reasonably decent service to sell. The trick was to know what specific difficulties each company dealt with, in respect of their present shipping contractors. They needed to show that they had solutions; they had to get in with the benefits above and beyond the now trivialised difficulties that these company had experienced, or could expect to, and then hit them with standard guarantees.

'It's in the approach and knowing where each shipping company falls short. None of these salespeople can deliver this information off the top of their heads, that's where you need to be for you to be at the top of your game.' Mark truly believed it was something that was easily accomplished.

Joyce accompanied him as he turned out the lights; both men were tired but exhilarated too. Mark had yet to give the board his final decision on America, but they were meeting in the morning, and that would put an end to that. He was heading over to meet Emily at the recording studio, and hopefully, from there, he could take her for a glass of wine and something to eat. It was going to be a surprise to her, but it was his only chance, she had dodged him at Siobhan's place; rushing out the door to her band practice an hour early. What needed to be sorted out between them had to happen tonight.

Emily was still hung-over from her night with Laura and Siobhan. She had been thinking about Mark's situation and had come to a conclusion, that she was against the idea. America could be a dangerous place, and he would be isolated for long stretches of time; it was playing on her mind more than she dared to admit.

An acquaintance of hers had been talking about a drum soloist who had become suicidal on tour; the isolation of his travelling alone had created depression and anxiety in the drummer that proved to be too much for him to battle with, the guy had taken his own life in the end. She felt that Mark needed to question what he was doing; he had suffered isolation before when Arthur died.

His workload was tremendous, and the pressure on him could easily become unbearable if he had to cope with executives that were of the same ilk as Mournaghan, he'd be in trouble. There were no guarantees that he wouldn't have to deal with that crap again, and moreover, in America, he'd have much more on his plate. She was continually finding reasons for him not to go. None of these reasons she could openly admit were her own, not even to herself.

The recording studio was brightly lit at the front entrance where Mark waited as handfuls of musicians flooded in and out; he recognised two of her crew. They were decent lads and acknowledged him directly.

'Is Emily in there? Have you seen her?' Mark asked after the usual, how are you? Greetings went back and forth.

Are?

'She's on her way out; I doubt she'll be long.'

When she did come through the door, she looked utterly dishevelled. She was nervously gathering her emotions and had forgotten what she was searching for in her bag. When she saw Mark, her face lit up with curiosity. 'What are you doing here?' She was surprised.

'I thought that I'd take you for a drink and something to eat.'

She had planned to ring him in the next few minutes and ask him to meet up, but she kept quiet about that.

'So where do you want to go?'

'There's a nice jazz place over in Smithfield,' he suggested.

'Sounds good to me.'

'Why don't we walk until a taxi passes, there's nowhere around here to get a taxi is there?'

'We can walk and find one. It's fine by me.'

They made it by foot to Smithfield in under a half an hour; there was not one taxi that drove by on the way, but they weren't concentrating on the road. They had talking to do in respect of the record contract that she had signed just days ago, so that kept them busy.

As they entered the Jazz club, they were hit by a blast of the mellow saxophone. The pair were escorted to a table with an excellent view of the musician. The guy was French but had brilliant English, his accent charming an already bustling crowd.

Mark and Emily could barely hear themselves think. They were both exuding nervous energy as neither were ready to say all that was going on in their minds. They ordered oysters and white wine; it had been a while since they had hung out on their own; there was sometimes a third party if not a fourth.

Emily began to fill him in on her evening. It had been a hard recording session as one of the band members had been getting at her, she admitted. She was drained from all the backbiting. The record company had wanted to sign Emily but not the band, though they had agreed to allow her to use the guys for the first leg of the tour.

Most of the band members respected that, but one guitarist had his nose put out of joint. After one hairy interaction, he was swiftly told that his ego wouldn't carry him to the next session, he needed to put a lid on it. Emily had no time for that crap; it was what it was, and she had no way of changing that. Mark was fascinated.

She was in no form to talk of studio antics. She needed to call Mark out on America tonight; she was planning to get on the blower to him after band practice, it was a good job he showed up when he did. In saying that, the issue of America was still clouding their exchange, she needed somewhere quiet if she was going to get her point across.

She made it plain once the oysters were out of the way, that his excursion to the States was now a sore topic and she was worried about him. She told him the story of the drum soloist and her fear of him suffering through more top executive shenanigans.

It took a while, but he did everything in his power to convince her that he had no intention of consorting with executives. He was to work as an independent; feeding back information to the board of management here on his progress. He was going to be keeping his eyes down when it came to any vexatious demons; the hallmarks of Mournaghan style behaviour were detectable by now.

Mark already had a picture of where he'd be working in his mind. Jokingly, he said he'd try to exude some fitting witticisms in the company of his new floor staff. Mark hoped that there was at least one savvy article that he could adopt as a friend. He planned to be open to that in small doses, but he was going to be careful, and if push came to shove, he could find quaint restaurants to eat in and explore the cities alone.

He talked about Siobhan's chutney business to lighten the mood and keep things at a ground level. He could tell that she was searching for another reason to stop him from going, but there was only one reason for him to stay and both knew it. He pretended that he was completely unaware of the progress that Siobhan was making and steered their news in that direction for the meantime. The night was young and the pub fuller than he'd expected. He was convinced that this was not the opportune moment, not just yet.

Emily wanted to see Siobhan going full time at the market trading; she had now seen first-hand what the museum job was doing to her friend.

Siobhan was coming home exhausted from the job, and the difference was day and night when it came to the market scene where Siobhan showed a fresh vitality.

'She lights up when she's at the market; she leaves to go there in a good mood and comes home in even better form.'

'That's great.' Mark was relieved.

'The curator job just bores her stiff. I'm going to go around the restaurants with her and hand out sample chutneys when she's ready. The restaurants aren't that interested in her sweet preserves, but hotel and bed and breakfasts might be enthusiastic.'

'She'll need an industrial kitchen when it properly takes off, health and safety-wise.' Mark advised.

'I've talked to the owner of the daytime cafe where I had my first gig. He's interested in renting her his kitchen one or two nights a week when she's ready for that. I left him a jar of chutney, and he rang me tonight to put a wholesale order in, Siobhan was delighted.'

'That's great; she's going great guns then?'

'I hope it works out for her, Mark. She'd need transport, a run-around, but she's saving for that. She knows how to squirrel money away, that one!'

'Did you enjoy the wedding?'

Her cheeks were flushed with embarrassment, but she managed to keep her composure. 'Yeah, it was great. Alfie rang me, and we went out for a drink before he left.'

'He cornered you into that one I'm guessing?'

'He gets that I'm not into him.'

'Good.'

'He seriously thinks he can get a tour off the ground in Australia, a three-week tour. I tried to explain that I'm tied to a label, but he thinks I can bring the label in on it. He's persistent I'll give him that.'

'He always was ambitious Alfie.'

'I have a meeting with the record company next week, so I'll put it to them then, that's as much as I can do? Australia, eh?'

'And you were complaining about me going to America?'

'If, and it's a big if that I go to Australia, it will be with the band; I'd not be alone.'

'That is true.'

'Look, Mark, do what you see as right. I've given you enough of my opinion in respect of America, just make sure that the management at your place organise one visit at a time, so if you're not happy you can still station yourself back here.'

'We said we weren't going to talk about this in the middle of a jazz club.'

'Fair enough!'

Within the hour, the bar was packed to capacity, the French jazz musician took a fifteen-minute break, but the buzz in the place didn't slow. There was plenty of eating and drinking going on. Mark suggested that they nip outside for a quick smoke and Emily was totally on for that. She was longing for a cigarette, and the very mention of one set off an instant craving. Mark ran to the cigarette machine while Emily put on her coat, she asked the waitress to leave the wine glasses where they were and bring seconds, the oysters were done and dusted, and they were lovely.

It was nippy enough outside, even standing under the heater. They huddled together to shield the flame of the lighter and leaned in with their cigarettes. Emily had to sit on a chair as the nicotine entered her bloodstream; she was feeling a little dizzy though she laughed it off.

'It's the nectar of the Gods when you haven't had a smoke for a while.' She remarked.

He raised his cigarette. 'To the nectar of the Gods then!'

Emily was a pleasure to watch; she teased him on his choice of trousers and the recent cut to his hair. She was different to Laura and Siobhan in so many respects, younger at heart and yet much more sensitive to global inequalities. She always had an ear for those who suffered in life, but that was part of her trade as a musician.

He reminded her of the first night that they shared together when they met the fox on their walk home. She talked of Morocco and brought back for him the characters that they had come across, ones that he had forgotten, a Welsh guy that they had spent the whole day with, having talked about community practice and its merits.

'Work has been good to you with its ups and downs... It's turned you into more of a man.'

'I don't know how you can accredit work with that. I had to grow up at some stage and stop arsing around. You, Miss Emily, have changed me beyond any of that.'

'Me. In what respect?'

'I can't say. I'm sworn to secrecy.'

She looked at him curiously, and he stared back, holding her eyes to translate some form of sentiment before breaking the silence again. 'Work had something to do with it. I have changed; I had to learn how to stand on my own after leaving Arthur's business, and losing him was an upheaval.'

'Good for you then if America is what you want, once you still find time to hang out with a struggling artist?'

'That's my biggest worry.'

'You're too sweet, Mark.'

'No, I'm not.' Mark pulled away irritated by her remark.

'You love being able to control where your future is going.' Emily jested.

His hands began to shake. 'No! That I can't control! I'm failing miserably when it comes to what I want out of life.'

'Nonsense!' Emily responded, knocked back by his sudden change in temperament though she was blushing.

'You think America is what I dream of now? What? To chase money? You don't know me if you think that. You don't know me in any way shape or form.'

'Just, calm yourself there!'

'I want companionship, the honest, straightforward, compassionate kind. I want respect and yes, a decent salary, an ethical life.'

'That's well and good Mark, but...'

'But, what Emily?'

'Well, you have that, and so few see this level of opportunity?'

'You can never make up your mind.' He growled at her this time.

'Why do I have to make up my mind?'

'None of it matters if I'm alone. Look to my mother and father, look at Joyce; they go home to something of real value. I want to hold the woman that I love and know that she loves me back with the same level of intensity. That's what I want.'

'That's hard to find?'

'It's standing right in front of me, and well you know it, as time transpires I am more captivated, and less able to look beyond you. It's been going on too long, and we've never even kissed. What man in his right mind, I ask you?'

'I'm sorry, Mark.'

'I'm afraid of losing you, of never getting back to where we are here, right now, that's without even moving things forward.'

'Don't, Mark.'

'Why not, let's have it out? I've lost you otherwise?'

'Don't be cruel.'

'Cruel? You don't realise… I walk the floor of my apartment trying to find a way to turn things on their head. I need to let you know how much I'm struggling with the idea of both of us being separated, of life without a 'me and you'.'

Emily stood and looked at him angrily. 'How can you?'

'What?' He was appalled. He'd just opened his heart to her.

She shot back at him. 'You think I can get out of my contract at this point? Two days ago, I signed it, I made them wait until after the wedding. You didn't want me; you wanted me to succeed.' There was a dedicated silence between them. He could have fallen to his knees.

'You don't have to pull away from your contract; I can stay. At least, that way I'll be here when you get back from your tours.'

'And that will sit okay with you six months down the line?'

'You're saying that you care, that you give a shit; that I'm not out of touch with reality here. You're saying that you have feelings or what, Emily? Be completely honest; everything hangs in the balance. I don't give a damn what people think.'

Emily stood firm, trying to figure out a way to backtrack what she had just admitted, indirectly or not.

'Mark, I'm not saying anything. You have this idea of me in your head that's a hundred miles from the truth. I am not this brave and mysterious person that you see me to be.'

'Emily, please.'

'I'm not strong enough! Before I met you, I was sure I wanted the relationship my parents had, the lifestyle they created, and you turned that on its head for me. You need to go to America. I could be touring for years. What have we done?'

'I don't care if you're on tour, you can tour for as long as you need to, Emily.' She could see that Mark was losing the run of himself, he was breaking wide open.

'Enough with this talk, Mark.'

'Why do I keep doing this to myself? Do you care?' He cried out.

'Stop it. I care. Christ, I care.' She was coming to realise that her feelings lay way deeper for Mark that she had ever dared to admit to herself. 'I'm heartbroken by the idea of you going away. There's the truth. But we have dreams to pursue!'

'America is not my dream!' Mark reiterated 'You are. I don't need that level of success. I am happy working here; I love Dublin.'

'Mark, you have a family you can help, and an opportunity that will secure your life in a way that Ireland never will. This country can be brutal, how many have a solid career? You don't know what's around that corner, three or four years from now you'll have the security behind you to make these choices but this, it's a once in a lifetime thing America.'

There was no one in the smoking section; no one left to take heed of what was going on between them; his eyes were wet with tears.

'Just tell me you love me? And I will wait, or we can meet, I will be back and at least for now...'

She put her hand over his mouth, shook to the core, she lowered her head as he waited for an answer. Being with him on a casual basis would break her that much she knew. There was a big part of her that wanted to ditch the touring idea and get a regular job, a part of her that wanted to give in and leave it all behind to be with him, but she was caught up in a contract now. She couldn't go that road; they had too much to lose, their dreams would crumble. 'I won't do it, Mark. We can't promise each other that.'

'Just be with me tonight, give me something to hold onto of you.'

'I want to, Mark but I can't. It would break both of us.'

Mark's neck fell limp, his head hanging, he was split in two. She could see the pain jolt through his body; she waited, rocked where she stood until finally, he lifted his head. She cleaned his wet and broken face with her hand. She whispered to him. 'Stay my friend, please, don't turn your back on me.'

He held his breath and thought before he shook his head. 'This is all wrong.' He wiped his own eyes, and she took his hand away to hold it in hers against his chest.

'Please, let's sit on a chair; we can look at the sky together.' To hold her hand meant such a great deal to him. She led him to the far corner of the smoking section that overlooked the pavilion. They sat in quivering silence before she took the cigarettes from his pocket and lit one up in front of him. The moon was full; the rhythms from the jazz club muffled by the sound of the wind on the street.

'We will always be friends, Mark, if only that and nothing else, then it won't be sad. Life will guide us.'

It was a while before Mark spoke, but when he did he choose his words well.

'It's easy for you to say, you're a potential rock goddess now, not a struggling artist anymore.'

'Folk, it's folk music. Jesus Mark, can you not tell the difference yet?'

Mark smiled, his life had been about music from as far back as he could remember, but his heart was heavy.

'I can't just let it go at that; I need to fight you on this. I have never loved this way; I have never felt the need to be close to anyone, not to this extent.'

'We can't change where we are in life; we cannot turn our backs on these openings; they might never come again. I can't be with you and watch you leave, and I cannot make you stay, I cannot be the reason that you abandoned your dreams, as much as I love you.'

'You're not listening, Emily…It's not what I want.'

'But it is what I want for you.'

Emily was already somewhere else in her mind; she knew that she would cry hard before the night's end but not in front of him. It had been a long time, but she knew the feeling well. What sort of woman was she to turn her back on something so powerful, so undeniable? She knew that beyond tonight there was no going back on her decision.

She would ring Siobhan and tell her she was staying with a friend. She would go to her old apartment for the night. Tonight, of all nights, she needed to be alone, knowing that she had the choice to hold him in her arms. She had waited so long for that moment and not even known it, and yet there she was ready to kill off the dream; to put it to bed for once and for all. She couldn't face Siobhan or talk to her about it. Her musician lodger would need no explanation, the walls were thicker than at Siobhan's, and there was a radio she left behind, it would give her time alone to let the pain out. She knew all too well how to manage her grief.

America was it now; there was no going back after tonight. He would give the news to the board in the morning. He would never again allow himself to get carried away; it was time to bury his feelings. Part of him resented her, but part of him knew that she was right.

The jazz musician put his lips to the saxophone as they re-entered through the side door. Two fashionable troglodytes had slipped into their seats and moved their wines to one side. Mark and Emily made their way to the bar, but they weren't there long. They downed their drinks, paid their dues, and the bouncer advised them on the best place to pick up a taxi.

'Don't leave me like this Emily, stay with me tonight. We could be dead and buried by next year, to miss the opportunity to know love this great, who are we kidding?'

'I feel the cruelty of it, Mark I do, but I couldn't withstand it. You need to do this thing; you can make such an enormous difference out there in the world.'

She stood and looked at him before they shared a lasting embrace.

'You mean more to me than any living person right here, right now.' She let go of his hand; both of them were ill-prepared to go their separate ways, both taking different taxis.

Emily broke down in the back seat, choking on her tears as the driver pulled in at the given address.

'There's such a thing as playing too hard to get, love.' He had watched their interaction at the taxi rank. 'Do you want me to come in with you, I can keep you company?' She couldn't believe her ears. He asked again.

'What do you say?' She stepped out of the taxi and readied herself to howl at him. 'Rot in hell, you creepy, snide, bloody God-awful low-life.'

She kicked the car door closed and took her bag to the front of the car, using it in a vain attempt to try to smash the windscreen. He quickly got out of the driving seat, but she ran. He shouted at her. 'That's seven Euros you owe me, love if you're not up for it like.'

Her body was stiff with tension, her eyes stinging with tears. 'Get out of here before I do you damage.'

'I know where you live, you silly woman.'

'And I have the number of your taxi, you fool, just get lost, creep!'

The mascara was rolling down her cheeks; she emptied her purse and threw coins on the ground for him as she ran for the door of her old place, keys at the ready.

'I hate this bloody country.' She shouted. 'Do me a favour if you can, hit the next lamp post, yeah?' He scrambled to get his greedy mitts on the money.

'Piss off now, you,' she wailed, 'before I ring the guards.'

The following morning Mark went in front of the board of management to tell them that he would be taking the position. He wanted in his heart to leave straight away and avoid ever having to see Emily again, but the management had other plans. He would be working with the sales team there first, for two months which would see him in Dublin, until at least the new year.

Chapter 40

Emily burst through the door; she couldn't wait to tell them her news. The record company she originally signed with had decided to offer her a two-album contract on the back of the progress she'd been making on the first album. They had offered her ridiculous money, but she was expected to go on tour just after Christmas for eight months. She had arrived back to a melancholy atmosphere, her overexcitement flying in the face of what her three friends had just discovered. Oden and Lucile were hunched around the fire while Siobhan was in the kitchen making tea.

'That's great.' Siobhan called out.

'Don't worry, I'll still be home midweek for the larger part, and I'll be keeping up my rent payments while I'm gone.'

'I can't allow you to do that.' Siobhan replied instinctively.

'I'm about to sign up for a two-album contract, it's a serious contract, besides I need a base and I'd only be paying the mortgage on my place. I'll be back and forward; I'm not disappearing just yet.'

'We'll talk later.' Siobhan stated calmly.

'You can come out to see me; I've concerts here in Ireland, more gigs in England, I'll be hitting Europe, Asia too.' Oden and Lucile were quiet. 'What's going on?' Emily at this stage realised that something wasn't right.

Oden left the fireplace to approach her, checking in with Siobhan before he said a word. 'It's Elliot, Siobhan got a letter today.'

Emily immediately turned to Siobhan, her hand against her cheek. 'Christ. Are you okay, pet?'

Siobhan stood firm. 'Your news is more important. I'm delighted for you. This is a big scoop.'

'Forget the record contract, what did he say?'

'It's an enormous opportunity.'

'Jesus, just tell me!' Emily was sweating it.

'He's coming home.' Oden stepped up and informed her.

'But it's not six months yet?'

'He's coming home next week to be here for the Christmas holidays.' Siobhan stated.

'And is he going back?' Emily was white as a sheet.

'He didn't say. I got a letter in the post.' Siobhan wasn't fit to elaborate.

'So, tell us, the record deal?' Siobhan asked again. Oden and Lucile stood quietly looking on, not knowing what to say.

'I want to know what he had to say. This is unbelievable.'

'Don't be over-thinking it, Emily. He had to come home at one stage. I was going to have to face it somewhere along the line, and I'll be following you around the country. You can count on that. We all will, won't we, guys? I'll have my van in a few weeks.'

Oden and Lucile were standing by the fireplace in silence.

'Have you talked to Elliot's parents yet?' Emily enquired.

'Yeah, I was speaking to them this morning.' Siobhan looked like her face was burning up.

'What day is he due back?'

'The twenty-second of December.' Siobhan replied looking pensive; her thoughtfulness strained by a deepening dread. 'Laura has a hospital appointment that morning.' Siobhan continued. 'Mark is taking her. Hopefully, they'll get to the bottom of those headaches. I take it you've not told him your news?'

'Mark, no, not yet, I'll ring him this evening.'

'He'll be made up for you, Emily.'

'Did you tell Mark that Elliot wrote you another letter?'

'I told him that Elliot is coming home, yeah?'

'I don't know what to say here, I'm stunned. How did Mark respond?'

'Much as I expected, he'll be glad to see him home. He wants to get to grips with why he left the way he did?' Siobhan just shrugged.

'He can go to pot as far as I'm concerned.' Oden insisted, his frustration visible from the other side of the room. Emily and Siobhan looked blankly at Oden both astounded and concerned.

'Siobhan, can I have a word with you upstairs? You don't mind, do you guys?'

Oden and Lucile looked over at them. 'We're fine here.' Lucile advised her on both their behalf, taking Oden's shoulder.

Siobhan was hesitant but followed Emily to the stairs. She was sitting on her bed within minutes. 'There's too much fuss being made of this, Oden is beside himself I thought you'd never get home.'

'What did the letter say?'

'That he's coming home. That he regretted leaving the way he did before he had even got off the plane. He didn't call because he knew there was no mending what he'd done.'

'Okay!'

'He said that he'd carried a heavy heart through what was otherwise an eye-opening experience.'

'Hum!'

'He doesn't expect things to go back to the way they were, but he's hoping to find a means by which he can make amends.'

'Like that's easily done!'

'Don't make it harder for me, Emily.'

'I'm sorry.'

'It was a sincere letter for the most part.'

'Go on...'

'He says he's still in love with me, but more so now.'

'So, what's the plan then?'

'I never stopped loving Elliot, Emily. In truth, I never stopped being in a relationship with him.' Her eyes filled up. 'Even if, it's just to draw a line under it and move on. I don't know if he's been with anyone else, but it's unlikely don't you think.'

'Do you ask?'

'I don't know if I even care. When I saw Elliot's handwriting on the envelope, I felt sick; I was trembling with hatred. I'm confused, Emily.'

'Did he give any inclination as to whether or not he's going back to the missions?'

'No, none.'

'Maybe he got thrown out; it's only been... what?'

Our Diligent Souls

'Four and a half months.' Siobhan reminded her. 'Why would he get thrown out?'

'Just play it by ear, love. There's nothing you can do, other than judge how you feel when you see him face to face.'

Emily wrapped her arms around her mate, but there were no tears.

Oden jumped up as they reached the bottom of the stairs. 'Are you okay, Siobhan?' He made his way over to the kitchen where Siobhan was retrieving mugs from the cupboard. He needed her to know that he had her corner.

'Listen, Siobhan; he hurt you in the way he handled it. Don't mask that!'

'I've had more regrets than ill feelings towards Elliot, Oden. Or I had until I seen his handwriting this morning?'

'You need to protect yourself, Siobhan.'

'Come on, it's time for coffee... We have Emily's news to celebrate. We're going around in circles here, what is in the past is in the past to a degree at least, back down now.' Oden knew she'd heard enough and said no more.

Emily and Siobhan settled in for the evening once the two others had left. Oden and Lucile were still so very young, rubbing two pence together to make a shilling, living on loves young dream. Siobhan envied that. Lucile had transferred over to games development but was two years behind Oden in college terms now. He could be a mover and shaker in the near distant future, and she could still be up to her eyeballs in assignments; it was all ahead of them.

They had started sleeping together. Siobhan couldn't but notice the way they moved around each other. Elliot would have had them hung, drawn and quartered if he was even to get a whisper of that. But Siobhan wasn't with Elliot anymore, and his opinion didn't come into play. It wasn't for her to spell out the importance of contraception either.

It was a long drawn out evening, neither woman wanting to talk about their relevant news. They were getting ready for bed when the phone rang. Emily picked up the receiver.

'Hello.'

'Is Siobhan there, please?'

'Elliot! Is that you?'

Our Diligent Souls

Siobhan walked over to the kitchen counter where Emily was resting with the phone in her hand.

'How is she, Emily? Is she there?'

'I'll see if I can find her, one moment, Elliot.'

Emily wrapped her hand around the receiver before she spoke.

'You don't have to talk to him now. The ball is in your court. If you're not up to this, that's okay. I can tell him you're not here or ask him not to ring again. You can do this face to face when he gets back. It's up to you?'

'Let me just catch my breath.' Siobhan requested. She stood there for a few seconds before carefully taking the phone from her friend's hand.

'I'll go upstairs if that what you want?' Emily asked.

Siobhan nodded. 'I'll be up in a minute.' She could hear Elliot's breath on the phone long before she dared to speak.

'I got your letter.' She said officiously.

'I waited for a few days before I called to make sure it had arrived.' He stated.

'It arrived today.'

He hesitated, hoping that a short silence might heal the tension.

'How are you?' He asked.

'Do you want an honest answer?'

'Yes!'

'I'm good in myself. The letter set me back. It was a shock to see something arrive from you after four and a half months.'

'Are we okay?' He asked again.

'Boy, but that could be very simple for you.'

'I didn't mean it in that way.'

'I'm still angry with you... I'm not sure it's even easy to say your name.'

There was silence at both ends of the phone.

'I have missed you so much.' His voice was shaking, but she gave no reply. 'It's been tough. Talk to me, Siobhan?'

'What do you want me to say, that everything's forgiven? I'm not the same person that I was before you left.'

'I don't expect you to be.'

'What is it that you expect?'

'I didn't want to hurt you. It was never what I wanted.' In all honesty, he wasn't sure what he wanted when he left. It was a flight of fancy, a selfish act; he couldn't justify his actions even to himself.

'Then why leave that way? What did you expect?'

'I was losing my will to live, Siobhan. It took months of working here to come to terms with that, to realise where I'd landed myself, to start to get my mind around the scale of destruction that I'd left behind me.'

'And never once had you the courage to lift the phone?'

'No.'

'Why not?'

'The pain I had caused.'

'Was I to blame for that?'

'No, not in any way, Siobhan.'

She corrected him. 'That's not entirely true, Elliot.'

'There's hurt to be mended. I know it's my fault, Siobhan.'

'I've coped.'

'And I love you even more for that. I haven't been with another woman or even thought of it, the day's move at full throttle here. It's been physically demanding, repetitive and beyond that more crushing is the fact that it's a cruel world here. Crueller than I'd ever have imagined.'

'It was always going to be the case, you and the missions. It was your dream, Elliot. I wasn't consulted.'

'I make a difference here... few stay, Siobhan. I am more equipped now. Through all of that, I couldn't escape the thought of how I'd made you feel, nor could I run away from what it is to work here. I'd never have been able to look myself in the eye.'

'And they're letting you take leave?'

'Yes. I've been catatonic with grief.'

'Because of what you've seen there?'

'And what I've lost in respect of you.'

His words were humbling, it had played out as she'd imagined, but her contempt for his actions was immovable. She could empathise with him but was disenchanted; her capacity to rescue was void and hollow. He had created a coldness in her that was justifiable, a coldness that called a bluff on the sincerity of men, of mankind, of anyone outside her circle of trust.

'The little time I do have for myself is full of memories of our life together. Life without you, without a confidante... It's dark, Siobhan.'

'I confided in my friends, those that are left. You had too many secrets. I was a woman that could be completely blindsided. I discovered that when you left.'

'I know the pain that I have caused.'

'I stood in the way of your dreams, Elliot. There was a time when we were both on the same page, but that time has passed. It passed long before you left. I was just not up to speed with that. I was out of the loop as it were.'

'I felt trapped.'

'I understood that from your parting letter.'

'None of my feelings for you have changed, Siobhan. All our hopes for a family, what we had, it is of enormous value to me now.' Siobhan was silent as he talked. 'I'd give anything to close my mind and erase the things I've seen, to be by your side again.'

'Your respect for me had worn thin before you left, Elliot. I will never risk that again.'

'I want to be with you? It is harder here, harder than you could ever imagine, it was only ever you and me. I never wanted that to change.'

'Your trip to the missions was about you, Elliot.'

'I know that, Siobhan.'

'I have found ways to improve my life; I've found upsides, but nothing that I will be grateful to you for.'

'Think back to the Christmas before I left Siobhan, we were happy, were we not?'

'You abandoned ship. You dropped leaflets and one self-absorbed letter, and split.'

'I was wrong.'

'And so was I in some respects, but it doesn't diminish the pain that you caused, nor the vengeful way you took off.'

'Vengeful?'

'Have it either way, does selfish sound better? I knew it was going to be tough over there for you.'

'How come you could see that and I couldn't.'

The truth was that she knew him better than she knew herself. Now, she could see beyond him to a life she better deserved. What they had was finished. She had thrived without him and was free to continue to do so. She could hold her head high; she could put herself first. Elliot was owed nothing but a stake in the house, and that was well on the way to sorting itself out.

'It's laughable Elliot, saying you want your old life back, it's not enough. I can't say hand on heart that I want you back, to me you coming home it's just another ploy to keep me on side in the interim? Are you going back to the missions?'

'Well; I have to...'

'Enough said, Elliot.'

'We have to be straight with each other, Siobhan.'

'Wasn't that our last slogan, Elliot? I wanted a family, I wanted all those things with you, but my world has opened up.'

'We can make it work, Siobhan.'

'Can you picture that in your mind, how do I ever feel secure again? This doesn't go away. What, I keep shut? I keep looking over my shoulder waiting for you to take off again. Hello?'

'It doesn't have to be that way.'

'You put the boat on the morning tide, Elliot, and you sailed it out to sea. There is no going back for us. I have to go.'

'No, don't go, can I call you tomorrow?'

'Elliot,' There was a cold, empty silence. 'We can meet and talk when you get home, we have practical arrangements to make, but what I know is that here right now on this phone, we no longer add up; I've never been surer of anything in my whole life. I'm sorry, but please don't phone again until your back in Dublin. Good night, Elliot.'

'Siobhan...'

'Good night! Do not attempt to phone me; you can call to the house when you get back for Christmas, a Christmas that I expect to enjoy with my friends. There are practical issues to resolve like I said. Respect that, if you can.'

'Siobhan, don't?'

'Good night, Elliot.' She repeated as she lowered the phone. Her tears had dried up; she stood there in silence accepting the truth, what they had ended the day he got on that plane. Holding on until he finally found it in his heart to call, it had served its purpose. They were no more, and that was the end of it.

She moved quietly around the kitchen and made herself some sweet tea, she didn't want to relay the details to Emily, not now, not ever. Siobhan thought about the success of the business, and the fact that she'd soon be able to leave her day job, she thought of the new friends that she had made and all the gigs she got to go to with Emily.

There it was, after four and a half long months; she hadn't the time or head space to allow him back into her thoughts, whether that was to last forever only time would tell.

Chapter 41

When Elliot rang the doorbell, it was his mum that was first to the door, his sun-kissed skin disguised his apprehension. 'You're welcome home, son.' She brought him through, and once he had passed her, his mother turned to press her body against the door, leaning in gently until the snib clicked. Facing the sitting room, she spoke again. 'Don't know why you had to go over there without telling us in the first place, but you're welcome home.'

Her husband automatically stood up to hug his son. 'Stop fussing woman, for God's sake.' He turned and whispered in Elliot's ear. 'You had your mother very worried.'

'So how was it?' His mother asked abruptly.

'Yeah, it was an eye-opener, mum.'

'I bet.' She replied.

'There is so much we take for granted, son.' His father added.

Elliot was getting a mixed welcome. 'You've both been alright then?'

'Nothing to worry yourself about, son... Sit next to me, please.' Elliot took a chair and pulled it up alongside his father as he sat down. 'Is Oden at home?' He asked.

'I'd leave him for now... He'll come downstairs when he's ready.' His father advised.

'I've missed him something awful, dad.'

'As, he has you, son. But you stepped on a few hearts when you decided to leave. You've bridges to mend.'

'I'm fully aware of that, dad.'

'Good.'

Elliot's mum wandered into the kitchen to bring back a tray of delights that she had ready in preparation for the occasion.

'So how have you been, what did I miss?' Elliot asked.

'Not a hell of a whole lot, son... Not a hell of a whole lot. You must be exhausted? But you look well.'

'It was a long flight alright.'

'Will you be going back?'

'Yes dad, for another nine weeks after Christmas beyond that I don't know. I've come back to see if I can patch things up with Siobhan. I couldn't take another day of wondering. I made mistakes in respect of Siobhan; it was the wrong way to go about things.'

'You've missed her then?'

'Heart and soul, dad.' He replied, holding back tears as he wrapped his arms around his father.

'You know what you want to happen going forward?'

'I do, I very much do, dad.'

'Well, I hope for your sake that you're given a hearing, it's not something that you're automatically entitled to, not at this stage, but I'm guessing you know that.'

There was a familiar silence between the two men as his mother made her way back from the kitchen.

'I'm going to go up to see Oden.' Elliot stated, slapping both hands on his thighs before standing up.

'He was very hurt, Elliot, take my advice and tread lightly. Ah?'

'Where are you off to?' His mother asked, disgruntled. 'I've just put the tea on the table.' Again, his father stood up; his wife looked as if she might drop the tray on the floor with annoyance; she had made a trip to the bakery especially for Elliot's return. 'Well I'll be snookered; I didn't get two sentences in, he has no manners, my son.'

'Sit on your chair and give it a rest, woman. The lad needs to talk to his brother.'

'A Bakewell?' She offered sarcastically, handing her husband a plate with his cuppa.

Elliot knocked three times on his brother's door but got no answer; he waited before pushing the door open to pop his head inside.

'Can I join you?'

Oden was sitting on the floor in front of his Xbox. He looked around to catch a glimpse of Elliot's face but made no response when turning his head back to the screen.

Glad to have at least been acknowledged, Elliot sat down on the edge of Oden's bed.

'Are you going to talk to me?' He waited a minute, but there was no response. 'Or at least listen?' Oden threw a quick look back at him again.

'I never meant to hurt you or anyone else for that matter. I just didn't see any other way. Please, don't lock me out.'

Again, Elliot was met by silence.

'I was going to Australia; I was going to be out of reach there too. I understand that I went about things the wrong way, I knew what I risked. Talk to me, please?'

'I have nothing to say, go away.' Oden muttered.

Elliot was choked up. 'Please, don't be nasty.'

Oden paused the game; he didn't move but kept his back to Elliot as he hunched to deliver his words. 'I always admired you, Elliot.'

'I don't need you to admire me, Oden. I need you to be a decent brother. I needed to get away, trust me when I say I did not set out to hurt anyone.'

'You have no idea how this played out; you have no clue. Siobhan is a braver person than you'll ever be.'

'You've no idea what I've seen, or what I've been through over there, Oden.'

'And you have no idea what you put people through over here, your closest friends.'

'I do know, Oden.'

Oden turned bitterly to face him. 'No, you don't know, that's just it... You have no real idea of the hurt you've caused. You want to listen to yourself, with your 'needed to get away' routine. People relied on you; they made plans with you, you led them a merry dance. I had never thought of you as conniving.'

'I came back to make it right, Oden.'

'Good luck with that...' The room went quiet. 'Look Elliot... I'm your brother, so maybe, just maybe time will heal what goes on between us.'

'I hope so.'

'But... Siobhan, Emily, even Mark, they have the right to walk away; I don't have the luxury of that option. Siobhan nearly lost her job. Emily left her home and moved in with Siobhan to support her; she had the wedding ordeal to get through and the months of wondering why you'd not called. Mark was there for her, Lucile and Laura too.'

'I'm so sorry, mate.'

'You didn't even call the parents; you could have talked to me.'

Elliot didn't know where to look; this was hard talk for Oden.

'I've been sick to the stomach, Elliot. You said you loved her, but we're those the acts of someone who cared? They've looked out for me; they've talked me out of being angry with you when all I wanted to do was to punch you in the gut.'

'Don't talk that way, Oden, that's not you.'

'You don't have the right to tell me what way to talk or think, not anymore. My respect for you is shot, do you even get that?'

'I've never seen you hurt or angry, Oden. You're changed.'

'Well, it's you that has altered me, not that I even care.'

Oden made no further comment on the matter. He had changed; the happy-go-lucky nerd was gone. It was only then that Elliot fully realised what he was coming home to face. Elliot had at the early stages in the missions imagined the worst-case scenario, he had even gone on to convince himself that time had healed wounds before talking to Siobhan on the phone. Now gauging Oden's attitude, there was a lot more to lose.

'Mum's made tea.' He said nervously

'I'll be downstairs in a minute.'

'I'm genuinely sorry, Oden, genuinely.' There was nothing more he could say for the minute, he stood up and quietly took leave of his brother.

At the hospital, Laura had been given a bed; she was being kept in overnight. The doctors and nurses had fussed around her for most of the morning, running every test imaginable. She had a small seizure in front of Mark the night before, but she swore it was her first ever. He had insisted that she stay at his place just in case.

Our Diligent Souls

Mark talked to Imelda on the phone that morning and got her to cancel a meeting with the management; there was something seriously wrong with Laura's health, and he'd known it for weeks. He was there for the duration, for as long as it took. He was angry with, himself truth be told that he hadn't pushed her into a proper check-up earlier.

'Maybe we should contact your folks, let them know you're in the hospital.' Mark suggested.

'Don't be stupid, there's no point in worrying them yet, it might be something and nothing.'

'I doubt it's nothing after the seizure you had last night; I'm not trying to worry you. I just think they should be kept posted.'

'Not yet, let's hear what the doctors have to say first, yeah?'

'As you wish Laura, but for the record, I'm not comfortable with that, if I were your parents I'd want to know.'

The phone rang again but this time it was Emily, she was calling to say that Elliot had arrived home. Things had been strained between them since their night in the Jazz club, but she was doing everything in her power to hold on to their friendship. He couldn't help but make the odd disparaging remark; he still felt blown out by her and needed to preserve what remained of his sanity. He left Laura's bedside and made his way out to the corridor to talk to her in private.

'No one has seen Elliot yet, apart from Oden. He went over to his parent's house first; he's staying there over the Christmas from what I could make out. He's due to head back to the missions for at least another nine-week stint once the holiday's season passes. Oden has no idea how he got to leave.'

Mark was more concerned for Laura at that moment in time; he let Emily know that she'd had a seizure. He rhymed off the list of questions that the doctors had asked. Laura was sicker than she'd let on to him and now she was refusing to call her parents. He felt they should be there as the barrage of testing was in no way ordinary or routine; it didn't take a genius to see that it wasn't just something and nothing. If Mark got a chance to talk to Laura's father, he was going to make a serious issue of the fact that she had been working way too hard.

Emily offered to head over to the hospital, she could at least cover while Mark went to work to square things, but that had been sorted. Laura had been told that she'd be kept in overnight; he mentioned that a pair of pyjamas might come in useful. Mark agreed that Emily should drop over, but on her own, too much fuss and Laura would get frustrated and send him packing.

When he returned to Laura's bedside, the nurses had been and took more blood.

'Christ! Are you okay?'

'Feeling like a pin cushion, but yeah, I'm grand.' They had done a brain scan earlier and a series of non-intrusive tests.

'Emily's going to pop by later; she's bringing you night clothes. Can you think of what else you might need?'

'A little sleep, maybe.' Laura suggested.

'Are you sure?'

'I can't keep my eyes open, Mark.'

'Fair enough, I'll leave you and check in later, you just rest, yeah?'

Mark went to the coffee shop on the hospital grounds to give her time to fall asleep. Later, he went outside to the front gates to smoke and gave Elliot a ring on his old cell number, just in case.

'Elliot?'

'Mark, how are you, mate?'

'Same old, welcome home buddy. I hear it's a fleeting visit.'

'It is, but I should be back home soon. Well, that depends on how I fare out with Siobhan tonight.'

'Good luck with that.'

'I'm not sure what I'm going to say to her?'

'Slow the thinking, mate, just approach it with as much humility as you can muster. Laura's in the hospital tonight, so I'm out of reach until that's sorted.'

'Is she okay?'

'I don't know, Elliot; I genuinely don't know.' It was good to hear his voice again; no doubt he would have lots to talk about, around his adventure. Mark had missed him.

'I'm going to propose to Siobhan, tonight.'

Our Diligent Souls

Mark's eyes dilated at the very thought of him proposing. 'Mate, I don't know if that's such a good idea.' Mark was one hundred percent, there were no two ways about it; Elliot was about to make the biggest mistake of his life, he was puzzled not knowing how to spell it out for him.

'That's the only plan, Mark. I bought the ring two months ago, and I've thought of nothing else since.'

'Elliot, I can't help you other than to say that you hurt the woman intensely, and on top of everything else, she'll be worried about Laura tonight.'

'I can't see any other way of making this right, Mark. I've missed her in a way you couldn't comprehend.'

'Elliot, she'll know that something serious is going on over here. It may be a case of poor timing, abysmal timing.'

'And when is it a good time after the way I acted?'

'Not tonight, that's for sure or this Christmas, Elliot, you'd be throwing a hand grenade at her, seriously.'

'I don't know, Mark, she has wanted this for a very long time.'

'Not this way she hasn't, mate? Pulling out a ring is the wrong approach; you were never one for bad ideas before this whole missionary thing, maybe Australia too. Look, I can't emphasise it enough, leave the ring at home. Use the sense that God gave you or you will never find your way back to her. Do you hear me?'

'I do, I'm sure I do... I hear you.'

'Thank you for that; she wouldn't take it well. She's been through too much as it is, Elliot. Honestly.'

'Are you okay with me, Mark? I know you've been rallying around her.'

'How close were we, Elliot? I lost my best friend, my Friday nights.' Elliot too had lost his Friday night out when Arthur had passed. Mark hadn't helped the situation before he left, he was aware of that. 'I had time to be there for Siobhan, the missions' thing that was rock-and-roll, mate; her head was spun out and understandably so. You get that?'

'I get that. Thank you for taking care of Siobhan and for the advice. You may be right?'

'We have catching up to do. I'm going to be living in the States off and on for the next year or two. I'm due to leave in the next month.'

'What?' Elliot was surprised.

'Siobhan's new business is going great guns, and Emily's off on a European tour with the record label.'

'Siobhan has a business?'

'I better get back to Laura, mate.'

'What business?'

'Chutney and jam...'

'Ah. Okay.'

'No, it has taken off. I have to get back to Laura; I have to go, mate.'

'Give her my best, will you?' Elliot offered up.

'I will, of course, Elliot.'

'Right, Mark.'

'Good luck with tonight, my friend. You'll need it.'

'All I can do is let her know that I didn't set out to hurt her, mate.'

'Okay, and no proposals?' Mark hoped he was on board with that, but there was nothing more he could do for now.

'Got yah!'

Elliot was preoccupied with his relationship difficulties. He hadn't even asked what was up with Laura, he had needed someone to lighten the load, and he'd missed Mark. He wasn't sure what he was going to do or say when it came to seeing Siobhan that night, not if he was to abandon the proposal.

None of them had any idea that Laura had been vomiting as regularly as she had, nor had they any clue to the extent of her dizzy spells, she'd been well out of sorts. Most Laura's confessions to the doctors were news to Mark; they left him wondering why she made so little of it. He again checked in on Laura, but his friend was sound asleep, and there were no doctors in sight. He went back to the coffee shop to bide his time. She needed someone to be there for her when she woke.

Emily rang later to see what floor they were on when she arrived at the entrance to the hospital. Mark was on his third coffee and had been up to check on Laura twice; she was still sleeping. He met Emily on the ground floor having persuaded her to join him for yet another coffee.

Our Diligent Souls

'She wanted to sleep; the doctors are supposed to be round to talk to her at eight. It's only seven now. They did too many tests on her, Emily. She's just drained.' Mark was suffering, and for the first time since the Jazz club, he needed Emily, friend or otherwise, his detachment seemed pointless.

'Are you okay, Mark?'

'I'm genuinely concerned for Laura, but we don't know what's wrong yet. It just not normal, I never saw that much blood been taken from a person in one sitting, and she had scopes and scans. I genuinely don't know.' His hands were trembling, so she stretched hers across the table to provide shelter. He lifted his head and forced a smile as they tipped fingers briefly. He quickly moved back to his coffee.

'There's no point in worrying until we see, Mark.'

'I was talking to Elliot.' Mark told her.

Emily had more to add to the story. 'He arrived at Siobhan's house just before I left. I had very little to say to him. I just got out of their way.'

'When was that?'

'A half an hour ago, I left and got a taxi here.'

'I hope he doesn't make a fool of himself.'

'In what way?'

'I don't know, just the way he was talking. Nothing. He's only back; he misses her. Look, it's up to them at the end of the day, right?' Emily was concerned.

'Siobhan's only starting to find herself again; if he knocks her over, I swear...'

'Come on; you loved Elliot too once upon a time, he was a solid friend to both of us.'

'You're right of course.' Emily couldn't argue.

'You got pyjamas there?'

Emily took the small rucksack from her shoulders; she had almost forgotten. 'There's wash gear too, creams and stuff.'

She passed over the parcel, and their focus returned to Laura.

'Will we go up to see her?' Mark suggested.

Our Diligent Souls

Laura was on the third floor in a private room. As they approached, they could see the doctors go through. 'They're early, do you mind if I go in to see her on my own first?'

'No, I'll wait here.' He asked her to hold onto the parcel; he said that he'd be out as soon as the doctors were gone. Emily found a bench in the corridor and quietly lowered herself onto it, ignoring the general traffic as she attempted to gather her nerve. She experienced fear and anxiousness each time she went on stage, but here, she was left alone in the corridor to deal with it alone

Laura was sitting up in the bed with three doctors to her left. 'We wanted to wait until someone was here by Laura's side.' They explained to Mark as he took the chair beside her bed and held her hand.

'What is it?' Mark asked.

'Are you a relative?'

'He's a close friend.' Laura intervened. 'It's fine.'

'Laura, this isn't going to be easy for us to say or you to hear.' The doctor stopped there and looked again at Mark with worry.

'I'm glad he's here, please, go on...'

'Laura, we found a grade four tumour in the front lobe of your brain, I'm afraid it's inoperable.'

'What are you saying?' Laura was alert but confused by what she thought she heard.

'We can offer you radium and chemotherapy, but the tumour is too great to see any lasting benefits from that.'

'What?' Laura sat up in the bed. She unconsciously freed her hand from Mark's. They gave her a second, and he took hold of her hand again.

'I'm dying? Are you saying I'm dying?'

Mark lowered his eyes briefly.

'I'm afraid the seizure you experienced last night may be the start of more to come, it's hard to say, the vomiting, the dizziness it may be part of the experience I'm afraid.'

Laura and Mark sat in defeating silence as the doctors stood and watched.

'How long?' She barely whispered.

The doctor looked at his chart. It was the Asian doctor that shared the news; he was very understanding. Mark's eyes filled with tears though his expression remained flat. She could barely comprehend what was being said.

'Three out of ten people see a full year with this kind of a tumour.'

'A year?'

'Three out of ten.' The doctor reiterated.

'And the others?'

There was another battle with silence.

'The tumour is large, and the cancer well developed at this stage, it was not going to make any difference had we caught it earlier, with the position of the tumour it was never going to be operable. The cancer has long since been progressing through your system unnoticed. I'm afraid there's no good news here, Laura.'

'Are you saying that I've less than a year?'

'It's not an exact science Laura, but the likelihood of you seeing a year is not there.'

Laura shook her head. 'No, that can't be right?'

'We're going to keep you in for a few days, start you on chemo and radium and see if your body can tolerate it; it could buy you more time. We'll see how you cope and take it from there. Are you okay, Laura, do you need us to ring anyone?'

Her mind was frozen as she gazed into the doctor's face.'

'Laura?' He repeated.

'Yes, my parents please, if you could explain this to them.'

The doctor hunkered down at the side of her bed and whispered looking up into her face. 'You're very brave?'

'Yes.' She looked like she was resisting the urge to push him away.

'And you're sure you want me to contact your parents?'

She was getting annoyed. 'I'm not up for that; it shouldn't come from Mark either.'

'We will call them then. We do have your parent's numbers on file here, you're next of kin?' The other doctor checked and confirmed the number on her file. 'We will contact them, and hopefully, someone will be at home.'

'When will you tell them?'

'We'll be finished our rounds in the next fifteen minutes; we will try to ring and catch them at home then. Is there anything you need to make you more comfortable?'

'New pyjamas.' Laura suggested without much thought.

The doctor smiled.

'Emily is outside with pyjamas.' Mark addressed the doctor. 'She'll be fine here tonight; I'll be with her until her parents arrive. Thank you.' Mark lowered his head in respect.

'Thanks.' Laura mumbled, shrugging her shoulders with a dazed expression. The reality was still hitting home.

The doctor was clean-cut and handsome, and he got it. His eyes were full of empathy as he reached out and touched her elbow. 'I am sorry, Laura. It's never easy news to deliver.'

'I appreciate that.' Laura's expression was still dazed.

The doctors hovered for a moment before leaving; a single tear ran down Laura's cheek while Mark tried to hold it together. He sat facing her on her bed and leaned forward to take her in his arms.

'Laura, Christ.' He held her with great warmth and tenderness, looking over her shoulder at the bed frame as she sobbed, weeping quietly into his chest. He was still as a mountain then, his mind empty. Eventually, she pulled back and smiled at him. He loosened his hold as she lifted her face.

She shook her head and lifted her hand up to touch her shoulder as she looked at him. 'It's okay.' She said sitting awkwardly in the hospital bed. 'You know I don't like fussing.'

'I don't know what to say to you, my friend.'

'You know, just thinking out loud,' Laura looked away, 'how many times have I closed my eyes and wanted to be with Stephen over the past few years and now when I just began to find life again with you and the girls, my wish is granted? Is life not peculiar? You being here with me now as well?'

Mark was struggling to hold back his tears; he raised his face to smile softly. 'Emily is here too; she's waiting in the corridor. What do you want me to do, love? She's brought night stuff for you as well.'

'Tell her and send her away, Mark, I'm sorry, I'm not ready to talk about this yet. Please?'

He kissed Laura's forehead and sat waiting until she was ready to indicate that it was time for him to go and see to Emily. 'I won't be long.'

Emily was troubled as she watched Mark approach. His shoulders were hunched as he made his way to her, she could see his tears.

'Holy shit, Mark.' Emily's arms were ready to receive him.

He stood back and tapped his foot nervously; her hands fell by her side.

'It's cancer.' She stood there limp as he lowered his chin into his chest.

'Mark!' She slowly lifted her hands and pressed them to both of his cheeks as he sobbed quietly. It was a momentary lapse as he reared his head and gently took her hands away.

'It's inoperable; there's no good news.' They stood there. 'It's progressed too far.'

'Mark, I'm so sorry for Laura, and her family.'

'She's not ready to see anyone; she needs time first. It hasn't sunk in yet.'

'That's fine.' The two friends faced each other attempting to absorb the news. 'Will you ring me and let me know when it's a good time for us to see her. If you think that she might need anything?'

'I will let you know?'

'Trust you to get landed in the middle of this. Laura's such a good mate; we're all going to have to cope with this but you, you have got to keep heart and soul together here for everyone concerned, especially Laura.'

It was the second time in as many weeks that she was forced to witness his heartbreak. He steadied himself, clearing his throat.

'The doctors are calling her parents; they're going to fill them in. I'd imagine they will be here within the next hour or two, that's if the doctors can get through to them on the phone.'

'Try to get sleep tonight. Leave Laura's parents to it when they arrive, you can always get back tomorrow after work.' She lifted his chin up with a gentle touch. 'Yeah?'

'I'll be here tomorrow; work can manage.'

'Well, if you're sure but let me know. I can be here too; we can take it in turns. Laura's parents will want to be by her side throughout; you need to be prepared for that. You'll have to leave them to it when they arrive.'

Our Diligent Souls

Emily was so shattered by the news that the skin on her face felt swollen and cracked as she walked through the main gate. She loved Laura as did Siobhan, how she was going to tell the others was beyond her.

In the home they'd built together, Elliot had made no progress with Siobhan. He was confronted with the same dogged determination that he had been met with on the phone when he called from the missions.

It was strange being in the living room knowing that it was no longer theirs, the leather sofa had been masked by a load of Emily's knitted throws, and it was somewhat less domesticated. There were books piled high on the floor, and the dining area was set up to work as an artist's studio, with an old bed sheet covering the table.

Siobhan needed to keep their conversation practical. His attempts to wear her down and talk, they were getting him nowhere. She allowed his pleas to be understood, but it only strengthened her resolution; she gave back little hope in return.

'I have places to be, Elliot; I've things to organise for the market tomorrow.' Elliot was just like Oden in that respect, when he had a point to make there was no escaping his forced opinion. It wasn't healthy to keep tolerating this same crap; neither of them knew when to let it go. 'I need to talk about the house.' She said. 'I went to see the solicitor and the bank manager. I had an evaluation done on your share of the property.'

'I told you, I don't want money from you, the property is yours. I thought that was settled. Can you let me at least try to put things right?'

Siobhan made her way to the small dresser in the hallway and removed an envelope that she had put aside.

'I have written confirmation here of the property value and the full breakdown of what is owed to you. There is a cheque there for five thousand Euros.'

'Where did you get five thousand Euros? Mark told me the chutney business was going well, but you can't have made that much ground, I'm only gone a few months.'

She took a deep breath to steady her temper. 'That's my first payment for your share the property, it might have been more, but I'm buying a van for my business. I will get the rest to you in due course.'

'Seriously well done, you're remarkable, but I can't take this.'

'You may need it if you come back to start life up here again. I don't want what's not mine.'

'That's not what I want.'

'No, but that's what you're getting.'

He was grappling with her attitude. 'If it's going to be this way between us, how will we ever work this out with our friends? You can't dismiss me in that sense; I'm not an outcast yet. At least let's figure out how we can salvage a friendship from this.'

'We can't do that until you give up on the idea of us being together again.'

Elliot withstood the tension between them. 'Okay, then let's start there.'

'You'll accept the cheque as part payment on your share of the property?'

'I'll put it in the bank.'

'Well, at least we can shake hands on that.' Siobhan put out her hand, he found the whole thing very odd, but it was what she needed from him.

'Can I hear where you are with the chutney business?' Finally, she offered him a coffee and in a distant manner defined the processes she'd gone through with her business. She did everything in her power to stay as guarded as possible, but he knew the right buttons to press, and the talk soon became insightful.

She hated the fact that he was turning on the charm; his observations filtered with their shared memories. He had tried to catch her with humour but stopped; he could tell at that point that she wanted him to leave.

He asked after Emily and wanted to know the story with her recording contract. She briefly explained the one album contract that had turned into a two-album record deal. She talked over the tour route and mentioned the supporting acts that she and Emily had handpicked on nights out together. All the way through, her tone was officious. She removed their cups and gently placed them in the basin.

He asked after the couples that they had spent their weekends with before he left. Siobhan relayed what had happened when she explained how he had gone, their ability to lift a phone had escaped them. She remembered Mark's comment about the same couples who were looking for playmates for their future kids; it was another thing she'd forced on him. They had called and made the occasional enquiry after her well-being, without inviting her anywhere or mentioning upcoming events. Sharing that with him now was near impossible.

'We need to talk about how we're going to manage our relationships with friends, Oden, Laura, Emily, Mark. Brian and Alfie when their home.' She needed to cover that ground with him.

'I won't get in your way in respect of you seeing other people, Siobhan if that's what you want. If we're out with the guys, and you're on a date, I will make my excuses and leave. I will contain my feelings... I will give you your space.'

'I can respect that if that be the case. Given time, it will be easier to be around you, but for now, there's a hardness in me that has rightfully earned its place, and in truth, I'd prefer not to see you. I am bone weary when it comes to you, you understand?'

'Can I write to you when I get back to the missions?'

'Where is the point?'

'We could forge a friendship given time, Siobhan. We need to do that going forward; I don't want to break up the gang here. I don't want to live outside of it and end up on my own. We were very close, all of us through the years.'

'If you want to then, you can write! I don't know if I'll be able to respond, but I will make an effort. I'll pass on the news.'

'Thank you. It will make the time move easier over there.' She didn't want to make anything easy for him, but another part of her was frightened by the idea of him leaving altogether.

Just then, Emily arrived through the front door; she had more on her mind than walking in on a scene. Elliot and Siobhan looked at her without saying a word. There was no music, no cups of coffee in their hands; they were just two people sitting at a distance from each other wearing drained expressions.

The words were running through Emily's head in slow motion; she could barely hear herself think, let alone muster up the courage to say what she needed to say. She sat at the edge of the sofa and covered her face with her hands. Siobhan looked at Elliot; he was white as a sheet as it was. She went straight to Emily's side.

'Jesus, what is it?'

Emily took hold of Siobhan's arms. 'It's Laura. I only know the bare bones, it's terminal cancer, and it's very far progressed.'

'Laura.' Siobhan whispered. 'How far progressed? Do you know?'

'I didn't ask. I didn't get to see Laura; Mark came out and told me.'

'He's with her now?' Siobhan asked.

'Her parents are on the way.' Emily was choking on her words.

The two friends sat side by side, their heads tilted towards each other. Elliot didn't say a word; he was ashamed to have nothing to contribute.

'There is no chance, Siobhan. She's not got much time.'

Emily was rubbing her tired eyes. Siobhan was still holding her breath. They sat up and looked at each other's face before dropping their heads and pressing forehead against forehead.

'There is nothing to do,' Emily whispered, her smoky breath reaching Siobhan's mouth. 'We can't change this outcome, Siobhan, we just can't change it.' She whispered.

Mark called to the factory first thing the next morning to let them know that he'd be contactable by phone. He arranged to meet the board of management later in the day to give them the update on his progress with the sales team.

He hoped to have a heart to heart with the board in the next few days to see if they could swing a delay now, with him going to America. He might not be fit to carry out his duties to any benefit for the company, knowing that he had left Laura behind with her life slipping away.

He was losing his friend, and as hurt, as he was, he was planning to make sure that every day she had left would count. He was hatching plans to get the lads from her and Arthur's workplace over to the hospital to sing her a song. A song that they had once used on the ladies. Any opportunity to lift her spirits would raise his, friends too would feel bereft. They were part of the equation.

Mournaghan walked in through the gateway and strolled towards the stairwell.

'Here, Mournaghan,' Mark yelped, 'I've news. I clean forgot to tell you. It escaped me.'

'Escaped you how exactly?' Mournaghan's replied.

'You know the way the firm has eight depots in American?' Mark mocked. 'Well guess who's going to be heading them up, at two and a half time his salary with extra shares and expenses?'

Mournaghan looked stumped.

'Me! Six weeks at home, six weeks abroad, six weeks at home, six weeks abroad. And that's before the second salary hikes for the following one-year contracts in New York.'

Mournaghan was speechless.

'I'll have more shares than you. I'll be wealthier than you. I might live in a bigger house, maybe at the top of your road, might get bodyguards. I'll need bouncers.'

'You're dreaming.' Mournaghan quipped.

'I've signed the contracts.'

Mournaghan looked smug. 'We have six depots in American; you don't have the sense you were born with, boy.'

Mournaghan was strangely not up to speed as the company had opened two new depots in America eight months back while he was on time out and him a shareholder; he was evidently being kept out of the loop. Mark couldn't help but chuckle.

'You can be amusing I'll give you that. If that scale of opportunity was to happen here, you think that I'd not be aware of it?' Mournaghan bowed his head, jeering as he took off to join his colleagues.

Mark knew that Ralph wouldn't be able to resist, he'd make his enquiries. Mark felt fuzzy and warm thinking about the expression on Mournaghan's face when he found out the truth. He couldn't wait to tell Laura; he might even get a smile out of it.

Chapter 42

The days and weeks that followed were beyond sad as Mark attempted to alternate between friend and family visits. Laura never left the hospital; she suffered severe side effects from the chemo and radium to a point where the doctors decided that it was more compassionate to move her onto palliative care.

The seizures, the headaches, the dizziness, they all came and went; there were points where she wasn't fit for visitors; people had to be turned away. The hospital offered her care where she was, in her private room or in a hospice. Her parents naturally wanted to take her home, but stubborn to the end; her wish was to stay in the hospital.

Her parents were very private people and might have wanted to keep her last days to themselves. She wanted to be surrounded by life and laughter, having Siobhan and Emily's hands to hold to the very end. Her parents were at her side for the more significant part of the day, allowing the others to take a lesser role and return to work. The gang were there on different evenings, her old pals too, all of whom were happy to meet so many new faces.

Siobhan called around when she wasn't at work; there were days when she couldn't bear to be away from her. With Laura being Turner's daughter, Mark was given leeway to postpone his American trip. Emily travelled the length and breadth of the country to be back by her side, flying to and from England after gigs.

Laura was fading fast; she lost her hair but retained her humour. Siobhan's visits brought some much-needed frivolity to the room. Where needs must, Siobhan was always able, but out of Laura's sight; herself and Emily could be caught gripping each other in horror on the corridors.

They brought Elliot with them on one occasion before he left to return to the missions. Laura had asked for a funny tale from the pharmacy, forgetting that he had been away for the best part of four and a half months. He played along as if he had just left work that evening and got her laughing until she choked.

Within weeks, Laura looked less and less like herself as the life drained from her cheeks, but she was utterly graceful in defeat. Mark had managed to get her into a wheelchair twice and took her to the hospital courtyard to see the night sky, but a halt was put on that as the doctors were afraid it might trigger more seizures and set her back further. Not that any of it made much sense to either of them.

She was weak with exhaustion. As the weeks became a month, there were more and more visitors, strangers to the gang and close relatives who wanted time alone with her. She was sleeping for a large part of the time, so their moments together were limited and precious. Mark held her in his arms one night for a very privileged hour. He didn't want his free time back, she was a monumental part of their lives now, and none of them were ready to lose her.

Laura died on the eighth of January, six weeks to the day she was diagnosed. It had been a Christmas of extreme emotions. The gang had gotten to meet the many people that had been in her life before they came to be part of it. Everyone consoled each other with the fact that her suffering wasn't prolonged, and although she'd had an interesting last few months before she departed, Laura was now back in the arms of the man that she never stopped loving, her husband, Stephen.

Mark, Siobhan, Oden and Emily, they all felt like outsiders at the funeral though Laura's father approached Mark days later and offered him the opportunity to take over her shipping company. He'd said that Mark could ask for whatever he wanted in respect of a salary.

Mark thanked the man but declined; he knew that the Turners were capable of finding someone to step into Laura's shoes and he knew from Turner's conversation that they would not disband the company.

His memories of Laura were his own, and although he might see her father on occasion at T&E shipping, he felt it was not his place. Mark had already lived in the shadow of Arthur for some time; he knew instinctively that he needed to move on. There was no mistaking it; it was time to venture forward and see what other kind of life he might create in America.

Elliot had missed the funeral as he was back at the mission when she left them. He completed the full one-year contract before coming home to Dublin. It was something that they figured he needed to get out of his system and besides, outside of their relationship, Siobhan was blossoming into a canny businesswoman. Neither of them ever dated another person; they had other things on their mind at that time.

Siobhan and Elliot stayed good friends and wrote to each other when he was away. Siobhan bought out his entire share of the house with the proceeds of her thriving chutney and preserve business, which was by then operating full time. She had given up her job in the museum.

Eighteen months on from the day that he had left Siobhan, Elliot finally got up the nerve to propose. After the initial anger had subsided, it was clear that nothing had changed the way she had felt about Elliot, and she agreed. They moved to Australia when Oden completed his honours degree in games development.

Siobhan set up the chutney business there, and Elliot got a challenging job with a pharmaceutical company. She rented out the house at home through an agency which covered her mortgage; it gave her something to come home to if it didn't work out between her and Elliot, married or not. That fear of him wanting more out of life was something that never entirely left her, but Elliot understood that and worked hard to find new ways to surprise her with his devotion. He could only revel in her tender kindness, she stood for so much. Way beyond any woman that he would ever know; Siobhan was profound and good-natured.

Oden stayed with them in Australia for a while before deciding to go back to his mates in Ireland. He and Lucile had tarried along together until he got his degree, but once he left college, the relationship fizzled out. They didn't stay in touch. Lucile ended up in a same-sex relationship with a girl off campus and never looked back.

Mark bought his apartment in Dublin, but when the six weeks here, six weeks there went to a year contract in New York City, he rented his home out and got a healthy return. He made friends in New York and enjoyed what it had to offer though a genuine part of him belonged in Dublin. Mark missed his family being down the road and Joyce, and the camaraderie that was to be found north side of the city. New York had taught him much, but just as New Yorker's were the soul of their city, he was Dublin through and through.

It had been three, almost four years since he had set out for America and he'd built up enough of a tank to set up a business of his own though he thought he might hang in with the company for another few years.

Emily's touring went exceptionally well, but as her popularity grew Mark found it harder, and harder to stay in touch with her. When he went to America first, she refused to give him her new email address but begged him to send handwritten notes arguing that it was a dying art. It left long gaps in their correspondence, but she thought it worth it for the keepsake, and he complied.

Our Diligent Souls

As time transpired, he tired of the effort of trying to keep up with her, trying to find things to say that weren't work-related was hard, and what he was left with was a distant dream. He had met a few impressive, professional women in New York and they had become his type, women that had a look that you couldn't find in Ireland though his well-disguised ambition was always to move home.

Emily was in Dublin working on her third album when Elliot and Siobhan were preparing to go to Australia. Mark was then in New York. She hung out with Elliot and Siobhan when she wasn't working, and he got lots of second-hand news, he never asked Elliot or Siobhan to get her to write. He'd called her number several times, but with her schedule, as it was, it was hard to get an answer. When he did get a response, she was always in the middle of a gang of people or at some raucous after-party.

Elliot and Siobhan organised their wedding around the end of Mark's first one-year contract; he was nearing the third year of his American placement then. He came home keen to see Emily, but it ended up that she was roped into a big stadium charity event. She couldn't get out of it contractually, missing the wedding of her two best friends. They were extremely disappointed, but it was felt by Emily more than anyone else, there was nothing to be done. Mark took on a second one-year contract in New York and was gone again by the time Emily got back from her concert. He was seeing a woman in New York and was planning to propose to her at the time, but that wasn't meant to be.

He was in New York at the end of his second one-year contract when he got word that Emily was playing at Radio City Music Hall in Madison Square Garden. He had managed to pick up a copy of her third album and loved it initially. Something had changed in her, she was more open to love now, he couldn't say if she was in its full embrace, but the tone and sentiment of her music had altered.

He played the record when he could, though it left him feeling very much alone in the world. He checked the album's sales figures in its first few weeks, expecting it to take a nose dive but it had soared to the top of the chart. He put his thinking down to her having experienced a proper relationship, the asexual undertone in her lyrics was gone; it was that that made him think the new album would not succeed. The more he listened, the more at odds he felt about the recording, some form of irritation was rising in him that he didn't recognise, a cross between anger and longing. He had tried so hard to forget her.

He was due to return to Ireland two days before the concert was on but postponed the journey to attend the gig. It was a big thing making it to

Our Diligent Souls

Radio City Music Hall, and he wanted to see her play. He knew that her concerts in Ireland were a less frequent occurrence. It could be months before he'd see her live on stage again. By then, he knew most of the lyrics on her new album; he found it harder to listen to, his desire to see her perform the songs live, left him feverish and self-concerned.

He had a job trying to get his hands on a ticket, in fairness she hadn't sent any special invite his way so that they could meet up. She most likely knew that he was due home days before the concert, Elliot and Siobhan would have said.

Madison Square Garden was packed as he moved through the crowd, listening to a variety of excited punters talk about her lyrical wizardry and her majestic voice. He smiled to himself thinking back to her in her mohair jumper and jeans. He slowed in his pace as he thought of the fox, nervously recalling the infatuation that he felt that first night when she ended their walk so abruptly. Now he had no apartment to run home to, no plans to prepare himself for an occasion where she might visit.

His ideas then of love, of home life, they were very traditional. Their coincidental love of sweetpea made light of all the bouquets he had ever bought. Each vase of flowers taunted his indecision; stirring up the old ideas of the family home he'd wanted to create with her. He had daydreamed so often about the garden they would tend together, the fruits of their labour divided up amongst their friends.

He missed the simple railway, the first signs of summer travelling from Dundalk to Dublin at the front of the early morning bus. He craved the smell of chip shops, the gang, Joyce, and the comfort of feeling not yet fully evolved in the company of his parents. He'd even missed the damning humour of his old school chums. But above all else, he had yearned for Emily.

Radio City was a sight for sore eyes looking up at the entrance, to think that he knew her, the waitress and legal secretary once; he could sense her still where she had held him in the corridor of the hospital weeks before Laura had died. He remembered with great clarity their trip to Marrakesh, the way the sun lightened her hair and coloured her face. Her eyes had lit up when she smiled, her fragile, sensual body calling out to him from her twin bed. He was a different person then. As he walked through the crowds, he was out there now with all the other dreamers.

In the shuffle, the chorus of a Leonard Cohen song flooded his mind. The song Alexandra leaving, the lyrics passing the chorus and into the verse. It was strange for him to remember the entire tune and yet there they were, every word edging him forward. The melody and lines ran through him as he walked through the crowd, purposefully searching out his seat, quiet in himself, the lyrics taking new meaning.

The venue was spectacular, the vibrant orange lighting, the semi-circle, dome-shaped ceiling that drew your interest to the stage. The long red velvet curtains through which she would appear. It took fifteen minutes for Mark to find his seat and still the song was there, leaving him moments after the support band came on.

He had barely taken the musicians in when they were finished; his mind distracted again, lost in this disconnected world where part of him was convinced that their relationship had somehow never existed.

He couldn't help but wonder if she might catch sight of him in the audience if she might know instinctively that he was there. As Mark took in the sheer volume of the crowd he knew that he was dreaming; not if he stood on his head would she see him, he was there without hope or solution.

The thought dawned on him, he could have Skyped Elliot and Siobhan to tell them that he was going, and they could have got in contact with her straight away, but it was too late for that now. He hadn't been able to reach her by phone in months. He had been busy preparing to head back to Dublin. Besides, he'd stopped humiliating himself in front of his friend's years before.

He had delayed his departure so that he could catch a glimpse of her, his sweet, untouchable Emily. Now he would see her from a distance as separated as they indeed were. He wondered how much she had grown as a performer from that tiny bistro on Wexford Street in Dublin.

Her first song rang out through the darkness, the music intro silencing the crowd, the sound of her voice echoing familiar lyrics as the curtains pulled back and she wandered out onto the stage, microphone in hand without any introduction. A treble emanated through her gallant lungs to leave the audience aghast with anticipation.

He recognised the tune immediately; it was a song from her first album, the same song that she had once dedicated to Siobhan with Laura, Elliot, and Oden in the audience at that very first gig. They were without mistake the most glorious years of his life; he understood that now, though he had always thought the idea of a heyday limiting. He had transformed from a carefree apprentice to a man, surrounded by friends. He'd won the respect of his team and conquered his battle with Mournaghan. He hadn't thought of him in years.

Our Diligent Souls

Emily wasn't ready to be with anyone then, and now, she was a more sensual beauty having visibly matured from a young, opinionated girl to a fuller-figured more balanced woman. She had since known passion in her own right, in her own time. Her voice was even stronger, the hair on his neck lifted in shock waves. Only once had he experienced that effect, once when he'd listened to Tori Amos play the open piano on stage.

The audience rose from their seats to applaud her, above the whistles and yelps she welcomed all, her deepened voice claimed overwhelming joy at finally having made it to Radio City Music Hall. She had more to say for herself, her seamless rapture with the audience equivalent to that of a seasoned performer; she had grown in that respect.

He edged forward to catch every word, she was introducing the songs on her new album as she went through all of them, one by one. Her hair was untidy, her mind more experienced, she had a musical sophistication. But it was still there, just, that natural part of her; the relaxed freedom in her movements, and the uplift in her heel when she sang into the microphone. The points where she closed her eyes to immerse herself in emotion, she was breath-taking.

He sat back in his seat. It was a sensation like no other; to watch the woman that he had loved more vital, more relevant now in her own way. For him, this was a real and decidedly precious opportunity to be even this close to her again. She was in her element while he looked on, she sang as many as six songs, stopping to explain the origins of each idea.

From this, he took a whole other picture, the where and why she'd felt compelled to write each song, the characters she had met along her journey, and the wonders of the world that had made her essential self, more visible. She was so much fun, and his heart was bursting with happiness for her.

There was a short moment where she asked for a glass of water and jovially entertained with a story of the first time she'd visited New York when she was six years old. Apparently, she had arrived with her nanny and was brought on a tour of this very building.

'On leaving this glorious place, my nanny offered to buy me my first coca cola. The luxury of which I had until then, been denied. She had allowed me to pick the venue, so I would never forget this small act of defiance; a secret neither of us ever shared with my parents.' Emily coughed, creeping away from the microphone. Mark was enthralled.

'God must have known my nanny,' she went on to say. 'We paraded the avenues in search of the perfect place to have my first coca cola… and of course, I picked the scariest looking pub you could ever find, but she had promised?' Therein Emily had become part of a collective. They were a crowd of people who lived to have her back; he could imagine it without much effort. The owner Cassandra who kept in touch with the little six-year-old from that day on, always writing her a note or inviting her over. Emily raised her glass, 'To Cassandra,' she said, 'another who replaced a mother, my naturally outrageous kind of friend.'

The song that followed almost brought a tear to Mark's eye as he thought back to how it was always there, this young woman without relative of any form, it was still with her. She had denied herself so much in fear of tempting faith; she was risk-averse. He remembered them talking on the street in Belfast when he'd offered to take her to his hometown, a thing he never did.

Emily's friendships were everything to her, bonds that she would never gamble with, knowing what it was to be truly alone in life. Mark welled up as he watched her, he would find her and make good on all those years they had been apart. He would make sure that she would always have him to turn to as a friend, sweet heavens permitting.

There was again a lengthy introduction to the next song. 'I sing this little number for the man that shared a secret with me, he showed me that I didn't have to be my parents, that I could chart my course of love. I let him go ahead, in the hope that someday we would meet when we'd taken all our chances. In the words of Leonard Cohen,' Mark sat up in his chair struck by the coincidence. 'May the light in the land of plenty shine on the truth someday.' This song is for the dreamer that can't settle until they know that their fella has properly moved on, right?'

The audience cheered, and wolf whistled then yelped at the top of their lungs. She swayed with the intro before her song filled the stadium. He was in awe as the music reverberated through him, recognising the song but from what album he couldn't say, it had been a while since he heard it though it had stirred something in him from that very first note.

He joined in on the lyric until the words slowly left him silent, it was their song, the song she had written for him, the song with their secret. The same song she had sung to him at that very first gig, the song about the time in his Dublin apartment when he had carried her to bed, the night that she had tried to kiss his neck. They were both too vulnerable to take advantage of each other. The lyrics had become transparent; he had only ever carried with him a line or two from the tune and thinking back he'd only ever heard it once.

He was adrift in that seat, his heart broken but perfectly still, his eyes unwilling to look away. The notes soared as he felt the emotion ring through her lungs, through him; he was utterly transfixed. She lowered her voice to finish, her free hand extended to gently pat the air. He trembled watching her; fully aware. As she reached the last note the applause hit the ceiling; he sat motionless, wanting her in a way that he had never wanted her before, vital and inspiring.

'That's a song I keep for my live performances.' She seemed breathless. The audience cheered again, and she smiled in appreciation. It wasn't on her first or her second albums, or even her third one; she didn't have anything left for a fourth album by now she said playfully. The audience jeered and booed as she tipped her mic and raised her shoulders. 'Well maybe, who knows.' She shook her head, taking it all in.

'I sing that song to the universe, in the hope that someday I might lay this lifestyle to rest, no joke. Let's get on with the music. Yeah?'

'Yeah!' The audience lifted in a ripple, filled with humongous cheer.

'I can't hear you?' She called out.

'Yeah!' They crowd rattled, laughing and prodding each other.

Emily scratched her head and confessed. 'A bit Butlin's that one.' She lowered her face to muffle the sound of her laughter. The drummer stood up to catch her attention, shaking his head. Mark smiling; he could see what was coming. 'Oops!' She said in jest, the band cringing behind her. 'Butlin's,' she shared briefly looking back at the band. 'It's an old Irish style holiday camp that attracted the critically challenged and poor of pocket. We all were there, at least once.'

A great roar came from the back of the hall. 'Hi, Dee hi!' They yelped. 'Hoe, hoe, dee, hoe! She responded, over wroth with uncontrollable laughter. 'That's the Irish contingent,' She pointed out, pulling herself together. 'A note to mention that the Irish crowd are always positioned in the cheap seats at the back. Half the fun, right lads?' Their whoops and screams hit the ceiling.

Mark shrivelled in his seat, 'Please no!' He whispered, peering through splayed fingers.

'The Irish parliament...' She went on to say. 'We won't get into the pig's arse they made of poor Butlins with Direct Provision, but you, my lovely punters, can go and check it out on bonkers.ie, where I guarantee, you'll unearth Irish bureaucracy and its many sociopathic delights.' The drummer was having a small seizure attempting to shush her with his snare drum. The lead guitarist found a comic use for his mother's old tambourine,

Our Diligent Souls

shimmying it to the heavens and back down to the floor. Mark thought right there that he might wet himself laughing.

God forbid Emily might start in on the pope and the papal policies; she was a big fan of Sinead O'Connor. 'There are no two ways about it, the woman had a notorious set of lungs, she still loved a smoke.' Elliot remembered Emily defending Sinead with authority.

'Enough of that!' There was a brief moment before her voice filled the room, and Mark took it, jumping up from his seat to holler. 'You're a legend Emily Rosemary Ann Johnson; I loved you before I ever laid eyes on you.'

She heard him call her name, just. Her microphone jolting nervously upward on the stand as she peered out into the crowd searching for some form of an outline. 'Here!' He shouted, but she'd never had any sense of direction. 'Mark?' She uttered his name as the rhythm guitarist struck up the opening bars of a bloody great song.

As the band called her back, Mark fell back into his seat; the neighbouring punters stretching forward to have a look at him. He leaned in and gave them a wave; his smile reaching his toes. No other person on the planet knew her full name; she had sworn him to absolute secrecy.

Mark knew then that she still loved him; he could barely contain his excitement as he struggled to remain seated. She had a concert in London the day after tomorrow and would be back in Dublin soon. She hoped to chase down an old friend of hers who had finally decided to move home. There was no doubt or delusion that this was happening. 'You better believe it,' he thought he heard her say.

Mark knew he could get her new address from Elliot, he could dodge her while he and Elliot connive the most outrageous proposal. It was real, he was secure in the minefield of what had just transpired, his heart exploding as he recalled her passionate sentiments.

As the crowd piled out, Mark waited, watching as fans from the far end of the arena tried to make their way past security. The two uniformed bouncers were having none of it, moving the crowd swiftly on. As the Emily fanatics grudgingly disbanded, Mark stood up and approached with a small measure of trepidation. A bouncer was called backstage to deal with some situation or other, and this had given him an opening; there was only the one bouncer left at ground level to tackle.

Mark was aware that he was under the bouncer's radar though he pretended not to notice, slowly shifting forward, he readied himself, removing two one-hundred-dollar bills from his wallet. The muscle-bound bouncer swaggered as he coped an eyeful, standing up fully to check the vicinity for onlookers. The native New Yorker, rubbing his thumb downward under the shoulder strap of his walkie-talkie before he tilted his head to one side to send a message. 'Will you send out Irish?' Mark was left poised in waiting.

The second uniformed lad made his way through the stage curtains; quickly side-stepping the stairs to join his colleague. He didn't open his mouth until he reached his co-worker in person. 'What's the story, pal?' Mark was impressed, the guy was from Dublin going by his accent.

The bouncer threw a suspicious glance at Mark. Wanting to give a full read of the situation, he turned his back on him as he conversed with his protégé. Eventually, the Irish lad slapped his two feet on the ground, displaying the width of his chest to address the situation. 'Can I help you, pal?'

Mark drew in additional air and paused. 'Two hundred says she doesn't know me? It's yours or between the pair of you, just tell her it's Mark from the shipping company.' Mark twisted his wrist to offer up the dollar bills that were held between his palm and lower fingers. The two lads looked at each other as Mark stood tall. 'I can go to three hundred at a push.' He added eventually.

The Dublin lad squinted, his face moving closer. 'It's hardly my job's worth. Get away from about me, pal. Ask me arse with your three hundred like.' The lad rallied him on, carefully shifting his eyes and Mark's attention to the security camera at his back. The young Dub licked his lips, retentively waited for Mark to reply.

Mark was deflated, he reckoned he'd been beaten as he nodded cynically; he was in too good of form to press the guy any further. 'Your loss, mate.' He turned and walked. This Dub's eyes widened in disbelief as he pulled back in confusion. Just then a call came through his walkie-talkie, he answered watching Mark climb the steps and veer out of view.

Just then Emily strolled out, to walk along the edge of the stage, peering down at the empty seats before turning to security with a blank expression. The young Dub stuffed his hands in his pockets, kicked his chin out as he grumbled to himself. His American counterpart fell about laughing, 'The bloody Irish, priceless. You're all so outta sight.'

Mark stood at the entrance, Elliot's number in Australia ready on speed dial, sweating excitedly as he tried to focus on his phone. How could, and

Our Diligent Souls

why would he translate this anomaly to Elliot; he had a life of his own now. Elliot and Siobhan would only think he had lost the plot.

He lifted his hands to the night sky, a starless navy. He turned slowly in a full circle to face the neon yellow, blue and red signage that carried her name, Emily at Radio City. He crossed the slanting white lined grid of the traffic crossing; the neighbourhood was teeming with happy concert-goers who were upping their zippers to brace the bitterly cold weather.

He needed somewhere to continue his night; he'd try to find a snug spot, far away from her adoring Trojan-like fans. If he took as faith her talk of Dublin, then he could wait. He pictured her now as he imagined her years before upstairs in the spare room of Siobhan and Elliot's house, waiting for him to make up his mind. He was leaving for home tomorrow, he'd be back in Dublin soon, a man with every option in his pocket. He could leave it up to her and figure out what way to take things from there when she arrived.

Revisiting the vocals of Alexandra leaving, he took strides along the side streets, collar up as he sang, the lyrics all but leapt from his person. Mark didn't recognise the avenues as he walked on, he'd only ever been that end of New York twice. Nothing mattered but the song inside his head and the wildly appropriate lyrics that applied, he couldn't deny it.

The rain began to lash, the thunder rattled soon after, moments in just for an instant, lightning turning the colourful streets to black and white. Mark's entire being; electrified by the city and the night that was in it. His breath ran shallow as he ground to a halt, it was only then that he became aware of the numbness in his cheeks, his dripping hair. Looking over, he was standing near the doorway to an authentic looking New York bar, the kind that Emily would have loved. He needed shelter.

He pushed the door inward as a few elusive characters lifted their drowsy heads, only to sink them back into their beverages. The barkeeper was polishing up some glasses, but as Mark strolled over, he transferred to a damp rag and swept the counter clean. Mark stood back and briefly scanned the shelving before he brought the man's attention to a Haut-Armagnac, a masterful brandy of sorts from the foothills of the Pyrenees, 'The brandy, a double when you're ready.'

'Do I look busy?' The barkeeper asked sarcastically, double checking the bottle before he spun it to the counter. 'No ice.' Mark requested. The bartender nodded and stoically poured a double shot of the costly white Armagnac. Mark thought of Alfie in his Bondi beach bar at once.

He might someday return to this spot and bring back all that New York had given him, Mark thought. He pasted over a one-hundred-dollar bill.

Our Diligent Souls

He would have opted for a pint of Guinness, but no half-assed produce would serve him tonight, not when he'd be back in Dublin so soon where Guinness was the babe's breath. He took note as a woman of some senior years slipped out of her raincoat from the other side of the counter.

As he moved away to find a seat, Mark spotted a young folk musician who was chatting to a handful of well-dressed suits, his fingers cupped around the neck of an old guitar. Mark took his drink to a booth at the furthest corner of the lounge. He placed the brandy on the table and slid into the soft leather seat. He took the brandy tumbler in his two hands, the treasured liquor at arm's length.

He peered through his window, speckled with metallic-coloured raindrops that were brought to life beneath a Cold Beer sign. Opaque antique perspex moulded decades ago was positioned at the top of the window. He caught an odd internal notion in his reflection before slanting his head to meet the lip of his drink. There was a box of matches left behind on the table; he could see Emily in that Smithfield jazz bar, neither of them knowing that it would all just now make sense.

A raindrop caught his eye as it slid down the window pane, tripping over another one before they veered off in different directions. Mark needed time to study the new variants that would shape his future; his well land plans just options now as his thoughts encircled the woman that above all others, he had taken his time to get to know.

In the background, the folk musician's sales pitch faded as he began to play familiar cords, there was a lull descending as the accent-less Austin player introduced himself. The young man cleared his throat with a significant nostril sound before entertaining his tidy audience; a swarm of money makers. Mark raised an eyebrow at the sound; the noise clearly indicated a cocaine habit though it didn't appear to have registered with his clientele. Such reckless abandonment might have been seductive to Mark as a younger man if he hadn't had work to contend with.

Recognising the retrofit of an old guitar solo that the player had claimed as his own arrangement, Mark smiled to himself. He turned away, placing his sleepy ear on the stub of his palm to wonder where Emily might be at that moment. Refusing to scold himself for not covering all exits, Mark delineated Emily's earlier movement from the gig, bringing her words on stage back to life. The sweet familiar resonance in her voice echoed within him as he thought back to the night of her very first gig.

It would have been her first time to sing that song in public, she'd sang it to him then, not just to some audience where he might have been. That was the moment she'd first confessed her emotions. She had been trying to bring him home, before the contracts and the critical choices. He had missed it, wounding her then; it was only now that he could sincerely take it into his heart, after so many years.

Struck by self-loathing, he tried to empty his mind, he sat in silence listening in on drunk conversations at a distance until the lyrics of Cohen made a return. He fell back into the navy leather booth and let his mind drift.

As he sat up to look through the window, he followed the tired steps of a young executive who'd stopped at the entrance of a building block across the avenue. The young man's face lowered to the sidewalk before he found the energy to gather his keys and climb the steps.

A throat cleared, startling Mark as he turned around sharply. The old woman who had slipped behind the bar to remove her raincoat earlier was perched at the end of his table; her wrists facing the window, her hands gripping the table's edge as she leaned towards him. He checked her face, then his three-quarter full glass, returning to her with a puzzled expression. He held back as she slipped into the booth to sit facing him.

'You're in the middle of a unique experience.' She stated as if she could see all of him at once.

He shifted suddenly, thinking for a moment that he'd heard Emily's voice. The woman's face lit up with a soft ancient smile. 'Your imagination is in overdrive, dude.'

He moved up an inch in his seat to address her. 'Aren't you a little old in the tooth to be calling me, dude?'

'You're some buachaill. This woman, she really must be something?'

'You know once upon a time, a Dublin taxi driver said as much to me.' Mark replied wistfully.

'Now, that doesn't surprise me.' This time she was smiling.

'Why, am I suddenly obvious?' He asked.

'Only your brogue is obvious to me, sweetheart,' she glanced beyond the back of his seat. The old woman turning back as she moved in to whisper. 'Tell me everything?'

'Emily?' He responded, her name seemed to whistle on his lips.

'That's a very sweet name to be calling me.' There was a moment before they smiled. His laugher took over, dark and natural. She shook her head.

Our Diligent Souls

'You don't know the half of it.' He barely stated, thinking back on Elliot's definition, the modern classification of his then asexual Emily. 'I've had the greatest night, that much I can claim.'

'So, tell me about it, Stud?'

'You really are a very strange lady.' His Armagnac eyes filled him with laughter, 'Go on, I've seen the movie.'

She could barely keep it together. 'So, you have a thing for this Emily then?'

'A small thing, yeah.'

'You're kidding me?'

'A bit... It's been a bloody nightmare; to have gone this long without her in truth.' He was forced to admit it as she smiled knowingly.

They silenced each other to listen in on a woman's voice as it drew nearer, he remembered the gentle light-hearted tune. The expression on his face struck her; through his eyes, she knew that it was hard to credit moments such as these. 'For it's only love, yeah it's only love, that can take a foolish heart and turn it inside out.'

He remembered the Dublin crowd at the big wedding, he had taken them in from where he'd sat at the dance floor window four years ago. Slightly shaken almost tearful, his eyes glazed over as he reached for the box of matches that had been surreptitiously left behind. Taking them in his nervous hand, he rattled them at his ear, smiling softly at the strange old lady.

'Yeah, it's only love, yeah it's only love, that can take a foolish heart and turn it inside out.' Tears were in the singer's larynx as she came closer, he lowered his eyes afraid to look, to even dare to dream.

The shapely figure of a woman slowly edged into view, dressed in an old green woollen coat, her long unkempt, now brown and golden hair, plainly parted to the left, a cigarette clasped between her slender fingers.

Pretending to look for a light; she raised the cigarette to her lips. The box of matches in his sweaty hand. He had all but forgotten his companion at the table. The old woman whispered. 'Light her up there; this is my kitchen.'

Emily's smokey voice was still full of humour. 'Jesus Cassie, it was just for effect like?' She placed the cigarette on the table.

'Aha!', he spouted catching the old woman's name to recall Emily's talk on stage that night, about her nanny and the spot she had chosen for her first rebellious taste of coca cola, as a six-year-old. 'Cassandra?' He mumbled, looking directly at her.

   Cassandra moved, hoisting herself up out of the seat. She lifted her lovely old Irish schoolroom stick from the window ledge beside them, with its shapely hook of old gold. Groaning, she stretched out to catch the window blind by its bottom centre loop and pulled the blind down. 'It's looking like an after-hours,' Cassie spoke loud enough for a bedraggled crowd to applaud. 'Hah!' She muttered, even the old doll's intimation sounded sweet.

   'You need to be cautioned.' Emily said laughing, tapping her top leg from where she stood.

   'Knock me over with a feather,' Cassie joked. 'If it isn't Emily.' She reached out and tucked a stray hair behind Emily's ear.

   'I take it you were there tonight then?' Emily asked Mark.

   'You know this eejit?' He asked sarcastically, referring to his new best friend, the old lady.

   Emily bumped him up gracefully on the seat and got in beside him as he leaned in to inhale her perfume. She drew back laughing, 'Really? It was you that just sold me down the river.' He seemed concerned though in truth he was just mildly curious, having been surrounded by her love. 'Emily Rosemary Ann Johnson, I ask you?' She reiterated, lifting his hand, her fingers tingling as her chest rose and dropped like a child's. He was trembling, at the glimpse of teary starlight in her eye. 'How about we agree you stay Emily Rosemary Ann... Johnson, for just a little while. I know that I will want you forever and a day...' She whispered, 'Yes,' before they shared their first kiss.

Made in the USA
Columbia, SC
03 June 2018